THE UNSATED

A NOVEL OF ANCIENT EVIL!

BY

RJ BARKLEY

OUTER FORCES PUBLISHING

Copyright © 2021 Book and Illustration by RJ Barkley

OUTER FORCES PUBLISHING
16824 44th Avenue W, Suite 130
Lynnwood, WA 98037

ISBN 978-1-7372534-1-9 EBOOK
ISBN 978-1-7372534-0-2 PAPERBACK

Cover Concept and Layout by RJ Barkley.

Cover Art by pantelispolit at Fiverr.

Special Thanks to Scott Kingham for Supplemental Cover Design, and Layout Technical Support.
Grateful Acknowledgments to Lois Hallock & Laurie "Stabby" Hopkins for their help in editing this novel.

Extra Thanks to Marion McElhany for Additional Help and Support.

DEDICATED TO MY WONDERFUL WIFE,

FARA DAUN

"How Can I Help?"

Without her encouragement and support, this book would not have been possible.

THE UNSATED

TRAVELS THROUGH *TERROR* ON THE EDGE OF *THE OTHERSIDE!*

AN OUTER FORCES NOVEL

A story relating the numerous Adventures of a certain Sergeant Travis Lehrman and his various Associates and Adversaries, while traversing the Lands and Waters on and about the South Eastern Coast of America, circa mid 1865 A.D.

TABLE OF CONTENTS

PROLOGUE

Ever had a day that was so good, so fine and nice, so extraordinary of a memorable time, that you just didn't want it to end? That wasn't this day. This was a day that by all rights, all that is great and holy, you wouldn't ever want to even begin.

Now, this day of fighting was almost at its end, and so was the last living man on the ridge.

Dusk. Dusk and smoky. The quiet of a rural spring day folding into twilight laid upon a silent cacophony of struggling shadows. Darkness and blindness, too much to see and not enough, joined by combat in muggy silence.

Reaching out, finding thin purchase, and pushing against a dark something nearby. Hard shoving, but not enough to roll himself over and squeeze his face up from the smooth muck holding half of it captive.

"Damn."

Weakness became pain as Artillery Sergeant Travis Lehrman struggled against the hundreds of tiny invisible shackles betraying his will. Red-rimmed agonies shooting from fingers to spine. So easy to just lay where he was, alongside a ready-made grave plowed by an enemy cannonball.

Another shadow loomed briefly, attached to a pair of legs that smothered the orange horizon as they jerked, the chest and other parts above them pierced by enemy lead, then collapsed between him and the far, far West. The uniform was red, but neither the enemy's men nor those of his side wore that color. Who could be wearing that?

"*I need to ask this fella where he's from.*" A simple request, surely, made impossible by the realization that the red-suited soldier felled directly beside had no ears to hear, no tongue to speak, no mouth and no eyes, no head as such to think about a cogent reply to such an easy, fair, and logical question.

"*Damn if he ain't one of our boys.*"

Trying again to push away from the exposed lip of the hill where he lay, he finds the body of his brother-in-arms a more solid bedrock than the bloody goo and mud he is now embedded in. Placing his hand against the still solid shoulder of the corpse, he shoves himself away, rolling deeper into the narrow trench so thoughtfully excavated by the projectiles of enemy cannon.

A moment of clawing in to bury himself another inch more is rewarded by not losing any of his body's bits or pieces as a fusillade of canister shots detonate not far away. Several one-inch-lead balls strike the earthly remains of his former comrade, pushing it over on top of him, a martyr's blanket.

"Damn."

Sleep or unconsciousness, even sweet catatonia, is refused by the man buried under dead bleeding bones and flesh. He knows what comes next.

After some time, the light fades and other senses awaken. He hears the approaching voices of jubilance, anger, defiance, and revenge. Not the voices of his compatriots. These other men have the hell-rasped accents of the enemy he has fought for almost four years. The enemy who takes no prisoners.

The newcomers walk among the dead in failing light, stepping past his army's shattered defenses. They laugh and joke while prodding the heaped corpses with their swords and bayonets to find any survivors, whom they promptly execute with blade or, less often, bullet.

"Gee Oh Dee! This one here's a horror!" trembles the gullet of a high-pitched two-legged scavenger. He pecks like a flightless crow amongst the broken-up bodies for loot and baubles.

"Wal, we ain't got no time to stare at the dead ones. They don't need killin' twice! Spear the ones still movin' and snatch their bindles before the officers climb this ridge. Grab your spoils before you don't have a chance to. It's gonna be dark soon." says the more veteran Corporal, all of 19 years old.

"Oh, Gee Oh Dee, I won't ever stop seein' that!"

"Stop starin' over at that there then, Little James! Looky, we'll find us some rum or whiskey tonight and you'll forget all about it. That's what I know.

"You sure about that, Billy Bill?'"

"Ha! I know what I know, and it works for me. Every time."

Inhumed beneath the shattered husk of his former compatriot, Travis breathed shallowly, ignoring the moist air of corruption beginning to seep from it. He managed to catch a glimpse of the prowling thieves. Knowing he was under pain of merciless death should his discovery by these enemy bandits occur, he nevertheless marked well their aspects, voices, and names, vowing appropriate requital to them, should he

3

ever have that privilege.

He was well buried and covered in layers of gore. Their eyes passed over him, but the scavengers moved off, still discussing their evening plans for counting their purse snatchings and the hoped-for medicinal doses of rum and whiskey.

Soon after, loud speech and heavy hoof beats announced the inevitable arrival of the holier-than-thou officers on horseback. As they clomped up the hill past his army's dead and broken defenses to have a look-see around the carnage, he felt they would crest nearby.

Sure enough, his eyes caught the waggling of a tall feather rising above the ridge. Knowing that the vainglorious plume was likely attached to the cap of an enemy officer, he pushed his face deeper into the blood cold muck, preserving his corpse-like aspect beneath the muddy edge of the cannonball's deep rut.

"Waaal, this ain't nearly as bad as what some of the boys said."

"Bad? This is what victory looks like, Colonel Jones."

"Yessir, General."

"Seein' the blood and guts of the enemy strewn about like this means they'll not ever fire shot, shell, or shrapnel at our boys again! That's a good thing!"

"Yessir, General."

"These broken trees will grow back. Looks like a particularly sumptuous view of the river from here too. Maybe I'll requisition me some land and have a new house built up here once this damnable war is done for and gone."

"Yes sir. I'd fancy returning here tomorrow

when the sun's come back up. Not too much more to see this evening."

"Colonel Jones, we'll do just that. I want to see what's left of their fortifications to fathom how the enemy somehow managed to hold out as long as they did. Devil's own deployment here killed more of our troops than I'd counted on. You'll be writing those letters to the families this week."

"Yes sir, General."

"I've seen enough of this, enough to make out the basics. Let's get back down before it's too dark for the horses. I fancy the bivouac's been set up below by now. In fact, I do believe I'm smelling our dinner if I'm not bedeviled."

"You're not mistaken, sir. I'm smelling it too."

"Let's be on our way then."

1. DEAD MEN GET NO STEW

Cold, trying his best to hold back shivering, Sergeant Travis Lehrman clawed as slowly and silently as possible from beneath the earthly remains of his comrades in arms.

"You won't need this anymore." he whispered, peeling the red stained gum-blanket off his former trench-mate. He wrapped it tightly around himself to help thwart his chill.

"Got to get back to my lines, but I need food, or I probably won't make it."

Darkness had overtaken twilight. There were no stars, but the lights of the enemy cook fires shone brightly below. Aching hunger and the aroma of food drew him, stumbling and moth-like, to those flames.

"Ain't no moon tonight. I can do this. Get in, grab some chow, get out."

Green smears and blood-black mud caked his body, but he didn't care much about how he looked, he didn't plan on being seen. One step, wait. Another step, wait again, close to the trees and shrubs, minimizing any motion that might catch an eye... *"One more step, slow and steady wins the stew..."*

Before he moved again, he was overtaken by someone not caring whether he was seen. Footfalls muffled by the moss carpet of the forest; the man's off-key humming of a popular marching song was Travis' only warning not to make another move toward the cookpot.

The enemy soldier passed by in hungry ignorance some twenty feet away, confident of the day's victory and his army's position on the over-run battlefield. He didn't bother to look left or right into the forested shadows that concealed a sworn enemy who was more concerned with capturing a bowl of soup than a prisoner. The interloper strode to the stew bucket, looked around, yelled.

"Alexander? Where are you now? There ain't nothing for me to put my damn soup in!"

From inside the cook-tent comes a frustrated reply, "Aw, curse your soup, Corporal! You know you're supposed to be bringing your own cup and silver wit' you! Where'd you lose 'em this time?"

"Don't rightly know but I didn't lose my appetite along with 'em. Be a good egg now and give me another batch would ya? I've gotta get back to my post."

"*Back to my post!*" Panic and a punch of hunger gripped the fugitive's innards as he realized the sad facts: either a stolen stew supper or a better chance to sidle past the ring of perimeter guards.

But not both.

"Damn your growling stomach, Corporal! If you'd shown up a few minutes later, I could have had both chow and my escape through the gap in the line that your hungry self is making in the human chain around this place. Looks like I have to choose food or freedom."

Darkness and its proffered escape beckoned brighter than the now fading fantasy of a warm meal, so he moved away from the source of mouth-watering sustenance and out toward the area the Corporal had come from. Travis moved silently with a tempered alacrity, thinking of good luck, bad luck, and the heavenly timing that had kept his head on his shoulders during the earlier cannonade while his chums were bursting into gobbets around him.

"Might be hungry, but dead men get no stew. I got nothing to complain about."

Ignoring the ravening pit within his stomach and guided more by faith than by the remaining faint glow on the horizon behind him, he stole into the dark, away from the stew and the mortal enemies who guarded it.

He tramped as quick as he could, as slow as he must, for as long as he had to. He escaped past the guards and then went on. Sergeant Travis Lehrman only stopped after he had already fallen twice from exhaustion, knowing that he had better crawl under some brush or a hollow log, rather than pass out in clear view of any pursuers that might come next morning.

A buried notch inside a fallen tree trunk sufficed. He crawled deep into its crevice, uncaring of the rotted bark that chipped and broke around him. He pulled the gum blanket tight and slept.

Awakening before first light... cold, damp, sore, still hungry and with a runny-nose cough, he roused and trudged toward the far glow of dawn.

After many more days and the nights between them later, Travis faintly smelled the sea upon the occasional gust from the east.

Having laid low behind enemy lines after escaping over a week earlier, Travis had stayed off roads but within sight of them, traveling mostly in the almost dark of dusk and dawn, or occasionally during the day along game trails within forests that imitated the gloom of night.

Not having done too badly as a fugitive on the run, he'd managed to come by some worn but clean clothes to replace the ripped and bloody rags he'd been wearing, along with the odd bits of food from here and there, either caught or liberated, just enough to keep him going.

Possibly the best of all, after a particularly heavy thunderstorm that had lasted several days, he'd taken full advantage of getting a bath in a fine small pond fed by several small waterfalls pouring down the hillside. The sharp bite of the ice-cold water had seemed to clean him from the inside out.

His hair and beard were getting long, and though that was annoying to him, right now it was more than enough to not be covered in blood and bits of bone. To be both clean and not in a Prisoner of War Camp was God's own blessing.

Returning to his own lines had proved impossible. Cut off deep within what had now become enemy territory, his several attempts to penetrate the shifting border had come to near disaster every single time. The frustrating thing was that the ground the enemy controlled kept growing, expanding into what had once been friendly areas at a faster rate than he could walk, even if he hadn't had to remain stealthy in his endeavors to remain undetected.

Earlier, while sleeping in an earth ditch during the day, as had become habit since he'd taken to traveling mostly at night, he awakened in the afternoon to faintly heard bugle calls. Those notes were familiar. Quickly scaling to a perch high in a gargantuan old elm and there hidden by its profusion of leaves and sturdy branches, he'd seen his country's flag carried above a small mass of men in the great distance. They moved with desperate purpose.

He began to plan how to join his comrades, hoping to get in another lick at the foe, but then the clouds of smoky dust pluming across the battlefield parted for an instant. It was clear long enough to reveal great swathes of enemy uniforms, many of them upon horseback, filling the space between him and what was left of his army. He knew any attempt to pass through their hordes would ultimately prove fatal.

"Can't just fade out o' sight and sneak by those motherless bastards like an ole' Will-o'-the-wisp, not today at least. Better just stay here, where I'm up and out of the way in case some outriders pass by."

Minutes built into hours as inexorable shadows laid blankets of counterfeit gravestones upon the mounting heaps of bodies. All he could do was watch.

"So damnable hot now, but worse over there. Our boys are taking a lickin' like a chicken splittin'. Wish I could help but I've got no rifle or musket... not even a pistol or saber. I'm worthless, 'cept for keeping my head down for now. If the enemy catches me back here, I'll hang as a spy before sundown, no two ways about it."

Ongoing all the while, were the sounds of battle and the diminishing number of souls fighting. Cries and screams, yells of defiance and defeat, all mixed with the dull steadiness of rifle and musket volleys. He knew which side had the preponderance of rifles, as the sounds from their numbers remained steady while the muskets withered, choked on blood and old iron.

Prudence had well served him these last weeks. But now, perched high in the sweaty atmosphere of motionless leaves, it seemed as if action, any action, would be preferable to baking alive while watching his countrymen fight and die.

His mind spun in the heat, while a hallucination of impossible victory painted its picture for him. A quick clamber down the tree and a run toward the backs of the enemy might work! Who knows how many he could kill with merely the righteous strength of his bare hands!

"After all, I just might could turn this battle around, if I have a spark or two of luck! Don't nobody know what they can do until they try!"

Sweat poured off his heat-addled skull while his delusional plan took on a reality it didn't possess. He felt a need to do something, anything, to help.

Travis' hazy mental mirage decided him. He could no longer abide the intolerable sight of his army's crushing defeat playing out before him. It was time to move; to attack.

The first part of his plan was unexpectedly difficult. He'd sat still for so long that his legs tingled pain and paralyzation almost as bad as the snakebite he'd gotten as a child.

Gritting his teeth against the tormenting needle points shooting within his extremities, he sees, through half-shut and sweat-soaked eyes, an unwelcome apparition whose presence slaps his motion to a standstill. Only his heartbeat still pounds, a thunder louder than shrapnel.

The enemy. Here. At this very tree.

A few seconds observation confirmed that the soldier had not yet perceived him. Travis was still safe among the branches, but for how long?

Cursing his body's weakness but thanking the ingrained caution that had delayed his movements just enough, he knew he'd nearly made a fatal error. His mind snapped back into focus on the here and now.

"Stupid! Stupid, stupid sod! Who was I to think I could take on a whole army and win, even if I attacked them from behind! Insanity! If I'd started down this trunk even a minute ago, this soldier would've seen me! I'd either be shot through the gut dead, or caught and named a spy, then dragged off to the gibbet with a rifle to my neck! Lord, please give me strength to do what needs doin'."

It seemed almighty providence had, perhaps, placed into his power the upper hand... despite the newly arrived interloper on the ground being armed.

The soldier was in no hurry to join the ongoing fight beyond the low-lying hillocks to the north. Instead, he relaxed, taking refuge from the punishing heat of the sun, and gazed placidly around the general area of the large tree with little urgency. He even glanced upward into the maze of branches and leaves that veiled the immobile man watching him. Satisfied at his seeming privacy, he placed his rifle upright against the tree, laid his haversack nearby, then walked around the large tree trunk opposite his gear and began to relieve himself.

He was directly below Travis.

The enemy began humming a song that was

close to every man's heart on the side that Travis fought for. But he made a mockery of it, spitting and cursing while doing so. He sneered out loud, making a crude joke to amuse himself.

"So much for you dead boys. We're waterin' the blooms for your graves over there with your blood, jus' like I'm waterin' this ole' tree. Ha!"

It wasn't so much what he said, it was how he'd said it, twisted with a cynical and insulting laugh, which sent a choking cry of hate and rage through the man hidden above.

Travis sprung without thinking over the large branch upon which he'd been sitting, directly through the mass of green and spindly breaking branches to drop like an avenging Gabriel onto the still-pissing man below. As he fell through the stinging foliage, he instinctively covered his face with his hands, bringing his elbows out to either side of his head. The right elbow, guided by luck more than intent, struck the startled man square and full, perfectly sharp between the eyes, just as he looked up toward the noise. No glancing blow was this but an almighty stroke with the force and power of more than ten feet of drop behind it.

Both crashed to the ground in a messy heap. Only one rose to his feet. The other now sprawled awkwardly supine, utterly motionless.

Testing his arm to make sure he'd broken no bones, and finding himself in relatively good shape, outside the painful bruise of the elbow that had proven so deadly to his surprised opponent, Travis decided that he was in excellent condition compared to the man crumpled inanimate before him.

"Better see if he's as expired as he looks." He

reached down to check the pulse.

There was none.

The enormity of what he'd accomplished washed across him, bringing a heretofore never experienced clarity to his immediate focus. Survival and escape had taken on two distinct attributes.

On one hand he had liberated a quantity of priceless kit and matériel. On the other, he'd killed an enemy who had surely had orders and a mission and would be expected to report back to his superiors within a reasonable time. Should he not, his absence would be noted and, sooner or later, investigated.

Travis immediately moved close to the tree trunk, knowing that even at this distance from the battle, a stray glance by a pair of sharp eyes might discern his presence, if not his identity as an enemy of the more numerous and powerful, and unfortunately the closer, of the two contesting factions.

Staying low to the ground and on the opposite side of the tree from where the fighting still raged, he pulled the personal and military items off the dead man to perform a quick inventory.

Hardtack, salt pork, an onion, and a small quantity of what looked and smelled to be genuine coffee beans were within the haversack. Travis, having by necessity skipped his meals for the last two days, gratefully began to eat. He continued to separate the other items into what he could take with him or must leave behind.

The first item he immediately strapped to his waist was the belt, and more importantly, the sheath attached to it containing a precious Bowie knife with the coveted D guard. The heavy blade was a length of sharpened steel more akin to a short sword than a piece of dinner cutlery. He knew that these types of man-killing blades had originally only been manufactured and distributed to his own army. Knowing that the knife he now took possession of had already once been a battle prize removed from the cooling body of one of his countrymen, he was satisfied to have been able to return the favor. Whistling in admiration at its balance and keen edge, he carefully replaced the blade within its thick leather sheath.

Next to put in the "keeper" pile was a small but finely made spyglass, two Colt Army pistols, several heavy caliber lead bullets, a powder horn, and percussion caps. A fine set of prizes, indeed.

He checked the pistols and, surprisingly, found them to be unloaded. He quickly loaded each of the weapon's six chambers with the powder, ammo, and percussion caps required, smeared the chambers with some bacon fat from the ration to prevent a chain fire, then returned them both to their holsters.

Carrying on the inspection of his plunder while still jawing away at the slowly dissolving hardtack in his mouth, he discovered that the boots of the dead soldier, whose more lightweight stature had undoubtedly been a factor in how easily he'd been dispatched by the surprise blow, were too small to be of any use to him.

"Can't have all the good luck at once I guess, but it would surely be pleasant to have some new boots that didn't leak. Of course, I should be grateful I've any foot coverings at all, worn out as they are. Ha! Best of all, I'm still alive to

bellyache about it!"

Finding a blanket and ground cloth secured to the haversack by a goodly length of thin but surprisingly strong and supple rope, the beginnings of a plan germinated. He knew that an enemy search party would at some point come by this hiding spot, so he knew he must be hidden away, or preferably, be *far* away. More importantly, the dead soldier and what was left of his kit must be concealed as well.

No shovel or pick to be had, not enough time to dig a grave of meaningful size anyway, there was only one solution: if he could not go down, he must go elsewhere. Upward it was; once again, the large elm invited him to enter its concealing maze of green. He considered, then concluded that, if he had been welcome to enshroud himself within its leafy mask, there might also be a place there to veil his unwanted charge.

He hefted the corpse, concluding that it was, unfortunately, too heavy for him to lift and carry up the tree while he was in his current malnourished and weakened condition. However, the discovery of the rope lent wings and possibility to his scheme. Tying the rope around the torso and under the armpits, he cinched it tight, keeping the arms battened down to not catch on the branches, and the rope well in place.

Next tying a small loop at the opposite end, then taking that with him, he climbed to the first large branch above, slung the rope over it, and placed his foot squarely and securely inside the little rope sling. It squeezed fast the worn leather of his boot as it tightened painfully around his foot, but it held, and his greater weight pulled the dead man on the other end up as he slowly descended. There was a minor struggle near the ground as the body momentarily caught on the edge of a branch, but a persistent and lively final pull yanked the corpse over it far enough to not come crashing back to earth.

He immediately removed the loop from his boot, wrapped it around his wrist to maintain tension, and climbed past the dead man to the next likely branch above, where he began to repeat the process, ascending and dropping several more times, pulleying up and down in a macabre semblance of some childhood game that might have been played under more joyful circumstances.

Ascending to a pair of branches robust enough to hold the body in a secure V-shaped hollow between them, he removed the rope, and placed the stiffening arms and legs into the most natural-seeming position possible, turning the head out toward the continuing battle, as if he'd just been observing the action when some unknown death had overcome him.

"Too bad for you. If you'd caught me up here first, I'm sure I'd be lookin' something like you do now. At least you get to watch your boys lick the hell out of mine before the sun goes down. Luck o' the draw. Just the luck o' the draw."

Satisfied with his work, but knowing he was at a continuing risk of discovery while he remained unhidden, he glanced upward toward the next layer of potential concealment, another twenty feet or so above him.

"Sun's gonna be down soon. Dead fella is missing from his post and nowhere to be found.

18

There's bound to be a search party of some sort out here tomorrow. I need to get this situation buttoned down before dark."

Scrambling to the ground, he looked around for anything unnaturally out of place, for the odd anomaly that might draw the enemy's attention, prompting their investigation of the big tree.

The sun had slung low on the horizon, long shadows portending its imminent disappearance. He looked around the area with a focused desperation, his heart pounding. Nearby the gun belt and other items he'd determined to bring along with him, the long, heavy rifle was the only offender. It leaned upon the tree trunk, stoically awaiting its fate.

"I'd love to take you with me but you're gonna have to go upstairs too. When your dead as a boot-nail owner is eventually found up there, you gotta be with him, like he was fixin' to use you before he died. It's not such a strange thing to have not been issued a pistol, but everyone knows it would be contrary for a soldier to be without his rifle. A search party would know someone else was involved, somehow."

After grabbing the pistol belt and other gear, he climbed to the first branch, carrying the rifle awkwardly over his back. The edge of its leather sling dug like a dull saw into his neck. He paused before climbing into the thick green mask above him, and from this vantage looked down one last time to make sure he'd left nothing that might attract unwanted attention. He could see that the grass was still squashed down, with only a few small scars of scraped dirt remaining as a memorial to the enemy soldier. He figured that a heavy dew or some few splashes of rain would most likely dispel that little evidence. The air smelled as if a squall might soon visit. He shrugged. It would have to do.

When he reached the cradle of branches where the dead man now kept his sightless vigil, he transferred the rifle, pulling it off himself and then looping the sling around the other's stiffening torso into a passable imitation of how a sniper might have rigged his weapon as he aimed. If nothing else, the weapon was well secured from falling.

Overhead, the branches and leaves made another green ceiling, above which he should be able to hide from anyone who discovered the body here, unlikely as that was. Night was quickly falling. The battle had been reduced to occasional angry snaps of gunfire as soldiers shot between the shadows at invisible specters of doom.

The wails of a mortally injured man shouting for his Ma reminded them all of their ultimate fate.

He ascended through the final thick layer of leaves, finding the branches still sturdy enough to support his weight. The last deep red of the western horizon provided enough light for him to be able to tie off the grommets of the gum blanket around the trunk and to a branch making a serviceable hammock. He clambered into it, tugging the ground cloth over as protection from the rain he felt would soon be coming.

After eating another chunk of greasy meat, he wrapped the blanket around himself. He was done with this day, utterly enervated, yet more comfortable in his perch high in the big tree than he'd been anywhere at any time in far too long. The food in his shrunken belly undoubtedly helped.

Travis closed his eyes, belched once, and slept.

2. WAR'S NO DANCIN' WITH SALLY

The light rains heralding the storm that had begun to gently kiss the moribund battleground quickly invited their big bullying brethren. These were ferocious gales that swirled in from the Atlantic. They attacked the land and everything upon it during the dark hours after sunset, their squally cannonades of hard windswept rain more horizontal than vertical before crashing to earth.

His treetop's tidy and snug hideaway had slowly become a soaking mess as the storm breached the protection of the interlocking leaves above him. Rain dripped, dropped, and dribbled tiny lances of dank chill upon him.

Travis had unconsciously pulled the wool blanket over his head several hours earlier. The army-issued covering was sturdy, and still kept him somewhat warm, even after becoming soaked. The ground cloth gave no protection from the cold runnels of rain that cascaded down the tree trunk and seeped quickly along the rope lines, much like hungry rats boarding a ship.

Pure exhaustion had kept him from waking as his makeshift hammock slowly pooled with storm water. Hours later, he stirred to logy wakefulness in the gray dawn. His first thought was that he'd pissed his pants.

Every muscle, joint, and bone in his body protested as he slowly rose and moved about his temporary roost, steadying himself to carefully teeter on two slick branches while assessing the situation.

No, he wasn't marinating in a puddle of his own making after all.

The gusting storm showed no signs of abating, unlike yesterday's mayhem on the battlefield. This morning showed little action from either side. Sleeping soldiers, collapsed beside cannon on the field of muck-soaked silence, were indistinguishable from their dead brethren already sacrificed upon the alter of Ares.

The miserable overnight watch by each side's pickets continued into the morning. They each peered futilely through driving rain for troop movements or clandestine activity from the other. They saw none, there was none. Nary a cookfire had yet sparked in either camp. The wet permeated all; it bogged and thickened both mud and time.

Travis grabbed blanket and haversack, tipped his former bed to one side to empty it of water, then sat inside it again to enjoy a mean breakfast. As the sun rose beyond a sullen sky, the sheen of green and brown verdure around him slowly brightened. His mood didn't.

Green, blue, brown, gray... all were offshoots of the same tree. But while one tree grew strong and thrived, the other had turned implacable destruction inward, threatening to destroy itself to their shared roots. When the violence was over, it left the survivors to mourn, and afterwards, rebuild their version of a new and glowing path toward the dream of a more perfect union, or so it was said.

Was any utopia on Earth possible? Seeing the shattered skulls and bullet-broken bones still mired in the battlefield, and very conscious of the dead man he shared the tree with, Travis thought not. Each bright new future had been founded on collapse and ruin, with each fated to die in turn. Men were men, granted the infinite ability to find complaint amid plenty, and the cunning knack to procure new ways to enjoy hate. There could be no satisfaction.

He knew the heavy murk that obscured him from easy detection would be curtailed as morning unfolded. Both camps would awaken soon, their colonels and captains eager to join once more in honorable battle upon the unburied corpses of their former charges.

The corporals and privates might have different and possibly more selfish ideas, but sergeants, such as himself, who by hard lessons had usually learned how to survive the worst of it, would goad and bully and prod them to their country's duty. It was the same in every army.

Realizing his musings had gotten out of hand, that time was a-wasting, and to delay any more increased his peril, he swallowed the bit of hardtack and dried meat he'd been chewing. He drank from his canteen to wash it all down, then popped a few of the precious coffee beans in his mouth, not being blessed with a way to properly prepare those luxuries. He vowed to himself he'd correct that problem at the earliest opportunity.

On his way down the tree, he paused at the artifice he'd created of the dead soldier. The angle of the rifle had gone askew, so he readjusted it, compensating for what the winds had upset during the stormy night. He then gave a quick salute of respect to the dead man.

"If it hadn't been you, it'd for damn sure have

been me. You would have sure as hell gut shot me with that fancy rifle, just doing your duty. Just like I did. You or me, just the luck o' the draw."

As he'd hoped might happen, the overnight gales had obliterated all evidence of yesterday's death struggle near the base of the tree. He prayed it would be a long time before discovery of the body. There was nothing more to do but to move on. Centering the kit and pack on himself, then adjusting his cap as well as he could against the rain beating into his face, he moved quickly away from the slowly stirring camps on either side of the battlefield. He slogged east, toward the ocean, to what he hoped would be a chance to rejoin his army.

Making sure he kept as far off the edge of what sometimes seemed like a back road, but was becoming more and more just an overgrown trail, was a chore. The muddy little path wound through a landscape of bushes and trees amid high grass clearings and abandoned farms. He didn't gripe. Its very difficulty of navigation made it into a series of concealing oases for him as he moved along.

He had, so far as he knew, been successfully invisible to detection while he traveled. He was thoroughly committed to his plan of doing whatever was necessary to avoid dogs, soldiers, and civilians, in that order.

His plan was simple. Travis hoped that the enemy incursions would be stopped by his country's military, somehow, at some point before reaching the Atlantic's shores. He hoped that he'd be able to sneak along the edges of their lines, make it to the vicinity of the ocean, then loop around to contact his forces and rejoin whatever was left of his artillery unit, or, more likely, be assigned to another.

To do that he had to avoid enemy outriders as well as any civilians newly sympathetic to the enemy; traitors who were willing to curry favor with the occupying authorities by trading information about suspicious personages.

Therefore, he could trust no one. A good policy most times, an absolute imperative now.

Sergeant Lehrman carried on.

Days later, his leaky boots continued to annoy him. Every time it rained, each step through the grassy mire pumped filthy water across his toes. There was nothing he could do about that, of course, except to not think about them.

Squish, squish, squish.

Travis considered, *"Best to not think at all."*

His broken march of caution continued. He became ghostlike, a brownish-gray smear of unremarkable dull. Irregular waves of broken clouds blown in from the still-unseen ocean sent soaking sheets of stinging rain to harry him and anyone else so foolish as to challenge their sway.

All creatures save one recognized with inborn instinct their natural subservience to the unyielding and humorless dominions of nature upon the earth on which they lived. All creatures this day kept those covenants, dozing in clusters of their fellows, staying warm inside their burrows, or dry within their nests.

Except for a two-legged outlier who numbly maintained a slow and mostly steady pace up and down low rolling hills, through the streams of muddy water that cleaved the tiny valleys between them.

Travis smelled the danger well before he saw it. Carried by combative winds, it was a noxious tinge of something very wrong that overlaid the stink of charred wood smoke.

Any pleasant memories that he might once have attached to prior experiences with cook fires and the comforting circumstances they generally afforded, such as security, warmth, food, camaraderie, and coffee... especially coffee... were cauterized from his mind as his body went on high alert. He ceased all movement. Sporadic gusts continued to carry their evidence of the nearby perfidy to him on the rainy wind.

Listening intently for sounds of distress or attacking cavalry, Travis attempted to ascertain the direction and distance of the smoke's source. He nestled into a large bush several feet below the top of the small hill he was on, blending into its pale green grayness as best he could. He guessed that the danger was on the far side of that rise but couldn't be sure.

Best to sit for a while and wait for the danger to reveal itself. Evil always did, it couldn't help doing so.

The occasional acrid smell of cinders and burnt... something... caught his attention. That was enough for him to remember...

"It was two years ago... that village by the river's oxbow at the bottom of the hill... the westernmost farm... "

Two years ago, a dispatch had arrived. His army's infantry had recently overrun and

28

occupied an enemy fortification miles away. That position was strewn with many still useful enemy cannon and supplies. The generals had decreed that those big guns needed to be uprighted, **turned** around, and re-aimed toward their former masters, who were even now regrouping some distance away, slowly preparing for a counterattack.

Time had vied fiercely against his side. More men were desperately needed there, as the contested field was only lightly held by the remnants of the infantry that had overwhelmed it by sheer force of will and bloody determination. His artillery unit had been ordered on a quick-time march to take control of the enemy cannon in hopes of holding off attempts to retake the hill, making it possible for more reinforcements to arrive.

As a result, he and his men were traveling separately from their own slower-moving teams of horses, which were dragging their own heavy caissons, limbers, and cannons up a less steep but more winding route toward the crucial position.

Thus were the circumstances that Travis and his fellows found themselves in when they came upon the massacre by the river.

Beyond them, at the position that had been over run, the enemy had not stood and fought to the last man. Under unrelenting fusillades from, seemingly, all directions, angry groups of frustrated and frightened men had abandoned their positions and desperately rattled off in every direction to escape the onslaught.

Some few of the deserters met a large man on horseback dressed all in black, who convinced them to join up with him. The group found their way to a long, lazy curve of the river, where a tiny civilian village of no military value lay.

Enraged by their recent deadly setback and, presumably, shamed by their chaotic retreat, emotions and pain conspired together in the renagades to enflame a red-rimmed vision of revenge upon the nearest representatives of their hated foe that they could find. The large man with them encouraged such ruminations.

The farms of the oxbow were first in their path.

Then as now, the conflagration's smoke and smells announced the deeds well before they were seen. A shivering and fearful witness to the horrors perpetrated there, the very air itself paused to catch its breath between inhalation and gasping, puking exhales. Gagging, those nearby drew shallow gasps of air past flapping skins of clammy atmospheric thickness, their lungs sullen and protesting.

Charcoal stubs of once-sturdy barns and houses still smoldered, their blackened outlines on every former homestead. Nothing had been spared before the big horseman and the other raiders left.

As the soldiers marched past the destruction on their way to secure the cannons, they saw many carcasses of dogs, spitted by sword or shot through. A very few still whined in half-dead pools of fur and blood. These stared angrily at the moving line of men. Their remonstrative gaze pierced the hearts of the soldiers as the small bodies seemed to silently cry out.

"We tried to stop them. We watched the raiders kill the humans that we loved. We

leaped high to rip out their murdering throats.
We sheathed their steel inside our small bodies.
We gave our all. WHERE WERE YOU?"

The devastation was too much for some. Several men fell out of line, stopping to search beneath a fallen wall that had plunged across a stone fireplace chimney. One had thought that he'd seen "something moving." What they found there was madness and heinous sin. Far to the front, upon hearing their shouts and screams of piteous rage, the commanding officer sent an aide to double back and find out what might be slowing down his column, which, of course, had already fallen behind the army's optimistic schedule.

The Aide spurred his horse to comply with his orders, angry he was being forced to wear down his mount unnecessarily. He hated to ride over the same ground twice, and angrier still that his charges would dare deviate from their marching orders.

Riding up to the scene of the recent caterwauling, he found that three men had already emptied their stomachs of what little their rude breakfasts had earlier afforded them, and now lay on the ground moaning. Another two had dropped to their knees in prayer, while several others stared blankly, faces twitching in witless spasms as their minds refused to accept what they had seen.

The Aide was no virgin newcomer to the chaotic blood spilling and sudden dissections of bone and internal connective tissues that all duty-bound fighting troops shared on the battlefield. He rode around the scene, although he himself had not yet observed its horrific centerpiece of sacrificial bloodletting. Cajoling and commanding by turn, he did his best to impel his men toward the objective, still miles away.

The Aide's horse danced back upon its hind legs. It, too, had smelled the blood and caught the hysteric fever of the men nearby. The horse yipped, swinging around in a circle almost drunkenly. The Aide struggled to keep it calm and hold his saddle as he yelled at the men.

"Tain't nothin' here to see! Get back! Tain't nothin' here to do no more! It's over! Get back! Get back to ranks and get marchin'! We got us a real fight to get to! You men there by that hearth! Get on yer damn two feet and get a god damn move on! This is an order! Damn yer souls, get going! Move on out now and march! March!"

Yet his outsize actions unwittingly drew more soldiers over to the vicinity of the atrocities.

It was the first of these curious new arrivals who was next chosen by the hand of uncaring fate to see what lay partially hidden, a once-human form now splayed, unrecognizable, across the desecrated hearth. It screamed a silent echo of an ancient blood offering, pierced alive upon a primitive alter dedicated to the implacable demands of unholy deities and their wild-eyed followers.

What was revealed to him as he joined the crowd was no more nor less than what his fellows had seen. Yet the horror remained. It sent him racing away, retching bile through his fingers, brushing past the others behind him, who were still crowding closer even as their officers tried to stop them.

Sergeant Travis Lehrman also moved closer,

ready to help as well.

Most of the men obeyed the orders. Some didn't or couldn't. One began to stand but fell back to his knees, sobbing into his palms as he covered his face. Sergeant Lehrman grasped him by his shoulder and helped him up, sending him on his way, only taking in the bloody tableau with a cursory glance past the still shouting Aide and a muttered oath of revenge against those who had defiled the laws of Nature, Man, War, and God.

Seeing that the cursing Aide had regained command of his horse, and that most of the men were recovering and obeying the orders to get going, Sergeant Lehrman approached his angry superior.

"Sir, respectfully ask permission to lead a search party for those who done this mess here."

The officer swung his beast toward him. Froth and bits of foam dripped from both horse and rider.

"Sergeant, you heard my goddamn orders! I see you've already got some of these dawdlers moving off in the right direction. That's good. Now don't go and spoil it all!"

"Sir, respectfully speaking, if what did this to our women and children ain't our enemies, what else are they?"

"I'd put a bullet between every one of their goddamn eyes if they was still anywheres round here! But they ain't! And we got nowhere near no damn time to go traipsing through the forest and hell's half acre looking for them!"

"Sir, that blood is fairly fresh." Travis pointed toward the ground leading into the stream nearby. "Those tracks ain't from our men either.

I watched 'em as I came up. They all stayed over here. Those tracks lead off into the water and I'll bet right straight up and out on the far side. We might could catch up to these devils if we left straight away."

The Aide sagged slightly in his saddle, while his eyes grew grim. His voice lowered. "Sergeant, I'd like nothing more than doing what you suggest. This was an accursed act. I've never seen nothing like it and hope I never will again. From the tracks it don't look to be too many of 'em, all on foot, 'cept maybe one, so a few of us on horseback could probably catch up and put them all in the dirt. At least it would be worth trying. If we had the time."

They both looked more closely at the muddy imprints leading off toward the stream. Four separate boot prints were clearly heading the same way, and, upon greater inspection, one set of hoof marks, which was stepped in and disfigured underneath them all, as if the men on foot were following directly behind their leader on horseback.

"Sir, looks like only one of them is riding."

"Yep. He'll have to maintain pace with his boys that are walkin'. They'll all be moving slower."

"I'm guessing that their next scheme right about now is to rectify that situation."

"How's that Sergeant?"

"They'll be lookin' for horses."

"Of course. That makes a barrel-full of sense, but it don't change the facts. Those facts say we got orders. You and me standin' here conjecturing ain't following those orders, Sergeant. We both know what needs doing. We

34

got ourselves enemies to kill, and they ain't here!"

"This might be our only chance, Sir."

"War's no dancin' with Sally at the goddamn hoedown, Sergeant! You know that. Listen, I know you're right but sometimes there ain't no room for right in this world. Forget all this. We just have to trust God will make Satan twice-roast 'em all in Hell."

Pointing past him toward some soldiers slogging along near the end of the line, he continued. "Now see those men? Get them damn lollygaggers steppin' double-quick till they catch up to the front of the line. We're gonna need every man we still got to hold that position up ahead. You know what needs doin'. You're a good man, Lehrman. Don't make me come on back here."

As the Aide rode away, still shouting for the men to speed up, Sergeant Lehrman took a final look at the tracks leading away to the stream. A few feet farther on, standing out on its own, one clear and unsullied hoof print invited closer attention. It was odd for some reason. He walked over to it, carefully avoiding stepping in or across any of the other boot prints.

Within the curve of the shoe, equidistant from the center, at about the eleven and one o'clock positions, were two "V" shaped notches, their points facing outward. Too symmetrical to be accidental flaws in the iron work, they could only have been forged within the smith's hot furnace to leave upon the land the imprint they did: a roundish curve with two obvious points attached.

Like horns. Like the Devil's own Horns. And if

he just slightly squinted, he thought he could see a moving, twisted smile that formed below them in the bloody water running slowly toward the little stream.

Meanwhile, several miles away, hidden by brush, hill, and tree, several figures diligently trudged away from the ravaged oxbow, all but one on foot. A large, mounted figure led them on horseback. His florid face was beset by blood-red lips stretched wrong by a scarred snarl. A strangely unhealed wound was torn along one cheek. It was covered only in part by his deformed and oversized cavalry hat. As he spoke, a white line of what might be too many teeth were revealed in profile.

"We need to move faster. The next batch of farms we come across had better have horses, enough for us all. If not, they'll suffer worse than the last bunch."

His odd accent, punctuated by choking hisses and groaning consonants, tightened the jaws and set the teeth of his men on edge, as usual. But they were getting used to that by now.

They replied in unison, "Yes sir, Captain!"

Sergeant Lehrman's recollections shifted with difficulty from past events to present circumstances. So much he'd seen at the little farmhouse by the oxbow had been writ oversized large in memory, it still seemed as palpable as if it had all happened only last week.

Neither he nor anyone else that he knew of had ever found out who, or what, had done those deeds, or for that matter, even who the victims really were, since it had proven impossible to identify them after the many types of desecration which had defiled their corpses.

The officers had, after heated discussion, relented, authorizing a few men to stay behind temporarily to give the civilian remains a Christian burial.

After the obviously human bits had been buried, a few words were spoken with a ponderous gravity. Then men shook their heads, and the dog carcasses were tossed into a shallow pit. The loyal beasts were honored for their sacrifice and courage with a perfunctory covering of earth. Without a look behind the men shouldered their kits and marched off to their own duties.

It was all considered another unfortunate, unnecessary bloodletting; it was just the War, just the War they all said. Case closed. Yet the atrocity remained, as did the memories. Travis would not forget.

3. YOU COULD'A MAYBE
JOINED US

B ushed and bone-weary, the Sergeant had slowly melded himself into the terrain of the stinging hailstorm. In his stillness, he became just another muddy clay gray shaded aspect amongst many within the shadowless riot of sameness.

Beneath his hat, the frozen bits of sky stung his exposed eyelids, running down cold unshaven cheeks as he slowly, ever so quietly, snugged up into the brushy patch of foliage. From here he could sit, and see, and wait. The closest crest of the hill he'd been walking next to was only ten feet or so above him, with the bulk of the bush intervening. He figured that he was as nondescript as possible, under the circumstances.

Only two things remained to do. He rummaged underneath his soaking blanket to inspect the revolvers, gently double-checking the seal of the pig grease he'd smeared over each loaded cylinder a few days ago. He made sure the percussion caps were seated in place and dry. After replacing the weapons in the holsters, he unsheathed the big Bowie knife.

The balance of it was perfect. The uncompromised heft of the finely honed blade lent at least the illusion of security to his situation. If he'd dared make any sound, he would have chuckled at the idea that he, stomach endlessly growling, almost bootless, and very much a potential prisoner of war behind enemy lines in his own country, had any hope of security at all.

Still, he folded his hands across his chest as he settled in, the hilt of what was, in essence, a short sword comfortably clutched and ready for silent killing, should that become a necessity.

Illusion of safety be damned. He was glad he'd sharpened it recently. That honed edge was no delusion.

Shifting winds whipped past his utterly still form, occasionally carrying traces of the smoky danger he'd smelled before. On the road below, nothing unusual or unexpected was in sight.

Now, the toll of his violent flight from the enemy, his scanty access to food, and lack of proper rest was coming due. He knew that the absence of obvious danger was itself a threat and that he, or a foolish part of him, might succumb to its facade and grant himself a furlough from alertness. Taking deep, silent breaths, he fought to yank away the blanket of chronic exhaustion that wrapped him more completely than the dripping wet of the rainstorm.

Not too much later, just as his eyes began to lose focus, he felt a rhythmic pounding coming through the earth. It was enough to jolt him back to the sharp reality of his situation. The thumping waxed and waned, yet always increased in strength, until at last he heard other familiar sounds as well.

A rider. The horse's jangling metal outfitting and the distinct sound of its hooves clomping their way nearer unmistakably announced both man and beast as they topped the crest of the small rise, about a hundred feet away. The man reined in his horse, then peered intently into the rainy murk overlooking the area where Travis lay hidden.

An idea washed through Travis' head when he saw the man on horseback. He wished he'd earlier had a chance to lash his knife to a long, straight branch. To have a sharpened pike, like the foot soldiers of old had used with bloody effect against the mounted knights that charged and trampled them, could be a welcome weapon even now in this modern war of cannons and gunpowder. It was impossible for him to manufacture such a thing right now, of course.

So, he waited, unmoving under the other watcher's eye. Travis was a grayish brown splotch of desperate intent upon a brownish gray hillside.

The rider focused his gaze beyond the straggling trees of the immediate area, scanning across the scattered copses yonder, then back to the low brush nearby. After his eyes passed over the Sergeant's hidden form without comment or reaction he turned, continuing his slow meandering along the rise.

Travis watched the rider, while the notion that each horseshoe was leaving horned impressions in the wet soil grew fearfully within him. He knew that if he got past this encounter alive and uneventfully, he would have to climb up to take a look at those tracks to verify or disprove his conjecture.

It was a long shot that those horns were there, and he really did not desire a face-to-face encounter with whatever sort of man or beast had inflicted the ugliness of what he'd seen back at that farm in the oxbow. But if Fate or God or even the stars and worlds themselves had indeed determined that it had fallen upon him to mete out justice for the oxbow atrocity, he would do his best to comply.

All of a sudden, both he and the man on horseback heard a clamor from across the rise. Human screams and animal shrieks rent the mist as they vied for supremacy with explosions of pistol, rifle, shotgun, and even the lower pitched blast of what Travis thought might be a cannon.

The rider swung around toward the fighting, spurred his horse, and was off.

After four years of warfare and fighting, Travis knew when it was time to move. He disentangled himself from his grassy shroud, secured his weapons and, keeping below and parallel to the hilltop's crest, scrabbled quickly on all fours to a position some forty feet away. He then turned and belly crawled up the slippery knoll to just beneath the top edge. The cacophony of gunfire, screams, and explosions continued unabated in the distance.

Carefully raising up on his side to peer over with one eye, a shock of terrible surprise tore through him, even as his soldier's instincts were vindicated. He watched the rider loop around, draw his shotgun, spur his horse, and return at a hard gallop directly toward the exact area where Travis had been hiding less than a minute before.

"That cussed devil saw me back there! Cunning bastard didn't let on!"

In one motion Travis dropped as flat against the hill as possible, drawing both pistols and aiming them in the direction he'd seen the horseman heading, just above where he'd been hiding. Time elongated strangely while he held his breath. He cocked both hammers back and waited.

"Come on you tricky son of a bitch... don't be shy..."

Muddy rocks and clods of clay sprayed in all directions from feverish hooves as the horse and rider crested. Simultaneously, a hideously loud boom announced the double load of both shotgun barrels spraying lead pellets in a much more focused path: precisely where this hunter's prey had been... but was no more.

The rider grimaced as he realized his error.

Travis adjusted his aim and returned fire, taking the second shots in this double-barreled duel of lead and steel.

Both hammers dropped.

The heavy slugs lanced, riding gunpowder flames. They pierced the black tunic of the rider to strike him square on, carrying his body from the saddle, but not off his horse. He had tightly wrapped the reins around his left wrist when he'd grabbed his shotgun to go in for the kill. Frenzied, the horse bolted, trying to free itself from the noise and stinks of burnt nitrates and death. It could not escape the latter. Its former master had become an awkward cargo of cooling blood and guts dangling limp and floppy... useless.

Travis watched the body bumping alongside the horse as it raced away. He replaced the pistols carefully in their holsters, then slowly crawled up the hill. The sounds of fighting continued on the far side of the crest.

No impending annihilation this time

threatened while he gazed over the hilltop.

In the distance, amid an almost continuous barrage of small arms fire, many figures on horseback scuttered angrily around a large manor house. It was obviously under siege. From what he could tell, there were no other horsemen coming his way. All the raiders seemed fanatically intent on visiting destruction upon those within the big house.

Travis remembered the spyglass. Pulling it out, he protected it from the rain and hail as he watched mayhem through its lenses. Amid the squall's sporadic lulls, he was able to see enough to piece together a rough idea of what was happening.

The big house had fortress-like qualities. Its heavy construction reminded him of the blockhouses he'd seen, temporary fortifications meant to help hold a strategic crossroads or high point.

"Or in this case, protecting a home and family."

Inside, the defenders were ensconced behind makeshift, yet effective, barricades of overturned tables, shelves, and thick couches. They had placed them strategically, blocking broken windows and smashed in doors to reinforce their shelter.

He saw a large cloud of smoke spew from within the house. A sharp and crackling report reached his ears several seconds later, announcing the discharge of what could only be a small cannon.

"Damned if those holdouts don't have themselves a swivel gun in there!"

It made sense. This house wasn't too many

miles inland from the ocean-going sailing ships of the Atlantic. Many pirates had based their ships among the hidden coves of the islands off the coast, plying their blood-soaked trade along the Atlantic seaboard and down south to the rich settlements of the Caribbean and back, raiding inland villages when times were lean, or when the buccaneers were just bored or drunk, or both.

One of the most effective short range defenses against boarding parties, or any hostile group attacking ship, home, or hearth, was a small cannon called a *pedrero*, or swivel gun. A muzzle-loaded piece of ordnance with a bore almost three times larger than a shotgun, it was loaded with a charge of gunpowder below a choice of solid ball, nails, iron scrap, or even rocks.

A deadly tool for a last line of defense.

"That place looks like it was built to fend off attackers. It may be that ol' Blackbeard himself might have paid a social call back then."

The sights and sounds of the siege reminded him of what he'd seen in the aftermath of the oxbow atrocities. Travis crawled back to the area where the horseman had been scouting before meeting his demise. The hoof prints were mostly mashed upon each other, slick mud runnels between their edges making indistinct the evidence of what he was looking for.

Creeping up to search the less water-soaked crest of the hill, he finally found a fairly well-preserved specimen, a horseshoe impression in the thin mud earth that left no doubt. He stared at it closely to make sure.

There were no notches.

"Maybe I've been imagining them devil horns all along...could be...could be. Who knows, it's been a long time. It would be deranged to weaken shoes like that, cuttin' into them. Nobody would ever bother to do it. Stupid to think I'm really ever gonna see something like that."

His instinct was to keep moving toward the coast, but he had more pressing matters at hand right now. Although the house in the distance was still returning fire, he could see its defenders were pinned down and outnumbered by the besiegers. He did not want this to become another massacre like what he'd seen at the farm. Those killers had done their deeds and gotten away with it. He felt he couldn't allow that to happen again.

"But what can I do to fight twenty or so of them? Not an easy chore. Of course, I've already killed one of them filthy raiders, so I suppose I'll just have to find a way to remove a few more of them. I was always outnumbered during the war, and It ain't no different now. I should be used to it. Ha! If the odds were ever on my side, I'd probably be a mite perturbed!"

Travis clambered quickly down the hill to where he'd left his provisions, still hidden under the cloak, and relatively dry in the unceasing waves of misty rain and hail blowing in from the ocean. He reloaded the empty cylinders in each pistol, marveling that he'd been spared this long during his journey.

"Can't remember how many times I've already been near blowed-up or shot through. I've eaten birds, gleanings, grass seeds, and trapped some few critters I never had a name *for to make a half-raw burnt supper. Now I'm within a split nickel of the ocean and a chance to report back to my lines, but these devils are in my way. I've had to kill twice already since that cussed overrun battlefield to get here."*

The pistols went carefully back into their holsters at his side, then the big Bowie was unsheathed, examined, and sheathed again. All non-essentials were packed tightly, hidden within the thick brush under the nondescript ground cloth.

"This fight ain't nothing new. I've just been doin' my job. Now it's time to do it again."

He pulled his hat down against the gusts of biting hail. He was ready to help fight off the raiders.

Staying out of sight as best he could, he crept along just inside the forest edge toward the house. About thirty minutes later, he was as close to it as he felt was prudent. He watched from behind the concealing trees and heavy foliage while the siege continued, waiting for his chance.

From what he'd seen, several raiders had already been taken out of the fight, dead or wounded and now immobile where they lay. It was difficult to see much of the defenders, as they hid themselves adeptly while continuing to fire their weapons, most often singly, but occasionally in volleys of three or more. The *pedrero* kept up its duty as well, the little cannon's maw making sure the riders paid in painful maiming if they dared approach too closely.

Just then, a pair of raiders galloped around the house, hoping to attack their prey from behind. But they hadn't counted on another man flanking them from within the nearby forest. As they passed the tree he'd hidden behind, the two horsemen came closer to Travis than any had before.

"Now or not at all. Time to earn my pay again."

The raiders slowed to aim their weapons at the house. Travis ran up alongside the nearest one. The raider hadn't noticed him. Travis leapt high, plunging his Bowie hard into the rider's chest cavity. The blade slid in underneath ribs, tearing its way through guts, and slicing into the raider's heart. The shotgun fell to the ground as he died silently without having had a chance to fire the weapon. Travis pulled the twitching corpse from the horse while dropping back to the ground.

The other raider cussed and whooped as he fired his rifle toward the house, a large puff of gun smoke momentarily clouding his sight, while Travis recovered the dead raider's bloody shotgun from the ground.

"Now it's your turn you son of a bitch."

From the corner of his eye, the horseman glimpsed his pig-stuck partner bleeding out on the ground, and the new threat that Travis posed. He reared his horse back, hoping to put its body between him and the shotgun's maw.

The dead horseman hadn't been as careful in prepping his weapon for use in the waterlogged atmosphere as Travis had been with his pistols. The shotgun's percussion cap fizzled as its hammer fell upon a dud. Instead of the satisfying explosion expected, the weapon sighed an acrid cloud of spittling disappointment.

"That'll teach me to trust another man's work. Damn him to blazes! Looks like this might be my last lesson!"

The war horse danced forward as it had been trained, front hooves slashing toward Travis. The shotgun was smashed out of his hands, spinning away to lodge uselessly in the mud.

Travis ducked and dodged away from the deadly animal's scything hooves. One hand almost numb from the blow, Travis used the other to yank the blood-soaked Bowie from its cooling human sheath. He swung the heavy blade to slash deeply across the rear hamstring of the rearing war horse, then rolled away as far as he could from the animal as its huge body spasmed with piteous cries.

Immediate results followed. The stricken horse crumpled in place, thrashing and uncontrolled. Its two-legged cargo was flung off to crash in an unwieldy clump of cursing antagonism. The stunned raider grabbed at his pistol, intending to kill this strange and deadly newcomer.

Events slowed down for Travis as time seemed to extend, drawn out into finite slivers of reality. He watched purple enragement contort the raider's face. Behind the writhing horse the raider steadied his hand and aimed directly at him, pulling back the hammer on the big bore revolver.

But he was too late for the kill. A rose bouquet bloomed above his shoulders, and he was done for; mostly beheaded by what could only have been a shot from the besieged house. What was left of him collapsed inward, a shattered clay vessel.

Sure enough, Travis looked past the wounded animal to see shadowed figures inside, some pointing at more threats beyond, others gesturing for him to come to them. All were yelling words of both encouragement and warning. He glanced toward the surrounding fields, and then saw the danger. Three raiders on horseback, sabers raised, were plunging through the smoke and pelting rain directly toward him.

There would be no time to outrun them to gain the relative safety of the house. His only chance was to stop them while they charged. He scrambled to his feet and readied his revolvers, grateful he'd taken the time to properly reload them earlier. He aimed both at the leading raider and fired.

Both shots went wide.

"Missed! Gotta do better than that!"

Still holding his aim at the lead raider, he dropped the hammers. Again, twin lances of flame blazed from the barrels. This time the saber dropped from the suddenly limp grip of the stricken man, who tottered off the saddle while the riderless horse veered away, fate directing its fearful gallop into the path of the next saber-wielding killer behind him. The horses banged together in a gritty plume of sweat and lather, forcing the rider to grab his saddle's pommel to prevent being unseated by the impact.

"Luck o' the draw right there. Let's do it again. One down, two to go."

Travis stood stone still upon the muddy red ground, his two pistols at the ready. The raider cursed and fumbled about, fighting to stay mounted while disentangling himself from the thrashing beast that had crashed into him. Meanwhile, the third horseman raised his blade higher, sneering as he thundered in to kill the stony eyed sergeant.

"I'm bringing your damn head back with me, stranger!"

Less than ten feet separated them when Travis fired. Only one of the lead balls struck his target. It was enough. Surprise and doom shadowed the raider's face, knowing he'd been mortally wounded. Still, he made a last attempt to chop off his adversary's head while the horse passed by. Travis crouched low below the slashing blade, sidestepping away. The dying man slid to the ground, while the other, seeing the fate of two compatriots, prudently decided to withdraw at a full gallop, at least for now.

Ignoring for now the ecstatic yells and shouts from the inside the house, he paused to listen to the last words of the man he'd just shot. Pink foam and gurgling streams of blood pouring from his mouth made them difficult to understand, but they were an unmistakable threat.

"You think you won, but I'll be back. We'll all be back. The Captain said so. We'll eat your heart for breakfast, and then again for dinner. Your soul won't never have no rest, feedin' us all for the rest of forever. That's all you'll be good for when we catch up to you, fool. The Captain will roast your liver hisself. You should'a never got sentimental about them there civilians. Feedin' us is all they're good for. I can see you're a soldier, you could'a maybe joined us."

"I don't kill women and babies."

"You ain't met The Captain yet, fool."

He died spewing a frothy red retch, face pale as paper, thin, crinkly.

Rousing from the unhinged threat, Travis turned his attention back toward the attackers. They seemed to have, at least temporarily, slackened their assault, perhaps to regroup and reassess their tactical situation due to the sudden loss of several of their men, and the deadly threat that the newcomer obviously posed them.

The gunfire from inside the house had abated as well. The defenders continued to anxiously shout for him to get a move on to come join them.

He debated only a moment. A small part of him yearned for the freedom of movement that he might find by escaping through the forest, but then a too close for comfort slug kicked up a trough of mud a few inches from his foot. New anger quickly decided him, and he was off running toward the relative safety of the house.

Then he saw it. One of the raider's horses was still nearby. He diverted his path to the beast and mounted up. He wasn't going to let those sons of bitches get one of their war horses back if he could help it. It felt good to ride again, if only for a short distance.

Sporadic shots once again came his way. He kept low in the saddle while he raced toward the waving men inside. An odd glint within the forest off to his left caught his attention, but when Travis looked over, whatever it was had gone, if it had ever really existed.

"What was that? Perhaps a motion, perhaps a pair of eyes... it was just a flash. Probably nothing. Can't worry about it now, need to get out of this open space before those raiders get

lucky!"

The house sat on a heavy stone foundation that rose a few feet above the ground. Above that the first floor was surrounded by a deck that ran along the periphery. A large shed took up the ground in the back, its doors slightly open. It was on the opposite side from the raiders and promised at least a partial haven for him and his four-legged plunder.

The fraught defenders urged him on ever more loudly as he approached them.

"C'mon, c'mon! Git on over here, stranger! They'll skin you alive if'n they ketch you out there! Hurry up!"

Travis took the advice. He rode hard, hooves flinging clots of muck and small stones aside as the horse thundered from the field, leaving his defeated foes to mindlessly drain their lifeblood into the sad, soggy mud. He urged the horse on, staying flat along its mane and withers to present a diminished profile to the enemy. Bullets clawed past his fast-moving target with an angry buzzing of near misses.

A defender fired his rifle from a blasted-out window toward another pack of slowly congregating raiders, then shouted at Travis as he rode by.

"Better hurry! They're starting to form up again! Get on over here quick like! They're coming!"

Slowing at the last instant, he brought the horse under control and into the dimly lit shed. Dropping to his feet he quickly hitched it up. No more bullets came his way, as the shed was partially screened from view by the house. But Travis figured at least one of the raiders had moved around the obscuring walls far enough to solve that problem.

"*Those cusses most likely have a bead on this door by now, waitin' for me to show my face so they can shoot it off. Let's find out.*"

He looked around the shed. A worn barrel lid lay atop a junk pile. Hefting it, he stepped to the door and flung it outside. A shot cracked from afar, piercing the old lid and sending splinters spinning.

Taking full advantage of the diversion, time again slowed into discrete slivers as Travis dove low out the doorway, hitting the ground to roll several times, then leaping up to hotfoot a ragged beeline into the house. The welcoming defenders cleared his path past the barricade, holding the door open. His ears were filled by encouraging shouts that overwhelmed the angry curses of the raiders he'd just bamboozled out of their chance to shoot him.

He entered.

Immediately afterwards, the *pedrero* bellowed its defiance at the circling killers, dissuading yet another raider who had strayed too close. Its roar greeted Travis before the cheering men inside were able to, a few of whom fervently pounded his back in admiration and shake his hand while congratulating his success against the two-legged hyenas outside.

His eyes began to adjust to the dimly lit impressions of the defenders under siege. Although some were smiling through the lines of stress that betrayed their precarious and deadly condition, most were not, and hardly bothered a glance in his direction as they continued to focus their attention and weapons upon the imminent danger outside. Looking around, he was impressed with the thick oak beams and heavy construction of the fortress-like old house. It looked like it might be a harder nut to crack than the facade it presented to the enemy's scrutiny.

The man closest to him pressed a greasy bread-and-bacon sandwich into his hand. "My name's Will, I own this place. This food ain't much but I'm guessin' you've been livin' rough and half-starved out there. This here chow should help separate your belly from your back. Help yourself to fresh water and some of those crab apples over on that table, too."

"The name's Travis. I rightly appreciate these here vittles but before I can eat, I'd like to know who it was blasted the head off the filthy swine that was about to kill me out there. That was the best shooting I've ever seen, and I want to thank him for saving my life."

Another "*CRACK*" echoed loudly from the rifle of a man snug behind a barricade of overturned tables. As he swabbed the barrel and reloaded, he called across the room to another man sitting low on the floor, his weapon poking out a slit in the several sandbags piled before him.

"Jamie got that polecat what was tryin' to kill you, didn't you Jamie?"

"Nah. I was takin' a bead on a sumbitch cross the field off to the right. Weren't me that got him. I thought it were Samuel brought him down, he's got the eagle eye here. You're the one that got him, right, Samuel?"

Samuel, a large man with a smallish head and, eagle or not, a pair of glum, close-set eyes, didn't spare a whit of interest at the social proceedings or the question. His rifle tracked slowly right to left, intent upon a group of three horseman quickly approaching in echelon, their weapons drawn, their intent clear and determined.

"*Boom*" bellowed his rifle. A fatal moment later reddish mist bloomed from the back of the middle rider. He scrabbled furiously at the air. Failing to find any purchase to cling a second more to life, his body tumbled off the saddle to become an awkward clot of flesh, draining into muddy earth.

Shaken, the other two riders glanced at each other. A decision both grim and deadly passed between them. They turned tail, retreating whence they'd come, knowing they might confront a greater danger there than the guns that pointed at them from inside the house. But after two years serving under the man they called the Captain, they both knew that... and were used to it by now... or so they thought.

All gunfire paused. Only the sound of rain splatters could be heard as the defenders watched the two black-shirted raiders ride back to their lair. A collective sigh of gratitude rose at this brief respite.

Samuel spoke up. "Weren't me neither that got whoever was trying to kill Mr. Travis. I didn't see the shot. I was reloadin'. I do recall there was a plenteous amount of gunfire at the time. I only looked up after hearin' all the whoopin' and hollers. I want to thank whoever made that shot too. I'm glad Mr. Travis is here with us. We're gonna need ever' man. Oh, and ever' woman too, of course."

The higher-pitched voice of one of the two working the *pedrero* spoke up. "That's right, Uncle Samuel, we're doing our part. Already got five or six of them."

The other woman looked up at Travis, catching his eye. She spoke up quickly, "It was seven, sister."

"Well, that's even better, Lorne."

Travis looked closer at the gun crew as they reloaded the little cannon. Sure enough, both were women, and each was the mirror image of the other.

"Twins! Well, ain't that unlikely!"

Just then, from across the field came shouting, and the yells of angry men. One voice rumbled louder than the rest. The words were unintelligible at this distance, but the meaning was clear: great disapproval.

Two gunshots rang out, neither aimed at the house. Very soon afterwards five more raiders burst from the concealing forest, riding toward the house. They split apart about halfway across the field, with three heading at Samuel and the other riflemen, while two galloped toward the opposite end of the house.

"We got these three, but them two's all your'n, Lorne." Samuel chuckled at his little rhyme as he finished reloading his deadly rifle. He spared a sad, momentary grin at Travis before turning back to aim at the approaching riders. "I got the back one, you other boys take front and center."

"Good as done, Samuel." came from one of the other riflemen nearby.

Lorne yelled across the room, "We got 'em aimed on, Uncle Sam."

When they got within range the twin's little cannon boomed again, discharging its load across the path of both charging horsemen. A scream wrenched from the leading raider as the expanding cone of rocks, stones, and rusty chunks of metal raked his side, leaving bloody gouges across face, chest, and arm. Watching him ride past, Travis thought he saw what might have been a dangling eyeball.

But somehow the wounded man did manage to stay on his horse. He circled away from them with an angry whirl of curses, threats, and agonized expletives. He was out of the fight, at least for now.

Not so the other raider. He came on. It seemed to Travis, even from the back of the house, hidden inside by its dimness, that somehow this rider was aiming directly at him, guided by a supernatural target that shone like a beacon on his chest.

He tossed the sandwich aside and drew his pistols once again. Trying to ignore the rifle pointing at him, he strode three paces toward his enemy, coming right up to the backside of the barricade. He cocked the hammers, aimed, and fired in one smooth action as he yelled his defiance.

"Damn you to Hades!"

The pistols' heavy steel mass took up much of the recoil of their discharge. Both barrels sped their spinning balls of lead poisoning toward the target. The rider received the delivery. The simultaneous impact of the bullets kicked him back in his saddle an instant before his finger twitched the rifle's trigger.

The two shots that tore through the raider were enough to yank his rifle askew. Its fifty-caliber bullet crashed into the ceiling inside, causing only a shower of painted plaster to rain harmlessly upon its intended target. The rifle slid from the dead man's grip, its butt landing in the mud just beyond the bottom porch step, its barrel pointing upward.

The horse bolted off, carrying the slumped body with it.

Travis brushed clumps of dusty plaster from himself while noting the hole in the wall above his head and wondered how that killer had been able to mark him so well from outside like that.

"Just imagining things, I guess. Ain't no way that's possible."

A short lull ensued as the raiders seemed to lose determination. They fell back to regroup and count their dead. This time, they weren't so anxious to attack again.

Travis relaxed, then saw the lopsided sandwich on the table back where he'd tossed it. He grabbed it. It was the best sandwich he'd ever had.

While he ate, he thought about what had happened earlier, outside.

"If the shot that saved me out there wasn't taken by any of these folks, then WHO WAS IT?"

His thoughts were interrupted as Will declared, "They must be takin' a fancy luncheon party over there. I suppose even demons pretending to be human gotta eat sometime. I suggest we do the same. It's died down quite a bit out there but even so, we need to stay at our posts. I'll fix us all some grub."

He made several more of the bacon and bread sandwiches and passed them out. Travis declined another.

"You know, Will, that I already had my share."

"C'mon Mr. Travis. You gotta keep your strength up, just like the rest of us." Don't be a damned martyr. I knew this day, or something else like it, would come. I've been storin' up supplies, hiding them in the cellar as I could. We've still got plenty of food and water left here." He pressed a bacon slab within its bready nest into Travis' hand. "I won't take no for an answer. I can see you've been missin' quite a few meals. You eat up now." After a moment, Travis nodded and ate the second sandwich.

Jamie called out. "Hey Mr. Travis. I've been thinkin'... you're pretty good with them six shooters of yours. But how would you like to get your hands on a rifle?"

"Well! You got another one laying around here? Yes, of course I would."

"Uh, sorta. Not exactly layin' around *here*, so to speak, but yessir, there's another one *leaning*, right out there!" He pointed outside. Travis could see that the rifle still lay where it had fallen. It was about ten or fifteen feet away, leaning upright against the porch's bottom step.

"This might be a good time for grabbing it. That weapon would be good to have." Travis began to move around the barrier toward the prize outside.

Samuel spoke up, an urgent rasp in his voice. "Hold up there. Those cusses over yonder may have stopped shooting at us, but they sure ain't stopped watching. I'm sure I can see at least three sets of their beady spyin' eyes back in the bushes, even through this bit o' rain and ground vapor." Samuel turned to Travis directly. "I'm sorry Mr. Travis, but if you go out there, you're gonna get plugged, surely you are."

This stopped him in his tracks. Frustrated, he knew that rifle would eventually be needed if they were to continue to have a chance, he almost continued outside anyway. But the evidence of Samuel's "eagle eyes" had been proven indisputable. If anyone could see into their enemy's domain, it was him.

One of the twins spoke up. "Uncle Sam, we don't have to go outside to get that rifle. We can reach it from in here."

It was Lorne. Her shoulder-length blond hair had been tucked up under a soldier's cap, adding to the illusion of her boyish mien. At first glance, no one would have thought that she wasn't a young man of fighting age, until she spoke, of course.

Having completed the re-loading of the *pedrero,* she rose and went to a shelf behind her, obtaining a length of coiled rope, fit and flexible.

"Before these horrible raiders showed up, my sister and I were practicing every day with roping, just in case any of the critters we used to keep out there might get loose and wander off." She began to loop it around her hand and wrist, ready for casting. "Now, I'm pretty sure I can spin this here rope over that there rifle's action, and we'll just drag it on up here."

She stepped up to just inside the thick walls of the barricade, out of sight of the raiders beyond. Standing on a wooden box to gain some height, she whirled the rope in tight, fast circles. Will, feeling that he was standing a touch too close nearby, took a few paces back. Travis watched intently, knowing that they needed that rifle, but concerned with what the enemies outside watching might do once they perceived the intent of the defenders to recover the weapon. He didn't want Lorne risking her life for something that ought to be his obligation.

Nevertheless, she flung the coil and the lasso flicked outward, its noose landing close by, but not over, the rifle. For a moment it lay there, beginning to soak in a small puddle of water, drizzle sprinkling the thirsty hemp.

Lorne quickly pulled the rope back, coiling it up as she did so. She cleaned the muddied end with a rag.

"Can't let it stay wet or it'll get full of slop and be too heavy to float the end out proper-like." She looked at Travis. "Gotta try again."

Once more the coil spun, again it released.

The small loop flew truly this time, arching flatly through its trajectory. It encircled the gun barrel, dropping over the action.

A cheer rose from the beleaguered household as she gently flicked the rope, tightening the business end around the rifle and then dragging it back, bumping up along the steps.

No shots came at them during this operation. This surprised Travis, as he'd expected their enemies to continue their trigger-happy spendthrift habits. They seemed to have unlimited quantities of both ammunition and men to expend.

"So, what's different this time? You'd think they wouldn't want us to have that rifle. So why aren't they trying to stop us? It's almost like they've something else on their minds."

He looked around outside nervously, seeking any unnatural movement or odd noise. Nothing was unusual, outside of the inescapable fact of being trapped in a makeshift blockhouse under siege by a small army of bloodthirsty killers.

Just then, Lorne dragged the rifle up and over

the barricade. It came clumping inside.

"And here it is. Not so much fun as ropin' one of our critters used to be, but a needful task." She took the rope off the muddy, red specked weapon and placed it on a nearby table. It thumped down heavily, demanding respect even while stained in blood-soaked muck. "You can clean it up yourself, Mr. Travis."

Will said, "There's a small table over there behind us you can use. There's cleaning supplies and rags already on it."

Travis picked up the weapon and got to work.

For the next five minutes or so a malignant calm settled over the defenders. They knew the fight wasn't over but began to relax from the high pitched awareness they'd known since the beginning of the attack. The household began to breath an involuntary sigh of relief. But only for a few moments more.

A raider burst from the shadowy bushes afield. Arms outstretched to either side, he carried four burning brands of oil-soaked flame and seemed to be guiding his horse by his knees alone. He came directly at the besieged house, his purpose plain.

A massive fusillade of firepower answered this daft charge. Every gun of the defenders fired at once, most striking the attacker square on.

His body shook, but did not waver, did not fall. Still the firebrands burned, still were they clutched in his hands. He came on, relentlessly.

Fear and horrible surprise gripped everyone who saw this display of unnatural power. A groan of dismay filled the once hopeful but now suddenly tomb-like room.

"He's gonna burn us out!"

"Impossible! He should be dead!"

"Reload! Reload now!"

Travis, having not quite finished cleaning and loading the newly acquired rifle, leapt up, heading toward the barricade closest to the quickly approaching attacker. He knew he had the only weapons still capable of firing. But he'd foolishly neglected to reload them during all the fuss of recovering the rifle. He knew he had only two rounds remaining, one in each pistol.

As the seemingly undead rider approached, his hat blew off, revealing unsighted eyes lolling in a bloodless face of eternal hate.

"That's one of the two raiders that turned back after we shot the third one dead!"

Travis remembered hearing the two gunshots from inside the forest and realized what the raiders had done. They'd made sure he wouldn't retreat this time.

"We didn't miss with those last shots, 'cause you can't kill a dead man! You already got shot dead as a doorknob after you went back to your boss! Then they tied you to your saddle and trussed you up like a turkey holding your own cook fires. It's all a trick! But who's riding that horse if it ain't this here fake phantasm?"

Travis got a quick answer. Suddenly, the second man who'd also fled sat up, rising from behind the propped-up corpse of the dead man.

Evidently this task was his penance. He ripped the blazing sticks away, then shoved the body aside to dangle half dragged. Supposing that all the weapons inside had already been discharged, he smiled at the deception.

Jabbering maniacally, he galloped close to the house, stretching his arms back to hurl the brands of flame toward its relatively dry porch. He knew they would burn there.

But now, out of the shadows stepped the newcomer with the only loaded weapons. He aimed his pistols square centered upon the attacker's chest. Surprise and consternation yanked the demented smile from the raider's face. He saw his death awaiting him within those barrels.

Yet, with even that knowledge, he still started to fling the deadly firebrands forward, propelled more by the distilled venom of evil pumping hatred through his veins than by muscle. Under the lash of The Captain's commands, and the thought of the unusually harsh punishments for failure, he was determined to complete those orders to burn down the house, even as he rode straight into his own demise. An almost inhuman screech of frustrated rage lacerated his throat. Things weren't working out like he'd planned.

It was too late for him to make any other decisions now. The first weapon Travis fired expended a small puff of impotent smoke, its small percussion cap hammerstruck yet futile. The second barrel did light up, a long flame announcing the discharge of its lead cargo. The projectile slammed into the raider's chest, stifling his scream. The new-born corpse dropped the flaming brands.

Two carcasses swung wildly alongside the maddened horse. It galloped up the several steps and through the door. Travis leaped aside as it smashed into the barricades, stumbling over them with some difficulty while still carrying its double cargo of dead meat. It continued through the room toward the light shining through the door at the rear, where Travis had first entered. He turned to watch it crash away.

Beyond the door, he saw different movements. He shouted.

"The open door! That door's open! They're behind us!"

Sure enough, before the words were even out of his mouth, the frothing horse exited, still dragging along its flopping human saddlebags. Four men paused to allow its passage, then stepped inside. All dressed in black, they began to disperse away from the door, guns in hand.

They were too late. The few seconds delay in having to wait for the exit of the horse had allowed the efficient twins enough time to reload their small cannon and turn it around to the rear. The sharp explosion from the *pedrero* wreaked agonized havoc among the group, exacting terrible wounds from all. The two invaders closest to it fell where they stood, flesh shaved and twitching.

One of the other two gurgled frothy screams attempting to hold his shattered throat together and simultaneously fire his pistol at his tormentors. He failed at both tasks, finally dropping to his knees to suffocate while his lungs filled with his own blood.

Meanwhile, the raider who had been farthest from the two sisters' barrage had only had one arm caressed by the explosion of bent nails, glass shards, and rusty iron scraps. Its cartilage and bone devastated, the useless appendage oozed blood past dangling tendons as it flopped around uselessly. He began to fire randomly throughout the house, screaming.

One bullet brushed past Travis' left ear before it crashed into the wall behind him.

"If it ain't me, no one's gonna be able to stop this devil. Time to do what needs be done."

Charting his path across the room, Travis circled quick and low around the furniture, hoping to come up on the weakened side of the last standing invader that had been flayed by the blast of the *pedrero*.

A good plan but one brought low when a table knocked about by the passage of the horse shifted. He slammed his knee into its edge. He grunted, drawing the deadly attention of the gunman, who fired off the pistol's last cylinders in his general direction.

Travis had already dropped behind the shelter of one of the dirt-filled barrels, ignoring the pain in his leg. The bullets slammed into the shielding earth. The gunman dropped the hammer once more, but the hollow *"CLICK"* exposed to all that his pistol had transformed from a death-dealing instrument of almost supernatural powers, into a mere club.

Undeterred, cursing, he dropped the inert clump of wood and steel, then smoothly yanked a second, fully loaded, pistol from his other holster. Blood from his grated arm spun off in random arcs as it flipped about, seeming like a fish on a pole.

Travis unsheathed his Bowie and moved forward fast toward his antagonist, its sharpened point a guiding compass of doom.

The pistol had been raised just enough for Travis to grapple with the wrist that held it. The raider was a strong man, but so was Travis, and even with the privations of the last month, he was able to match his strength to the rabid ferocity of the injured man. He held tight the wrist and kept the pistol down, pointed at the floor, while its owner pulled the trigger in frustrated rage. Bullets smashed harmlessly into the heavy wood flooring below, even as the raider screamed.

"I'm a gonna kill you all! Die! DIE, *DIE!*"

With never a sound in reply, Travis brought his long blade of sharpened steel to bear on the raider's midpoint, forcing it inexorably under the protective curve of ribs, piercing his innards to release a gushing flow of blood so dark it looked almost black.

The twilit eyes of the mortally wounded man focused one last time. He smiled and spoke quietly to Travis.

"It's hopeless for you. The Otherside always wins, and our Captain is The Otherside. You have no chance against him. As for you, stranger, *Blestemul Morti.*"

Those last two words banged as boulders cracking. The gun dropped from his hand. He died.

Although daylight still illuminated the squalls outside, a dark cage of deepening chill began to swirl around Travis as he wiped his blade off and returned it to its sheath.

Echoes of the dead man's final utterance persisted, words that brought visions... infinite rows of granite slabs clashing one upon the other, scudding down a steep and frozen mountain pass, forever.

He stumbled as the tendrils of darkness multiplied around him. The cries of concern from his new compatriots became muffled and

68

squashed. Spots and then layers of blackness jumbled his senses while he staggered away from the bleeding-out corpse. He stumbled incoherent through the open back door and beyond before he fell.

He felt himself flying upwards within the cupped hand of a power beyond any he'd known. The dark mists solidified into a transparent shell around him. The Earth receded, suddenly far away, while the leering moon grew grotesque in size, a grayness spinning beneath him as he brushed past its dusty surface.

Travis flew on, carried through the aether, disoriented and helpless on this journey of spectral sight and terrifying wonder. He crossed beyond a frozen portal somewhere within the infinite curtains of time itself. He uttered a silent prayer, and then another few for good measure. Soon, exhaustion swept over him. Unconscious, he traveled, dragged along time and space within the fissures of the Between.

4. THE GREAT DEEP OF TIME

"ARRIVAL."

The voice woke Travis. He lay prostrate upon frozen ground, cold and confused. He turned over to find himself under a whitish blue dome of sky surrounded by jagged mountains, the size of which he'd never before imagined.

The sounds of battle, familiar but oddly unlike any he'd heard, echoed all around him, yet out of sight. Around a blurred corner lay shadows garbled by a broken sun, dark outlines of men fighting on horseback. He rose slowly to his feet, looking for whomever had spoken, only to have a wave of nausea and dizziness force him to sit down on a boulder. There were many such large stones strewn about the hemmed-in plain of what he guessed to be a mountain pass.

His head began to clear. The raging battle clashed, its ferocity rising as the numbers of wounded cried out in greater numbers. His own person was held safely in this dream, for surely it must be a dream. He was, he knew, in a makeshift blockhouse under siege, not among peaks so high and jagged that their mere existence defied reality.

"Who's killin' who out there?" Listening more intently as he recovered, his understanding gelled when he realized there were no sounds of firearms or gunpowder. Just steel upon steel, and the thick hollow thumps of ax and arrow into flesh. *"And with what? Ain't nobody's firing*

71

cannon or musket. Nothing."

Unpainted chiaroscuros upon the splintered granite walls showed horsemen's swords falling and rising methodically amongst their enemies. Spearmen came forward, trying to stanch the slaughter, but were cut down in droves of cruelty, their necks, chests, and eyes pierced by unceasing flights of arrows. Grinning horse archers drove their mounts in close, unleashed death from their compound bows, then rode back out again to nock another projectile, over and over.

Travis marveled at the havoc and bloodshed that could be done to human bodies without a single shot being fired. *"My God, what a brawl...*"

"Your LORD has few adherents in this realm of the great Deep of Time."

The voice rumbled around Travis, more firm than an iron blade in bone.

"A world is changed by both action and words, Soldier Travis Lehrman. I must tell you that here upon this battlefield of frozen dust, your ancestor spoke a vow that must be fulfilled... but has not been. We of the Outer Forces have given you an opportunity for both action and remedy."

"Opportunity?! I'm supposed to thank the outer who-sis for what? These mountains, this battle... and fixing something my relative said and never did? Makes no sense to me! Where is this, and who are you?"

"My name is unimportant. But... it would be more illuminating to ask me 'WHEN'... "

Travis obliged the disembodied voice, "All right. WHEN is this? And not to be rude, but who the hell are you? Why am I here?"

"As I said, my name is not important, but since you and the other beings of this world seem to put considerable importance upon them, you may call me One. This is the year of your Lord 865. An oath was recorded and sealed in fire by an immutable curse... yet never achieved. We deemed it important enough for you to be brought here from your time and place through the fissures and pathways of the Between to fulfill these words. Now, you are here at the when and where this vow will soon be spoken by your ancestor."

"What words? What curse? Why am I here?"

"You are here to kill the commander of an invading mercenary army that betrayed your forefather."

"What?! Who do you think you are, dragging me off from a fight I care about to another I don't!"

"To repeat, you are here to kill the commander of an invading army that betrayed your ancestor. And to clarify, both fights you speak of are against the same foe, merely separated by time and location. If you destroy this enemy now, your fight in the When from where you came will never happen."

"What you say is... confusing, but, alright, Mr. One, nice to make your acquaintance... I think. But I don't believe I heard you correctly about something else. What year did you say this was?"

"The year of your Lord 865."

"No, no, no. It is 1865! This isn't 865. I'm an artillery sergeant assigned to a battery in the year of our Lord 1865! We were completely overrun, wiped out, except for me! Since then,

I've been tryin' to get back to my lines."

"And you have succeeded, Soldier Travis Lehrman. Accept these facts. Before has become Now. Here in this time and place of the year 865, THESE are your army's lines, for you have been returned to your own bloodline by the power of the Between. You will be safe here, at least until you face the enemy. We of the Outer Forces have given you a chance to keep your people from being destroyed by the hordes who have followed The Otherside from beyond far mountains unseen. You must stop these invaders that your progenitor failed to halt before."

"Sounds like a battle I've already been through, but listen Mr. *One*, this ain't my war. This is all just a dream, or more likely a nightmare, like you must be."

"Open your eyes, short-sighted one. This dust is not a dream, nor is the bloodletting of the invasion happening before you. This is a war against all your people... and your very world. A war that seeks to bring suffering and undead horror upon these lands for another millennia, should you fail again."

"Again? I've never been to this place!"

"Your ancestor knew the stakes for which he fought but was betrayed. You will take his place when you must, then you too will know."

Screaming sounds that could only be curses, one of the defenders stumbled past the rocky outcrop that shielded Travis and his unseen companion. His body was there and yet not there, allowing Travis to see through its diffuse form to the boulders beyond. The warrior carried a gore-soaked spear. The leather straps of his armor hung ineffectually, sliced free in battle. Two arrows protruded from his body, perhaps not fatal yet, but surely agonizing as he continued to curse and jab his spear around him, parrying unseen enemies. The language he spit was unlike anything Travis had heard.

"Arrows? Who are these people? Indians? What's going on here?"

"Hear me well, Soldier Travis Lehrman. In these lands and times, a King could not hold back invasion from his sworn blood enemies to the West. So, to stop them, he invited the army of his Eastern allies into his realms. They arrived, and after many brutal battles, the invaders from the West were vanquished. After their great victory, the grateful King arranged to pay his allies the gold he'd promised them. He had a magnificent hall built upon the field of victory, stocked with meats and delicacies. It was to be a sumptuous feast of celebration and the ceremony of payment."

Travis shrugged, "Seems about right to me. A deal's a deal."

A noise like ten-thousand human sighs came from *One*, disturbing the frozen soil beneath the boulder on which Travis sat. The unseen voice continued.

"But unknown to the King, his Eastern allies had become indolent and cautious. They did not want to lose their men in battle for another leader's cause. So, they in their turn had hired a mercenary army from the North to fight in the front lines for them. Their warriors were powerful, but treachery rode with these blood-thirsty Northern men. Their horse archers tracked down the soldiers who were bringing

75

the payment to the feast. They ambushed and killed them all, stole the chest of gold, then blamed the King for cheating them when it did not arrive."

Travis grunted, "I've heard of worse, but go on."

"The allies believed the evil leader of the mercenaries, who demanded payment of the very gold he himself had stolen. The common soldiers were lied to and became angry, believing they'd been cheated for their service. Both Eastern and Northern armies threw themselves upon the King."

"Two against one. No wonder the King is losing. Is that what this fight is all about?"

"Yes. In part. They attack here and now in the pass of these mountains with their combined forces to claim the value of the gold they were promised. For the soldiers from the North, it is a frenzy of land-taking. For their leader, of captives and blood sacrifice."

"Land-taking and blood-*SACRIFICE?!*"

"Indeed. And this is where your ancestor swore the oath that has brought you here. Rather, he WILL swear it shortly; an oath that binds you to fulfill his duty if you are able."

The sky darkened, hearkening a false sunset, for the shadows cast by the sliver of sun remaining lay short upon the ground.

Travis looked around, confused. *"It looks as if it were almost high noon. But how can that be when the sun is setting? Or is it really?"*

The shimmering warrior before them continued combating his closest adversary, both of their forms becoming more substantial by the second. Other enemy fighters nearby were

76

gloating and insolent as they also solidified from the mists of time.

Travis stood up, his weakness and dizziness gone, now replaced with a growing stupefaction as he watched more and more battling men appear. It was as if the winds blowing between the towering peaks were scooping up the many centuries of icy dust that filled the pass, forming their lives anew from this frozen clay. He looked around behind him, anywhere, for something that might anchor him to the reality he had so recently been a part of. Nothing familiar was to be seen, there was nothing here for his being to grasp onto.

He shook himself, trying to escape from what he desperately wanted to believe must be a nightmare. But he remained, stubbornly embedded in this ancient world, assailed by the stench of pooling gore and filth and blood that slicked the frozen landscape.

Warriors screamed as the sky darkened. All around them, the mountainsides shaded from steel blue to the cobalt of midnight. Stars winked into sight beyond the towering peaks to either side, and directly overhead. The mottled sun, which had so recently shone its icy radiance the length of the pass, had almost gone out.

In its stead loomed a last forlorn sliver of rapidly decreasing brightness.

"Alright, Mr. *One*, alright! You win! I'm here! You say that you and some others brought me here for a reason! Now, what am I supposed to do?"

"Go forward into the fray as I instruct. You must step into the footprints of your ancestor as he falls. Your planet's star will be eclipsed by

77

then, just as he utters his oath."

"Hellish. This is hellish and horrific. Alright. I'm here. What then?"

"You must kill The Otherside."

"Kill?! The what? Kill the eye? The other's eye?"

"Listen carefully. You must kill THE OTHERSIDE! He is first chief among these warriors before you! He is their leader!"

"With *WHAT*? I don't have any of them spears these boys got, and I sure as hell don't know how to shoot no arrows! Besides, there's over a thousand men fighting out there, how am I supposed to tell which one needs killin'?"

"He is distinctive. He is large and mounted with the other horse warriors. The Otherside will draw your attention even before he murders your ancestor. After that, you must shoot him with your projectile weapon. Hear me, Soldier Travis Lehrman, you are being given a chance to excise an emissary of eternal evil. As for your other question, your weapons are at your waist."

Sure enough, both pistols hung secure in his holsters. He remembered the last time he'd used them. He'd emptied them into the attacking horseman who'd been carrying the torches.

"Guess you don't know how these things work, Mr. *One*. These pistols are empty right now! I have to reload 'em. Until then, they're pretty much worthless, and it don't look like we've got much time left until I'm supposed to do-si-do with whoever you say is my great-great old grand pappy out there. I'll never get 'em loaded up by then."

"Wrong. One weapon still contains a

78

projectile. You do have time enough to replace the small explosive cap that failed to work earlier with a functional one. That task must be done now."

"Ah, of course!" He'd forgotten about the misfire. He could fix that instantly. In the growing gloom of the approaching eclipse, Travis reached down and hastily pulled out the pistol with its very last ball still loaded. He removed the faulty percussion cap, blew out the cylinder hole to allow the sparks ingress to detonate the waiting gunpowder charge within, and placed a new one carefully over the nib. Spinning the cylinder into the proper position for firing its one last bullet, it was ready, only needing to be aimed, cocked, and hammer dropped.

This Otherside son of a bitch was gonna get a surprise present from a thousand years away.

Even as he finished his preparations, doubt remained within Travis. *"I'm thinkin' like a pigheaded mule! I must be going mad with some sort of fever dream. I shouldn't believe any of these here horse droppings I'm seein'! I'm gonna wake up anytime now and have another bacon sandwich at that house, that's what will happen!"*

But his wish was not to be. Here he was, and here he stayed.

Around him the attackers and defenders looked fearfully to the glowering sky above the mountain pass. Their phantasms now became solid as the millennia-old dust coalesced into life once more. Life that, perversely, made its only purpose death as they fought to kill with blade and bow.

The unseen voice of *One* burst loud, an

irresistible bugle call, jostling urgent action upon Travis.

"Then has become Now. Into the fray. Destroy The Otherside!"

"Where am I going?"

"The spearman that you first saw is he who is your primogenitor. He is the son of the King that was robbed and cruelly cut down by treachery. It is he, and his royal family hidden many miles from here, that you must fight for. It is he that The Otherside kills as he who swears the Oath you are now responsible for. We have brought you through the infinite folds of the Between so you may fulfill that vow."

"So, he has a family that somehow lives through this and I'm... "

One rumbled at him, a quaking from all directions, shaking his guts and stinging his skin.

"Yes, they survived, and now you are their last descendant. All others have died. We sought you for many years. You are the last who may fulfill the oath. You are the last hope, Soldier Travis Lehrman."

To Travis, the voice of *One* overwhelmed the sounds of the battlefield like a cannon firing double-shot loads of canister at point-blank range. Yet, none of these ancient soldiers he saw seemed to hear it. It was like he was tucked away, just around the corner of Time.

Travis thought, *"What was it Mr. One said, about us being safe inside something called the Between? Maybe that's why they can't hear or see us."*

One spoke again. *"Gaze above you. Soon, the radiant blaze of this world's star will be unleashed! To be revealed, what you call the sun must be either directly above, or have its mundane light blocked by an eclipse. Then your sun's power to fray The Otherside's strength will be unleashed as its outer radiance pierces every shadowed crevice of the evil one. He will be weakened enough that you may kill him before his flesh is renewed."*

Travis did look up. The sun was only a tiny sliver peeking from behind a dark disc, yet still blindingly bright. "I'd heard about this kind of thing, but never thought I'd see one. That's the moon, covering up the sun, isn't it?"

One didn't bother to answer the question. *"Our time grows short. Can you not feel it? The boundaries between the ages that we straddle, and the level of power The Otherside may wield will be vastly weakened by the energies of the coming eclipse! You must act. Now... into the fray Soldier Travis Lehrman, NOW!"*

Travis felt that he was motivated by forces higher and more powerful than any before. He was getting orders from a greater general than he'd ever seen or saluted. He marched directly forward toward the beleaguered spearman at the melee's center.

That warrior fought ferociously, cutting down every man he faced. Yet the arrows loosed from archers hidden afar still at times managed to slip past his armor to strike the flesh within; Travis could see that he would soon succumb. For every adversary he cut down, he lost ground and precious blood. Step by blood-slicked step, he retreated before the invading swordsmen and the hulking horseman behind, who goaded the footmen on, swinging his axe at them and shouting what Travis guessed could only be threats.

"That's my thousand greats old grandpa? He don't look a lot like me. Well, he knows how to fight and he ain't no coward. He and his folk, my folk if what Mr. One says is true, deserve to win this war."

Raging battle surged everywhere. Close packed warriors were hampered in their defense. They couldn't move their weapons effectively without injuring their countrymen. Yet Travis pushed forward through them in the eerie dimness.

"Only seconds more remain, Soldier Travis Lehrman."

An arm's length away from his goal, he swerved past an enemy spear thrust and took a long final step, surrounded, and now pinned in place by a wall of bloody shields held by the dead, corpses so close packed they still stood upright amid the many bleeding, desperate warriors surrounding them. Travis now stood directly behind his great-ancient grandfather. The warrior took no notice of his descendant.

Above, the last sliver of light disappeared. The sky blackened with Totality.

"IT IS TIME!"

Past the high snowy peaks, he saw the sun transformed. A giant ring of frozen fire surrounded a hole in the sky, a black portal, now open to other worlds not of our reality. The blazing corona now visible around the sun seemed alive as it silently pulsed arcane energies down upon the battlefield. Its pale brightness invested every shadow that the powers of The Otherside might lurk within, forcing them out, weakening him.

The Otherside angrily summoned black, snowy flakes from the frozen sky in a vain attempt to bring his healing shadows back, but these only succeeded to coat the battlefield with a tainted, oily froth. The evil one on horseback tried to escape the shimmering pure light above him. He could not.

Warriors fell to their knees; some sank even lower to their bellies. They ululated their tribe's mourning songs of death and threw the frozen dust upon their own prostrate forms in madness, calling for the mercy of the gods they saw revealing themselves above, mercies they themselves would not have considered giving one another only moments before. All were stricken by the heavenly signs, save the three beings arrayed in their deadly tableau of inescapable fate: Travis, his ancient predecessor, and the alien nemesis before them.

Now, standing just beyond the shoulder of his ancient ancestor, Travis finally saw The Otherside in detail. There could be no doubt that this was the accursed *THING* that he had been brought here to kill.

A heavy jaw hinged open and shut below twin slits cut in a narrow, sharp nose. Thick folds of jelly-like skin wrapped eyes that surrounded black, pinpointed pupils. Grinning with the confidence of certain victory, the Otherside twisted open an over-toothed smile. Waves of putrescence wafted past a few strings of matted hair that fell below his iron battle helm.

Travis reached down, readying his weapon as his eyes narrowed upon the creature before him. *"Can't tell which one is uglier, that son of a bitch waving his axe around, or the horse he rode in on. I wish I had me one of my old unit's six-pounders pointed in his direction instead of this here pistol, or at least a few more bullets loaded. But I guess I should be used to it. As usual, I'm outnumbered and outgunned, and right now, outspeared, too. So. Let's do what I can and hope for the best."*

The leather sandals of his ancestor shifted in the frigid dust. Slick hail pellets crashing down from the frozen heavens made solid footing an increasing challenge. Yet the spearman stood strong, his battered armor soaked in red gore, his weapon at the ready.

A grim baying like a thousand hungry dogs burst from the horseman, who swung his battleax forward. "KNEEL to your new KING! You and yours are hereby FORFEIT! I said KNEEL, cur!"

"Your evil hordes may conquer us for now, but we shall NEVER kneel. I swear upon the graves of all my people, of the future, past, and present, that even if it takes a thousand years, we will fight and will defeat you! Your essence shall be crushed, and the pustule of your memory banished to the very edges of existence!"

The huge battleax swung again. The spearman stepped forward to fling his spear toward the horseman, but this time his foot landed upon an ice-coated stone. He slid uncontrollably into range of the swinging blade of doom. It struck him alongside his helmet in a stunning blow. His eyes remained focused long enough to watch his spear fly harmlessly past his target's head, only a finger length away.

He had missed.

Abominable cracking noises masquerading as

laughs pulled The Otherside's cheeks apart, revealing dead white incisors and too many sharp canines within a stinking maw darker than the frozen sky overhead. The entity's voice rattled like a thousand spider's claws, all clattering in hunger while wrapping up their sticky-netted prey. "So Weakness babbles to Strength, cur. Our land-takings shall continue! The Punishments we now visit upon your people will be increased a hundred-fold for your temerity!

The King's son stood undaunted, "Your treachery and foulness will be avenged by my people, no matter the time or price! You will never know who hunts you from behind with the sharpened stake of vengeance, demon! *BLESTEMUL MORTI!*"

The axe carried by The Otherside leapt forward once more, the motion almost faster than Travis could follow.

The defiant spearman's head separated from his body.

"Did I just watch my ancestor get killed? This is more than a nightmare; I can't wake up! But now, do I really want to? As long as I'm here, I know one thing, that pug-ugly critter that just chopped up my great old gran-dad needs a special kind of killin'!"

Defiant to the very last, the dead spearman stood straight before toppling onto the windswept earth, his lifeless husk no longer subject to the miseries of the battlefield.

As the spearman died, Travis completed his transit between worlds. No longer standing outside the threshold of this reality, he crashed into full existence. Blinking the stinging hail from his eyes, and attempting to ignore the mounting cold, he knew he wouldn't have long to complete his task. He drew his pistol, aiming it at the creature that had just decapitated a member of his family.

The invader was taken aback by this revenant from the future that had suddenly appeared. Travis stood resolutely in the footsteps of his murdered forefather. The merciless axe waved nervous paths in the air between them, as The Otherside remained unsure of what he should do next.

One spoke again, drilling its words into his brain. *"Then is now. You must act, Soldier Travis Lehrman! This is your last chance for another thousand years!"*

The weapon's barrel pointed between the eyes of his tormentor. Travis cocked the hammer and the one loaded cylinder rotated into its proper firing position. But the feral eyes of The Otherside sparked an unholy red. Time slowed around them, stalling almost to a stop. Travis pulled the trigger, but the small lever of steel beneath his finger now seemed to weigh a hundred pounds. Nevertheless, he kept up the pressure, waiting for it to release the hammer, for spark and then ignition.

"My last chance for a thousand years that Mister One feller says. Don't think I like them odds."

The axe kept up its slow meanderings. From well behind the front lines, an archer had recovered his wits, lashed by his master's unheard compulsion. He rose from the ground, loosing an arrow. The feathered shaft came out of the shadowy ranks in the rear with an inexorable mission to kill. It was perfectly aimed to fly harmlessly past the axe-wielding form of The Otherside, targeting only Travis.

The external slowing down of time which gripped the man from 1865 only affected his body, not his mind. He watched the plodding approach of the arrow with growing terror. It was an iron-tipped, razor sharp broad-head designed for maximum damage to human bone and brain. Travis knew his peril. He desperately tried to move his head off to one side, but the enforced lethargy of motion persisted. His muscles seemed as taffy, his bones heavy rods of lead.

Only a few feet remained between his face and the approaching arrow. He just couldn't move fast enough. The pain of his finger squeezing the barely moving trigger had become a scalding ache that wrapped living ropes of agony around his arm.

He kept the pressure up.

Everything happened at once. A tiny tremor from the pistol announced the hammer's release. Just as it struck the percussion cap, the arrow reached Travis' head. He had managed to twist away enough so that, instead of it piercing his eyeball and brain, the deadly missile scraped a bloody rut of hair and flesh, furrowing his skull as it passed him by. Mute rivulets of sweat and misery clawed his nerves while he strangled a scream, but he could not keep an involuntary spasm from reaching his limbs.

This time the percussion cap did not fail. Its tiny flame sparked down the center of the nib, igniting the powder within the weapon from the future. The superheated gasses demanded release as they exploded down the pistol's barrel pushing away the lead projectile in their path.

Travis felt himself twitch from the shock and pain of the arrow's wound. His perception of time stretched out again, slowing even more, and the bullet's path snapped into focus for him. He could see it spinning away toward his enemy, but his painful shudder had thrown off the aim from his original target of The Otherside's head. Now that bullet sped toward the great mass of the leather and armor-clad body astride the horse.

"Okay. I still may be able to take him down with this bullet to his heart, or whatever passes for one inside him."

The sickness of slowness seemed not to affect the horseman in the same way as it did Travis, or most likely the man-like monster was just faster. As the bullet approached, the random motions of his axe ceased, and he yanked the weapon in toward himself, keeping the edge of the blade directly between himself and the approaching ball of spinning lead.

To Travis, after all the earlier nightmarish nonsense, almost everything that now happened became a cruel joke. He watched, dumbfounded, as the bullet hit square upon the axe edge. Like a tiger's deadly caress of a fawn, the sharpened blade held by The Otherside gently split it in half.

One-half of the lead ball spun away to slam harmlessly against the stony sheets of canyon walls, ricocheting into the barrens. The other piece deflected upwards toward the face of The Otherside's. But, as Travis had managed to avoid the arrow's killing blow, so did the demonic horseman mostly evade the projectile.

He was very fast, but not really quite fast enough to dodge the burning lead. The erratically tumbling half-bullet struck just to the side beneath his cowled nose, tearing the fleshy cheek and breaking away several of the too-many-teeth as it ripped a path along the edge of his face. A deep and bloody trough was gouged from lips past ear. Black ichor and meaty shreds of an earlier meal dropped from inside, staining the armor below.

Yowling fury doubled and re-doubled from the ravaged mouth. Incoherent spittles of hatred tried and failed to find words with which to curse the puny two-legged vessel of impudence which had maimed him so.

As the agonized horseman thrashed upon his saddle, Travis fell forward, bleeding and exhausted, to see the hoof marks being stomped into the hail covered ground. All were crescents with two sharp marks embedded in them, exactly like horns, exactly like those he'd seen beside the massacre at the farm.

"That Mr. One was right! This is the same enemy we're still fighting a thousand years from now!"

As this new realization sunk in, he felt himself diffusing from this Now, pulled away by unseen forces to be dragged over disappearing ancient warriors and weapons.

The corona's purifying light vanished as the eclipse ended, its powers of universal illumination exchanged for a waxy sunlight that beat down upon stunned soldiers not yet able to climb to their feet. Their leader injured, yet still alive and craving revenge, the armies of The Otherside would now bring another ten centuries of loathing, death, and torment to the hapless and hopeless.

One was silent in towering reproach.

Travis had failed.

He felt himself a tiny particle moving within what seemed an infinite translucent tube. He forced his eyes farther open to look past clotted blood now crusted hard and blinding. Panoramas of people and deeds both mundane and heroic played out in faded colors, while the shuffling of the temporal fabric of the Between twisted him ever forward toward his former place and time.

He was a numb and cold body, head a thick hank of fiber and meat.

"At least it's still attached to the rest of me. Unlike some I've seen recently."

Spectral images of lived-in lives lurched past, some hidden, some revealed, a deck of cards played for the highest stakes. Sometimes winners, frequently losers, but most often just the pedestrian paths of ordinary people, dying at the end while steeped in a multitude of petty regrets.

Explorers and monks, heroes, saints, bakers, stonemasons, kings, and thieves, all at work...this and more he saw. They did what they felt they must do, where they were or wished they weren't. Climbing mountains, crossing rivers, founding settlements that were better than before, or leaving intolerable towns and dukes behind.

A wide ocean traveled, land fought upon, victories and defeats, new oaths uttered and trusted, betrayals and bloodshed, all were revealed as the past unreeled before Travis. Yet, always rooting below were the loathsome snouts of The Otherside and his minions, ever seeking to twist good into evil by blood sacrifice and unholy feasts of flesh.

Then *One* returned and spoke. Travis recoiled as he watched the progress of his enemy throughout the many years since the failure in the pass.

"Fate has proclaimed The Otherside's malignancy to fester and feed upon humanity for another thousand years. However, you will meet again. You will have another opportunity to destroy him, but the life force of the many he has fed upon has led him closer to supremacy. It will be a more difficult encounter next time. You are a military man. You must know your enemy better even than you know yourself. Behold."

The torn face of The Otherside appeared. As promised, he did his best to bring re-doubled terror and pestilence to the lives of every being possible. He fed upon on his victims, becoming stronger every century, never growing older or injured. Yet, his facial scar from the battle in the mountain pass refused to heal.

He kept the recruitment of his lieutenants an on-going task that drew the ambitious and gullible to his flame like gnats. Promises of plunder, earthly pleasure, and long life, with the evidence of that fulfilled for some, convinced many over the years to swear fealty and slash their palms to grip the hand of their new Master, mingling their blood with the green-yellow fluids that seeped from his ancient wounds.

His men did live longer than the humanity they had turned away from... if they didn't perish while doing his bidding. But his underlings never really lasted long enough, and The Otherside had learned that after having served him, their winnowed life forces were of a sour and thin sustenance. But sometimes one had to make do, and foolish replacements were always easy to come by. It seemed that most everyone wanted more than they were willing to work for, and The Otherside promised his new recruits much.

He had used a multitude of names over the centuries, but most recently he had, for the time being at least, settled on *The Captain.*

Travis started, remembering what one of the dying raiders had said: "*You ain't met The Captain.*"

Although, it was true he'd never met the being who styled himself by that rank during his own time, he knew he would recognize him. And his gut knew, even if it made no logical sense to his mind, that he'd already fought this so-called Captain face to face in a mountain pass a thousand years ago, and more than that many miles away.

His journey became monotonous, watching the never-ending sheets of water passing beneath him. The bloody rut ploughed along his skull throbbed but had stopped bleeding. His battered body grew less numb as it flew above the saltwater expanse while also moving forward through the temporal curtains back to his present time. On occasion, ships of more primitive style could be seen, singly or in fleets, some peacefully at sail, some fighting and locked in battle with others. He flew past them all.

Yet he could not escape his growing discomfort. As he moved over the ocean, the great blue sky above locked him perpetually in the center of every horizon. He became a midpoint toward which all earth's pain was focused.

Below, the ocean's creatures lived their lives and stoically accepted their deaths within the watery jungle, as the shipboard men skimming the surface in their tiny wooden tubs found their profits, losses, glories, ignominies, and sometimes, new lives of hope amid old deaths of futility. Those events he saw as they had happened. His attention was brought to a galleon, built sometime in the 1600's, sailing under what he thought might be a pirate's flag. It moved westward at high speed, sails billowing.

Yet, even in this mid-ocean freshness, a decaying stench permeated the quickly moving vessel. For from it came memories of recent meals... of rendered fleshy human soups and nightmare ovens roasting brains in eyeless skulls. All, of course, washed down by the unholy wine of every victim's distilled fear.

A sense of bloated and unceasing hunger emanated from inside the ship's deepest inner hull. Stripped of their meat, piles of greasy human bones surrounded The Otherside as he fed. His distended belly slowly filled with warm blood and still-twitching flesh. He was... almost... pleased by his meals, but, as usual, remained unsated.

Increasingly weary of the drearily monotonous flavors of blood he had consumed for over a thousand years in the Old world, The Otherside had taken his most faithful minions and Underlords west to the New World in search of exotic tastes, pleasures, and power.

Many promising tales of these far lands had

93

traveled into the hidden folds of the jagged lands he had ruled for centuries. They told of warm islands and sandy coasts far from the chill, land-locked mountains in which he had for so long hunted down his sacrifices. It was said that these new lands were filled with infinite varieties of the two-legged creatures he craved, droves and droves of them. They said it would be an unending banquet of human meat and feasting.

Above the ship, *One* finally returned to Travis. *"This is all you can be permitted to experience at this time. Perhaps it has already been too much for you. I hope not. Yet the risk is worth the reward for you to better know what the stakes are. The pain you feel is merely a silken shadow wrapping your neck, a whispered distillation of what the conquered peoples of the mountain have been enduring for the last thousand years beneath the yoke of The Otherside."*

"Yes. Since my failure at the mountain pass."

"This is not the time for remonstrance or excuses. Time past was penetrated yet unchanged. We may not there return. Those gates have now been closed. However, time present and future remain potential portals to victory. All our efforts must now dwell there. You have learned enough. Be on your guard!"

Another burst of pain struck Travis, but as *One* ended his communication with him, his suffering ended instantly.

"And here I was thinkin' I'd be waking up from this world of phantasms and just get back to fighting the real war again. That seems a lot easier after dealing with all this nonsense about worlds and other sides, but no such luck, looks like."

He shook his head at the thought that an artillery duel between cannons trading double-loaded canister shot with each other was a less arduous task than facing the monstrous power of The Otherside, who'd been growing in strength for a thousand years according to *One*, so now was an even more deadly foe.

"To Hades with that ugly S.O.B. My ancestor's oath might never be fulfilled, but I'll damn sure try."

Flung from the ancient battlefield of the Old World westward above the ageless sea, he was propelled by the outerworldly power of the entity known only as *One*. Travis rode the Between across curtains of time and space back to the There and Now from whence he'd come.

He knew there would be more fighting at the house under siege in the year 1865, but he also knew he'd get another chance at killing The Otherside. That was enough.

He finally passed out; his face bent into a crooked smile of revenge.

5. SPIRTUAL LEATHER

Travis returned from whence he'd been plucked. Within, but not of it, his consciousness was once more encompassed by pain, now of a more personal nature. No longer floating within a vision or fighting a nightmarish demon, he lay crumpled on the uneven wooden floor of the backyard shed, face up with a view of the ceiling and the hind-quarters of the horse he had earlier tied up in here. That animal patiently stood, while the sounds of fighting coming from the house continued sporadically.

It was dim inside the shed. From what he could see of the sky through the partially open door, night had fallen. Before he'd passed out during the raiders last attack it had been late afternoon. How many hours had it taken to cross a thousand years of ocean and mountains? It didn't matter. Crawling to his feet he accidentally touched the side of his forehead. Caked blood from the raider's grazing pistol shot had hardened messily in a shallow gouge from eyebrow past ear. At least, that might account for the wound.

"Or... this could be from some prehistoric cave man's damn arrow, I suppose."

Weakened by both blood loss and the intense visions his rattled mind had endured, pain clamped his head. It was a sharp fetter that served to keep him from moving too quickly. Anytime he did so, vertigo spun the world around like a roulette table, confounding his motion.

97

"Need to get movin'! Can't lay around here waitin' for a parade! Need to find out what's going on at the house and get some help to them now!"

At that thought, he checked his sidearms. Both pistols were still with him, fixed snug in their holsters, gun belt strapped tightly around his waist.

"But they're both empty! Gotta do something about that, soon."

Lashed by his sense of duty, Travis forced himself to stand upright. Crimson lights from outside gave a flickering illumination nearby the door.

He carefully placed one foot in front of the other while his hand scrabbled along the horse's tack, steadying himself. As he moved forward, his fingers brushed a length of formed leather tubing strapped along on the horse's side. He froze. Unable to see much of it in the dim red light, he nevertheless knew what it was. He untied the end of the leather case and drew out its precious content. The container wasn't long, nor was the Spencer carbine it held.

"A rifle scabbard and repeating carbine? How could I have missed this? Course', I was getting' shot at when I rode in here. That's always a mite distracting."

He moved closer to the door, inspecting the carbine in the dim red light. Its shorter length made it easier to handle than a full size rifle. It was a deadly piece of manufacturing, with a lever for repeating fire, and a load of seven cartridges in the tube that ran from the back of the stock into the chamber.

"I'd hate to be lookin' down the barrel of this

here Spencer. No fun, no fun at all. Wish I'd had this with me up in that frozen pass. HA! That big bastard who chopped off my great-gran' pap's head wouldn't have stood a chance against a few shots from this!"

A desperate chorus of garbled screams and enraged shouts came from inside the house.

"This carbine will give those folks over there a better chance. No matter how ill I am, I have to get over there with it straight away."

Cautiously he peered out the door. A scene of growing devastation and defeat met his gaze. He could only see a few figures moving within, smothering flames as best they could. The raiders were nowhere in sight.

"Seems like they managed to finally get a firebrand lit, and then left. Or not. Them boys don't seem like the type to let their enjoyment of the unfortunate circumstances of others go to waste. Sick folks like that are always so unhappy, they try to make everyone else around them feel even worse, just so they can tell themselves they're better off than them."

Recalling his vision, he remembered that *One* had told him that The Otherside drew his strength from drinking in the fear and pain of his prey, so it was in his twisted interests to make every victim suffer as much as possible. His henchmen were always more than willing to help make that happen.

"Well, if that's true, or even if it ain't, it don't matter to the facts. The facts are, right now, that they want to kill everyone here. I need to get me a handle on this spinning head, then do what I can do. I'm guessing those raiders are all out there hiding on the far edge of the trees,

sitting nice and comfy and enjoying the evening's entertainment.

He sat down on a barrel, reviewing options amid injuries.

"Seven shots. Got to make them all count but that'll be hard at night. I don't know how many more of those fools that so-called Captain still has working for him. Can't really be much more than seven of them left, from how many I saw running circles around here this morning, and how many have been killed."

He knew that his dizziness wouldn't allow him the strength to run out into the darkness to circle around the field, flank his enemies, and pick them off one by one as he'd like to. Instead, he decided to get back inside the house to help whoever was still left inside put out the fire.

If the house could be saved, it remained at least a semblance of a haven for them and the defenders would have far better odds against the raiders.

"Ka-*Chunk!*" He worked the lever, chambering one of the heavy lead slugs. Crouching down, he opened the door slowly. Staying low seemed to keep his head spins at bay.

No bullets came his way as he creeped outside the shed. It looked as if the flames inside the house had almost been brought under control, yet a red glow still shone. He kept low as he moved toward the house with an unsteady trot.

Travis was almost there when a flutter of unknown motion off to his right caught his soldier's eye. Dropping, he rolled along the ground up to the house until his side touched its heavy stone foundation. He lay prone, gripping the carbine, its stock solid against his shoulder, ready to fire.

"Not all of 'em are sitting pretty, back there in the dark. Looks like we got ourselves an over-achiever here."

The raider sneaking around the corner was dressed as most of them were. He wore a dark uniform with no insignia, heavy boots, and an oddly contorted kepi also undistinguished by any identifying marks. His creeping form was illuminated by blood red light upon his right side that faded to a black cloak of darkness on his left. He carried a burning bucket of tar oil in his right hand.

"Yep, he's planning to kindle more flames on this side of the house."

Travis sighted the carbine upon the raider's chest. Illuminated on only one side by the burning glow of flame, his target seemed only a half-man; a one-legged human cleaved down the middle, lost to both this world and the next. Now this living apparition began to swing the flaming bucket, intending to throw it inside the house.

Travis squeezed the trigger. The carbine's report was loud and decisive, final as a hammer stroke upon an iron spike.

The recoil shoved Travis. He re-aimed while he worked the action to eject the spent copper, seating the next deadly round in the carbine's chamber.

His target needed no second shot to help it die. The bullet had struck during the mid-motion of flinging the flaming bucket, convulsing his arms to send the burning pot upwards above him, instead of toward the house. After he fell, shot clean through by the carbine, the sticky liquid flames dropped back down upon him. All the tar and burning oil he'd meant to injure others with now cascaded in burning torrents over his expiring body.

He keened a broken wail of imminent death, quickly reduced to a dribble of frothy whimpers. The raider squirmed, weakly twitching his arms in futile defense against the inevitable.

A tableau of otherworldly revenge suddenly stepped forth from the blood-black night to embrace the dying man. Travis watched, his eyes growing wide as he saw a hellish scene appear, as from beyond the veil. With silent screams of revenge, the clamorous spirits of all those that the raider had abused and killed crowded round, their toothless mouths jeering as they awaited their turn to punish him. They cheered as the burning tar boiled out crisp gobbets of still living flesh, swinging cudgels or heavy knouts of spiritual leather across his writhing form as his physical body melted into stinking fatty oils.

The spirits were preparing their long-awaited tormentor to join them.

Spine shattered by the fast-moving lead from the carbine, the raider was helpless as he burned away to final doom. Travis heard his last phantasmic scream, a question of what his life might have been had he not drunkenly joined a group of his fellow toughs to pledge his fate beneath the yoke of The Captain's commands those many years ago.

But the uncaring Fates that he had worshiped since that time did not, and would not, answer his pleas. As he had disregarded the pain of his many victims, so now the shrieking spirits ignored his, inflicting even more agonies as they sought vengeance.

Thought ceased as the boiling black tar he'd sought to fling upon his victims now melted down eye sockets into his shriveling brain. He passed from this world's commonplace torments into the not so gentle ministrations of his bellowing welcoming committee in the next. The raider's burnt husk finally folded in upon himself, a perforated accordion collapsing. Incoherent sour notes chuffed from the charred corpse, his last words. The specters surrounding the body continued to wreak their revenge upon his agonized soul, while all slowly faded from view.

Soon, only the once-human offal remained, a stinking slop of desiccated ruin.

Travis kept his carbine at ready, keeping an eye out for more attackers that might be sneaking up, but his sights remained empty. No other enemies arrived to share the raider's fate.

"Looks like he got what he deserved. It's another killer down. But how many more to go? Seems like a battalion out there, but that can't be, or they would have overrun this place already."

It had been only a short while since Travis had taken down the raider. He remained on alert, the carbine at ready. A few patches of flame still burned around the house above him. Voices from within seemed urgent, but not desperate. After a few moments of silence, he heard footsteps from the porch above, followed by a soft voice of inquiry.

"Mr. Travis? This is Lorne. Is that you?"

"Yes. It's me."

The footsteps came closer, almost to the edge

of the porch. "I knew it! I saw that evil man who was carrying the fire pot get shot clean through! I knew it had to be you! But where are you? I need to tell you something!"

"I'm down here. In the dirt. But you shouldn't be standing. We don't know where the raiders are. They could be anywhere. In fact, they could be drawin' a bead on you right now."

She popped over the edge of the porch, lowering herself down to lay facing Travis, as snug against the stone foundation as he was. Lorne whispered with urgency.

"We heard atrocious noises just after the last two attackers tossed their firebrands inside the house. I think we shot one, but he still managed to run off. They both got away, running back to the forest. A few minutes later, while we were smothering the fires, the most frightfully wicked sounds came our way from off in that direction."

"What kind of sounds?"

"Horrible, ghastly yelling, like the most cross and impatient schoolteacher whipping his students for failing a class. And then, well, then there was a lot of shouting and more curses, and then horses."

"What do you mean, 'then horses'"?

She leaned closer to Travis, determined to make him understand.

"Horse sounds, whinnies and snorts, you know how they go about puffing and huffing when they're saddled up. Those sounds. Then a few gunshots, and lots of galloping. Sounded like at least ten riders, just riding off into the night. Lots of curses. Then, it was over. There wasn't no one else out there for at least the last half-hour till that one over there showed up with his fire-buckets. That one you shot."

Travis looked over at the body. It stank of char, death, and melted fat.

"Well, Lorne, I can't believe he was the only one they left behind. I can hardly believe they all left, for that matter. Those kinds of men, once they think they've got their fish in a barrel, they ain't about to stop shootin'."

She thought over what he'd said. Disappointment crisscrossed her turned-down face while she reluctantly realized its truth.

"Those hateful men. I'd hoped so much they had decided to run off and leave us in peace. I'm so tired of the shooting. I never wanted to have to kill anyone, and now I've done that at least three times today! Please, let's go back inside. We need to help with everything that still needs doing."

She started to move away, then stopped, catching herself mid-crawl. She drew back to the wall, close to him, and placed her hand lightly on his shoulder. "I mean, I, myself need to get back to help. I didn't mean to speak your mind for you. But I do hope you'll come along inside with me Mr. Travis. You've been immensely helpful, and I'm sure you've helped save some of our lives, even if you were knocked senseless for a while. You sort of staggered backwards and fell outside after that bullet grazed you."

She tore a strip of mostly clean fabric from her dress and wrapped it around his head, covering the clotted wound gouged along his scalp. "I hope that helps. You were almost killed by that shot. I'm glad you weren't."

He still felt vertigo wobbling around the edges of his consciousness, and knew that the sooner he had a chance to rest and eat something, the better fighting shape he'd be in. Travis started his reply to Lorne, but he didn't have a chance to speak.

The world blew up.

An explosion wracked the air above them. Waves of heat washed over the edge of the porch to envelope the pair below. The air was hot, but only carried the smallest portion of the blast now spreading out in all directions from the detonation's center inside the house. Both of them were spared.

The house was in ruins. Its thick walls were scorched and strewn about; the heavy timbers that had survived repeated assaults now laid out like so many insensible prize fighters. Only the solid stone foundation of the porch had saved their lives.

Fires flared above. There were no screams. There could be no survivors.

All thoughts of rest or recovery became impossible. He knew they had a small chance of escape, but only right now, while the fires still blazed, before the raiders came to pick through the ruins.

Lorne shuddered and tried to speak. Words could not come. Her eyes were dry while her face contorted; shock holding tears inside, grief at bay. He grabbed her shoulder with his free hand, never taking the other off the carbine. Six cartridges left. Six shots at freedom, maybe.

Her body jerked, locked in battle with disbelieving convulsion. Bereft of all anchors to her former life, she refused to accept what had just happened. She could not seem to move, nor would tears come.

"Lorne! We must go! I know what you're feeling. It's hideous I know, but we HAVE to go NOW! If we dally there's only death, but if we can get away from this place, we'll have a chance to live. Lorne...We have got to move *NOW*."

Shaking, unfocused, she reached out to clutch his shoulder with a desperate grip. "My sister and uncle. They're in there. Everyone I care about is in there. Or was. Why am I still alive?"

"I was the only survivor when my entire battery was wiped out. All dead except for me. I don't know why, either."

"But why them, and not me?" Now the tears began. They streamed down her face to mix into the anonymity of the uncaring earth below.

"Don't think about it now. Those were good people. I've come to believe that I was spared because the Man Upstairs still has a job for me to do. That keeps me going, but we must move. You'll have time to think about all this later, but only if we can get ourselves out of this now."

Travis spoke gently but with the military insistence of a sergeant to his charges. "They'll be coming back soon, Lorne. That kind always wants to gloat. We MUST get a move on. Come on, it's time to saddle up, soldier." With difficulty, she turned her eyes from the devastation and nodded. Remaining vigilant to any unwelcome company lurking about, he backed away from the foundation. Keeping the carbine to hand, he firmly guided Lorne with the other.

Lorne's trembling slowly subsided but her grip on his hand never loosened. They ran in a low crouch from the burning ruins toward the shed. The animal still waited inside.

"Saddle up? What are you talking about?"

"The horse is our only chance to get away. We need a quick escape. Running into the night on just our own power won't get us far. We must ride."

They entered the shed. The horse, unfed or watered for some time, was not in the best of condition. Travis deemed it still rideable, at least for a while. While helping Lorne get astride the animal, he looked around the shed's murky interior, Nagging the back of his mind, he had a vague sense that he had earlier seen something worth taking with them that might prove useful.

Then he saw it. A wooden hoe hanging on a hook by the door. Its long and stout wooden shaft was tipped by an unusually pointed end, bent over at about a ninety-degree angle. It had been made to cut deeply into the stubborn roots of invasive foliage and break up hard packed clods in clay clotted fields.

He knew that if he could bend that tip around to face forward, he'd have the silent killing tool he'd been considering since he'd survived the debacle that had wiped out his battery. It would become an old-fashioned pike that might still be useful in this modern world of gunpowder weapons.

"Maybe it was only a dream, but those soldiers up in that frozen pass were doing a pretty good job of holding off that big ugly fella's army with just these things. Not that they were facing cannon or rifle, but sometimes that's not an option either. This will get someone's attention no matter how wet the powder is or if you've shot your last bullet. And... it's quiet."

He quickly strapped the pointed shaft along the side of the horse, then mounted up just behind Lorne. He knew the animal wouldn't be able to carry them any great distance in this fashion, but he hoped it would be far enough. It would certainly be farther than they could walk on their own. He slung the carbine's strap over his left shoulder, keeping the weapon in front of him. It was somewhat awkward, as it pressed into Lorne's back, but he wanted it immediately accessible if needed.

To spare the horse he shifted his weight as far forward as possible. He noticed a longish scar across the beast's neck, but the beast was strong and seemed to take the double riders as routine. He realized it had likely carried an extra passenger in this fashion many times, after many raids. *"Of course! This mount is familiar with carrying more than one rider. That dead raider would have dragged his trussed-up prizes up here for later amusements back at the camp. For that alone he needed killin'."*

He took the reins and leaned into her, speaking softly.

"Are you ready?"

She answered slowly, livid rage smoldering into icy revenge beneath her words. "Ready? Everyone I loved... murdered. How can anyone be ready for that, for all that's just happened?"

With no reply possible, Travis grunted a grim assent. He pressed against her as he took up slack in the reins. The horse nickered when he set it forward into the night. "Wrap your arms around its neck and stay low to it. I'll keep us moving in the right direction. Just relax and don't fight the rhythm of the horse."

All emotion was absent from her every syllable as she replied. "Don't worry, I won't fall off. I've ridden before, even if it wasn't like this. I'll be fine, or I won't. It doesn't matter. Like you said, let's get a move on."

Travis knew roughly where he'd left the rest of his gear, hidden under cover in the brush along the hillside. There would be no trouble finding it during daylight, but at night it would be a different story. He had noted a peculiar tree, one with a triple trunk. It was about fifty feet away from the bush, across from the narrow path he'd been following before his deadly encounter with the horseman. If he could see the odd tree tonight, he thought he would be able to find the bush where the goods were hidden.

Lorne kept her face turned away from the blaze. Travis did too, but for a different reason. He didn't want to lose his night vision. The incessant rainy drizzle had finally given way to the chill of clear skies. The moon shone intermittently from behind scudding clouds driven west from the ocean. He scanned the field and forest around them as they moved steadily farther away from her former home and refuge.

He hoped that everything he'd left was still hidden. All the food they had for the immediate future was there, little as it was. The most important item, of course, was the powder and reloads for the pistols. *If I'd had those earlier, a few shots extra might'a made a difference in that fight at the pass. And if what Mister One said was true, and I'd managed to kill off that Otherside character back there, maybe none of this evil would have happened today! Lorne's family would still be alive, and we wouldn't have to be skedaddling off into the night."*

Muttering under his breath in anger and frustration at the fleeting thoughts he'd had, he caught Lorne's attention.

"What did you say?"

"I didn't know I had."

"Not much you didn't. But it seemed that, whatever it was, it made you shiver clean through. Scared me, like. Just a little."

"I was thinking about a nightmare I'd had."

Vicious night flowed past them. She did not speak. He continued,

"I had a nightmare. After I'd been shot at back there, almost killed. After I was laying there, bleeding and comatose, I had a nightmare, Lorne."

The horse kept moving. It went for many paces before she leaned back toward him and spoke with harsh whispers.

"I grabbed you, Travis. Dragged you back, away from the gunfire. Set you near the rear of the house, and then went over to reload for... sister."

Her jaw set hard as an iron band, stifling tears. She continued through gritted teeth.

"I thought you were safe back there, at least as safe as anywhere. Later, I looked over again, but you were gone. I saw the door swinging on that shed and figured you had maybe gone there but... I didn't see how. You had a lot of blood on your head. You didn't move or open your eyes at all. It made no sense for you to be able to move much, let alone walk back to that place."

The moon brightened behind swift changing patterns of translucent clouds; silver shinings lured inland at speed from the unquiet ocean.

"You're right. I didn't move, least not any ways I can remember, to get back into that shed. It felt like someone moved me, but not until later, after the whole nightmare was over."

Exhaustion crept closer. Neither spoke. His thoughts rambled and split, reformed, then washed away again. Their entire world was now upon the back of the creature beneath them. Travis forced himself to focus on their immediate surroundings, not some delusion of mountains and warriors and a monster called The Otherside.

Concerned about finding their food and supplies, he thought he should be able to spy the odd triple-trunk tree that was his landmark, if they got up onto that crest that surrounded this field.

But that would also put them up high enough to appear in perfect silhouette against a waxing bright moon. A fine target for anyone out here that cared to look.

"Or anyone who was ordered to look for us."

He took the horse closer to the edge of the trees in an elongated arc around the large field that pulled them increasingly into the relative safety of the shadows. They continued in the general direction toward his hidden cache, the horse swaying as it walked forward, gently rocking them side to side.

Time itself felt immobile and unchanging. As they continued their escape, the dark ground seemed to slide eternally from front to back beneath them. He looked up and shook his head to dispel the illusion, taking several breaths of cool air to clear his thoughts.

"I can't fall prey to slumber. Neither of us

need more false visions to come our way. I've certainly had my fill. One nightmare is enough, especially with all the real horrors befalling so many today."

The horse slowed. The soggy ground held many puddles of liquid mush left from the long days of rain. Travis heard the hooves of the big beast splashing, pulling up the clawing mud as it trod along. He worried. If he could hear it... so could their enemies.

"Nothing for it. We gotta get farther away from those killing grounds back there. And we need those supplies. Have to keep moving."

Deeper breaths and quiet shallow snores announced Lorne dropping off to sleep. Travis fought hard against that impulse even while waves of fatigue threatened his balance atop the horse.

"She's asleep. If I can't stay on, she won't either."

Before them, the land tilted up. He knew the danger of climbing the ridge, but at this point it didn't matter, somehow. Cold and numb, crumpled, he gave the horse leave to climb the small hill. At the crest he paused, scanned the far field, now awash in moonlight, and spotted the tree of three trunks. He moved the horse forward, across the rise and down to the rough path he'd been traveling earlier on foot.

"There! That's got to be it. A bush just this side of the crest and large enough to sleep under."

As he pushed them through the undergrowth, her remained on the alert, even while images from the day's events swirled through his mind in a disjointed panoply.

He awakened Lorne when he dismounted to lead the horse the rest of the way.

"Are we here? I mean, are we there? Wherever it is that you wanted to go?"

"I believe so, yes. Wait here just a minute, please."

He clambered over the rest of the way. The bush was the correct one. He dropped low to grab beneath the ghost gray cover still wrapped around it; reached inside.

Everything...save one small case... gone.

At his sharp intake of breath, and the drop of his shoulders, Lorne carefully slid to the ground. She went to Travis. He knelt in front of the little shelter, a metal box in his hands.

"What's wrong? What's that?"

"Bullets, lead, and molds to make more. Gun powder."

"Didn't you leave something else here? Food?"

"Yes. It's all gone. But we can't worry about it now. We must keep moving."

She sighed, then took a deep breath before speaking. Grim exhaustion thickened her words.

"Mr. Travis, this horse is done in, and so are you."

The moon had risen much higher. Time, which had seemed so malleable before, had now sped along. They were deep into the night. With great effort he rose. She was right. He went to the remove the saddle and blankets from the horse.

"We're still too close to the raiders, but you're right, in our condition it will be more dangerous to keep moving at night. There's a flat dry space inside those bushes, and it still has the tarp covering to shield us. We can both squeeze in, sleep for a few hours, then get going at dawn."

He removed the bit and tack, laying it and the saddle under another brushy area. Knees buckling, the vertigo and tunnel-vision crept along the edge of his consciousness while he trudged back to the makeshift shelter. Lorne was *very* right; he was on the edge of collapse.

Then he did. Dragging his battered body forward on his hands and knees he crawled the last few feet to squish himself inside the tiny space, sagging unconscious into the dirt next to Lorne. She rearranged the blanket to cover them both. Then, attempting to remember her sister's smiling face but failing, she fell asleep crying silent, but very wet, tears.

6. BACCHANAL OF BLADES

A two thousand year old malicious consciousness swirled within its own corruption. It plucked, poked, and prodded amid the ruins of the destroyed house. Searching and seeking, the stygian manifestation of The Otherside had sent his wraith into an astral form. Now his laughing evil soared above the dirt of Earth, covering more ground than he or his riders could on horseback. The man-like creature knew that two of the humans had escaped his wrath. He was determined to find them.

The disembodied being flew both high and low through the dark sky, peering across the landscape with shadowy eyes. A gnashing of over-large jaws underlined his hunger for more sustenance, always the overriding imperative of The Otherside.

He loitered here and there to inspect any anomaly that might conceal the prey he hunted. The sprawled forms of Travis and Lorne were unaware of their peril as The Otherside's malignant senses crept closer and closer to their tiny refuge. He would soon find them.

Then came a sudden shout from another being also roaming through the astral lanes, loud as a thunderclap.

"Get back!"

The shout awakened Travis from his troubled sleep. Its timbre was similar in tone but different in type than that of Mr. *One*. That voice had been male, this one was decidedly a woman.

He heard orders snapped as if from a mighty

Queen, her terrible lash of power and punishment implicit, should her commands not be followed. She repeated them again.

"Get back and away!"

Her attack took the foe by complete surprise. With no time to parry the blows of her blade, The Otherside was injured during their brief combat.

Pummeled by the pommel of her mighty curved sword, tears of alien wrath oozed from the smashed, bony orbits of The Otherside's bleeding eyes. He realized he must regenerate his wounds, and that meant cutting short his search this night. He would find the two he sought later. For now, he had another priority. He must discipline his men for their failure in allowing his prey to escape. He left.

The Otherside's pressure of foul wickedness departed as well. Travis, still exhausted remained cheek down in the muffling clods of wet dirt. Soon, he began to sleep again, deeply, dreamless. Rest had finally come, aided by an unknown yet friendly force.

During the spectral battle, Lorne had awakened to the sound of cracking bones and a gasping fetid dampness that clammed the air. She had held herself silent, shallowly breathing, while praying for whatever was outside to pass.

Mosquitoes and gnats had appeared, their buzzing a vindictive cloak around their heads. The bugs bit sharp, drawing blood unabated while the malevolent presence drew closer above them. She remained silent, and not slapping or shooing them off, somehow knowing that the strange and foul whatever-it-was outside had strength enough to crush them both, should it find them.

But then, as if from a distant room, she had heard a woman's voice of command, then a quick clash of clanging steel upon iron. There came a shuffling of purpose from the baleful presence, then it drew back. Looking out, she saw a dense spectral cloud pass before the shining moon, dimming it, yet no shadow pressed the ground beneath. The groaning entity receded into its malicious rift of astral unreality.

Abruptly, both the biting bugs and the palpable sense of evil disappeared. Relief. Lorne began to breath normally again.

Then a calming new voice spoke, and a woman in armor appeared, translucent among the stars. She stared at Lorne while sheathing her sword.

"For you and the one with you, the danger is past for this night. The evil that was here has gone to inflict his malign punishments upon others. You two must leave in the morning, for tomorrow his wounds will be healed, and he will eventually think to return here. We will speak more later. For now, you must sleep. Sleep now."

Lorne swooned back into the arms of healing torpor.

They knew no more terror that night.

Morning twilight, faintest prelude to an early dawn, shimmered a lighter blue along the eastern horizon. Not far inland from the ocean over which the sun now announced its imminent return, the ruins of what was once a wooden home still burned in places, feeding the chill infamy with a smoky char from wood, flesh, and hair. Other ashes smoldered and stank as they faded into slow red death.

Not so far away, Travis awoke first. He turned over, wiping off his flattened cheek that had lain the night pressed into the earth. Tightly spooled pain clamped his every tendon, bone, and muscle. He stretched, thinking.

"Sleeping face down on dirt is never the best option. At least we're alive."

More chill awaited outside the meager cover of their shared blanket, but he knew that seeing to the weapons was an overdue task more important than staying warm. He sat up slowly and carefully, making sure the blanket stayed covering Lorne.

As he awakened, Travis looked through the meshed branches of the makeshift hut, out toward the brightening blue skies of the east. Then he noticed the itching. Stinging welts were strewn along his hands and arms, their many red bumps each plumped up over a hundred mounds of swollen flesh. They built upon and atop one another, tiny volcanoes of two or three angry red punctures apiece. There had been no more room along his arm for the ravenous insects. It felt as if the bites had been poured, dripping with terrible acids, along his arm in a caustic stream from above.

As best he could, he forced himself to stop bothering at his bitten body. He got to work on what he knew should have been done a day ago. As the sun rose in a cloudless sky, he cleaned both pistols and made short work of loading them, measuring powder, setting patches, and ramming home the lead.

After gently settling the percussion caps on each cylinder, he smeared them with grease and replaced the pistols in their holsters. Now he double-checked the rifle's action, and its stock of cartridges. Without doubt it was the finest and most deadly weapon they had, as long as it could be fed. After its precious ammo was consumed, its worth in battle would be no more than an awkward club, lesser than even the long garden hoe with its sharpened point he'd taken from the shed.

"That's right, I'll still need to find somewhere to pound that point straight. Not here or now, we need to move out soon. But I can do another chore that needs doing."

He pulled the big Bowie knife from its sheath. It balanced perfectly in his hand, as usual. He began sharpening the blade's already keen edge. Somehow its mere presence gave a more visceral sense of security than any of the firearms did while holding them. His mind knew the foolishness of that chimera, yet it persisted.

"Delusional. What am I thinking? Any one of these here guns could literally tear a man to pieces with just a few shots, and from a hundred feet away. Gotta get in close and make it personal with the Bowie, but if you try that and the other fella has a pistol, you just better forget about it. 'Course, without the bullets and powder you end with the same mischance I found myself in up at that pass. One shot, one chance. It was only one shot. I had one shot left from the twelve I should have had. That didn't work out well."

He kept up the blade's smooth, rhythmic action to and fro along the small whetstone that traveled with the scabbard, gently checking its edge on his thumbnail every so often. Hunger tightened its rough cords around his belly, but he knew there was nothing for it. He was glad he'd eaten that extra bacon and bread yesterday.

The sun peeked over the horizon; he'd have to wake Lorne soon. They had to pack up everything and get a move on. Too dangerous to stay. Someone knew they were here. The same someone who had taken everything but the reloading kit from his stashed bundle.

"What am I rambling on about. Can't seem to get my thoughts straight this morning. I'm thinking that battle in the pass was real. I know it wasn't any more real than that nightmare from last night. This foolishness must be caused by me getting hit in the head. But... something happened with that food yesterday that has only one logical explanation. Someone's out there, watching us, but it can't be the raiders, or they would have already killed us in our sleep."

He looked at the fiery red blotches up and down his arms. Welts covered almost all exposed skin and the backs of his hands and fingers. He could feel more across the back of his neck and behind his ears. He knew if he scratched at them too much, he'd want to claw his skin to shreds, so he again forced himself to ignore the itching pain wrought by the hundreds of little punctures.

"It was all so awful real, that hideous dream last night, and the evidence of some sort of attack is right here on my skin before my eyes! And, if it wasn't for that odd voice, that new voice of someone that fought with and told the whatever-it-was to get away, I might have been eaten alive by those bugs."

The blade's edge was more than satisfactory. It could have been used to shave with, had they the time. He replaced it within the sheath. As he looked up, he was startled to find Lorne awake and watching him. He took a deep breath and spoke first.

"Good morning, Lorne. We need to pack up and get going, but I didn't want to wake you."

"Why not? If something needs doing, don't wait for me."

"It was a very difficult day yesterday. I figured you needed your sleep."

"That was nice of you, but whatever stole your food and gear from this camp knows we're here. He, or whatever it was, might come back. If we're killed by this thing, it won't matter how much sleep we got. I think we need to go."

"I think you're right."

They gathered up what meager goods remained. Lorne finished, and crawled out, carrying the blanket with her to roll up outside. Travis noticed several coffee beans from his former stash that had fallen in the dirt, impossible to see at night. He picked them up, cleaned and then pocketed them.

"So, whoever carted off the supplies took time to open up everything to see what they were getting. That means they were out here during the day, after I'd fought with the first horseman, certainly well before Lorne and I got here last night. But why did they leave the ammunition box? Too heavy? Or maybe they just had no use for it since I've still got both pistols."

As he was finishing up the packing, an odd thought came that, perhaps, made more sense. *"What if they knew I needed it? What if they left it behind because they wanted me to have it?"*

Finished at last, he exited their shelter into

the bright chill of early morning. No fire, no coffee, no food, just another day like many others.

"And any other day I would have kept on moving east, 'cept now we're almost as far east as we can go, and I've got another person to worry about."

"You don't have to worry about me, Mr. Travis."

"What?" He spun toward her. Sunlit dawn shone over the low hills directly behind her, casting an aura round her body, leaving her face in shadow. "Was I speaking out loud?"

"You were muttering a bit, like you always do."

"Huh. I've been traveling alone for a while; guess I've started talking to myself. I never noticed. I'm sorry Lorne, no offense meant. I've been trying to link back up with my army but haven't been able to get past the enemy lines and their patrols. This is a war we're in, and it's a rough journey. For both of us. Under the circumstances, I'm concerned about you."

He looked behind, nodding toward the disaster they'd escaped from last night. He didn't mention the burnt house or her family. "This war just made your life even rougher than mine." He moved off to one side of her, the sun now a thin patch of warmth on his cheek. The streaks of dried tears along her sooty face showed in detail. "Do you have any relatives living hereabouts we can get you to? I'm sure you'd be in much better hands with them than out here starving with me."

"Mr. Travis. They, those folks back there, were all I had left. Everyone else had already been

124

killed, one way or the other. My mam, she died having me. With my sister... gone... I'm the last of my line."

She took a step toward him. Tears washed down her cheeks as she flung herself forward into his chest. Her silent sobbing wetted the front of his shirt. Travis, taken aback, kept his hands lightly holding her shaking shoulders.

"Best to let her cry it all out right now. Wish I could do more for her but there's just nothing for it if she's got no family left." He looked around their surroundings while she wept, considering their predicament.

Under other circumstances, it would have been a beautiful spring morning, and was shaping up to be unseasonably warm too. However, pleasantries and other comforts were impossible to enjoy right now, especially as hunger clawed his insides, reminding him of their priorities.

"We've got to find some food soon. Neither of us had much to eat yesterday."

After a few minutes, her quiet weeping began to diminish. She began to relax, and Travis stepped back when her shaking subsided. From behind, he heard the faint sound of a horse breathing. He turned about, keeping himself between what he'd heard and Lorne, his pistols were already drawn and aimed toward the threat, whatever it was.

He quickly relaxed when he saw that it was only the horse they'd been riding last night while escaping. It slowly walked toward them, comfortably chewing a hank of grass grazed from the nearby field.

Lorne's mood changed, excited to have

something else to focus on. She exclaimed happily in greeting and ran to the horse. She wore a smile and demeanor that were both perhaps a bit more jovial than the circumstances warranted.

"Well, she's right about one thing. Since we've got a horse, it'll be a durn sight easier to carry our gear. That'll help us move faster. I don't think we're very far inland from the ocean. Hopefully, we can get there in another day or two. Then I can report back to my officers and get some new orders. I hope. Until then, at least it'll be good to dry out after that deluge we suffered all last week."

He looked over at Lorne, seeing her in a new light. He realized that his situation had become much more complicated.

"Her only home's been burnt to the ground. All her kin have been killed. She ain't got nothing but the clothes on her back. Except me. I'm all she's got now. If I hadn't showed up to try to help them, she wouldn't be alive. If she hadn't come outside the house and crawled down under the porch to see how I was after my skull got creased, she'd have been blown to bits along with everyone else up above. So, in a way, I'm responsible for her. I'll do whatever I can to help her before I get to my lines, but I also have my duty, and I'll soon have my orders. What happens to her will be up to God at that point. But I hope we can find some friends or neighbors along the way that will take her in before then."

"Mr. Travis! Mr. Travis! Please come over!"

Lorne knelt by the saddle he'd taken off the horse and set down last night. He over went to see what had roused her excitement.

"See here! Isn't this what you were looking for last night?"

Amazingly, the missing satchel that he'd carried for so long had been returned. It was a miracle, yet one not without disquiet. Obviously, someone had returned it last night, while they were both wrapped deep in the sleep of total exhaustion.

He dug into the sack and checked carefully to see what was still there. It seemed that all the contents had been removed, then replaced, with one exception. Almost everything was still there but a small portion of the bacon, which had been replaced by several small apples. It was a welcome trade, yet disturbing to think that a person, even of good intent, had been so close to them while they were vulnerable as newborns.

But what other choice had they last night? If they hadn't crawled inside the tiny shelter when they did, both of them would have soon slid headlong off the horse to sleep where they fell. They'd been on their last legs.

Someone out there had known it. They were being watched, perhaps even now.

Keeping the disquiet from his voice, he answered her question. "Yep. It is the bag that was missing. We'll be able to have breakfast now. Nothing fancy or too tasty, but it'll keep our bellies from getting wrapped around our spines."

He wasn't as worried as he probably should have been, but the cold fact was that they would both be dead right now if their mystery visitor had wanted them so. Thankfully, whoever it was had left enough food for Lorne and him to have at least a few small meals over the next several days. Time enough for them to get miles away from here before having to either hunt or scavenge for their supper.

The sun had risen over the eastern ridge of low-lying hills, clearing out the leftover chill amongst the shadows. The growing heat washing over them was a slowly opening oven's open door that promised noontime enervation.

For now, they needed to get going, especially if they'd have to take a break later in the hottest part of the afternoon. Travis saddled up the horse, which seemed docile and no worse for wear after carrying them both last night.

"Glad it can fend for itself, must have found some water out there along with the grass."

"Miss Lorne, I think we've got everything but that covering over the bush there. Would you mind rolling that up while I finish with this saddle and the other gear?"

"I can do that. What are you chewing?"

"Coffee bean. We do it in the Army when we don't have time nor water to make a proper brew. It's crunchy and better than nothing. Do you want one?"

"Sure. I've had them before."

"Have you now? That seems peculiar."

He proffered the tin. She grabbed a few beans and began crunching on them while packing away the old gray blanket that had covered the hut. "We used to buy bags of them from the traders."

The horse was loaded. He pulled out a portion of bread, tore it in two, and handed her half. "It ain't much for now but we'll eat a better meal later. We need to get moving. You get on up in the saddle, I want you to ride."

She crammed the bread in her mouth, and hoisted herself on the stirrup, chewing as she easily clambered into the saddle.

Speaking around the bread, she asked, "What about you? We're not riding together, like last night?"

"Last night was an emergency. I don't want to tire the horse today. It's going to be getting hot soon. Besides, it's not good practice to make a horse carry two riders very far, especially over unsettled ground like this."

They got moving eastward along the trail that was little more than a scratch in the ground that the occasional animal kept clear. Travis led on foot, while Lorne rode behind. She spoke.

"We could go around the field and over to the road I was telling you about. The road the traders used. It goes east all the way down to a dock at the ocean."

"What traders are those?"

"They'd be driving those big wagons coming from the ships. Usually two horses pullin' it, but sometimes it was so loaded up they needed four. Those drivers would whip those poor critters something fierce when they came on by the roadway out over on the back side of the field beyond the house. They carried all sorts of bags and crates in their wagons, full up with things that usually smelled good, but sometimes not, and sometimes with words on them that I'd never seen before and couldn't read. I asked once and they told me them words was French or Spanish, or something else that I can't remember. All I know is that I never learned any other languages. Da never bought any of their rum. He called it the demon's disciple, wouldn't allow it in our home. We'd always buy what we could of the other things they sold, but most of their sugar and coffee and tobacco went all the way to the sutler's tent by the training post. Whenever we had some extra butter or milk, we'd either sell it to the traders when they passed by or take it to the camp. We got paid better if we carried it to them ourselves, but it took some time to get there."

"Training post? An army post? How far is that?"

"I went once. It took all day. We had to leave at dawn to get there and back before nightfall. I'm glad I went, but it was a bit frightful. I'd never seen so many men and guns and cannon."

He stopped before a particularly low hanging branch that crossed their little trail. "Miss Lorne, I'm glad you told me about this. If there's an army post back that way, it's my duty to get there. My battery, and as far as I know, our entire brigade, was destroyed in a fight weeks ago. I need to get back to a commanding officer and report in."

"Mr. Travis, I'm sorry to have to tell you this, but that post is done shut down, and I've seen no traders here for at least a year now. The last one that come by didn't carry much, not like in the old days. Those traders who did come by told us that there weren't ships willing to bring in goods from the islands out there no more. Said it had got too dangerous. Said most of the captains didn't want to risk gettin' themselves blown up by the blockade and sent to Davy Jones' Locker."

He considered the possibilities. If he insisted they turn back to see for certain if any of the army camp still remained, it would take at least two days, more if they stayed off the main road, which he would. But he figured it would take about the same time to get to the ocean, even remaining on this this narrow rabbit trail.

It was better to keep going, keep to the plan. He pushed the alternative course of action out of his mind, along with a low-hanging branch before them. Lorne ducked under it and they continued eastward, to the ocean.

"How'd you know so much about these traders and that there army base, Miss Lorne?"

"Just growing up. Riding our horses. Visiting the neighbors, going to school. Most of this land roundabouts here is our property. Was, I mean. It was our property. I imagine it ain't no more."

"Why do you say that?"

"Well, my paps and mam and older brothers, they... ain't here no more, Mr. Travis, and even my uncles and my sister have left, too. Gone upstairs to Jesus, all of them."

There was a silence. She did not cry. "I don't know what will happen now. With the house gone, there's no reason botherin' to stay. Even them raiders could see that. If they couldn't have it, they made sure nobody could. I reckon they're long gone."

"I don't know about that. Someone's still around. Someone that I think watched that whole fight. "

"Nothing worthwhile here to fight for, anymore."

"Well, Miss Lorne, upon general reflection, it seems to me that it's you who owns all this land now. That's worth fighting for, I'd say."

She looked at him oddly, shook her head, then glanced behind them, back toward the general direction of the burnt-out house.

"Perhaps, but I've got no way to prove it. I saw the deed once. Da kept it inside his desk, locked in a drawer. It was a very heavy desk, big and strong, but made of wood. That desk is ashes by now."

Very quietly, she began singing a hymn under her breath. He'd never heard it, but that meant little. He never had been much of a church-going man. Eventually, her songs turned to hums, then even her humming ceased. She dozed in the saddle as she rode.

Balmy morning warmth became woolen midday heat. He began sweating unpleasantly. So different from the cold he'd been fighting for so much of his travels!

It wasn't so bad when they passed through shade underneath the occasional leafy canopy, but he was becoming a sweltering mess in the direct sunlight. Uncovered skin seemed to redden visibly.

Lorne stirred out of her muggy lassitude to make a suggestion.

"It's gotten right hot, Mr. Travis. I know where there's a pond not too far off from here. It's a place my sister and I would go swimming." She looked at him straight on. "We're covered with burnt ash and dust and... other things, both of us. We could each use a good washin' up, at least I know I could." He raised his head to answer, but she spoke again. "I wouldn't mind taking that lunch you promised earlier this morning. This would be a good place for that too, I think. I'm sure it'll be easier to travel later after it cools off a trifle."

He nodded but didn't speak. They kept up

their trudge between alternating patches of warm shadows and the bright heat between them. The perturbations and general foreboding that had for weeks goaded him toward his goal seemed more removed this day, but that was most likely another chimera. He knew from his experiences over these last few years that any illusion of even momentary respite would usually become a harbinger of some more painful difficulty, another new challenge of life or death to be dealt with by bullet, blade, and blood.

However, Lorne was right. They both were sullied and unkempt. And, most concerning to him, either would be easily noticed by anyone down-wind. For the time they'd have to spend traveling out of their way to clean up, removing that danger alone was worth it. Of course, a short lunch would be welcome too.

"Miss Lorne, I like this idea. Let's get on over to this pond of yours. Even if that army camp were still up there, I couldn't present myself to a commanding officer while smelling like the back of a bear cave."

Relief brushed across Lorne's face. She nodded and turned the horse off the trail they'd been on. Travis followed several wary paces behind, keeping watch for threats as best he could.

She led them a short distance across a grassy patch of ground to enter a small opening between tree branches. A dirt path led deep into the thicket. As they continued toward the pond, the breezes outside that had offered sporadic cooling had dissipated. Mugginess hung heavy from every branch and leaf surrounding them.

The land between the trees was mostly flat,

but in a few directions, rolling shrub-covered knolls kept sightlines short. A dense quiet settled over them as they paced along. Even the normally heavy hoof falls of the horse were lighter, almost mute.

Lorne turned to him, slowed, and pointed ahead toward a pollard tree. "That peculiar tree's right nearby the pond, Mr. Travis. My daddy and uncle chopped those branches off for firewood a few years ago. They grew back funny like that. I never exactly knew why. But since then, it's always made the waterhole easy to find."

A sense of concern, and then outright agitation increasingly gripped him as they continued closer toward the promised solace of the pond. It was probably for no reason, but he wished she had whispered, all the same.

He grabbed the reins, stopping the horse. "You say, this pond is just over the little hill by that funny lookin' tree?" He did whisper, hoping his example would carry his concern.

"Yes."

"Alright. You just hold up here a moment."

"Why?" Her voice began to rise.

"I can't rightly say. But... well... Lorne, I've done a lot of hiding out this last month. A place like this looks to me like either a perfect refuge, or a better ambush."

He reached up and pulled the Spencer rifle from its scabbard. "You give me just two minutes to reconnoiter the situation. Stay here, please."

Without waiting for an answer, he turned and swiftly moved past the tree, keeping low as possible. He crawled up to the edge and peered over.

A numb maw of stillness extended across the

silent body of water, its motionless surface only some fifty feet across at the widest point. The pond's perimeter pushed back against the land, draped here and there with oddly shaped rock formations, some half in or out of the water. He watched intently, casting his eyes back and forth for any motion. It was dappled dark beneath a green canopy that held sunlight behind leafy shadows. Their intertwined branches above made the tiny lake a passable impersonation of a castle dungeon.

"Now, how in hell and damnation would I think of that? I ain't never seen a dungeon before... or a castle."

Nothing moved. Nothing at all.

"Okay, there it is then. I don't like it, but... all clear, best as I can see. Better safe than sorry. I'll go get Lorne. We'll eat and get cleaned up."

His uneasiness, however, persisted as he crawled backwards away from the water, down the little rise a few feet, stood up, and turned around. He jumped with surprise. She was already there, standing by him, holding the satchel with their food. She held it out to him.

"You eat first. Sorry Mr. Travis, I surely didn't mean to scare you."

"You didn't. I'm fine."

"Didn't look fine a second ago. I'm very sorry. I shouldn't have come up on you so quiet like that, but I've such a craving for cleaning myself up, I just couldn't help getting here as soon as possible. Everything's alright over there, isn't it?"

"Yes, seems so. I smell a tinge of something... off, but perhaps that's just me." He looked at her, then reached for the satchel she still held.

"Enjoy your lunch." She dropped the food in

his hand and walked away toward the pond, out of his sight.

He sat down and slapped together a small ration of more stale bread and bacon fat. He was still chewing his first bite when a horrible shriek of dismay came from beyond the hillock. It was Lorne. He dropped the sandwich and grabbed the Spencer, running off hard, guided by her sounds of distress.

"What was hiding over there? What did I miss? Damnation! Whatever it is will pay if she's hurt."

They met near the ridge top. She had mostly undressed but had grabbed her pile of neatly folded garments as she retreated from the pond, holding them up, covering herself as she ran toward him. Terror and tears mixed on her still unwashed face. He held the rifle at ready, scanning the area for enemies behind her. There were none he could see.

Briefly she paused her headlong scramble.

"Blood! Blood water, Mr. Travis!"

Naked fear pushed words past chattering teeth. She stared at him, eyes shocked, angry and wide at the desecration of her childhood sanctuary.

"Blood! Everything has turned to blood!"

She turned to run back toward where they had left the horse. He noticed that her feet and ankles were mottled, splotched with crimson, as if she'd been wading in wet barn paint.

"Don't try to think now. You can figure it out later. Whatever caused this might still be down there."

Very slowly he crept toward the pond. All was still, just as it had been only a few minutes ago.

The pond's sickly odor was now explained. Decaying revulsion tattered every breath. He wished that he'd taken more time to reconnoiter earlier. That would have saved her from this ugly scene.

He was angry that he'd risked their lives to save a little time cutting corners on security procedures, just because they'd both been in a hurry to get cleaned up. The truth was, of course, that he knew better, should have done better. It was entirely his fault. He wouldn't let that happen again.

A narrow edge of sandy soil rimmed the pond for most of its diameter. He could see the footprints where she had begun to wade in, a red-splashed area by a fallen tree trunk. Near her footprints he saw one stocking on the ground where she must have dropped it. He picked it up, saw no blood, so put it in his pocket to give back to her later.

Again, he noticed the oddly formed rocks. He stepped over the log to get a better view of the closest formation.

Only a few paces forward, then time and vision came to him in thin-cut slices amidst the gloom. He stopped, grinding teeth and fighting rising bile. Staring between... what? A rock formation? Maybe or not. No. Stones don't bleed. Yes. These had. Blood water.

The reality of what lay before him became distinct.

It had been a long time since Travis had been physically nauseated. He'd killed men, both at a distance and up close with his own hands. He'd seen more limbs and brains and guts destroyed than could be counted. He'd heard the dying's last mewling agonies made public throughout the night. But this, all this around him, almost voided his nearly empty stomach. Stumbling under the throes of his new-found vision, he gripped the carbine tightly, his only sense of stability in a world now sharply tilted toward Hell.

It was a bacchanal of blades.

Everywhere within sight, the arcane twist of horror festooned the tiny red pond with a heinous stew of decapitated male naiads. Everywhere he looked, the clumped shapes he'd originally thought were rock formations were, in fact, mutilated clots of flesh, all that remained of the many headless soldiers who still wore their dark uniforms. Everywhere and everything nearby the pond was slaughter and ruin.

Their blood had fed the soil around the little swimming hole, as it drained out the sacks of their earthly shells into the once-pure waters of the pond. Holding himself and his stomach in check, he moved among the headless dead, confirming the horror of what he did not want to believe.

"There are at least twenty men in here. Every one of them decapitated, looks like. This took some time. How could this many men let themselves get bushwhacked and killed ugly and stupid like this?"

Moving amidst the carnage, Travis noticed that although mutilated corpses were plentiful, there was a severe paucity of heads. None were to be seen. All had been gathered up and taken by who or what had done this. A very large bag or two would have been needed.

"These men were obviously soldiers. This

could only have happened if they were killed all at once. Why are they all dead? It makes sense that one poor son of a bitch could be surprised, the very first one. But it would have been impossible for the rest of them to not have fought back against... whatever it was... while that was happening."

He slowly paced among the unmoving clumps of rotting, headless death. A few corpses had fallen so their high-topped boots were visible. What he hadn't noticed before was what was on those boots.

"Black iron spurs... these men were all the Captain's raiders! Looks like every one of these bastards is wearing those peculiar spurs. This explains where they went last night after they exploded the house. But why are they all dead? What could possibly kill this many heavily armed men all at once? Where are their horses? And where in Hades are their heads?"

Shelving those mysteries for now, he prepared to leave, but then saw an oddly organized collection of human carcasses on the other side of the pond, also headless as far as he could tell.

"Those bodies over there are the only ones that seem like they might have been moved after the massacre. All these others over here dropped down right where they died."

Again, he checked the carbine, then looked carefully around once more before approaching the bodies. *"I know that whatever did this to a couple dozen armed men ain't going to be worried about the likes of me, but it can't hurt to at least be more careful than I was earlier."*

The ground was boggier here than elsewhere. These several bodies were piled one on top of the other. Travis stared at this further infamy before him, knowing something was different from the others.

"Mr. Travis."

He spun around, jumpy, and nervous. Again, he'd been surprised by Lorne's silent approach. He relaxed his hold on the weapon and lowered it.

He saw that she had bathed, managing to clean herself up somewhere else, along with her clothes. Standing beside her, the slather of filth that still coated him seemed even more oppressive. He ignored that discomfort.

"Ma'am?"

Lorne continued, "I've eaten and, even better, gone upstream to the crick that feeds this pond. Can't we get moving along, away from here? What are you still doing in this horrible place? These men are all dead, just like my sister. From the looks of their uniforms, they're probably some of those that killed her. Please can't we go on soon? I'm sure you'll wish to wash up too, I can show you where the fresh water is. Oh, and I ate the sandwich you made, thank you."

Seeing the anxiety in her quick-stepping motions and blurted words, he guessed that she was close to a state of nervous palpitations from the many shocks she'd just been through.

He'd seen it a few times in some of the men after a particularly ugly battle, sometimes immediately, other times days or weeks later. Some men drank rum or whiskey as a cure, but he'd seen that using drink would often make it worse for themselves and those around them. He was glad they had none here.

He knew the best thing was to go along with

her suggestions, and get her to a safer, less distressing locale as soon as they could. But she was right, he did need to clean himself up, and his clothes too. The creek would also be a good time to fill up the water bag, and they would be needing that. He didn't worry about his missed lunch. He'd be fine with a bit of bread and jerky while he walked.

"Lorne, you're absolutely right. We do need to leave. This is so very horrific, it's hard to imagine how it happened. I'm worried that whatever did it might come back. I came over here to see if there might be a clue as to what we should be looking out for. I've been trying to figure out what it is about these particular bodies that seemed different from the others, but I can't put my finger on it."

She gave the stacked corpses near them one quick glance. "Mr. Travis, there's no blood."

He looked at the closest heap of stacked bodies, then over at the ones he'd seen earlier. Sure enough, the others he'd mistakenly thought were rock formations were marked by dark stained swaths of dirt and grass beneath them, many laying in thick puddles of their clotted blood.

But these other bodies had not bled out.

"You're right Lorne. Their skin, it's so pale. There's no blood on the ground, and I'll bet there's no blood left inside any of them, either."

"It's like a beast chewed them off."

"What? Chewed what off?"

Looking more closely at the nearby corpses, he noticed that while all the other bodies he'd seen had seemed to have lost their heads by the clean stroke of a straight blade, the wounds left in the upper torso of these men had been inflicted differently.

She continued. "Their heads. Chewed off. All these necks have jagged scrapes on them that look like a big bunch of teeth dug in all around and... just chewed them heads off. Clean off in one big bite." She looked at him, whispering. "What on the good Lord's earth could do something like that?"

Although a shadowy suspicion flickered in the back of his mind, he answered, "Lorne, I can't rightly say for certain."

"Maybe a tiger... or a lion?"

He bent down to inspect the jumbled dirt in the area around the bodies, looking for tracks he knew weren't there. "Them beasts could probably do something like this, but I don't believe there are any tigers or lions around here. Now, maybe a bear. I've seen a few bears. They're strong enough to rip a man apart. But mostly if we give them a wide berth, bears leave us alone. I don't think any swamp gators live about these parts and I don't know anything else that could... "

He trailed off. There it was, again.

"Mr. Travis, what is it?"

"Something I saw before. A long time ago. Very long."

"What is it?"

He stood up, numb, yet a part of him terribly vindicated by the discovery. "It means we need to get moving. Now. I'll tell you after we're on our way."

The impression in the damp earth was clear: two small but telltale upside-down "V" marks were both there, plainly cut into the upper curve of the horseshoe.

It wasn't just a fever dream or nightmare. The Otherside was real after all.

7. DON'T FEEL LIKE FIGHTING TONIGHT

Several hours had passed since they had left the bloody terror of the red pool behind. Long shadows cast ahead of them as they rode on. Travis was glad he'd taken the few minutes back at the upstream creek to clean up and to at least rinse out most of the blood, muck, mud, and soot from his clothes. He'd been a mess. Afterwards, the afternoon heat had dried them both.

It was a good opportunity to talk as they traveled, and they took advantage of it, but a long silence stretched out after he'd told her as much as he could about the demon-horned horseshoe. He'd explained where he'd first seen it at the massacre down by the river a couple years back. Now, he'd seen that it was here as well.

But when he tried to tell the tale of what he'd done at the mountain pass by the power and behest of the being he knew only as *One*, his words simply failed him. He'd grunted a disjointed string of syllables and vowels that made little sense. Finally, he gave up, saying it had just been a nightmarish vision of violent confusion, no doubt brought upon by his head injury. It was a sober and sane explanation which he still wished to believe himself, but could not, now.

There were too many similarities, too much coincidence, between this scene of sick degradation and the earlier killings at the oxbow farms.

"I've never had any dreams or delirium like that before, never been flying around or seen sword fighting on mountains. It's madness. Hell, I've never even thought of mountains like that before, and why would anyone wear sandals to go fight?"

Looking down at his own worn boots, he suddenly remembered that many men he'd known had gone into battle without any shoes at all.

"Might not be so bad, them sandals. Better'n nothing, that's the truth."

"What's the truth, Mr. Travis?"

"Am I muttering out loud again?" He laughed at the thought, then spoke.

"Sandals. Just pondering sandals, that's all."

"That's very strange. I had a dream last night. There was a woman walking by who wore sandals. She wasn't very old, but not young, either. It was night, with a bright moon. I could see she had long dark wavy hair. It hung down in curls behind her that shined so pretty. At first, I thought it was wet, but then I discerned that it wasn't at all. I don't know how, but suddenly, I knew it was some sort of oil. It smelled nice but wasn't like anything I've ever smelled before. When she first walked up, she looked mean, like she was scolding someone I couldn't see. She made a face at whoever it was. Then she saw me looking at her and smiled. Then she looked around again. She nodded, then walked off. Those sandals she had on were laced all the way up to her knees. And her dress wasn't like anything I've ever seen before either. It was all very peculiar. And... " She trailed off.

"And? What else was peculiar?"

"She carried a knife. A big one."

Travis started, worried, and reached to his belt, affirming that his own big Bowie was still there. It was.

"What kind of big knife was it? Every seen one like it before?"

"No. I've never seen anything like it, except, I guess, in my imagination, or a drawing in a book I've forgotten about. Don't know how I'd make up something like that. It did look real, and it did look different... but it did look like it would *work*, if you know what I mean."

"I think I do, Miss Lorne." He remembered the short swords he'd seen used during his dream, or travels, or whatever that vision had been. "What did this big knife look like, exactly?"

Travis glanced up at her. She was silent, pondering the question. It had, again, been a long day. He was glad they'd gotten as far away from the ugliness as they had. But he knew it wasn't enough distance. Twice as far would have been half as much as he would have liked to have traveled.

"But here we are. We've done the best we could, under the circumstances."

Awaiting Lorne's reply, he noticed that the land they were traveling through had changed. There were fewer large clumps of underbrush, which would make it more difficult to build a shelter that would blend in with their surroundings. Still, they would have to find somewhere safe to sleep, for soon it would be dusk.

He scoffed to himself, *"Safe! With headless*

raiders, blood-drained corpses and ghosts dripping acid on us while we sleep, where can we be safe? Well, we're still alive and moving, so that's better than the alternative."

They would just have to make do with what they had. He checked his weapons again, a habit now become ritual.

Finally, Lorne spoke.

"Mr. Travis, that woman's knife I was talking about, well, it was very pointed, and very curved, of all things. It wasn't like a proper officer's sword, or even like your own big knife. It hung from what looked like a beaded belt off her waist, or maybe it was a belt made from beads, since she was wearing a lot of them. A lot of beads, thick as armor."

He thought back to the swords he'd seen that were used by both sides during the fighting. "I know that most cavalry swords do have a curve to them."

"I've seen those. Before the war we'd sometimes have officers over for dinner who wore a sword. Their blades did curve a little, but this was nothing like that."

Travis spotted a small thicket of brush off to one side as they came around the base of a hillock. He led them off the trail toward it.

"We can talk about it during dinner. The sun is going down. It's time to set up camp." He looked at her again. "I've also been having very odd dreams lately and had another one last night too."

"Yes, let's talk over dinner. But please Mr. Travis, not about too many horrible things. We've seen enough of those recently."

They set up their little camp and ate another

mean supper, but after Lorne had gone to sleep, Travis sat motionless, not quite ready for sleep yet. The fresh breeze swept across his face, a small chill pleasure after the day's heat. At times he smelled the salt air that was carried inland. He knew they were close to his goal, and he chafed at the delay. But they were still moving, still alive. He pushed the images of decapitated men out of his consciousness as best he could.

"Doin' better'n than those tore up sum-bitches back at that swimmin' hole. Lord Almighty, that was a wretched sight!"

They had eaten, filling most of their guts with another ration of the dried fatty meat and rock-hard cracker bread. Nothing fancy but he had no complaints, not when it was the only thing keeping them alive.

"Keeping us alive. That's what I've got to do. Food, shelter, and keepin' us out of the way of... whatever it was... whatever it still is... that chewed those men apart back there."

Lorne revealed her presence only by her regular deep breathing. They had taken advantage of a shallow nook in the hillside behind dense brush. He'd protected that hidden space from the elements using their gum blanket and tying several branches together. Now, Travis sat inside, gazing past the gray edge of the waterproofed fabric into the clear night sky, listening to evening sounds.

His thoughts kept returning to the whatever-it-was that was following them, and how to best deal with it to survive. He knew he didn't like the real answer, plain as it was to see.

"We'll never be safe as long as we're hiding here and there trying to stay out of his way.

Retreating in good order can be an effective tactic for the short term but won't ever work when the enemy is hell-bent to chase us down. That allows the enemy to keep the initiative. Ever since we ran from the house, I've been trying to keep Lorne safe, but at some point... I know I've got to turn and fight, I suppose, since I failed the first time. I must fight that creature again unless all that really was just a fever dream. But... I don't think so."

He closed his eyes, remembering the many dead spearmen strewn in broken heaps around the last stand of his ancestor. The scores of arrows that protruded from their bodies was a testament to The Otherside's obscene victory. Travis cursed that creature's thousand-year reign of terror ever since then.

"Mebbe it's time to start huntin' him down, find him first. Killin' that so-called Captain, or The Otherside, or whatever name he's callin' himself these days, is gonna be the only way to keep him from getting us. He's gonna be following me, maybe for another thousand years, no matter where we hide."

He thought he heard a solemn affirmation to his thought from afar. Or, it might have just been night winds glissading across the surrounding foliage.

"Yesssss."

For several minutes he listened intently. Holding his breath, he sought to detect any other natural sounds that might be mistaken as words. Hearing none, he felt exhaustion creeping up to claim him. He lay down next to Lorne and slept. There were no visions.

Overnight came and went. They slept and

woke. Rain had replaced warmth. Now clouds hid the sun.

Dawn. Travis hadn't really expected this kind of rain again but was glad he'd gathered up the loose branches and other wood nearby their tiny camp last night, bringing them inside to keep protected from the dew.

"At least now I'll be able to make a small fire. It's cold and damp, but the perfect morning to boil up some of those coffee beans I've been packin' around."

He remembered that they only had the one battered tin coffee cup. That was fine. They could share.

Later, they moved eastward into the rain, and the day had become a gray muddled mess. Each step was the same as the last. Occasionally he would glance over at Lorne, still riding, covered by the gum blanket to keep her dry. A bubble of gray mist seemed to surround them, reaching out to about thirty feet in all directions, beyond which little could be seen. Mostly he stared ahead and downward, watching the land they walked upon, hoping to prevent any missteps.

The good news was that if there were any raiders left lurking about, there was only a small possibility they'd be seen within the murk... unless their pursuers, literally, stumbled over them.

Of course, the bad news was that there'd be no possibility of escape. He'd be forced to fight it out, alone against many.

"But when was that ever different for me? I've been fighting against uneven odds ever since the army marched through my town and called all the fellers out of the fields. We had to

sign up us right then and there! Marched us off without a fare-thee-well and we were on a train to camp that very night. I was loadin' up caissons and strapping feedbags on the horses the next day."

Pushing those thoughts away, he staved off midday hunger with a few bites of another ration. They kept moving. There was no reason to stop in the rain, and nowhere dry to do so. He was still chewing the last of his biscuit when he noticed that the gloomy daylight had brightened ahead.

Curtains of rain and gray opened and closed before them while random gusts of salt air swirled and spit. Beyond lay a much different vista.

Step by step, the tiny caravan of two humans and one beast slowed tentatively to a stop. Quick, teasing winds cleared and closed, then re-opened, shifting cloud banks before them, bestowing evidence of their goal one instant, proffering their senses only a shuttered wall the next. An almost tearful awe clasped them both. They were finally within the dominions of the Atlantic, or, at least the brutal expanse of its blustery edge, where an iron pall of broken rivets moved as whitecaps, bruising the green blue waves below.

Glimpses of the great waters before them were increasingly frequent. They were here. They had made it... the ocean.

Lorne slid from the horse to stand beside Travis. He stared through the squalls, immobile. She took his hand.

For several minutes neither spoke. Finally, a raspy whisper came from the man. "I'd heard the ocean described many times. And, after seeing some paintings of it, I thought I knew what to expect. But there's a difference between listening to tales of the sea when sitting around a fire after supper or looking at a picture in a frame on some parlor wall, and... *this Ocean.*"

Lorne released his hand, then spoke softly, "It is a sight to see." She turned to him. "I'm proud of us. I'm proud of you. We managed to get here, even after everything horrid that's happened."

He coughed a sour laugh, then looked at her, "I believe you have the heavier burden, and I praise you for how well you've held up. Thank you, Lorne."

The horse whinnied, bringing him back from his musings. He knew they couldn't stand there forever, gawking. All three moved forward again.

Later, he spoke again, "This is my first time being at the ocean. In person."

"That's what I'd guessed, but what do you mean by, 'in person', Travis?"

"Oh. Well, I've dreamed about it, that's all. Of course, it's not the same."

"You must have a vivid imagination. But I'm surprised you've never been to the ocean before. That's unexpected. I'd have thought a soldier would have gone everywhere and seen almost everything."

"I've seen a lot, no argument there, but I only went where they told me. All my battles were on solid ground. I suppose the generals never saw fit to assign me to fire my cannon at ships. And of course, I ain't no sailor. So here I am."

"Here we both are."

They looked at each other with amusement, sharing a gentle pause. Travis offered her a hand for her to mount back up, but she shook her head.

"I think I'd like to walk for a while. You should ride instead."

"I'm doing fine. If you're walking, I'd rather give this horse a rest."

"You know, Mr. Travis, even with boots like that, you're a real gentleman."

He laughed. "That's right nice of you Miss Lorne. The fact is, these old boots have gotten me this far, and what's left of them should get me where I need to be."

"And... where's that, Mr. Travis?"

"An army supply wagon." They both laughed.

He pushed away a depressing thought, *"If there are any supply wagons left."*

They walked on, winds lashing nettles of rain across their faces.

Travis scanned the countryside around them for any signs of his fellows or the enemy. He saw little that was man-made, save two burnt foundations of long-dead buildings and a few broken fence poles. The countryside, bereft of humans, held flying and small four-legged creatures in plentiful numbers. The squirrels, hares and birds ignored the pair of two-legged interlopers.

Travis had hoped to find someone in his chain of command. An empty world holding him sequestered hadn't been his plan.

"Destruction. No matter how far I go it's always the same."

Yet here he was at his goal...finally. After weeks and miles of walking, he'd been encouraged by the hope of reaching this place. He'd done everything necessary to get here, hiding when he could, killing where he couldn't. But now, with neither military or civilian in sight, and with Lorne's wishes to consider, Travis decided that they both needed to recuperate and plan their next move. Obviously, they couldn't continue east, so it would have to be either to the north or south.

"And what will Lorne want to do now? She said she had no more family. Where will she go? Do I want her to go?"

They still had time to build a shelter before the sun went down. Previously, he'd walked as far as possible during the daylight hours before finding a place to sleep. Making a rushed camp before nightfall had always been a ramshackle event when he'd been alone. But if they were going to stay here a couple of days or more, they had time to get a few things done. Shelter, as usual, topped his list of priorities, but as they only had about another day's worth of food rations, they'd have to steal, fish or hunt to fill their bellies.

"I don't want to waste bullets on shootin' game. Maybe I can get that spear point straightened out and use that instead."

Turning away from the beach, they went back inland, up the slight rise into low hills and brush. He wanted to get off the exposed sand and dirt to build a leeward facing refuge before dark. When they found a likely spot, Lorne unsaddled the horse.

"Mr. Travis, I was thinking, there's quite a few of these small branches laying around, and there's lots of grass to tie them together. I think I can build us a rabbit trap."

During lulls in the rain, they'd sighted a

several of the creatures. Usually, the rabbits held themselves completely frozen while attempting to hide in plain sight, a tactic Travis knew well, but a few times they'd seen or heard them scurrying through the high grass while fleeing from some unseen bunny terror.

"Or maybe they're just chasing after something better than what they've got to deal with in the here and now. Sounds familiar."

"Miss Lorne, that's a great idea! I can't think of anything better. We're gonna be needing more food soon and fresh meat would be a blessing. While you hunt them rabbits, I'll set up our camp and then work on another little chore that needs doin'."

Lorne started off, but after only a few steps, she stopped abruptly and spun around.

"Just one thing, Mr. Travis. Before I start on this, I'll need to borrow your knife. There's a lot of branches I'll need to cut, and I'm not about to be gnawing through them all."

Travis only hesitated an instant before handing her the big Bowie. It felt odd to not have it in his possession, but this seemed like a safe enough area. He could hear her cutting brush and working while he built their camp.

"Safe enough? Like that pond full of headless corpses back there? I looked that over. I thought that was safe too. Another mistake like that could be deadly, but I can't be everywhere, seeing everything, all the time."

After building their little hut, he realized he couldn't hear her working anymore. Glancing around, there was no sign of her. He climbed up from the bottom of the hill, his slight concern tightening into panic, until he saw her putting down a cage, well away from their camp.

"There she is! Looks like she's setting the trap. Roast rabbit will be a welcome dinner... if these cages work out, of course."

While watching her work, he realized how much they'd both been through.

"We do need a break. Too much death. Too much loss. Not enough rest or food, or love. She's lost her entire family. All of them, gone. She's handling it well, but for how long? I need to get back to my army to report in, but I'm not making the best decisions after that head wound. I'm not thinking as clearly as I should be. I could easily make a mistake that will get us both killed."

He climbed a few paces up to the top of a hill. The strong smell of salt thickened the breeze. Standing tiptoe, he could just glimpse the vast waters beyond the tall bushes that stood between him and the beach.

"I'm jumpy and imagining things that aren't there. Like that dream of the woman the other night, talking to something outside our hut? Jumping to conclusions about demon horns on horseshoes? And that Mr. One fella, telling me about somebody he calls 'The Otherside', who's an evil bastard who makes his followers call him 'Captain'? Or being sent on a mission to kill that same fella a thousand years ago in a frozen mountaintop pass? But I failed then, so now Mr. One expects me to try killin' him all over again? It's madness. If I told the boys in my old battery about any of this nonsense, they'd all just laugh and call me a drunken fool and an opium eater."

"Mr. Travis. I'm almost done."

He started at her sudden presence, yanked out

of his daydreams. More evidence that he needed rest.

"I should have heard her comin' before she was on top of me like that. Anybody could've snuck up and run me through like a pig. Or, in this case, maybe more like a confused little rabbit."

"Here's the second trap I need to place. The first one is already set up, over there behind me. I'll put this one up the hill a bit in front of me. That's where I'm going now. I just wanted you to see it first."

She held out a trap. It was woven with the thin and supple branches that grew everywhere around them and tied together with long strands of tough grass. A gate above the opening would drop down to close whenever the prey inside knocked over a stick at the opposite end.

"The 'dead end', you might say." He chuckled silently to himself at his jest, then spoke aloud to her.

"Very ingenious. I'd hate to be a rabbit anywhere within fifty miles of here. You are a formidable young woman, Miss Lorne."

"I appreciate that, but don't thank me until we actually get a couple of them trapped and roasted up for supper. You can do the skinnin' if you don't mind."

"Not at all."

"I found plenty of sticks and driftwood around here to build a fire and brought back as much as I could carry while I was cutting the grass and branches for the traps. It's in a pile just over there, near where I was working. That knife is sharp as a wonder, Mr. Travis, even if it's a little big."

"What's the use of having a knife if it ain't sharp? I'll need to hone that edge again if you're done with it."

"I'm happy to sharpen it if you'll show me how. But I need it for one more thing."

"What's that?"

"We still have some of those small apples left inside the satchel, don't we? One of those will make a more than acceptable bait. I just need to cut it into some small pieces. The critters will smell the juice and won't be able to stop themselves from goin' right on inside for a nice meal. Well, that's my supposition at least, but it used to work well enough out in the fields around the old house, so it should work here. There's enough of these rabbits living here, that I reckon more than a few of them must be looking for something extra to eat."

He got her the apple. She baited the traps. She had set them both far enough away that activity at their camp shouldn't spook any critters. Beside each one she marked the spot by staking a tall branch nearby, then tying a strip of yellow fabric she'd cut from her dress to it. Both little streamers jutted up a foot or so above the surrounding grass, fluttering unmistakably in the breeze. She didn't want any difficulty in finding the traps later.

Back at their camp, Travis worked on the hoe. He finally got the blade bent back enough by jamming it in a crevice between two large rocks, and slowly working it back and forth, occasionally hammering it straighter with another rock in his hand.

"I guess I'm a stone age blacksmith now. It would be nice to have a real anvil and hammer,

159

but this will have to do."

He bent and pounded the iron point out straight. It wouldn't be the strongest spear ever made, but it would hold together long enough to pierce animal and human flesh.

"Nice to have another silent killing tool in addition to the big Bowie. We've only got so much gunpowder and lead left. Can't be wasting it trying to kill game. More important is for us to keep our heads clear, not be hasty, and only use it against the two-legged beasts, if need be."

Remembering the bloody scene at the pond, he knew that it was important for them to keep their heads, in more ways than one.

"Something's out there that wants both of ours, literally, but I aim to permanently dissuade that monster by any means I can."

He'd seen plenty of mauled and mutilated bodies from both sides while manning his batteries. Double canister shot generally produced some of the worst horrors, being designed for the manglement of humans who were getting too close and personal while trying to kill you.

"They were just' doing their jobs, same as me. Every soldier knows if you don't advance when they tell you to, you'll probably get shot after the court martial. Dead now or later, makes no difference."

This time he did hear Lorne approaching. He had just finished sharpening the blade of his improvised spear as she walked into the camp with one of the traps. It already had a rabbit inside.

"That was fast!", he blurted.

"It was uncanny! I'd just finished setting up the second trap, when I noticed the first trap's marker moving about! I ran over and there it was!"

"Looks like we'll have something good to eat tonight!"

"Amen to that Mr. Travis! If you take this one out and get it ready to cook, I'll set this trap back and see if we can't catch another one."

They ended up with five rabbits for their supper that evening. Lorne left the two empty traps out overnight. Going from a steady diet of bacon fat and rock-hard cracker bread to a meal of fresh meat was a welcome luxury for them.

After dinner, they relaxed as the evening twilight surrounded them. The stress surrounding the recent carnage of bloodletting, disaster, strange events, and even stranger visions slowly lifted from them both. Their camp was hidden behind a hill from any unknown eyes on sea or beach. Nevertheless, Travis had kept their cook fire as low as possible, while still keeping it aflame. He wished to avoid attention from anyone, or anything, that might be prowling the open sand or sea. He would quench the tiny flames soon, before they turned in for the night.

Lorne turned to him.

"Mr. Travis, I have a question for you. I'm wondering what's left of this war." He looked up, saying nothing. She continued. "I know you've been fighting for a long time. From all you've seen, how much longer do you think the war will last?"

He remembered his last battle. Morale had been dropping for months beforehand, while

161

desertions mounted. He understood why men left, especially if they had family, but he didn't, and looked at the situation as just another job.

Even if he hadn't been paid for months, he'd usually been kept fed, and he felt it his duty to keep fighting, no matter what. Too many of his friends had been killed for him to just throw his hands up and sneak off.

On one hand, he had been damn glad to be away from the monotony of the backbreaking field work he'd done since childhood. On the other, that boring farm job didn't get your face peeled away, stripped down to the skull-bones, like he'd watched happen to one of his loaders hit by red hot iron fragments. Afterwards, that man had lived too long.

"Mr. Travis? Did you hear me? I just asked you a question."

"Ah? Yes. Sorry, I was just thinking. Thinking long and hard about an answer. I've been wrong about a lot recently. It's... difficult to say."

"And? What do you think? Will it be finished by year's end? Do you think it will be over before 1866?"

He felt the fire's heat withering. The embers nestled inside the tiny cook-pit seemed to dim before his eyes. What had been crackling flames only an hour ago were now barely warm.

"What I think is... that what I think don't really matter very much, Miss Lorne. But since you asked, from what I've seen in this here life, circumstance tends to push men to do its bidding, not the other way around."

"That's not much of an answer, Mr. Travis."

"No, I suppose not." He grabbed their one coffee cup, reached over to an exposed patch of sand between clumped grasses and scooped out a cupful. He pointed to the fire. "See those embers? If they could think the way men do, and who really knows if they can or can't? Well, I'm sure they'd like to continue doing their jobs and still be flames burning hot. They'd still be cookin' our food and keep on fighting the cold off."

He dumped the cup of damp sand over those few embers, extinguishing them. Dregs of heat and light crackled into the dirt.

He turned toward her, again considering his answer before pointing down to what was left of the fire. "There's more chance of those dead cinders cooking us up a whole goose than for the pains that have been inflicted by this war to be forgiven or forgot. I'm guessing that even after one side raises the white flag of surrender, the cannons go quiet, and both armies go home, there's still gonna be so much hatred left in people that this war will last another hundred years or more in some form or other. Hate makes people fight. Hate or insanity, maybe both."

The purple silence of the young night pressed closer. They sat just inside the opening of their tiny hut; on the same sides they'd grown accustomed to during this last week of flight. Tonight felt different. Tonight *was* different. After a long pause, Lorne spoke softly to him, her hand suddenly touching his face.

"I see. That would be a pity."

She moved close to him. His body warmed as she drew her hand along his cheek, brushing the hair aside, whispering close.

"I hope you don't feel like fighting tonight."

He didn't.

8. OVEN OF THE DAMNED

Dreams. Flying again. High vistas lucid and real. He soared south along the coastline while eternally breaking waves came from far a' sea, soaking sand with rhythmic marches, echelons lit bright and clear by the midnight moon.

No other presence could he sense, save the two sparks of life behind him where his sleeping physical form lay embraced with another.

Then he was moving out to sea, darkened shoreline quickly left behind. He flew along placidly, the center of a moving dome split by the horizon into moon swept waters down below, a starry blackness above. Travel was swift and guided, once again, by unknown forces beyond his control.

A small landmass loomed ahead, then in a moment, just below him. He slowed, now moving at a languid pace above what he somehow knew could be his only destination... the island of The Otherside.

Not so very large, yet large enough, it was covered in palms and jungle vegetation. He saw only a single town, although there was plenty of room among steep mountains and hidden coves for more settlements, if needed. It spread along the shores of a protected harbor, the homes and factories burrowed up into the sides of the angled hills that surrounded it. A high wall that stretched from hillsides into the ocean kept visitors out, or its people in, or both. He noticed a pair of ships docked at the harbor, with room for more.

Two different regions outside the walls caught his eye. Within the town and on the ships were ordinary lights, candles, and oil lamps, burning with the glow of any modern mid-1860's civilization. Yet, several hundred feet outside the wall to the east was a cleared area whose very ground seethed with a dull ruddy glow. On the opposite side of town, over a thousand feet beyond the wall to the west, was an area which seemed, at first glance, to merely hold the upturned hull of an unremarkable old shipwreck rotting in the jungle. But when he tried to discern any details, it defied his focus, instead becoming to his eyes a nothingness upon... something else.

Its glowing sheen reminded him of the quality of light he'd seen before during the high noon of summer, and, strangely enough, during the eclipse at the battle of the mountain pass.

After several attempts, he found that he could discern the strange region's oddly illuminated outline if he looked slightly away, to see it only with the corner of his eyes. Using this technique, he noticed it was at the end of a short zigzag channel which connected to the ocean. He thought he saw a small dock within, perhaps a boat tied up as well, but couldn't be sure. Whatever was there, it was well hidden.

Finally, he had to look away. It was too difficult and tiring to stare at something, while looking away at another thing. When he looked directly at it again, all of its other worldliness vanished, becoming once more just a decrepit hull of decay, unworthy of a second glance.

The strangeness of the island was evident.

Nothing less did he expect.

Motion caught his eye. He turned toward it. While he'd been preoccupied with the mystery of the western enclosure, a cavalcade of floating horrors had arrived above the ocean. In a long line that led back toward shore, translucent souls of shimmering orange were dragged along by unseen masters toward the glowing red ground of the eastern region.

Each had tucked within its elbow's crook, its own embittered, frantic head.

Weeping red gore, the severed heads gnashed and gnawed their fetters with dry broken teeth. Their feeble attempts to bite through their bonds were, of course, in vain. Years ago, they'd joined The Otherside, signing inexorable blood oaths of fealty. Now, glazed eyes glossed dull, tortured orbs burned red, the branding iron within their skulls glowed hot, still wielded by their unholy owner.

There were no second chances and no mercy when he ended their contracts. For each man, that had happened when head had been nipped from neck. Now they must fulfill their final covenant.

Time to pay up.

Along its unseen tracks, the floating train of torment slowly, with agony and regret, swept the former raiders of The Otherside along.

Travis twisted round in his airborne seat to get a better view of whence they came. There it was. He knew he could see it only by the extra-normal vision granted him by Mr. *One*. Far back, much more than a hundred miles away across the waters, beyond the many hills and brush, was their place of origin. Seeing it, he was not surprised.

They emerged from the selfsame pond of blood red death where Travis and Lorne had hoped to bathe. They came, one by one plucked out like laboratory specimens by the half-grinning rictus who wore a Captain's cavalry hat. He plied tweezers of soul-sized proportions as he emptied his former minion's spiritual remains from the clotted pool.

"Again! He's here! The Otherside!"

Sensing the thought of his name, the bestial Captain shifted, jerking away from his work with an annoyed grunt. He glared about but kept looking toward the general direction where Travis still steadily moved in random arcs above the island.

"You're one pug-ugly ol' son of a bitch now ain't ya?" Memories of his last bullet being sliced in two flashed past his mind's eye. *"Damn it all. If only I'd had one more bullet back at the pass, we wouldn't be having this little encounter."*

The orange procession of headless souls on their way to serve their master's final whims paused when a hissing growl from inside their former Captain's yellow-seeping cheek was heard. Then high-pitched shrieks surrounded Travis as a black-on-black cauldron of bats arose to pester his aerial viewpoint, a squealing swarm of flapping wings that agitated obscenely whenever the monster spoke. His mutilated tongue occasionally poked out through the torn wound, a thick snake spitting disapproval from inside a wet cave.

"I do not 'ENCOUNTER' the temporary beings of this realm!! I COMMAND and RULE THEM ALL!! Your crawling brethren are but

pulsing tubes of mortal liquid!! Such filth is fit only to obey my bidding and slake my thirst and hunger!!

"Some discharge their duties well as they lighten the burdensome details of rule!! I promise MUCH to those that serve me well, and REWARD their petty DREAMS of glory, gold, and women!! Indeed, I even grant some select few a lifetime so EXTENDED they OUTLIVE their GRANDSONS!! Can you not see my towering BENEVOLENCE?!!

"I allot much POWER to each of them while they still live, yet ALL that and MORE is EXTRACTED at their DEATH!! BEHOLD now their repayment!!"

It was a floating nightmare. The slurred words of The Otherside hit hard from all directions upon Travis, a syllable or sound from every thrashing bat that swirled nearby, peppering his astral form like buckshot. Finally, the tirade ended, and the man-like creature returned to his hellish task of disposal.

The line of decapitated souls began moving again, reaping their final fortunes. The wan luminosity flickering within the severed skulls increased and slowly incandesced to a more terrible brightness the closer they came to the end of their last journey. That same unrelenting force that had torn them from the bloody pond of death now also positioned them above their ultimate exit. It was the beginning of their forever sojourn, eternally encased within fire.

Still more came, awaiting their turn high above the burning rift. Each was still at first, then wildly animate with the terminal fear of a trapped rat. Every one of them, at the last, held its own severed head tightly to its ruined torso like a child might grip a favorite doll for security from the night.

Yet there was no safety, nor any cooling ministrations from the kind hand of merciful succor. Eyes now incandescent, heat poured from the unseeing sockets, rising past the melting point of bone.

Hair, flesh, and face dissolved forever. Each skull, still gripped in a desperate embrace by its own cadaver, deformed from an infernal heat and sank into its once proud and haughty chest.

One by one each was dropped into the glowering slash that led into the bowels of the earth. Around that pit grew a smear of gurgling dark soil, wounding the beach with red-rimmed anguish.

Those skeletal hands, when earthly flesh had once garbed their pale white forms, had often brandished braided whips for their master's beastly pleasures. With excuses of anger, or revenge for trifles, or for no reason at all, over the years each had held a slew of bloody, spiky clubs, made for tenderizing human flesh.

That time was done. Those fingers now dripped a rendered burning char, their last remaining earthly meat and marrow. Bones digested one another, becoming immobile stumps forever. Soon each sternum caved in to pierce the shriveled heart within.

Metamorphosis was complete.

The grilled husk of former humanity was now fused solid, twisting helplessly inside its own cocoon of melted bone and hate. It hung above the pit below, imploring even the merest trifle more of this existence, until it plunged swiftly

170

downward.

Travis watched, horror struck, yet noting the similarities he saw playing out before him with his own wartime experience.

"I once fired a load of shot and ball through a spying enemy balloon. It crumpled the same way when it fell."

A flash of blinding red burst loud, echoes of a shrieking bawl. Then a rush of smoke in darkness, smothering it all.

It was over. For a time. Until the next shattered soul was dragged forth into position, its separated head cupped within slagged hands. Its final purpose now was to fulfill its contract with The Otherside, the false man they'd known only as the Captain during their deluded lives.

The cycle of midnight doom continued to repeat itself, over and over.

Travis grew ever more revolted by the unholy spectacle before him. He could not stop that, but he determined to at least rid himself of the fluttering annoyance of bats that still swarmed about.

"I may not be able to stop The Otherside from frying what's left of his men, not that I could or should, but I can knock these bats away!"

He yelled in frustration, then grunted and swung his fist wildly at the black-winged tormentors. He thought of some far ancient ancestor, who might have shouted at a cluster of barking crows or jays while standing outside the entrance to his cave, dispersing them a short distance, but unable to shoo them away completely.

Though not flying quite as close to him, the mass of leathered wings and lice-coated fur still swarmed nearby, their gibbering forms remaining just out of reach.

But now, in true dreamlike fashion, the spear he'd pounded into deadly shape back at the camp now appeared within his reach. His hand closed upon it, and he lashed out at the malevolent creatures chirping about him. Time and again he struck down five or ten or more of the tiny harpies.

Ignoring losses, they seemed to laugh at his distress, their high frenzied squeals a piercing counterpoint to the slurred rantings that once again rumbled from The Otherside's unhealing maw. He pointed at his former soldiers, gloating over their broken ruination.

"Thus DEMONSTRATES the staggering PENALTY for disobeying the REALM-WRECKING SINEWS of my POWER!!"

Travis snorted in derision, not much impressed at the mad rantings. He redoubled his efforts against the bats, sweeping a deadly arc among their chattering midst. He cudgeled their numbers over and over, finally clearing the air around him. They either fell broken or fled from his blows.

The bats were gone. He could once more see the firmament's clean host of stars, crowned by the moon's shining orb. But even its pure celestial light dimmed and shuddered, recoiling from the ghoulish spectacle still taking place.

The Otherside swung his ruined face from side to side, dark hooded eyes losing focus. His gloating convulsed into twitching rage.

"Now UNSEEN!! Yet I sense you STILL, transient worm!!"

The Captain's huge form lashed out,

backhanding several of his former minions away. Thrashing and gnashing, those headless specters found themselves batted toward Travis.

Disembodied heads cradled inside melting arms; the once-human apparitions became crackling fireballs that spun wildly across the velvet heavens as they raced toward Travis. Their blazing craniums cackled insanely, raging aflame and infernal.

"I've a notion it will be a very bad idea to let any of these ol' bastard's burning skulls get too close to me."

Sputtering flame, they careened toward him from the oven of the damned.

Gripping his spear with both hands, he used it like a club, swinging first at the closest melting blob of bone.

He walloped the burning center of that foul mass, blazing it away to strike another of the group. Fusing, they spun away from him, their once separate torments now bound together, a composite ghoul, each sharing the other's splintered hate. Together, they would trudge lockstep to straddle hell and earth forever.

Travis had no time to concern himself with their unholy fate as two more demonic cannonballs of fire spun toward him. Yet, he knew that both ghastly incarnations would miss him. He gave thanks to his gunner's training and his knowledge of trajectories.

Indeed, they passed him by, then burned out dark into the night. Two more souls to wander earth, forever without light.

The next former minion The Otherside had slapped out of line came toward Travis fast and sure, direct, and deadly. Its human-fat had rendered into something resembling a writhing wall of expanding molten lard. Charred edges burning red, it closed with malice upon him. The spinning mass had spread out into a pinwheeling sheet of melted flesh from which Travis knew he could not dodge.

But at the last bare second before impact, Travis felt another force, lent by a strength and will not his, grip his arm to thrust the spear he carried forward into the vileness of the rotating thing.

The weapon's iron tip haloed bluish-white as it pierced the profane veil. It broke the churning liquid gore apart, dissolving it into a godless phantasm.

Silent howls retched, lashing inarticulate across the dread landscape. A final flame consumed the burnt particulate as another servile toady met his fate. His former master, whom he'd once saluted and called "Captain", now ignored his final suffering, too busy spitting screaming fury at Travis.

"GNAT of foolish IGNORANCE!! AGAIN, have you INSULTED me!! You are but a TOOL of powers you know NOT of!! You shall PAY with merciless PAIN for your IMPUDENCE!!"

The bats were gone, and Travis noticed that The Otherside had lost his exact location, glaring about only in the general direction of where Travis floated.

He spoke, watching to see if his enemy's eyes were able to follow him without the bats.

"Seems to me you have a difficult time taking very good care of your own tools, Mr. High-and-Mighty."

The Otherside sneered, his broken maw

insulting the night. Again, he directed his horrible gaze only toward the general area of where Travis was, peering intently here and there.

"He can't see exactly where I am!"

Evidently, as mighty as The Otherside thought he was, while in his astral condition he needed help from the creatures he controlled. But none of that seemed to matter to him now. He bellowed again, not bothering to use any night beasts to voice his rage.

"Tools... BAH!! A HAMMER is only so good as how many COFFINS it nails shut!! A SHOVEL is judged only by how many GRAVES it digs!! A SWORD is only so valuable as the EASE by which it SEVERS a coward's HEAD from trembling NECK!!"

"I've got to give you credit for that last part. That was quite the head choppin' party you had back there at the water hole."

"WORM, you cannot give me CREDIT for you have NONE!! Mine is not the only THIRST demanding to be QUENCHED!! The CULLING that you speak of was but a mere SIDESHOW, a MINOR feeding!! Those like you have VALUE below ZERO, for you offer NOTHING!! Meddlesome FOOL!! EVERYTHING you think you are, is LESS to ME than WORTHLESS!!"

Ignoring the ugly judgments but taken aback by the enemy's vehemence, Travis considered everything that filled his life right now. Of course, Lorne's image flashed through Travis' mind. Immediately he realized his mistake. Within this spectral world, focusing on the person most precious to him while so close to The Otherside allowed the monster to eavesdrop upon his cogitations. He quickly sought to banish any thought of her. He took conscious control of his memories, forcing himself into detailed ruminations of battlefields and gore, cannons and canister shot, along with all the terrible punishments he wished he'd inflicted upon this creature back at the mountain pass, to stop it dead in its tracks so many centuries ago.

But the only problem was, once formed, how does one unthink a thought?

A gloating laugh rasped past sharpened reptile teeth. The Otherside had indeed reached into the thoughts of Travis to taste his deliberations.

"AH!! SO!! Reality REVEALED!! The TRUTH at last!! I KNEW there were more of you COWERING WRETCHES inside that hovel than had been reported to me!! Those cowards FAILED to bring another MORSEL to MY TABLE!! They desired to keep HER for themselves!! Now you ATTEMPT to wrap your MEMORIES of her within your hidden BATTLE LUST!! Yet, she CANNOT remain HIDDEN from ME!! Mortal FOOL!! NEVER doubt that she WILL be MINE, mortal FOOL!!"

Angry with himself that he'd let slip the knowledge of Lorne and, worst of all, where she was, Travis retorted with a fire inside him that he hadn't known before.

"I'd hardly say those folks inside that house were cowering! They held out for days fighting your horse-riding savages to a standstill. They left half your men's mangled bodies in bloody heaps where they fell, until you decided... for some stupid reason... to kill off your own men after they'd torched the place!"

Fits of rage shook the twitching form of The

176

Otherside.

"SIMPLETON!! The day of your SUFFERING will soon ARRIVE!! Then shall we SEE how you BEG!!"

The Otherside cackled another lizard laugh. A scaly noose of fear formed around Travis as he fought hard to douse all thoughts of Lorne.

"COMPLIANCE with my WISHES must be sure and SWIFT!! Those men were CRAVEN and could NOT be TRUSTED!! I paid them well as I had PROMISED with REWARDS of their base DESIRES!! By MY largess, the power, gold, and women that they CRAVED were theirs in PLENTY!! They KNEW that in return they owed unthinking LOYALTY to my COMMANDS!! Yet later... while BESIEGING the dwelling by the forest these COWARDS dared to BALK at MY orders to ATTACK!! For that ALONE those spineless worms DESERVE all this that has BEFALLEN them!!"

The mad ravings of The Otherside continued unabated. Travis circled the island of nightmares as the unholy spectacle continued. He watched as the final group of headless ghouls received a charred baptism into their soulless eternity, caged within a molten underground realm. Only a few stains of putrid grease marked their passing from this world.

The last one fell away into the hellhole. Immediately afterwards the puckered lips of the fiery rent into which they'd been dropped was pulled together tightly, sewn by unseen threads. It was over but for a noisome stigmata left upon the groaning earth.

Eyes still searching all around him in a spooky hunt for Travis, The Otherside began fading into blurred outline, losing form, receding inside a gathering mist. Yet, the man-like creature's voice still bellowed.

"THE OATH that your cursed ANCESTOR swore against me was based upon a foundation SOFTER than the shifting SANDS below us!! After I KILL you that ANCIENT oath shall be declared NULL and VOID!! Your TERMINATION will come SOON... little pink WORM!! You are the LAST and must DIE before you spawn ANOTHER such as you!!"

Travis forced himself to laugh at his odious enemy. *"Ha! So, you say. But think on this, big mouth. Which of us doesn't have an unhealing wound after the fight at the mountain pass? That's right. And these days, you and your men haven't done so well either. You admitted you killed them for cowardice. And guess who helped make them afraid to keep attacking that house? Right again! You're just a loudmouth blowhard. Still haven't got it? Ha! Don't think too hard, you might hurt yourself!*

"You insufferable, mewling SWINE!! Your insolence is INTOLERABLE!! When will you learn that you have ALREADY lost?!! You CANNOT defeat one such as I, an IMMORTAL who outlives even the very EMPIRES of this lowly PLANET!! I will LEAVE now!! But KNOW that you shall DIE soon, WORM!!"

The Otherside became indistinct, then dissipated, leaving behind an obscene taint. The space that he had occupied shivered and shook in outrage, twisting as a dog might shake off fleas. Abstract nothingness filled that void, then even that anomaly vanished. Nothing remained but questions and anger.

"I know why The Otherside wants to kill me. Not it makes sense that nothing makes sense. He's utterly deranged!! Maybe that's what happens when you live too long. I don't know much about him, but I do know I have to take care of that problem for him.

Alone for but a moment after the so-called Captain's exit, Travis started when he heard a different voice. From out of the night, spoken clear to him, came a feminine voice edged with Damascus steel.

"I know some of the story. I will tell you what I can of this creature."

Travis remembered hearing this voice before, during another vision. It had been the night he'd escaped the explosion with Lorne. The night he'd been bitten by insects within the tiny shelter.

She spoke again. *"Yes, that was me. You both were very weak. The Otherside and his minions were seeking you. He suspected that at least one of his victims had wriggled free from his wide-cast net. Raging, he screamed his orders out to every baleful creature. He called all of those that claw and sting, those biting bugs and crawling pests that make their simple livelihoods inflicting torment upon others. Those nasties are easily led by such as he; they aid his will on land and in the air. Even some horrific creatures from deep below the sea will follow his commands."*

Travis felt himself moving faster. He swept over the large ship he'd seen at anchor, over decks and past its smokestack and rigging. Its sails were furled. He tried to read its name, but he went by it too quickly to be sure. He thought it might have started with an *"F"*, but that was all. He turned back to the woman speaking. She was quickly materializing, forming into focus before him in the air, looking much as Lorne had described her, a warrior queen wearing a large, curved sword inside a well-worn sheath around her waist. She continued her tale.

"You and your companion had concealed yourselves well, but with so many malign eyes searching for you, your fate was sealed, almost. Your lives, in pain and blood, would have to the fiend been forfeit, had I not obscured your essence."

Travis spoke, recalling her help. *"Ma'am, I... don't know half of what's going on here but want to thank you for what you've done. I remember that evil night. I was being burnt, bitten, and even getting what seemed like acid poured on my skin. The next day more than half of me had been stung by skeeters. I still have them bumps and itches."*

She shifted the sword belt on her waist. As it moved, her curved golden sheath reflected shards of moon light all around them. Sighing, she spoke again.

"Your thanks are pleasant but not necessary, as your presence here acknowledges your oath, and your will to fight once more against the being known to us as The Otherside. His men call him The Captain, as he fancies himself a great leader. He is not, but he is so powerful that his mistakes are overwhelmed by the sheer force he wields. Soldier Travis Lehrman, his destruction is needful, both to your world, and to my people of the Outer Forces. The stakes are high. You must destroy this so-called Captain."

Travis looked at the town of The Otherside

below, a crouching predator behind its defensive wall. The black talons of spreading mines and workshops clawed a deep abscess of suffering into the island's steep rocky hills. A suitable redoubt for a creature such as this Captain.

"Yes", she said, *"Festering within that island is a suppurating ulcer of evil. A stygian pall lays heavy, its miasma fueling treacheries and day-to-day atrocities. Over centuries, The Otherside has twisted the fates of uncountable human souls there. He and his Underlords experiment upon their victims' flesh, attempting to recreate them into perfect human slaves. Most die, but the still-living failures are exiled outside the walls, left to starve or feed as they might."*

Travis asked, *"What are these Underlords? Who are they?"*

"They are the undead ones, the once but no-more humans, the original elders of their nations who used their arcane knowledge to unlock the barriers between this world and those of the Other. It is from there that The Otherside was beckoned many centuries ago. He was brought across the barriers between realities into their lands to smash their enemies. He did so, but that was not enough for this beast, he was still hungry. Afterwards they lost their own people and country to his rapaciousness. As strong as they imagined themselves to be, they grossly underestimated his powers and were unable to compel him to return to the reality from whence they'd extracted him. Since then, the Underlords have been forced by his command to keep that doorway between the worlds open... for more than two thousand years."

Travis began to understand the enormity of the situation.

"*Do you mean to say this evil was going on for a thousand years before I had my first run-in with The Otherside? A thousand years before Mr. One dragged me up to that mountain pass? According to him, that battle beneath the eclipse happened in the year 865! Are you saying The Otherside had already been here a thousand years before that?*"

She nodded, "*That is correct. This has been going on for a long time, I'm very sorry to say.*"

Travis continued to think about this, then blurted out, "*That means this dirty son of a bitch was slithering around when Jesus was here!*"

The woman opened her mouth as if she were preparing to answer, but reconsidered, holding her silence. She gazed toward the island far below. He waited. After a while, she spoke.

"*These Underlords are granted extended life from him in return for making sure the portal between worlds remains open, as he maintains his powers of regeneration from contact with that realm. Only two celestial events that occur upon this world will temporarily negate those energies that protect him from harm. Meanwhile, he uses this world as his grazing pasture and hunting grounds. It is his supply of anguished fear and blood to feed upon. But even unlimited, it is still thin gruel for such as he... always hungry, always needing more... forever unsated.*"

Sighing, she withdrew the blade from its scabbard. The sword was just as Lorne had described, a sharp steel blade with a supple curve. Deadly. She used it to gesture toward the island.

"Not so very long ago, upon these watery tracts, a man your tales call Blackbeard swore fealty to a man he knew only as the Captain. For a short time, the pirate thrived, his earthly powers peerless, while he plied his evil trade. But soon... it was over. Ephemeral his name and fame and life became, his fate the same as every other common minion of the Captain... he was drained of blood and for eternity entombed."

Travis shook his head, then spoke.

"It's exactly what happened to those raiders back at that horrible blood pond. And, ma'am, respectfully, it looks like that there blade you're holding is built to do its share of choppin' heads as well."

She nodded, replacing it within the scabbard.

"Yes, his former lackeys were not merely sacrificed in rage, but also for example."

The nightmare of what he'd seen within the bloody pond repeated, yet again, within his mind.

"In rage? And for what example?"

"The rage consuming The Otherside has a simple explanation. It is his reputation's calling card, the fit and fiber of his being. Since called within our mortal sphere, The Otherside is in a constant state of hunger that is never satisfied, no matter how much he eats and drinks. For example, the first armies he'd led beyond the desert's mountains, had strict, severe, incentives. They decreed that just one misdeed or accident would foul all. None were spared the punishment, no matter how unfair. Now, his new minions have even greater cause to blindly follow his commands. The consequences of their

failure have been further reinforced."

Travis gave a sharp cough of a laugh. *"So, inside the logic of whatever passes for his mind, it seems that one bad apple spoils the barrel, huh?"*

She considered, then answered slowly. *"Yes. Yes, you might say that."* She looked at him and smiled. *"Your people's idioms are always amusing."*

He frowned at the humor, being caught up in the deadly seriousness that he and Lorne faced. *"Glad at least one of us can find something to smile about right now."*

The phosphorescence that marked the sacrificial site still glowed. To his eyes, augmented by outer-worldly vision, the pulsing pits of the yellow-green clearing were filled with parasitic chiggers of gross proportion. Their pincered maws fed upon the world's anemic, fleshy sores.

Travis spoke again. *"Where are we now? What else is down there, beside a soul eating pit?"*

"It is The Otherside's island base of workshops, dry-docks, and resupply. He has removed himself here for the time being. He must recruit again soon. He still has a small army to police the town, but after this latest purge, there is a lack of sycophants left to do his killing and bidding, save for a chosen few that have been with him since the very beginning." A shudder twisted through her. *"Those creatures are scarcely deemed human now."*

Travis began to ask another question but stopped when he felt his north bound movement slowing to a halt. He wanted to continue in that direction, to see more of the scars and pockmarks inflicted by The Otherside on the lands below. It was not to be. His control over his own actions was strangely restricted here within this world of phantasms. He knew there was a reason he'd again been brought within this realm by a force he could not control. But he also knew that his body still lay sleeping in Earth's reality, with Lorne by his side. What could he really do while asleep? Better to let himself be shown around like a visitor, than to fight it.

The woman spoke again. Her voice scythed deep furrows into his consciousness.

"You are free to step away from this ancient duty at any time. However, from your actions it seems that you have chosen to honor the oath your forefather swore. The forces that the eclipse released that day tied the battle of the mountain pass together through time and space and, yes, progeny. Your valiant ancestor fought this evil then... you fight the same evil now. Do not despair. Remember, you have already clashed with The Otherside, even wounding him. Over the centuries many men have tried to kill him, but all failed and were consumed. You've done well, Soldier Travis Lehrman, as these things go."

Travis remembered the anguish he'd felt when his last bullet was split and deflected by The Otherside's inhumanly wielded ax blade; to merely graze and maim his sneering visage... instead of killing him. He'd been told by Mr. *One* how the creature's chaotic evil would burn all hope alive for the next thousand years, searing compassion to a white-hot bone.

And yet, with so much at stake, he had still

failed.

The warrior queen moved close, imploring, *"Stop! Be of high esteem. Do not allow his infection of despair to penetrate your essence! Turn your mind away from thoughts that weaken your resolve!"*

Travis brought his head up and took strength from her advice. Her words brought new perspective to his thoughts about that battle of the mountain pass.

"You must know, this creature stalked through a rent in the fabric of reality. From his world amidst the Other, he'd heard a siren's call from a desperate kingdom on this planet. Their rulers were what might be called by some, magicians, by others, Technicians. They were armed with shallow proficiencies and high hopes of using their newly discovered energies to smite their foes. They attacked but their assault failed. In retaliation, their enemies swarmed forth, toppling the walls of their cities. Overrun, defeat was imminent. Crying in desperation, they called again upon their thin powers, hoping to find an overwhelming force that such a one as The Otherside could provide. They wooed him here with many promises to slake his hungers, and much more. When he finally burst through the door they'd opened, his expectations were high, and appetites... insatiable.

Travis listened; the night around him hushed.

"The laws that govern your existence here are harsher for its kind than those in the world from where he came. You, as well, would survive only with difficulty within the realm of The Otherside. Although his strength and speed

186

are great, at random times his senses have some difficulty here; then he must borrow the eyes or ears of earthly beasts. And he is always hungry, as his being must consume prodigiously or slowly whither."

She stopped and sighed, staring hard at Travis. She spoke again.

"At times he trades with others of his kind, or worse, from beyond the open door between our worlds, exchanging bloody human essence for the fiendish goods that he desires. The ill-advised kings had no idea of their fatal error when they called this monster forth. They had not tested their new knowledge to learn the truth about their weaknesses, so arrogant they were in their conceit."

Her hand gripped the curved sword at her waist with inhuman ferocity. She drew it partially out, then slammed it back into its iron scabbard so violently that a shock wave washed across his disembodied being. The clash of metal underlined the steel in her voice.

"They were like a furry tribe of beavers inviting a tiger into their village. They thought their sharpened little teeth were strong and powerful, but their foods were only shrubbery and other plants. They knew nothing else. But The Otherside consumes meat, blood, and bone. They had no conception of a carnivore. When they offered to him what they thought were sacrifices of honor to assuage his hunger, he spit their offerings of plant life from his maw into their stunned faces."

"Some of the braver kings turned their forces toward him, attempting to bind his power and force him back through the cursed portal they

had opened. But, without ceremony or much effort by The Otherside, they themselves were ingested, and their blood became his wine. The other kings, surviving his initial assault, and now near madness in their fear, pointed desperately at their enemies, beseeching him to feed among those multitudes instead."

She paused, staring up at the watching moon. Amid the silence, Travis asked, "He killed them all, didn't he?"

"Of course, he did. Mostly. As I said, he keeps a few of these ancient ones with him to maintain his connection to the realm of the Other."

She looked at him, softening her words.

"One of his tactics is to increase uncertainty within his enemies, as if spider eggs were hatching under your skin. Then they grow and spin the many-legged webs of fear. Be vigilant! Awareness of his cunning is the way to victory! He has grown and gained in power since your battle on the mountain, but so too have your weapons and the power of our sentinels to aid you. We will speak again, Soldier Travis Lehrman."

She looked away from him, her hand remaining on the sword hilt. She began to leave. Travis saw that she was fading from his presence. He shouted to her. She might be finished, but he had more questions.

"Sentinels and weapons? What am I to do? I have nothing more deadly to fight with than what I had in the mountains, really. Perhaps a few more bullets, that's all. I'm still left alone to face this monster; I have no army beside me. And now I must protect a woman as well. If anything, I'm weaker than before!"

As she slowly faded from his view, a narrow smile teased across her lips. She brushed a lock of hair back, then opened her mouth as if to speak, but changed her mind and stopped. The remnants of the smile still played across her face as she closed her eyes. More and many stars revealed themselves in her stead as she slowly faded from his view. Travis called out to her.

"Wait, please, at least tell me your name."

The smile disappeared; she opened her eyes to stare hard at him for more than a moment. Finally, she spoke.

"Alyssia."

She was gone.

The bright stars shone, yet a grim foreboding shaded his soul.

9. SHADOWED REALMS

Removed. Returned. Travis went from flying as a midnight hawk, soaring above the ocean, and conversing with what he thought might be a demigod, to awaken in the grip of cold flayed consciousness. He lay face up on his bed of sand and grass, staring into the night through narrow seams open above the makeshift door of their little hut. Lorne lay asleep beside him, breathing deeply, the slow rise and fall of her chest a living metronome. Outside, the fitful ocean cast salt and chill reminders of its presence upon all.

He wondered if Lorne were dreaming, perhaps having another encounter with the woman with the curved sword, who could only be the same Alyssia he'd just met. He would ask her in the morning after she'd awakened.

If he rolled his head just a few inches, he saw outside the hut a silvered curve. It was the same bright moon that had just dominated his perspective, when he'd felt himself a brother to it as they both shared flight within the same night sky.

Back here on the ground, Travis was as stunted in mobility as any other wretched earth-bound brute. Only memory held the vantage of his vision, a gaze of grandeur borrowed from the hawk.

Now he was humbled, his clod-like body held by muck and sand. Melancholy took him, a bully creeping up to strike its victim from behind. He fought back, remembering the warrior woman's words.

"Quite the depressing thoughts, and just the kind of attack that The Otherside would inflict upon those who oppose him. Alyssia was right, I can't fall prey to an attack of despair. I must fight this."

He made every to turn his thoughts around. He counted his blessings as best he could.

Part of him could still not fully accept these strange circumstances. Why was he fighting on the side of these outerworld beings who pushed him about, to and fro, whenever they fancied? After all, couldn't everything that had happened to Lorne and him be explained by rational means?

Besides, he already had a war to fight. He didn't need another.

These visions of flying and fighting and talking with demons and spirits, there had to be another explanation for that, didn't there? Hadn't he recently had not just one, but several injuries to his head? First, during his army's defeat at the ridge, he'd been concussed and bleeding so badly from a nasty head wound that he'd been mistaken for dead by the enemy. Of course, that wound had saved his life, but it had surely scrambled his brains, hadn't it?

Could there not be some form of head injury that might lead to his wild dreams and visions of battling an axe-wielding monster a thousand years ago? Or his conversations with an invisible man and a sword-wielding woman? Of course, there could.

"Of course. Head injury. That's all it is. I just have to heal up a bit and everything will be fine."

His body relaxed with these thoughts of normality while he idly scanned the night sky. It had not brightened in the east. But the nightmarish vision he'd just awakened from felt like it had taken hours, so it seemed it should be near dawn.

Yet, in the time frame of here and now, he could see that the moon had scarcely traveled westward since its rising. The hour was still closer to dusk than to dawn. There seemed to be no consistency with his sense of time whenever he was thrust into these visions, unreal as they may be, or not.

"A sacrificial island out at sea with an entrance to the underworld? Would I know it again if I somehow managed to sail there? Probably, but why would I bother? I'm sure I wouldn't be meeting any of my commanding officers there. I've made it to the coast now. My duty is to continue following my plan, not to gallivant about all over creation chasing some blood-thirsty creature from another world!"

He resolved to not worry himself anymore tonight with the problems of tomorrow.

Lorne's gentle breathing soothed him. Where their bodies touched, the warmth they shared gave hope for the future. Silently, he thanked God for her being alongside him, and the miracle of them still being alive after all they'd been through together.

But then he remembered what she'd said about the woman with the curved sword. During her own vision, she had also met Alyssia. Sharing an encounter with the same person while in their separate visions would be inconceivable if all this madness had been caused by just a wallop to his head!

Also, at the blood pond massacre, she had pointed out to him the fang-like teeth marks that shredded the blood-drained torsos. That was another impossibility. He knew there were no animals around here that could open their jaws wide enough to kill like that!

Except, perhaps, the unearthly maw of The Otherside.

He didn't want to, but he had to admit that what they were dealing with was as real as any cannon ball he'd fired. He would just have to believe.

He pushed away the ugly memories of the bloody little pond and fighting raiders. Exhaustion pummeled him. His eyes closed. He slept.

Time passed. The moon proceeded along its ordained path to settle below the western ridge before the first purple of dawn. Inside their tiny shelter, Travis slept on, exhaustion finally having taken its toll.

Hours later, Travis awakened to find he was still haunted by last night's dreadful horrors.

"Heads and melting bones, a demon's supper of souls in the cookpot... "

He pulled himself together, pushing the ugly disjointed recollections aside. Even more disturbing, the space beside him was empty and cool to the touch.

"Deal with the here and now, not the there and then."

He dressed quickly, then double-checked both revolvers. Each cylinder was loaded, ready for action.

"Not gonna get caught with only one bullet

left again."

He strapped the gun belt on, pushed aside the cover that served as the hut's door, and stepped into the gusty sea breeze. It was late morning, judging by the sun. Fresh winds scraped the oily clasp of last night's horror away. Climbing to the top of the nearest little dune, he scanned the immediate area for Lorne.

She was nowhere in sight.

"Lorne!"

He called her again, but the sound of waves bursting upon the shore was his only answer.

A narrow lane of crumpled grass led from their hut to a small thicket of wind-blown trees about a hundred feet away. Nearby them, a little marker flag fluttered above one of her traps. He guessed Lorne might be there, unable to hear him because of the muffling ocean wind. He walked in that direction, trampling underfoot the grass before him.

Everywhere was green new growth. Nature's pure and uncompromised visage surrounded him, bringing a sense of sanity with it. For the first time since his escape, he felt rested and able to relax, almost.

He laughed at the irony of his thought. *"Of course, if I weren't carrying two loaded pistols and a large steel blade it would be a different story. Yes, right... and If everyone were kind, rational, and trustworthy, weapons would be unnecessary."*

However, that was not the way the world worked. Might still made right, and there wasn't any amount of whining or complaining that would change that fact. He hoped things would be different someday. But for now, he must greet reality on its own terms.

He kept walking. The trees loomed larger ahead. Below them the trap's marker still flopped about in the wind. He heard an odd chittering sound.

"Lorne!"

There was no answer.

"For such an agreeable day it's unfortunate I should have to be this concerned about her. But I don't want to make the same mistake I made back at the blood pool. My lack of observation there would have gotten us both murdered if the killer had bothered to stick around, but he didn't. Our luck, his mistake. The Otherside is an overconfident bastard, and that's what will be his downfall."

A screeching pair of seagulls wheeled high overhead. Travis had almost reached the copse, its tree limbs unmoving among the wind-blown foliage.

More chittering sounds, this time directly ahead, low to the ground.

He stepped forward, then saw it as he leaned down. There was indeed a trap here, close to the tree, and inside was the mysterious noisemaker. It was a rabbit with mottled brown and white fur that froze silent when it spotted him. He began to rise but stopped when he heard an intense whisper.

"Travis! Don't move!"

He emulated the trapped animal, holding still in his crouch. The tall grass bristled in waves about them.

Even if he didn't understand why her voice was edged with danger, relief washed over him.

"She's here, and she's safe. So far, anyway.

But where is she?"

The wind blew continuously, distorting the sounds it carried. He looked cautiously around, moving only his head, slowly. Still no sign of her.

He gave his best impression of a stage whisper when calling out.

"Where are you hiding, Lorne?"

"Up. Up here. Look up. No, no, don't STAND up, just LOOK up!"

Holding his awkward position, he craned his neck back to see her sitting about twenty feet up in the crook of a large branch near the edge of the canopy.

"Travis, stay low like that and move around to your right a few feet, then come close to the tree and start climbing up. But STAY over on that side, opposite the beach!"

From his vantage point he could see that the tree's fresh spring leaves shrouded her from view. She was all but invisible among the branches.

"No wonder I couldn't see her. She took a lesson from what I told her I did. Nobody bothers to look up. Even me. Foolish! I gotta remember this or I'll get caught by someone more unpleasant than Lorne in the future.

He climbed up and sat himself beside her on the branch. They were surrounded by leaves, but she had cleared a small area that faced over the beach below free of them. Her voice was low and strained.

"You were still asleep. I decided I'd come out here to check the traps, clean 'em out, reset them if need be. Well, lo and behold, this one's got a critter inside! I thought, we've caught us our supper already! I was fixin' to get started on it when I started hearing a different sound, a whistle off in the distance. I thought it was another critter, maybe some sort of bird. I looked around but couldn't see anything. It wasn't too loud, and I tried ignoring it, but it kept up a regular caterwauling, you know? Annoying. I climbed up here for a better look-see. Had to move a few branches aside, but then I saw them. She pointed. If you look right through that opening there you can see a bunch of men down on the beach, settin' up camp. A big camp."

He moved closer to Lorne, squeezing in next to her to get a better view of the proceedings. Below, a few members of the unknown troops built tents or tended their horses. Others lounged about, while a few bathed in the surf. The camp seemed to be about a quarter mile away, perhaps a bit more.

"What do you think they're up to, Travis? They don't most of them seem too rankled by anything."

He waited before answering, wanting to get a better idea of what they faced.

"I can't see any insignia or markings from here, and they haven't bothered to raise a flag. Those men down there do seem to be uncommonly relaxed for soldiers. Undisciplined. Wish I'd brought that spyglass with me. I'll have to go back to the hut and bring it back to get a better look at what they're up to."

"Lorne, I can't rightly say just yet. They certainly aren't moving about with much urgency. You did the right thing by stayin' out of sight and keeping your voice low. With all this

198

wind, and them being close to the waves and surf noise, I doubt they could have heard too much, even me yellin' like a fool, but after everything we've seen, caution is our best policy right now."

"Travis, look at the tracks made in the dirt behind the wagons. They lead back to the road." She looked at him. "Maybe these soldiers are on our side after all. You can report in, get your orders and what not, like you've been sayin' you need to do."

He looked at her and shook his head. "Well, possibly. But things just don't look... military... down there. Something's not right."

He thought, *"Well, I'd like to do just that, but I have two problems if I do. I can't just walk up to an enemy camp and ask for orders or I'll end up a prisoner of war. And even if they are my boys, and I get orders that reassign me elsewhere, which I surely will, what is Lorne to do? With no family or friends that are still alive, where's a beautiful young woman going to go?"*

He looked back at the troops. They had set up only about a hundred feet back from the high tide line. He could see they weren't building anything too permanent. In fact, many of the shelters were tarpaulins, their bottom edges staked into the earth against the sea spray, tops tied to the supply wagons that had their wheels chocked tight. Most men were not working at all. Some had even taken off their shirts to loll about in the sun or walk barefoot in the ocean surf. Very odd for commanding officers to allow such frivolity.

"Even if their military discipline has completely broken down, those men wandering about aren't pulling their weight at all. I'm

surprised there hasn't been a fight by now between the those working and the others who aren't."

A small field kitchen was the only aspect of the camp that looked normal. Everything else that should have been there was either built haphazardly or just non-existent. The only reason for that...

"They're not planning to stay here long! And it doesn't look like they're planning to take much with them when they go, if anything."

Suddenly he realized why many of them were so indolent.

"Lorne, those men are going to be evacuated off this beach! They're just waiting for their boat to show up. That whistle you heard must have been a sergeant trying to get them formed up and working when they first arrived here."

"Can you tell which side they're on?"

"Nope. And even as relaxed as they all seem, I'm not going down there to find out."

"Something's bothering you. What is it?"

"Several somethings. For one, I don't see a flag anywhere. Every army raises theirs, one of the first things they do. For another, I know that there's a been a blockade out at sea for a few years now. If anyone's going to pick these men up, they're going to have to get past those gunboats, it's only easy to do if they're on the right side. Which means, for me, that's the wrong side. Also, I imagine those lazy men sauntering along the beach have already been given leave, or perhaps their enlistment is up and now they just don't care. Whatever it is, it's not any way I've ever seen soldiers under orders behave. Everybody always pitches in as best they can to help their brothers, even if they aren't ordered to. From what I see from here... well, I don't know, but something very odd is going on down there."

"What's that man doing? Looks like he's carrying driftwood."

"I do believe he's the cook. Even if these men don't behave like soldiers, they're still going to eat like them. That man's getting the cookfire ready. Speaking of fires... I hate to say this, but I don't think we can make a fire while that bunch is down there. We'll just have to eat what we've already got left over. Which isn't much."

She pointed to the cage below. "Well, what about our supper that's already been trapped?"

He thought about it. They couldn't eat it raw. The men on the beach might be there a few days, waiting for their ship. Or it may not come, and then they'd start searching the area for food themselves. Either way, a cook fire was out of the question.

"We can't keep that critter if it's goin' to go on chittering and chattering. If anyone does come near, the noise could lead them right to us. We'll make do like I said. We'll be fine. Let it go."

10. COLD RATIONS

Lorne watched the activity on the beach for another few seconds. "Travis, I think we should keep an eye on these men. If any of them decide to ramble on up here, we must know before they get too close. After I open the trap, I'll stay here while you go back to get that spyglass."

He gave her hand a squeeze. Lorne smiled and, after taking another long look at the men milling about on the beach, they both climbed down. Lorne released the rabbit. She had to pick up the trap to shake it out. It froze where it fell at her feet, staring straight ahead. It refused to move, even after she'd stomped her feet nearby it. But it had stopped being a noise maker, which is what they wanted. Satisfied, he started walking back to their camp to fetch the small telescope. Lorne climbed back up the tree to keep watch.

After a few steps he looked back.

The rabbit had vanished.

"It's your lucky day today little fella. I don't know if it will be for us."

After retrieving the spyglass, he walked back to the tree. It was a fairly clear day, and he could see through the thin haze a goodly distance across the waves. He paused in the high grass several times to get a view from different vantage points. He peered intently through the small telescope as he slowly scanned between shore and horizon.

"Nothing yet. No sail, no smoke, no mast, no flags. I know those motherless bastards down

there are waiting for a boat to come pick them up. They'll be here for at least a few days, most likely. It's gonna be cold rations for us 'till they leave."

He cursed under his breath, angry at the presence of the interlopers.

"After all Lorne's been through, just when we get a chance for her to calm down for a day or two and maybe get back to something like normal, then this bunch shows up. Like Lorne said, we'll have to keep a watch on them in case anything changes or, worse luck, if some of them get bored and bushy-tailed and come exploring up this way."

After his arrival back at their lookout, Lorne went off, declaring she would put together some sort of lunch. Travis climbed back up. Now, with the help of the spyglass, he gave the intruders below a much more detailed inspection. Once again, he found no evidence of any insignia at all, let alone a flag.

"They have to be the enemy because, so far as I know, my side don't have enough ships left to spit at, let alone be called any sort of navy. But are they the old enemy I've been fighting for the last four years or the new one that killed Lorne's family?"

Time passed, enough that his stomach told him that a lunchtime ration was overdue, cold or not. He had just decided to forego eating until dark, when he heard Lorne's loud whisper of urgency.

"Travis! Travis, get on down from there and come with me, quick!"

He climbed down out of the tree's little observation post, concerned by the seriousness in her voice. They kept their voices low.

"Alright, what's going on?"

"We've got to get back to our hut, there's more visitors comin' this way! But this time from the other direction! Please hurry!"

Relief flooded over him. These newcomers had to be a vanguard of his side's army. Finally, a chance for him to report in and get new orders. But what about Lorne?

"Guess I'll be askin' her to marry me, then she should get a housing allotment to take care of her. I've been meaning to anyways, especially after what's happened between us. She's a good woman, and a helluva fighter when need be."

"Lorne, that's good news! They've got to be our boys!"

"Please Travis, let's get away from here. We need to gather up our things from the camp, and then I'll take you up on the hill to where I first saw them." She turned and led him away.

"These new boys you just saw, did they have a flag with 'em?"

"Yes."

"You get a chance to see it?"

"Of course."

"And... ?"

"Why do you think I ran over here and got you so quick?

"Well... "

She stopped and turned back to him, exasperated. "Travis, It ain't our flag, so it ain't our boys."

When they arrived back at their camp, it was already too late.

Lorne still led the pair when they burst through the tall grass and other foliage that helped hide it from casual view. They stopped dead still at what waited there; three dismounted cavalry men. Their horses were tethered nearby.

One of the soldiers was already poking around inside their rude little hut, while the other two held weapons pointed directly at them, the muzzles gaping wide as cannons to their eyes.

The first man, the one who had been inspecting the hut, stepped back from it, and stood up straight, Obviously an officer. His hand rested, too casually, on his still holstered firearm. "Now, that's at least one good idea ya got there, sharpshooter, stopping like that. No quick moves, from either of ya. You can both jus' raise your hands real, real, slow and keep 'em there till we find out what we got us found here."

While raising his hands as ordered, Travis wondered, *"Sharpshooter? What's he mean by that?"* But then he noticed the officer's eyes looking past him, over his shoulder at the rifle that was slung across his back. *"Well, of course he'd mark the Spencer. And of course, he ain't gonna like that one little bit."*

The small tableau held static for another few seconds. Then the officer moved around behind his men to take up a position just off to the left of Travis. He still hadn't bothered to draw his own weapon.

"I'm going to have to ask you both some questions. But before that happens, I'll feel much better if you both are disarmed. Ma'am, very slowly, you are going to keep one hand on your head and unbuckle that there satchel you're wearing, then slowly lay it on the ground. Please don't reach inside it for any reason while doing so. You got that?"

"Yep, I sure do." Her voice was absolutely neutral. She got to work. Travis kept his eyes straight forward.

After she completed her task, the officer again spoke.

"Alright ma'am. Now if you would please do the same with your companion's gun belt and that there carbine he's carrying on his back, then we can get down to business."

Travis stood as still as he ever had while she performed the operation.

"Don't want to give these two any excuses. They both got a case of the jitters. I wonder why? We're obviously not much of a threat to them."

As soon as Lorne had laid the carbine down on the sandy dirt, the officer noticeably relaxed. His men didn't. They kept their aim steady on the couple. The officer spoke again.

"Now, if the both of you would be so kind as to back up three paces, then sit yourselves down, we can all have a nice conversation." Never taking his eyes off them, he gave another order. "Trooper Phils, as soon as they're sitting, pick up those items on the ground and bring them back to me. Please keep your pistol aimed upon them at all times."

The man on his far right replied, "Yessir, lieutenant."

The officer looked at Lorne, "No offense ma'am, nothing personal, just following the orders that I'm obliged to respect in situations like these."

Her voice still utterly without inflection, she replied, "None taken. We're all duty-bound to answer to our superiors."

After they sat, and their pile of belongings was spread out before the soldier, the officer began again. The two cavalry men stood to either side, flanking them. They had replaced their pistols in their holsters but kept their hands close by the weapons.

"Let's start out by getting to know one another, shall we? I'm Lieutenant Billings, and these gentlemen are Corporal Masonwright, and Private Phils. And you, ma'am?"

"My name is Lorne, Mr. Lieutenant, Lorne Davenport."

"No need to call me 'mister', ma'am. 'Lieutenant' will be just fine. And you are, sir... ?"

"Travis Lehrman, Sergeant, twenty-second Artillery Battalion."

"Ah. You claim to be a sergeant. So. The twenty-second Artillery, you say?"

"Yes. You'll find documentation among the papers in my wallet. If my uniform had survived, you'd see the proof there, too."

"That won't be necessary at this time. Interesting. You just said that if your uniform 'had survived'. Those are strange words. I find it hard to imagine the circumstances where a uniform that's being worn is destroyed while leaving its owner unscathed."

Lorne spoke up, "Mister Lieutenant sir, we are hardly unscathed. We've been through a lot, the both of us, and Sergeant Travis here most of all. He was helping us fight off the raiders who were attacking my family's house before the outlaws managed to burn it down. My family, God rest their souls, all perished. Travis and I barely escaped with our lives."

Travis noted that all three of the soldiers

watching them shifted, very slightly. *"Now that's the second time they got jumpy. They all tried to hide it, but something's settin' them off. At least he hasn't gotten round to asking about the Spencer carbine yet, even though he must know that only his side issued them. The few our boys had were liberated on the battlefield. Or in his view, stolen."*

"Thank you for adding to the discussion, Miss... I assume it's "Miss"... ? At her nod, he continued. Miss Davenport, I must ask you to please hold your horses while I'm questioning the Sergeant. You'll get a chance to air your thoughts later, I assure you."

"I'm sorry."

"No harm done, ma'am. So, Sergeant Lehrman, what brings you to this placid and remote little outpost? And without your uniform, which you say was destroyed, but you're still carrying your identification? With an attractive young woman? And in possession of so many weapons, so many *fine* weapons?"

Silence. Only the winds shook around them. Billings continued.

"I've seen a few deserters in my day, but you don't quite fit with what I've come to expect from them. For one thing, you have an honest eye, Sergeant, and I hope you'll prove me right. So, let's go on. You must admit, finding you two here, well, it's quite an interesting puzzle. Please, elucidate me."

"I'll be happy to relate my experiences, Lieutenant."

Travis began his brief outline at the beginning. The loss of his entire unit and almost his life when their position was overrun, his subsequent escape from enemy forces and probable internment in a prisoner of war camp, more travels and hiding, the frustrated attempts to rejoin his army, the burning of Lorne's house, her escape with him, the massacre at the horrible blood pond and, finally, their fleeing to this place.

Left out of the narrative of course was the incident at the big tree, as were his visions, nightmares, dreams and, of course, any mention of floating around the night sky, chatting with demigods, demons, or goddesses. Or whatever they were.

Or fighting ancient battles with phantasms a thousand years and ten thousand miles away.

After Travis finished his tale, all three soldiers stood impassive. Billings steepled his fingers like the strictest of old-time school masters while he considered. Eventually, he let out a long sigh.

"It sounds like you've had a rather arduous journey, Sergeant. And an especially difficult one for you as well, ma'am. My deepest condolences for your terrible losses. But back to our business. Under different circumstances, I'd be forced to detain you both, of course, but my orders now enjoin me to pursue a very different priority. My time, unfortunately, is somewhat limited, so let's keep on the subject please."

"Now, Sergeant Lehrman, where did you come into possession of this fine rifle? Please don't tell me it was given to you by Miss Davenport's very generous family."

Travis looked over at Lorne, who was already looking away from him and the others as she began to weep quietly. Billings sat, impassive, waiting for his answer. Before he could, Lorne spoke up.

"Lieutenant Billings, may I speak with you privately?"

Billings raised an eyebrow, considered the emotional Lorne, then shook his head in the negative. "Whatever needs saying can be said in the presence of all. My apologies to the lady, but these are difficult times for everyone. Please go on with the answer to my question."

"As you know, Lorne's entire family was recently... lost... and her home burned to the ground." Travis paused, thinking about that hellish night.

"Please continue, Sergeant."

Lorne was silent, eyes shut tight against memories. Tears still squeezed out, holy waters praying down her cheeks while Travis spoke.

"One of the raiders that she mentioned... "

Billings cut in, "These 'raiders', how many of them were there?"

"At least thirty, possibly even closer to forty. Probably no more than that, at least that I could see."

Billings nodded and gestured for Travis to continue.

"One of the raiders was killed and his weapon, this carbine, fell into my possession."

Lorne's hand shot up, like a child in school. Billings took note but shook his head. She relaxed with a frustrated sigh. Travis went on.

"I'd been traveling since my position was overrun. Mostly at night, keeping off the roads, out of sight of dogs and people. Trying to get back across your lines to mine, to report in, get new orders."

Travis paused, noticing how the three men all

glanced at one another, and Billings even raised that eyebrow of his again.

"Well, I'd been livin' in ditches and stream beds, in caves and brush for quite some time by then. I think I must have looked like a part of the earth itself, as covered with mud and muck and blood as I was."

Lorne looked over at him, then back to Billings as she began to speak. He cut her off.

"Miss Davenport. You'll have your opportunity. Please continue, Sergeant."

"What warned me was the smell, the smell of smoke. Not that I've never smelled smoke before of course, but this had a difference to it, something else, something just downright...well, I know this may sound witless, but to me that smoke yelled out loud, shout[ng... 'Evil!' Lieutenant, It was an evil far beyond what the business of war brings."

Billings leaned forward, asking, "What exactly are we speaking of here? You say 'evil', but actions can be interpreted many ways. The same deed that, for instance, saves a life, some might say is a good thing, but it might also be considered by others as justification to start a war, which ends up killing tens of thousands. Where is the good in that, Sergeant Lehrman, fifty thousand lives, traded for one?"

Travis closed his eyes, remembering the first time he'd been exposed to that same kind of necrotic smoke away from the battlefield. It was by the oxbow at the burnt out farm a few years ago. There had been nothing he could do while on that forced march, nor could he un-see the scenes of horror, the sting of murky gasses, or untaste the thick bile that had tainted his throat.

Those ugly memories persisted to this day.

"Atrocities, Lieutenant Billings. Many and various acts of savage brutality can indeed be defined as 'good' or 'bad', depending upon where the sympathies of the observer lay. But how can any civilized man claim, as you said, 'for instance', that the skinning of living men and women be anything other than what's defined as 'bad'? That kind of sick atrocity can only be described as an abomination against God and nature, a sin against the soul of a People and their Nation. It's the very definition of 'cruel and unusual punishment' if you will. A concept I imagine you're well aware of."

Billings growled back, "I suggest we steer this conversation away from the metaphysical and back toward the physical."

The Lieutenant paced in a tight arc, then abruptly stopped, staring at the couple, staring at the coupled sitting on the ground before him. "Alright, you seem a very capable man, Sergeant. I can accept you were able to evade capture for many weeks and hide yourself while traveling after your army's defeat in battle. Judging from what's left of both your boots and your cap, I can also believe that your uniform basically rotted off your back."

Travis hid his surprise. He had expected much harsher judgment from the enemy. "Thank you, Lieutenant. It has been a difficult time, but it's also a blessing. By all rights, I shouldn't still be alive and meeting with you now to tell the tale." He looked over at Lorne, then continued, "Neither of us should be, really."

"The battlefield is a capricious ol' bitch with guns on, isn't it? Pardon my coarseness, Miss

Davenport."

She said nothing as Billings waved his hand to include all of them.

"I reckon all present here have their stories to tell about angels and deaths and demons and miracles. However, let's get on with finding out where we are now. I really only need to ask you a few more questions."

"I've been assuming the only horses you ever had any control or command of were of the draught beast variety, which were used to haul your guns and ammo and such?"

"Now that's a very odd question. Not what I expected him to be asking about at all." Travis answered aloud, "Yes. We can't tote them guns on our backs, much as the generals would love to have us do."

They both shared a brief chuckle at the inanities of those exalted commanders whose rarefied opinions and orders sometimes flew in the face of reality.

Billings' face shut down like a strike at a coal mine. "Well, if you've had nothing to do with honest to god cavalry war-horse flesh, would you mind telling me where you came across that saddle that's hidden under that bush over there? As far as I know, draught horses don't generally need saddles, since they're fitted out for hauling, not riding."

Travis sat silent, angry that the truth he'd spoken had been twisted into what now seemed like a lie. Billings spoke up, louder this time.

"Please answer the question. Why is that fancy saddle hidden in the brush, under that patch of garment? Why, it almost looks like a big piece of cloth from a torn up uniform to me. But I may be

214

wrong. Maybe you can help me. What does it look like to you, Sergeant?"

Still Travis was silent. He knew he was so upset, that the best thing for him right now was to say nothing, rather than something that would give offense and make their situation worse.

Then Lorne raised her hand again.

Billings began to shake his head, then relented. "Oh, all right Miss Davenport. This seems to be as good a time as any for you to speak your piece. What would you like to say?"

"Sir, if I might, I'd like to tell you in private."

Billings motioned for her to stand. "Private Phils, you're with me and Miss Davenport. We'll all three of us walk out of earshot about fifty feet off in that direction where the grass is thinner and not so tall. Corporal Masonwright, please draw your pistol and maintain the aim of that weapon in the general direction of Sergeant Lehrman. And you, Sergeant, consider yourself temporarily detained for the time being, so please don't do anything that might cause concern or alarm in the Corporal. He's a bit touchy today. I think his digestion might be acting up again."

As Billings and the other two began to walk away, the Lieutenant turned back.

"Corporal Masonwright, if our Sergeant here becomes overwrought or begins to get het up about anything at all, your orders are to shoot him dead."

Never taking his eyes from Travis, it wasn't difficult for Corporal Masonwright to nod while simultaneously spitting another chunky aqueous stream of brownish-black tobacco juice in the general direction of his charge before speaking.

"Yessir, Lieutenant Billings."

11. CABAL OF BLOOD

Travis watched the little group in the distance as they conversed. Billings was impassive, his arms crossed and motionless. Lorne crossed and uncrossed hers, occasionally pointing back at him, or waving them in the air. Private Phils, a few feet away from the others, held his rifle casually. Almost too much so.

Travis kept himself relaxed while he watched. *"Don't know if he'd actually use that on her. Hope I don't find out. Hope he don't find out, either."* He took a deep breath, looked around their little camp, then spoke to his keeper.

"Well, Corporal, all things considered, it turned out to be a nice day today, even if I am a prisoner of war."

The corporal's grip tightened on his weapon while he re-aimed it with even more precision at a spot directly between Travis' eyeballs. A high-pitched bark of exclamation ejected from him, belying his large frame. It was as much a dismissal as a laugh. He spoke slowly.

"Ha. Ain't much chance of that. You ain't no prisoner of war. Not now. Didn't you hear what Lieutenant Billings said? You're detained. Under temporary detention." His words plowed slowly past brown teeth and the glossy black ovoids of tobacco spittle caught in the permanently wet corners of his lips.

"Why, yes, I did hear him, but I assumed that... " Travis stopped speaking as he was cut off by another dog-like bark from the large man holding the big rifle.

"Hey! Lieutenant never ordered me to have to listen to you, and I sure as hell don't want to talk to you. Let's keep it simple. You shut your gullet until Lieutenant Billings tells you otherwise, and I won't shoot you. Deal?"

Travis very slowly nodded, looking past the weapon to see the brown tobacco drops that speckled his unshaven face. For him, maintaining the aim of his weapon "in the general direction" of Travis, meant keeping it pointed directly at his head, even while quivering with barely suppressed rage.

"Now I know. Unlike Private Phils, there's no doubt that this Corporal Masonwright would blast me clean through if he thought I'm fartin' too loud."

The sight of the barrel's maw did have a definite muting effect. He shut up and waited.

After several minutes, the others returned.

Lieutenant Billings stood near their rude little hut, flanked by his two men. Lorne had gone to sit by the side of Travis immediately upon her return. Both Phils and Masonwright kept an uneasy vigil on their detainees. Occasionally, the tobacco chewing Corporal would spit another short stream of brown liquid, not exactly in their direction, not exactly not.

Billings finally spoke. "Sergeant, your companion has just exposited several details of the events you two have shared since you were first acquainted with one another. It's been very illuminating. I'm going to ask you to share your recollections as well, and then we'll see what we see. Please don't take offense at any perception you may have of me considering you a liar. These times are not normal, and the situation at present is much larger and more dangerous than you can imagine. I'm sure that you'll appreciate the fact that extra caution, on all our parts, is required."

Travis nodded, eyeing the Corporal, wondering if he still considered his promise to him active. He decided to respond to Billings anyway. "No offense taken. I'm sure I'd undertake the same actions were our situations reversed. I understand that any precautions you deem necessary to keep you and your men safe are required, Lieutenant. Besides, your boys have the pistols."

Billings barked a short huff of amusement, nodded, "Indeed we do, and until it proves a superfluous caution, indeed we shall. Now. Since you brought up the subject of weapons, let's discuss that. Where and how did you obtain the Spencer carbine that we found in your possession?

Travis sifted through his jumble of memories. So much had happened since then! It was almost like being asked to describe another man's life, it seemed unreal, like a newspaper story about a disaster that happened in some far off foreign land. Travis closed his eyes, thinking back. The raiders, the smoke, the fire... horses...

"The carbine! Yes, I remember it being on the horse I'd captured at Lorne's home during the attack."

He went on to answer the Lieutenant's earlier questions about the saddle, then described the battle at Lorne's house, the capture of the horse and carbine, and later using the very same weapon to kill the raider who'd been trying to burn down the house. "He died outside with a pot of burning tar splashed all over his face. Lieutenant Billings, I'd had a head injury, so I could be imagining all this, but from what I saw, it looked like a crowd of wraiths and phantoms were standing around him, cursing him to hell! They were... partially there, bodies transparent... angry men and women lashing his dying body with cudgels and whips. After he died, they faded away. At the time, that vision was more real than the bloody dirt and smoke and fire in the night around me. It was quite disconcerting."

Billings remained outwardly impassive, but Travis noted that his eyes blinked quickly a few times as he looked back and forth between Lorne and him. *"Did I just confirm or annul Lorne's narrative?"* Lorne sat, her face turned away, seeming to study an ant slowly crawling through the sandy earth.

"Let's move to the next point. I'd like to hear what you have to say about this 'swimming hole of blood', as Lorne described it. Continue, Sergeant."

Travis went on, detailing Lorne's horrific discovery of the ichor-filled pond where she and her sister had swum in better days. He went into detail regarding the decapitations of the many men they had found murdered there. Finally, he offered his opinion, when asked, about how he believed such an atrocity might have been so easily and quickly perpetrated against such a large group of robustly armed and obviously experienced fighting men.

"Lieutenant Billings, once I'd gotten over the shock of seeing, well, what we saw, I asked myself the same question. The strangest thing is, I'm almost certain that those were the same cavalry men who had been raiding Lorne's home earlier."

"Sergeant Lehrman, how could you know, if every one of them were decapitated."

"Lieutenant Billings, the uniforms I saw the bandits wearing when they were attacking the house seemed to be the same as what the dead men still wore at the blood pond. As far as I know, these raiders are outlaws, not operating under the orders of, or under the authority of any governmental military force. I never once saw insignia or rank markings on any of them. Yet, they were obviously organized, as they had uniforms and a semblance of military order. And those uniforms were distinctive by their plainness. They were without any colors or standard, and different from what either your army or mine wear. They were tightly fitting, not so loose as ours. The collars are higher, and they are all black."

Travis paused to see what effect his statement was having. Billings nodded and motioned for him to go on.

"Now, as I said earlier, I did see them making multiple attempts to kill the civilian inhabitants of Lorne's family. For my own part, I do admit to killing several of these men, in self-defense, while they were attempting to kill me. Again, Lieutenant Billings, that's how we came into possession of both the Spencer and the horse we rode to safety on." Travis briefly pulled the side of his cap off to show the large scab that covered the bloody rut from the bullet (*"or was it an arrow?"*) that had creased his skull.

Billings held up his hand. "My respect to you both, and my deepest sympathies to Miss

Davenport for the loss of her family." He began pacing in a tight circle, then stopped and spoke again, "This kind of behavior is not unheard of, unfortunately. I do know that both of our armies have orders in place intended to prohibit displays such as you have described, or at least to dissuade it. Sadly, sometimes things do get out of hand. They certainly did back at this blood pond that you both have described in horrid detail. Sergeant Lehrman, I have a question. I ask this as an opinion from a fellow soldier. How do you think all those heavily-armed and experienced fighting men were so easily killed and mutilated back there?"

Travis answered deliberately. "Lieutenant Billings, I've also considered that. The best answer I've come up with is betrayal. I believe they were told to trust new men that had just been recruited. Of course, they had not been told that these troops were to be their replacements. I'm guessing that the first order given to those replacements was to kill and behead everyone there. I believe those men inside the blood pond were all tricked."

"A cabal of blood," Billings muttered, and shook his head. "Not a commander I'd like to have."

"Nor I." Travis remembered watching The Otherside pitching these headless men's earthly shells into agony as their souls burned. "That said, I would not have considered it an honor or pleasure to have served alongside any of these men, either."

Billings looked Travis square on. "That I don't doubt. Finally, one last question. What was Lorne doing when you first met her, Sergeant?"

Lorne grabbed his arm tightly, but Travis never took his eyes off Billings. "She was defending her house, standing side by side with her twin sister, to help load and fire an old pedrero, a ship's swivel gun from at least a hundred years ago. Any raiders who got a notion they were brave and strayed too close got shot to Hades! Those little old cannons were very effective back then against pirates trying to board your ship. And make no mistake, Lieutenant Billings, just because those raiders were ridin' horses instead of sailing in a ship with a skull and crossbones on it, those men were, by every definition, pirates."

Billings smiled while he slowly unfolded his arms. "Phils and Masonwright, you men may stand at ease." While they lowered their weapons, Billings walked over to Travis and Lorne, who were still seated on the ground.

"Miss Davenport, Sergeant Lehrman, you are both free to rise if you choose to." Seeing Lorne begin to stand, he reached his hand down to her. "Ma'am, please allow me to help you up."

Travis stood without help. He didn't care that Billings was helping Lorne and he wasn't. He'd already helped by saying the right thing. *What I did was to tell the truth. Mostly.* Something had changed here for the better because of what she'd done, what she'd said. He looked over at the Corporal, who had at least lowered his weapon, but his beady eyes still tracked every move he made.

Travis was glad they were both still alive. Things could have easily gone in a different direction.

Billings suddenly barked an order, "Private, I

want you to go over to our horses and bring back all our saddle bags with food in them."

"Sir?"

"Do I need to repeat myself? You haven't become hard of hearing since we rode in here, have you?"

"No sir."

"Then get a move on."

When Private Phils returned, Billings had him leave the food inside the little hut. "When you're done emptying them bags out, strap 'em back on our horses."

"Yessir, Lieutenant Billings."

Shocked by this generosity, Travis asked, "Lieutenant, I confess, I'm somewhat mystified why you're doing this. It's much appreciated of course, but... "

"Say no more. My men and I won't go hungry. But you and your lovely companion have gone through some mighty rough spots. And now, the world is no longer as it was, even a few weeks ago. You'll both will find your situations upended for the foreseeable future. However, my men and I will soon be returning to our command to report back in, and there will be plenty to eat there. In the meantime, you've given me valuable information, whether you know it or not. This is the least I can do to help you until you can find your footing."

"Lieutenant Billings, you have our deepest gratitude, but I've a question that's been plaguing me. Why aren't you detaining us, and takin' me to a prisoner of war camp?"

The other men laughed. Corporal Masonwright's thin lips loosed a flurry of wet yaps past spittled brown stains.

Billings just shook his head. "Well, Sergeant Lehrman, my Captain would bust me down to a private, no offense, Phils! Anyways, he'd give me a barrel of grief for bringing you in and wastin' his time like that."

"Why would that be a waste of time?"

Billings replied, in kind, with a question, "Sergeant, do you happen to know what date this is?"

Travis shook his head. "I stopped keeping track. Never seemed important after the first few days of getting' on the run."

"It's May 24th."

When that revelation elicited no reaction from either Travis or Lorne, Billings went on. "I suspected it before, and it seems that I was right. You two really have been isolated. Perhaps you'd both better sit down again."

He walked close to them both, speaking dramatically in a loud, clear, stage whisper.

"What that date means is... the war's been over for two weeks."

For just an instant, Travis thought that perhaps he should have taken the Lieutenant's advice. As the import of the words washed over him, his knees weakened, and he swayed slightly on his feet. Lorne reached over to grip his hand.

Travis finally found his voice. "That's... quite the revelation, Lieutenant. It's good news, very good, even if hard to believe."

"I imagine so. Just like you, when I first heard the news, I had a hard time believing it. Thought I'd be passing this hateful bloodlettin' on to my children and their grandchildren, just like the hundred years war back in Europe went on and on."

225

"Guess we got off lucky then, us only fighting for four years, instead of a hundred."

"We'll all have to look at it that way. You wouldn't believe some of the new weapons that were coming out before the surrender. The misery and death would have gone on and on until we were all dead. I've even heard tell of a certain Mr. Gatling, who they say invented a repeating rifle that can replace an entire regiment."

"Lieutenant Billings, honestly, very little surprises me anymore, when it comes to men devising more efficient ways to kill one another. We've gotten very good at it, but I suppose there's always room for improvement. However, if you don't mind, I do have a question for you. Since the war's over, why were you and your men bothering to come up here scouting? You were obviously searching for something, and I'm sure it wasn't for us."

"No, of course not. We don't really care about what stragglers or deserters are up to. All that's changed now. What we're looking for is a large collection of men on horseback. Very dangerous men. These outlaws have been wreaking havoc in the area, not only upon civilians, but they've also attacked several of our smaller garrisons. They steal whatever valuables they can find and, worse, usually murder everyone they see. When we've come after them, these men are just gone, vanished into the air." He looked at Lorne. "After having heard both of your stories, I believe these are the same troops that attacked Miss Davenport's home and family."

Then Travis remembered the men on the beach.

"Lieutenant Billings. I believe I may have more important information for you. Just before we returned to camp, Lorne had discovered a threat not too far from here while setting her rabbit traps." He pointed north past the grassy hill, toward the ocean behind him as he spoke. "She had me climb up to a better vantage in a tree that overlooks the beach."

He pulled his spyglass out of his pocket. "From that tree, we used this to observe a large gathering of men that possessed a complement of horses, probably some of your stolen ones. They'd been setting up what seems to be a temporary camp on the beach. Across the hill, over there about a half mile or so, in the opposite direction of the way you came. From what I saw that bunch down there has no flag and no markings of rank or insignia of any sort on their clothing, which is neither blue nor gray."

"If neither blue nor gray, what color are the uniforms of these men on the beach, Sergeant?"

"No color at all, really. Its more the lack of one. As far as I was able to ascertain from my perch, their clothing is completely black. Every last man is wearing the midnight black."

12. SOMETHING ALWAYS BECOMES A DIFFERENT ANYTHING

After being told about the unknown force encamped on the beach, Billings had insisted he be given a view from their overlook, so Travis and Lorne took him to the observation post up in the tree. After they'd arrived, Travis swore, as the men's ship had already arrived, anchored close in, and they were loading their gear and material into the several skiffs pulled up onto the beach, for transfer back to the larger ship.

His guts tightened after he'd scanned the hustling crowd. In the center of the action, encouraging the workers with shouts, gestures, and the occasional kick, towered a large figure. His hat was of an odd cut, seeming somehow too short while it floated across his brow, yet as he moved, it flopped about, almost with a life of its own. It had a larger brim than any hat he'd seen before. His long black mustache was also overly thick and large, but even so it failed to cover the twisting red scar that still devoured his left cheek from mouth to ear.

The tall figure could only be The Otherside.

"Or, as his men know him, The Captain."

Travis didn't want to look at him too long, or even think his name for that matter. He remembered how the creature had been able to sense his thoughts before. That didn't seem to be the case now.

"Even if that bastard is still lookin' for me, this time I found him first."

"Good to know he's not invincible," he muttered as he handed the telescope off to Billings.

His former enemy settled in with the spyglass and scanned the activity. The skiffs shuttled their cargo back and forth between the placid shoreline and the waiting ship.

"What's that you just said, Sergeant?"

"I think I recognized at least one of them."

"Let me guess: the big man with the hat?"

"Yes. Too easy. That one really does stand out in a crowd."

Travis thought to himself, *"Or on a battlefield. We'll meet again, 'Captain', you filthy creature."*

Lieutenant Billings handed the small telescope back to Travis. "I've seen enough, Sergeant Lehrman. My men and I must return to report this. I only hope we won't be too late to stop them."

They made their hurried farewells. Billings and his men rode off to gather reinforcements, while Travis and Lorne climbed into the big tree overlooking the beach.

The raiders, being goaded and lashed unmercifully by their Captain, had been able to transport almost everything to the ship. A few horses had somehow managed to escape their round-up, galloping off inland to avoid being captured and loaded up for the trip across the waters.

The Otherside worked his followers to perform at an inhuman pace. They managed to finish up and slither off the beach only minutes before the punitive force that Lieutenant Billings brought back with him arrived at the scene. Lorne and Travis passed the spyglass between them while watching the chase and escape unfold.

Low in the water and already moving out to sea, the ship carried its rapacious seeds of woe and ruination to safety; their pursuing avengers back on shore were only able to ride helplessly back and forth among remnants of the abandoned camp with impotent rage. A few of the cavalrymen fired their carbines at the ship, but those shots were futile. They had been too late.

Billings and his men turned and rode back the way they'd come. As the lieutenant passed by, he looked up toward the lookout tree and snapped a quick salute to the hidden couple above. Travis returned it, even while knowing he couldn't be seen.

"He was a good man to us. He didn't need to be. I hope we'll meet again."

Travis and Lorne watched until the ship had sailed out of sight, then climbed down and returned to their little hut.

Later, twilight blue cast its blanket over the horizon. The last long shadows ran deep, snuffing out the sunlight within the folded hilly seams and small, hidden valleys around their camp. Travis was grateful for what Billings had given them, both the food and the war news. Or, rather, the lack of any more news about the war. It was now history.

Travis and Lorne sat outside the hut, finishing their meal. The rations had been eaten cold. They had decided to not take the risk of building a fire. Neither of them had wanted the slightest possibility of drawing attention to themselves, even though The Otherside and his raiders had already sailed off.

Or had they really?

"If I've learned one lesson, it's to never assume what The Otherside might do. With a creature like him around, something always becomes a different anything."

The sun had set. They had eaten. It had been a long day.

Lorne reached over to his head, tousling his hair. He turned to her. "I was disquieted for you today, Lorne. I'm so glad... things turned out the way they did. So much happening, with confusion and suspicion, so many things that might have gone wrong."

Hc took her hand in his own. It was a gentle encompassing, a firm grip of sincerity.

"Lorne, I was dazzled by the way you handled the lieutenant and his questions. They never seemed to end! But you kept your head and worked out the best way to convince him that we were who we said we were and had nothing to do with those raiders."

"I'm sure you would have been able to ascertain a workable solution with them as well."

"Ha! If having to deal with Billings and his boys had been up to me, I would have tried some damn fool antic. In all likelihood, that wouldn't have gone well."

"You're a strong man who knows how to survive. You've already proven that. Look how far you've come, what you've made it through since that last battle. You should have been killed when they overran your position, but you're the last survivor."

She stopped and pulled her hand from his to cover her face. The tears came, silently, no sobbing. A matter of fact statement of reality choked past her immobile jaw, "Just like me. I'm the last of my kind too. It's a lonely road, isn't it?"

He laid his arm lightly across her shoulders, considering his words. She slowly relaxed into him. Finally, he spoke.

"Lorne, never one day's gone by since we got away from them raiders that I haven't thanked God for his saving you."

"You should be thanking yourself for that, Travis. If it hadn't been for you shooting that raider, and then staying outside, I never would have come out and jumped down there with you. It was you that saved me. Just by being there, you saved me."

The starry twilight faintly illuminated them both. She wiped the wet from her eyes and took his face in her hands. Her swift pull brought them close. "Please, let's both get inside and warm up." With that, she kissed him.

Later, Travis was more than plenty warm. Entangled with Lorne, he lay dozing into a sweet, exhausted slumber. The events of the day blurred him away from consciousness. A kaleidoscope of memories swept jumbled, raw, images piecemeal through his mind. They flashed hither and yon, an honor guard devouring his mind's eye as they marched him off to sleep. He dreamed.

"Them boots n' hooves tramping along, shakin' the dirt right under me. Not too far from here. They must be off to battle. Where's the fight? Ain't none now, the War is over, or so

233

they said. Must be a parade. Not getting up for that."

Not so far away from where Travis and Lorne lay in their tiny shanty, hidden inside its bindings of branches, grass, and leaves, trod the heavy drumming of horses. It was neither a parade nor a dream. Just a small troop of horses that had run off from the uncaring raiders. They moved together, compelled to follow one horse, to seek what it sought.

That horse had been ordered by the arcane forces that The Otherside wielded to find the man and woman it had carried in their flight from the burning house.

The horses snuffled and stamped their way through brush and grass. If one slowed down for any reason, it was nudged by the others back to its duty. They moved in a large circle which centered around the sleeping pair. Yet they never came closer to the helpless man and woman than several hundred feet.

As the horses searched, they kept their distance from the couple, almost as if there was a large corral emplaced around the hut, and they were on the outside, rather than inside. Yet, it seemed to them, somehow, that they were never treading over old ground.

They couldn't know that they were being edged aside by a different power than The Otherside. Pushed aside by a series of invisible hands and crops and elbows, they were compelled to travel in a widening and fruitless circle before trotting away into the night.

The visions began for Travis almost as soon as his mind released one awareness in exchange for another.

Tonight, he wasn't soaring above the aether, discussing ancient secrets with what might be a demi-god, and trading deadly insults with a demonic creature. This night, his perceptions were far from smooth or ennobling. Movement and sense shifted from place to place, a blocky creasing of space that folded his view from beast to beast every few seconds.

He was experiencing what the several horses were seeing as they trotted around his tiny camp. Their vision differed greatly from what he'd known all his life. Their equine eyes were set widely apart, allowing a much greater field of view, granting an easier recognition of friend or foe, or in this case, a target being sought.

Travis became disoriented by his random shifts in viewpoint. From without, he sensed, as did the animals, a constant painful goad from an unseen whip. It was an uncontrollable compulsion to continue moving, searching. The dark of night proved no impediment. Every object of any size the small herd came upon was rimmed in red outline, while the ground itself glowed pale orange as if ablaze by internal subterranean fire, revealing the best footing for all four hooves to travel.

Their orders from The Otherside tolerated no alternative: *"Search until you drop!"* Within every malleable equine mind into which he was thrust, each shared the same desire to please their unseen yet demanding overlord, each knew what was required, and of course, dominating all else, each animal feared the terrible penalties of failure.

Travis watched the night pass by. Off to his left lay unseen territories, as yet unexplored. To his right was a sheen of faux memories hammered upon a forged reality. Within every beast his consciousness visited, he felt an irresistible pressure laid midway between shoulder and withers, a relentless push off to the left, away from where he and Lorne slept.

Then, a shout from elsewhere, filled with supreme prerogative: *"Veer off. Go! Move away from this path you have already trod. Do not retrace your steps. Go now! What you seek is far from here!"*

The horses complied. They obeyed this new imperative while still following their prior commands. Their belief in where they were now, and had been, was an iron certainty within every beast. The area of roiling mist they once sensed off to their right had now became a firm memory of blank empty grass patches scattered about a dry sandy hillside.

"Nothing more to see here. Be off with you all!"

They moved with one mind, hearing their new commands, following their leader. As Travis continued to shift between their multiple viewpoints, one set of eyes would vanish from his own perception, while the next opened for him.

Travis glanced over, getting a good look at the horse beside him. Just as they all turned away from the mist of false memories, his perceptions began to wane as well. He sensed that his connection with them all would end soon. But he'd already seen what he hadn't expected. It was a mark he'd seen before. A scar running across the beast's neck. Unmistakable.

The lead horse was the same beast he and Lorne had escaped on.

With this realization, Travis woke. A headache pounded behind his eyes. He stared straight ahead into the gloom, struggling to return to his own human perceptions. His mental connection to the herd-mind of the horses had paled but was not yet completely broken.

"That big animal saved us once. Has it been told to come back to correct that error?"

He listened intently. After a while, the tremors faded and the pounding echoes of the hooves diminished as the horses searched farther and farther away from the couple's fragile sanctuary, now hidden behind an unknown ally's shield.

Finally, the beasts were gone.

Travis came to full wakefulness. Lorne still slept beside him. Unmoving, he lay staring at a star that peeked past the tarpaulin covering their primitive hut.

Unexpectedly, that single bright star suddenly winked out. It was as if a stage curtain swung shut, or the long woolen cloak of a cab man had flopped down to obscure his carriage window. Little could he hear save the soft hiss of surf across sand.

Lorne shifted slightly beside him, sighing, then draped her arm across his. Her long, slow breaths resumed.

"We haven't spoken of it much since, but several days ago she did mention having a strange dream, of meeting an oddly dressed woman who carried a curved sword. Even then, I knew it had to have been an encounter with Alyssia. But the possibility of us encountering the same person within our separate dreams was utterly preposterous at the time. But now! It seems that this madness is reality. We really

have been contacted by... something else. Something from beyond this world."

The effects of having shared the senses of the horses had strained him. Now this strange evidence of a group calling themselves the Outer Forces almost snapped him.

"Madness. Real or not, these events are affecting me as if they are. I can't let this insanity destroy who I am, or my honor, and those I care for... and Lorne. She's become important to me...much more than important."

Abruptly, the star he'd seen earlier returned to dominate his gaze. The fast moving clouds blew past it, alternately dimming, then again quickly unveiling its uncanny brightness.

"Tonight, Lorne and I were both shielded from those searching animals by a deception, a wall of falsehood akin to what Alyssia had wrought earlier. But the commands I overheard tonight were from someone new. Perhaps another member of this so-called Outer Forces group who's not bothered with introductions."

He had no more time for introspection. At that moment came another disconnected voice, another woman, perhaps another warrior, so far as he could ascertain from its timbre and tone. There was no visible manifestation of her presence such as what Alyssia had formed. But the star that had caught his eye pulsed with a precise cadence as she spoke.

"You've guessed passingly well Mr. Military Man, but far from exact in detail. Yes, I'm one such as you, not such as them. I also carry the burden of my own unfulfilled oath, which unfortunately is unobtainable in this here and now, much to my regret. So, until I pass into

that ripeness of time, I've been enjoined to lend support to your quest. Ha! Maybe you'll find yourself working to help me with my own quest one day. Ha!"

Travis's mind spun and tilted while he replied, *"You've been helping us? For how long?"*

"There's never been no help for your "us". But for as long as you have needed it, I've been helping you." Unexpectedly, she burst out in laughter.

Her unseen hilarity caused much distress for the star overhead. He continued watching, as its blinking and dimming struggled to keep up with her roiling laughter. At last, she quieted, then spoke again.

"The other one, that female you call Lorne, she needs no help. My instructions were to assist you. But since she seems to enjoy your company... she's along for the ride, you might say. Ha!"

Travis could almost hear her shoulders cracking as they shrugged with indifference. He spoke.

"I must thank you for your help. What may I call you?"

"Don't you dare thank me. Thank the others. Thank the Outer Forces if you must thank anyone. As for how you should address me, I haven't decided yet. I don't know if I like you. Yet. Maybe I'll tell you when we meet."

Taken aback by the derisive tone she inflicted upon him with every syllable, Travis only managed a terse reply.

"I like to think I have something to offer, occasionally."

The star's brightness remained unchanged. A

239

long silence preceded his next question.

"*You said something about a meeting. When is that going to happen?*"

The star flickered. Her tone was impatient, as to a particularity dull child.

"*So many damn questions. Stupid questions! Why you think that I know? But I suppose I do. Ha! Okay. I'll have something for you that you gotta have, but they ain't given it to me yet. Sometime soon, I gotta do this thing, they told me, that's all I know. That's all I ever know. I'm done having to talk to you now. I've done my job.*"

She stopped talking.

Travis tried once more, "*Are you still here?*"

The star shone steady.

Travis pressed on, "*Well, I want to say thanks anyway. You may not care to hear it, but I need to say it, and I do mean it.*"

Sea breezes inexorably swept more clouds inland, slowly obscuring the star. Eventually, it dimmed away, darkness compressing the very atmosphere around them. The smell of salt water permeated the little hut.

Travis lay still, feeling more stunned and bruised than after his encounters with The Otherside.

"*At least with that ugly ol' carbuncle, I know what I'm dealing with. This snappy gal sounds like a big ol' box of mess. Obviously, she's been more than helpful, but she's just downright mean while she's at it. Somewhat mean, anyways. She wouldn't bother to even give me her name.*"

After considering the bizarre situation a bit more, he realized that her attitude mattered little if her aid had helped keep Lorne and himself alive.

"I'm being a short-sighted fool again. She's dealing with her own problems I have no conception of. No matter her name, she's probably already saved my life more than once before tonight. I owe her, and I'm going to acknowledge that debt, do what I can to repay it. Whatever she thinks about me is her own business that I can't change."

Lorne's soft breathing was a comfort. He turned toward her, seeing her dimly lit outline. Her warmth pressed his side. He finally relaxed, looking back toward the empty sky.

"After losing her family, Lorne is in need of any help she can get. Why did this woman say that any help she had given, was only for me, that Lorne didn't need any? She even laughed about it. There are many questions that need answers."

Sighing, he knew the explanations he sought were in the control of others. But he had to do what must be done to survive. It did not matter what others said or believed, but instead what their actions revealed.

"So what if she don't care for me. What she's done has helped keep me alive and in one piece, away from The Otherside! Because of that, I've been able to help keep Lorne safe as well. And that's the important thing. But now, she and I must live long enough for me to get close to that bastard, and then somehow kill him this time. That's the priority."

The war was done. His army was gone. The killing skills he'd learned as a soldier, irrelevant. Travis knew that the world had changed forever.

To make things more complicated, he wasn't the only one out of a job. There would be many men out there willing to do whatever necessary to make sure they got their place in the job line, ahead of him. When you looked at the situation from this point of view, it might not be quite so difficult to understand why broke and desperate former soldiers might decide that joining up with a bunch of wild-eyed galoots led by an unnatural being as fearsome as The Otherside wasn't such a bad idea.

"Well, it might be work for some, if you don't mind killin' women and babies. Or worse."

Dismissing such thoughts, he knew that in these after-war days, the mission he'd set for himself since his desperate escape was now rendered null and void, becoming an irrelevant fool's errand.

"Getting back to my lines was the only thing that kept me going all those weeks. A straightforward task but gone. Now I've stumbled into this mad pageant of soulless phantasms, hallucinations of horses, and headless corpses in bloody ponds. All because of some ancient oath and the insatiable evil of The Otherside. The world's gone from merely crazy to utterly deranged."

But no matter what happened from now on, even with what the angry woman had said about Lorne not needing help, he knew he had to look after her. He also knew that at this point she might even be in a family way, and if that was true his responsibility to her would be irrevocable.

"And if she is with child, that's fine, that's good. If I'm honest with myself, I know she's the

best person I've ever met. She makes living worthwhile. And since I don't know what I'll be doing for work in the future, as it don't seem that fighting The Otherside, or the Captain, or whatever he's calling himself today, pays very much, as long as I can be living my life with her, it'll be fine. If we can just get through all this, maybe soon it will be done and over and we can put this all behind. Find a preacher to get us hitched, and then somewhere peaceful to settle down and have a quiet life. Maybe we'll head to Texas."

He hoped that his night was complete, that no more surprises would come, at least before daybreak. Dozing off, the last thing he felt was Lorne by his side. *"With all the madness that's been going on, at least things have worked out as well as they have. I have to be grateful we're both still alive."*

He slept.

The next several days were as normal as any he'd had since being swept up and dragged off his father's farm by the press gang several years ago and forced into the army. The war had been ugly. He was glad it was done.

They decided to settle in beside the ocean for a short time to rest and decide upon their next course of action. The next several days were generally pleasant. Lorne resumed her trapping, so there was enough to eat. Travis, remembering the spear men at the battle of the mountain pass, continued to work on his armaments.

The piles of junk the raiders had abandoned

on the beach in their rush to escape the pursuing cavalry had proven to be an unexpected bounty.

He decided upon modifying his spear so that it might easily be broken down for transport when not needed. He didn't want to have to carry it in one hand, which might slow his ability to quickly draw his pistol.

Using the old tools and scraps of iron fittings found left behind in the ruins of the raider's camp, he got to work. He cut the shaft into three sections, then hammered out four small but strong circular iron rings. Two of them he made into locking rings for the spear shaft. The other two were smaller. Those he polished up as best he could, setting them aside for another purpose.

When he was finished working on the spear, the entire length of it fit inside a leather case just over two feet long, to be carried across his back. The sharpened iron blade lay inside a wooden sheath. When needed, all the sections would be fitted together, connected by the lock rings. He'd managed to make the ancient weapon tight and straight when assembled. After some practice, he was able to get it out of the case and put together, ready for use in under ten seconds.

Now, concerned about the condition of the firearms in the ocean's corroding mists of humid salt air, he made sure that the edges of the powder case were tight, with a well coated seal of grease around all edges. The carbine and the pistols he also inspected, and then, double-checked as well. Satisfied, he left the hut to join Lorne outside. They ambled down to the beach, looking for anything else that might prove useful.

Earlier, when Travis had been watching the raiders escape, he noticed that, at first glance, the various broken boxes, smashed cases, and split open barrels looked empty, just heaps of useless garbage; indeed, they mostly were.

When the cavalry had finally arrived, their attention was on the Captain's ship they'd missed catching as it headed out to sea. Obviously, they didn't care about a bunch of rubbish on the beach.

After a cursory inspection by a few privates who found neither weapons nor gold, the men had saddled back up and returned down the coast to their army's encampment for the sad task, Travis assumed, of reporting their failure to capture the raiders to their superiors.

He hoped none of them would return but knew that eventually they or someone else would. Lorne and he would only have a limited time to explore the debris scattered across the abandoned beach to recover anything else they might be able to use.

When they arrived at the beach, they saw that the scattered dregs were almost buried with wind-blown sand and driftwood. They split up to explore.

Lorne carried a long, stout stick. She usually used it to prod about into spaces that might be uncomfortable or indiscreet to put one's extremity into. This afternoon she was doing exactly that. Travis heard her shout from where he was engaged in fruitless scavenging some distance away.

She was waving at him, occasionally jumping up and down, beckoning him to come over.

"Must be a prodigious discovery to wrest that kind of response from her."

Lorne was as excited as he'd ever seen her.

When Travis arrived, he saw that she had used her big stick to lever off what was left of the lid. She pointed at the contents inside.

"Look here Travis, this box has a great batch of boots inside it!"

It was true. There seemed to be a variety of sizes, and many looked as if they had already been used, but for the most part they were in serviceable, if somewhat soggy and sandy, condition.

Travis looked down at what was left of his own boots, something he didn't like doing. He'd gone so long wearing what were really just ragged leather remnants, he hardly even noticed them falling apart around his feet while he walked anymore.

"Lorne, you're a wonder!"

"I had gone by this box before without another glance, it was so smashed down, it didn't look like there was any chance of anything at all, useful or not, being inside it. Today, no matter where I poked around, I couldn't find anything worth a nit before this, so I just thought I'd give it a look-see. It's not like I had anything to lose."

"But everything to gain! How many more are in there?"

"Come over to help me and you can see for yourself, you lazy man."

Before he'd gotten more than two boots out, she tossed the last one aside and sat looking at him. She smiled. He sat next to her.

"Well now. Looks like you had all that under control. Didn't seem to need much assistance at all."

"Oh, that's where you're wrong, Travis. I don't want just anyone's assistance." She grabbed his shoulder, turned him full on toward her. The heat of their bodies mingled in the gentle sea breeze as they drew together. "But I need yours."

Close by, yet distant in a sky above the wind-blown beach and crashing waves, sea birds cooed and squawked and circled, back and forth, back and forth, mimicking the ocean's surging tidal motions, forever heaving out to sea.

Later that evening, the two sat together before the dwindling flames of their tiny cook-fire, just outside the entrance of their hut. They were tired from the activities of the day and were now sated by a hot meal of rabbit meat accompanied by the food supplies left them by the generosity of Lieutenant Billings. They leaned together, lightly dozing while their shoulders touched one another.

Travis' internal thoughts broke his silence, two syllables of memory whispered in a quiet musing manner. "Embers... "

Lorne opened her eyes, "What? Travis, what did you say? Is there something wrong with the fire?"

"No. No, not at all. Nothing wrong with this fire."

"What did you say? It sounded like 'embers'. Why would you say that? Were you dreaming? If you're sleeping while sitting up, we do need to put out that fire, and crawl into our hut."

Travis remained sitting. "No, I wasn't dreaming, not so much anyway. Just thinking, remembering, perhaps some conjecturing, I suppose." He turned to look at her. He spoke slowly. "Lorne, have you had any more dreams lately? Not just the normal variety that you can't hardly remember the next morning, try as you might. I mean any more like that odd one you told me about."

She shifted slightly and took her eyes from his. "What dream was that? I don't remember, Travis."

"There was something about a curved sword. That's the main thing I recall you saying. A curved sword that a woman carried, and the strange clothes she wore. Robes or something like that. But you mostly seemed impressed with that sword, said it wasn't like anything you'd ever seen around here."

Lorne paused, blinked her eyes, speaking slowly. "Yes, I do remember now that you describe it. There was a woman wearing clothes that bore a more than vague likeness to drawings I'd seen."

"Drawings? What drawings are these? And where are they?"

Lorne retreated into herself, shrinking from her usual exuberance. "I saw the illustrations when I was in school, studying history. Ancient history, like Latin and the people who spoke it, those Roman folks back in Europe, a long, long time ago." Then for an instant, she brightened, speaking more quickly, "After reading those books and daydreaming about the people those pictures, I'd always wanted to be a Roman princess or a queen. Of course, I knew it was impossible." Her shoulders slumped slightly; her mien quieted once more.

Travis waited. She continued in a soft voice.

"My father had a large library of Latin volumes and... other wonderful big books that were full of illustrations from bible times. They showed a lot of pictures of those Romans too, and how people dressed back then. I used to look through them a lot, especially during the winter, when we'd all be sitting around the hearth. But... now. That's all gone. Father is gone. The house is gone. My family is gone. The books are all burnt. Those pictures I looked at... just black ashes."

She threw a pebble from the ground into the fire, with a bitter vehemence Travis hadn't seen before. "Only the fires remain, Travis, I know they do. All over the world, still the fires remain. They're still flaming, still burning the homes of children and no one cares. Even when the evil kills the parents and rapes their daughters, no one cares. No one cares, Travis. No one cares enough to put them fires out. And I know now, beyond certain I do, I know now that I'll never, ever get a chance to be a princess or duchess or queen or anybody fancy like that, ever, never ever! All I am now an orphan, Travis, and all I've got left is you!"

Lorne clung to his side quietly sobbing, violent, intense. Her silent despair quickly soaked the nook of his arm with tears.

Travis held her firmly, his arms encircling her weeping form.

Around them, shadows lost definition, spreading like black mercury into one another, slowly filling nook and crevice. Silhouette trees metamorphosed into primordial idols who flanked the darkening zenith.

Cheeks touching, sharing breath; the couple remained thus for some time their faces dimly lit by the dying fire. Chill gusts from the north cooled what the ebbing fire before them could not warm. Lorne's desperate clasp around him gradually diminished as she cried herself out.

"Now I wish that I'd never reminded her about that dream. We'd be asleep by now, and she wouldn't have gotten all upset like this. But... I suppose everything would have broken out later, like some of the men in my battery becoming agitated for no reason, weeks after a battle. Lorne's been through a lot, no denying it. And truth be told, this here, right now, is as good a time as any. It's not like we have pressing appointments tomorrow, or there's a train or boat we need to board on some schedule."

A long pull of air, then staccato sighs. "I'm scared, Travis. I need to tell you something." She kept her head buried next to him, not looking up. Her voice was a low rasp. "I knew you were going to ask me about that woman with the sword, the one I'd seen in the dream."

Travis tensed inwardly, "How did you know?"

"I had another dream about her later, well, really several other dreams, but I didn't want to believe what I was seeing, or what she was saying. I didn't want to go to sleep because she kept bossing me about, telling me what I was supposed to do, and after that I didn't want to talk to her anymore. But I knew I had to."

She finally looked up, new tears in her eyes. She coughed to clear her throat and continued. "I thought I was going mad, Travis. I thought that it was just a prank my mind was playing on me. I tried to believe that if you never... ,"

Travis spoke softly, briefly interrupting her, "Lorne, please, you don't have to tell me any of this if you don't want to. I'm sorry I even mentioned it."

"It's alright, Travis. We need the truth. Just

because we don't talk about something doesn't mean it won't exist. I've learned that now. At any rate, I was thinking that if you didn't ever ask me about her, like she said you would, then that would be proof, and I would know that she didn't really exist, and I wouldn't have to worry about any of the awful things she told me about."

They sat unspeaking, feeling the unsteady breeze splash across their faces. Soon, they both felt the first drops of rain at the same time. The night seemed colder than it had only a few minutes earlier.

She stirred and began to untangle herself from him. "Let's get out of this rain, please. I don't have any more tears inside me. I don't need the angels crying on me either."

She crawled into their little shelter. He stirred sand over the last fitful embers then started to crawl inside as well. The rain intensified. Remembering one last chore, he went back out to retrieve the boots they had recovered earlier. He pulled them from a wooden form where they'd stretched them out to dry, then rushed back inside.

The hut was more crowded with the boots inside, especially since they'd found two pairs of them that seemed they would fit them both when dried. Hers had been the smallest they'd found; his, the largest. After shifting a few other items around he made everything fit, with room enough for him to lay down comfortably, more or less. Lorne had already dropped off to sleep, exhausted.

After everything that had happened that underscored the harsh situation they faced, and all the difficult decisions that must soon be made, he looked forward to wearing something that should keep his feet safe and dry.

"Small victories. They're what keep you going in a world gone mad."

Outside the hut, heavy fat drops sluiced down. The little hut shook beneath the increasingly violent storm.

During these last few days of their sojourn, he'd had time to plug and cover over the open seams of their dwelling. Now, only the most minor of drips marred the hut's interior. Outside, the vast ocean rains pounded upon them with frustrated impotence.

"If I hadn't endeavored to make those repairs, we would be swimming in here by now. Just as if Lorne hadn't decided to go back to double check on those smashed boxes she'd already looked over before, she'd never have found these boots. Guess sometimes you have to make an extra effort and give another try or two or ten to get done what needs doing."

Having stumbled upon something positive to consider as his last thoughts of the day, he dropped off to sleep. Outside, the wrath of the tempest enfolded them.

He did not dream.

The next morning began as last night had ended, with saltwater winds still shaking their walls. The storm had abated but continued to be a drizzly mess that toyed with them and gusted hard at times. Travis was grateful to find only a few damp areas around the interior and did what he could to patch them from the inside. Building a fire was impossible, of course, but at least they'd kept the leftovers from their last meal, and still had much of the hardtack, cheese, and bacon that remained of their gift from the Lieutenant.

Travis knew that the exhaustion of their coffee supply was at hand, so the inability to make fire this morning was a bittersweet event, as it allowed him to save the last beans until they could. But that only delayed the inevitable, and he did not look forward to that day. The end of the coffee meant to him the symbolic end of civilization. It would force him to recognize that they were indeed isolated and alone, far from help in a very dangerous world.

"Don't matter any which or what way circumstances are pushing us around. The consequences of all I do now, or don't bother doing, are what I'm gonna have to live with the rest of my life."

He watched Lorne as she worked with her hands on the boots she'd chosen, wringing them this way and that, keeping them supple as they dried out. *"Now my decisions not only affect how long my own life might be, but hers as well. One thing is for certain. We can't stay on this beach eating berries and wild rabbit forever.*

He picked up one of his boots and began to emulate Lorne. The damp leather yielded with difficulty. He reached down and placed it against his own foot. The length was almost correct, perhaps a bit large, but all the others had been obviously too small. He kneaded the leather, twisting and pulling it this way and that. His fingers began to hurt after only a few minutes. He stopped to shake the cramping out.

Lorne turned and smiled. "Good morning Travis. Idle hands are the Devil's playthings."

"I wish mine were more idle. This leather is

253

stiff."

She gave him an amused look, back to her more optimistic self again, saying, "They played fine as fiddles yesterday, when we were on the beach... ", then laughed. He enjoyed seeing her happy. She pecked him on the cheek and briefly watched him work.

He grunted. "This is downright strenuous work. How do you keep it up so?" Leaning into the leather and ignoring the pain in his fingers, he twisted at it twice as fast.

A cloud passed across Lorne's face as her brow knitted closer together. "I kneaded a lot of dough, Travis. Ever since I was a little girl, I baked for the family almost every day at home." Turning back to her boot, she continued imposing her own will upon its insubordinate leather.

"Damnation all to Hades and back. I did it again. Isn't there anything I can say that won't remind her of that horrible night? No, I suppose not. But I can't always be walking on piles of needles and pins, watching my every word. She'll just have to get past it, and I'll just have to do my best to help her."

For the next half hour or so they worked side by side. They took comfort from each other's presence while the liquid sky flung its heavy sheets across their camp. Occasionally they felt the hut shuddering during a particularly aggressive gust. Yet while it bent, it did not break. They finished working the tough leather of their boots in warmth and dryness.

"Another small victory. Our breakfast may be cold, but breakfast we shall have. I cannot be less than thankful for our luck so far."

For two days the incessant squall restricted the pair to their shelter and immediate vicinity. It was an enforced curfew that gave them a chance to discuss subjects they might not otherwise have had the time for. They spoke of Texas, of plans for the future, and if there might not even be the possibility of such, considering the deadly motives of The Otherside.

Travis decided to tell Lorne of his ancestor's vow to destroy that creature, a thousand years past, and how that promise became his responsibility with the help, and the insistent prodding of the strange and powerful entities that called themselves the Outer Forces.

"This is as good a time as might come. Best for her to learn about the monster that's really chasing us.

He told her about his fight with The Otherside, and everything else he'd seen and done. When his story had once again gotten to the point of including Alyssia, Lorne interrupted him. "That's the woman that I dreamed of too, the woman with the curved sword, is that right?"

"So far as I can ascertain, yes. It seems like we've both had our own separate contact and interactions with this group. Usually at night when we're sleeping or, at least for me, after I'd been knocked unconscious. I think that if we both combine whatever it is we know, we might have a chance to understand what our best course of action is."

"Travis, you said that you were committed to follow this vow you'd taken and destroy The Otherside. If he's the leader of those that killed my family, you know I'll be right there beside you."

Frustrated, he spoke slowly and clearly. "It's a vow my ancestor made, not me. My very, *very* ancient, *ancient* ancestor."

She did not reply.

Her silence seemed to make the rain outside louder. "Lorne, yes, but only if... and these are all very big 'ifs', well, If I can believe all these ghost stories, and if I can believe I'm not a mad man, and if what all these protectors or guardians... these so-called Outer Forces people... are telling me during these visions is actually true, then, yes, I would prefer fulfilling that oath. I have always made every effort to be a man of honor. But... that is the precise reason I don't feel it's the right path for me now, after what's happened, I mean."

"What do you mean by that? What has happened?"

"I mean everything that's happened between you and me! Lorne, I want you beside me, but not if it means putting yourself into danger!"

He reached into his knapsack to remove a small object within a tightly wrapped cloth. "Lorne, I don't have a golden ring to give you just yet, but I swear I will someday. He paused, watching her in utter stillness, then continued, "But I figure that's no reason to delay asking for your hand in marriage."

He held out his open palm. "In the meantime. I do have this for you." I could only guess at your ring size, so it isn't perfect, of course. I'm no jeweler, but I can be handy with a hammer and such if yours needs changes."

He folded the cloth away from its contents. Laying side by side were two iron rings, curved and shaped and polished from the same metal scraps they had found abandoned in the beach camp.

Lorne stared at them, her breath catching.

"I made these last week while you were away setting your traps. I was working on the locking rings for my spear. I perceived that since I had everything already set up to shape metal, it would be a good time for this type of manufactory as well." Placing the larger of the two on his own finger, he took a deep breath, let it out. "Lorne, would you be my betrothed?"

After a moment, she found her voice, "Travis, my sweet one, of course I will!"

He placed the smaller ring around her left hand's appropriate finger.

"It fits!" they both cried simultaneously, then kissed.

Outside, the torrent was unceasing, uncaring.

13. THE SHREDDED REMNANTS

After another day and night confined inside the tight but mostly dry quarters with Lorne, Travis considered their situation. Without a steady supply of rabbit or other fresh foods, their sustenance now depended upon what remained from the largess of Lieutenant Billings.

"There ain't much left of that food; But as stale and tasteless as it is now, it's certainly been a godsend in helping keep us alive. It's going to be gone by tomorrow. If we don't get a break in this weather, we'll be getting hungry soon."

He listened to the incessant pounding of rain drops, as he had for the last several days. *"At least we've got one thing going for us, we're not going to die of thirst."*

The next day, both the food and the storm's fury ran out. They had just finished the last bit of breakfast crumbs and bacon fat. Lorne noticed the quiet first.

"Travis... "

He looked over, waiting for her to continue. She smiled instead, pointing upwards.

He blurted, "It's finished. The storm's over. The rain has stopped."

Lorne gathered up what she'd been working on and set it aside so she could crawl out of the hut. "Yes, and I can't stay in here another minute. I want to go up to the stream and wash up." She left.

Travis looked after her. "Alright. I'll be there soon but first I want to see how much damage has been done by the storm."

He pulled on the boots. They were somewhat large for him, as he'd suspected. But they were dry and almost supple, but infinitely better than what he'd been wearing. He'd make them work.

He took care to strap on his gun belt before stepping into the fresh air outside. *"Never know what's changed since we've been stuck inside. A whole new batch of raiders might be back down on that beach. Or even, God forbid, set up shop right around that bend over there."*

Before he left to reconnoiter farther away, he inspected the vicinity around the hut. Only a few feet away, a deep rivulet gushed pent waters from the hills behind them to the ocean. It had not been there before. Travis looked away, gazing around. In all directions, he saw that the tall grasses were bent horizontal, soaked with the heavy remnants of the storm. Their hut had fared better.

The little shelter had held up well through the long deluge. He again looked at the new stream rushing by only about a yard away from it and knew that they had been very lucky.

"If that ditch had been just a smidgen more over this way it would have cut right through the dirt underneath us. Instead, it passed us by, and we stayed dry. We wouldn't have been able to move away or repair anything during that storm. For whatever it's worth, as frustrating as it's been, I have to admit we've been fortunate. It could have been much worse."

Travis thought back to the night after the raiders had left. He was certain that if the barrier placed between them and the searching horses had failed, their lot would have become even more grim than what he now imagined as "much worse".

He knew that, even as The Otherside sailed farther away on board a ship already miles off the coast, he or his evil minions would have been able to bring mayhem to their lives, which undoubtedly would have been very short.

"We would have been dead or worse already. He's had a bone to pick with me, well, hell's belles, with my whole family, for the last thousand years or so. Ever since my great, great-old grand pap told him and his army to go to hell. Then I showed up and tried to shoot the son of a bitch dead, but only grazed him. Ha! I guess I'd be mad too if I had been running around being a mean-ass damn near immortal bastard, just doin' whatever the hell I pleased, and then some upstart son of a bitch appeared out of nowhere to scar me up. That ripped up cheek wound of his just never bothered to heal very well. It's too bad that eclipse in the pass hadn't lasted longer, might have done him more damage. But it's worse that I missed my best shot, of course. Who knows if I'll get another one, not that I really want to find out."

Travis quit his musings and took several long walks around the camp, moving outward in concentric circles. He wanted to cover all the ground within several hundred from the hut. He didn't want to be surprised by what might have shown up during the days of the long rain.

"We weren't able to hear much else than rain and thunder during the storm. If somebody did set up out here, we wouldn't know, and I want

to find them before they find us."

He kept searching, walking around the soggy mud puddles, looking for any sign of foot or hoof prints, but there was nothing.

Soon the ground would be dry again. He walked on, glad he'd already filled his canteen, which he kept under his left arm, high up as possible to prevent its movement or noise, with the strap slung over his head above his opposite shoulder.

After he'd finished inspecting the vicinity around the camp, he stopped by the hut, grabbing the spyglass. Then he made his way over to the tree that served as their observation post overlooking the beach. There was no sign of Lorne, but he knew she could take care of herself, as she had left with the Spencer carbine slung over her shoulder, and the big Bowie strapped to her waist.

"And I know that woman can belt out the loudest screams I've ever heard. If she finds any trouble, or if it finds her, everyone within a mile will know about it, and they'll be sorry they tried anything, that's a fact."

He trudged along toward the tree, with slowly drying wetness all around. He made a wide detour of a large pond that had formed during the storm. His boots were keeping his feet dry as he'd tromped about this morning, and he didn't want to test them further by sloshing through too much water.

When he arrived at the tree, he looked around carefully. Nothing much had changed. It didn't look like any fresh tracks had been stomped into the grass, which was beginning to stand up straighter as it dried out. He climbed up the tree.

When he got to the branch they'd used for observing, he sat. Looking up, he saw the "TL" mark he'd carved in the trunk just above his head soon after they'd arrived, when he was out here by himself.

He smiled at that memory, and at what had happened since that day now that Lorne had accepted his ring and become his betrothed. Everything that had happened ever since the battle had led him to this point and complicated what had once been a simple mission... evade the enemy, return to his own lines.

"Simpler times back then, or maybe I just wasn't seein' what was right in front of my face. 'Course when you're in the army you can't see more than what the officers want you to, you have to believe in what they tell you, or else, and you damn-all better follow them orders they tell you to. Mess up on any count of those and you just may find yourself buried with a bullet in your back. I'm glad that damn ol' war is finally done. Maybe life will be simpler now, after all. Except I suppose I've still got to somehow take care , if he keeps on after us, I suppose I've still got to somehow take care of The Otherside, and then marry Lorne. Or maybe, the other way round. Ha! Life ain't never more simple once a woman's involved! But she's worth it."

Whistling quietly through his teeth and finally feeling better about their general circumstances, he settled into his perch on the tree branch, happy that his new boots helped steady him among the limbs. He pulled out the telescope and scanned the horizon in all directions, then swung the instrument back to pay particular attention toward the north, the direction that

263

The Otherside's ship had fled to.

"Nothing but the gray haze of Poseidon sleeping out there, and best of all, not a ship in sight. That's a grand view to be grateful for, even now."

He turned his attention down to the beach. A bleak view of empty sand greeted his eyes. Every box, barrel, cart, or crate that had before been prominent was either utterly gone or displayed only a weathered and waterlogged fragment of its man-made origin.

"Anyone else that comes across this stretch of beach won't hardly know what's buried out there, unless they had been here before, and even then, they'd have to look twice."

Travis clambered from the tree, then went to the beach.

"If that storm did such a good job burying all that, maybe it's managed to uncover something as well."

The winds waxed and waned, occasionally flinging up gritty sand into his face. He pulled his faded red cap down as far as possible, squinting against the salty breezes. He didn't mind. The sea winds seemed to scour off the evil taint left by the Captain and his raiders.

Travis gazed slowly over the beach, seeing nothing unusual. He had just turned away to search to another sandy patch when a metallic glint caught his eye. It looked like a ring of metal, partially buried, about a hand's width across. *"There's something. Over by that bush."* He strode across the beach, leaving bubbling boot prints behind. His feet stayed dry.

Coming closer he saw what it was... an iron horseshoe, both ends buried in the sand and easy to mistake for a ring. He bent down to remove the curved metal poking above the sand. Turning it about, he found what he knew would be there: two small upside-down "V" cutouts stamped into the top curve of the horseshoe.

"I wonder how many faces this has crushed. Perhaps a friend of mine or a relative of Lorne's? Whatever he or it is, I hate that awful creature from the past, and the evil he's brought here."

Discovering this horseshoe brought back all the anger, uncertainty, and, if he was honest with himself, the ugly fear anything having to do with this monster from the past.

"Fear is probably the reaction of any normal living creature as well. But obviously that alone isn't enough to keep him from getting lickspittles to sign up for his army. I hate this situation he's put Lorne and I into. And I hate these awful horseshoes."

He walked to the shoreline, intending to toss the odious thing as far away as possible into the ocean. But just as he pulled his arm back, he stopped. A thought came insistent and clear into his mind.

"Hold up there, just wait a spell. It's not doing evil nailed on the hoof of one of his horses anymore. It's just a piece of metal now. But... perhaps... it will prove useful for something, later."

He examined it again, more closely now. Just a horseshoe, but something else besides the imprint of devil's horns was different about it. After turning it over several times he realized what it was. It seemed lighter than a normal iron shoe of the same size, if not more so.

"Odd. How could that be? Perhaps it's made from some other metal than iron, something as foreign as The Otherside himself. But what might it be?"

The mystery was too much to ponder excessively. Shrugging, he stuffed the artifact of evil into his shirt pocket and continued his walk along the ocean's edge. The tide was out, and wriggling sea creatures of all sorts had been stranded on the beach, unable to crawl back into their natural element, or hide in plain sight within a shell. It was a seafood banquet for the guests with two wings, who squawked and fought over the choice morsels laid before them. Travis watched the birds feasting on the helpless stragglers.

"A feeding frenzy. Looks about the same as when the raiders were attacking Lorne's house. That turned out to be a tougher crab to crack than they'd thought. Until they finally blew it up and burned it down. But that wasn't enough because it had taken too long for their beloved Captain... he'd wanted the women inside for himself. So, he ordered their heads chopped off for insubordination. He even took a few bites himself! No matter how much The Otherside says he pays his lackeys, it ain't hardly worth it."

Several groups of gulls stopped eating, deciding, for no reason Travis could see, to argue amongst themselves. They nipped sharply at one another.

"The gleaners always end up eating their own."

Realizing that he was woolgathering, Travis halted his lackadaisical search, bringing his focus back to what needed doing. Taking a few breaths, he looked intently seaward. Clean gusts blew inland over ranks of waves fading to the distance. At the far horizon floated a slowly thickening mist.

"More rain? After the buckets we got dropped on us for the last several days, I figured we'd have at least a short spell of dry weather and sun."

He pulled the telescope from his pocket, peered through it.

"Nothing. No thunderheads, and sky's not too darkening. I'm no sailor, but it don't look like another storm's coming up just yet. Just to be safe, I'd better head back and make any repairs to the hut that might be needed and tighten everything up."

He turned and walked back up the sandy slope toward camp. When he got to a point just past the hill's crest, he paused at the bottom of the lookout tree. He looked toward their camp then back to the tree. After a short hesitation to weigh options, up he went. He climbed past the sitting branch, their usual spot, which commanded a good view of the beach, but only a limited view of the sea. Up and up, he went, up to the highest branch that could support his weight. Among these sparser leaves, Travis could now see much more of the vast ocean beyond. He again pulled the spyglass from his pocket.

The far mists leapt closer for inspection; gently lumbering seas blurring into gray; the occasional seabird. Altogether, it was nothing out of the ordinary, and yet... a disquieting ache gnawed his bones. Travis tamped those emotions down and kept still, slowly moving the instrument back and forth, as he scanned the horizon. Finally, he returned it to its case. A very real ache had replaced the pain of premonition he'd felt earlier. He felt at least one of his feet might be asleep; those toes were jammed into the end of the boot.

"Time to get going. No shame in getting spooked in the first place, but it's my own damn fault if I stay that way. I've watched over my shoulder for hobgoblins long enough."

As he disentangled his limbs from the tight nooks of the tree, he glanced once more into the distance. The slightest stain of brown discoloration caught his attention. He stopped his downward motion, staring intently at the suspect area, which at first glance was just an innocent smear upon the horizon. But his suspicions were on high alert. He shook his head and, once again, brought out the telescope.

When he raised it up, he saw what was to be seen. He cursed.

"Damnation! He's at it again. But why am I not surprised?"

Off the edge of the world, it came square upon the shore, full sails taut and snapping, single stack amidships belching black.

"That coal fire plume was the smudge in the sky I'd almost missed. I'm glad I took the second look, but... Damnation! Once again he's back!"

Travis now clambered down hurriedly, hardly aware of his foot that had been compressed while he was awkwardly perched above. He ignored the prickling numbness as he ran limping back to the camp.

When he got there, he saw that three rabbits were almost cooked. He hadn't smelled them or seen any smoke during his approach from the beach, since the wind blew from his back. Out of breath, he called Lorne's name. She came forward out of the cover of trees, riding the horse that they'd both assumed had wandered off a week ago.

"Travis! Look who's come back! She made a grand appearance just as I was finishing up cookin', and I couldn't help but jump up for a quick ride. She seemed awful glad to see me.

He thought back to his disorienting vision when he'd been randomly shuffled between equine minds as they had searched for them. He felt no such connection now, nor did he sense any taint of The Otherside anywhere nearby.

"But maybe... "

He looked down, reached, and turned the rabbits over on the hot embers, then slowly and as non-threateningly as possible, walked toward them both. Lorne still sat relaxed and excited, happy to have what she thought of as an old friend back. The horse just stood there, snorting at times, unconcerned.

"It almost seems as if the horse is waiting. Waiting for something... the other horses perhaps? Or the ship I just saw... rather, what's on the ship?"

Travis looked at the ground, seeking the tell-tale hoof-prints. There were several good impressions pushed into the moist soil nearby, all normal. He looked at the back of the beast, seeking the tell-tale scar.

Nothing. No scar, yet this seemed to be the same horse they'd escaped on. He could only assume he'd been mistaken, or this horse was a twin of the other one. Either way, they needed it now, scar or not.

"*No scar. Not any devil's horns on those shoes. Nothing at all out of the ordinary. Except the fact that after all this time this horse, or its double, shows up again... at the precise time a ship carrying The Otherside and his band of killers is bearing down on the beach. But, coincidence or not, we must get as far from here as possible, and this animal will help with that.*"

He looked up at Lorne, still astride.

"I see you managed the saddle all right by yourself."

"That wasn't any sort of problem. You know I've been riding since I was little, at least my recollection is that I already told you that."

"Indeed, you did. However, I'm very glad you got the saddle on. It will save us time. Lorne, I'm sorry to say, we must leave here. Immediately."

He explained what he'd seen while gathering up their goods to pack. She wasn't thrilled about the news but agreed with the plan. "*She knows the danger, and how high the stakes are. We aren't that far from the beach, and it wouldn't take a determined search party long to find us, even if they weren't on horseback, which they most likely will be.*"

They ate on their feet while hurriedly dismantling the camp. He commented, "I'm presuming this will be our last hot meal for some time. It's a shame we can't enjoy it more."

"That may be so, and I don't like this any more than you do, but if there's one thing you've taught me, Travis, is that if we weren't still alive, we wouldn't be able to complain about it."

"Ah, now that's a fact, since if I were dead, I'd nary be critical of anything in this world of here

270

and now. There is no escaping that great indisputable truth, indeed." Laughing at the doleful humor, he gave the horse a friendly pat while loading their tarpaulin across its back. The beast gave him no reaction. "She seems to favor you well enough, even if I'm to be ignored. Ha! As long as she carries the load we give her, it's not a bother to me."

After packing up, they did their best to obliterate any trace of the camp, then fled.

The couple rode within a black and white kaleidoscope of shadow and sunlight. The sun came and went, its light twisted by the many scurrying clouds that chased one after another.

Travis ignored it all.

He had decided they needed to make the best speed possible, their objective being the safest place they might realistically reach before the ship unloaded its horses and riders to form into scouting parties.

"His return can't be for anything else... that so-called Captain has a thousand year old bone to pick with me. This proves we can't run forever; he'll just keep hunting us. At some point, I know I'll have to fight him again. Before then, I must get Lorne to safety."

Though speed was of the essence, he could not risk moving faster over the weak and uneven soil.

"Cracking a hoof, breaking a leg, we won't get far if that happens. Better to keep it slower and steady and hope we have enough of a lead to reach Lieutenant Billing's army camp before those raiders catch up to us."

If the army camp with its soldiers and cavalry was still there, he was fairly certain they would want to engage the raiders in combat, since they'd already chased after the Captain and his hirelings.

Getting to that camp was their only hope.

For over two hours they put as much distance between themselves and their old camp as possible. Lorne sat ahead, Travis behind, his arms wrapped around her, holding the reins. Occasionally, he looked back over his shoulder for pursuers, even though he knew it wouldn't do them much good if he saw any.

They had made good time to this point. The horse had been fresh when they started so they had pushed harder than he would have liked, but felt their danger justified the means. He fervently prayed that the past storm's brutal pounding of wind and rain had kept the soldiers of Billings' unit from breaking camp and moving out. That army had to be there.

But they weren't.

Lorne and Travis soon reached the remnants of the army camp. It was empty.

"They up and left, the whole lot of them, even with that storm bearing down. They were probably on the move as soon as they knew they'd lost the looters and thugs down at the beach. Must have been a hellish march, even with the wind at their backs, but I suppose their commander's orders were to report back with news of the mission's failure, and more importantly, the last known position of the raiders. Ha! Not much luck will be coming of that since the Captain's last position was laughing at them while on a ship pulling hard out to sea! Things won't go well if those two bunches ever do meet again."

After a very brief inspection of the former army encampment, they'd moved on. A short time later they had seen a break along the forest line. It was a rude but wide dirt path leading inland, obviously the route that the army had taken. The couple decided to turn west, still hoping to overtake the soldiers.

They exited the sandy environs brushing the coast. The more solid ground made it easier for the horse to move on. Travis relaxed, but only slightly.

"This harder ground lowers our chances of laming the horse in some sandy sinkhole, which is good, but it also gives any raiders pursuing us a better chance to catch up when they find it. No matter, we must keep moving."

So, they did, as quickly as possible and for several more miles while the sky darkened above them. Lorne spoke up.

"Travis, I think this is the same road that I told you about."

"What road is that? Sorry, I don't remember."

"The trading road. I'm sure that it's this road we're on now. It came from the ocean and ran from there to that big clearing a few miles from my old house, where all the families from miles around would come to bring their extra goods to sell or barter, like mine did."

Travis nodded, thinking back. She continued.

"The ships would dock, unloading rum and food and such, but sometimes nice items. In fact, my father bought a beautiful hand mirror from them, he gave it to my sister for her birthday."

Lorne paused, her breath shuddering, then, "I told you about this road when we were still near the other end of it at the trading spot, because I thought it would be faster for us to get to the ocean this way." She shook her head, "But, you didn't want to use it."

"Ah, that's right. I remember."

"Now here we are again with an army ahead of us, and the Captain's scouts behind us with the both of us in the middle. We're ridin' too slow to catch up to the help we need ahead or to escape from the killers behind."

He thought more about what she'd said, then blurted out.

"Wait. Lorne, you said that the "... ships would dock.". What did you mean by that?"

"Just exactly that."

"When we turned onto the road from the beach, I don't recall seeing a dock nearby."

She paused, gathering her thoughts, then replied.

"Once, when a few families and ours had so much salt-pork to sell that the traders couldn't transport it all by themselves, we agreed to take what they couldn't in our own carts down the road to their ship. Father thought it would be a good opportunity for my sister and I learn something about business, so he brought us children along to the ocean.

"Do tell. But what about the dock that wasn't there?"

Slightly exasperated, she replied, "I'm getting to that, Travis. At any matter, my story's done. The fact is, when we finally got to the end of the road at the ocean, I remember that a ship was tied up at a dock. But I didn't think much more of it because a few other children had also come along with their families, and we all ran down to splash about on the water's edge. While we played, the adults worked, and moved all of the food we'd brought onto the ship."

Travis asked, "So, let me get this clear in my head. There were no smaller boats to ferry your goods from shore to the ship, like the raiders did back at the other beach?"

"Nope, not to my recollection. They just rolled the carts onto the dock and then moved everything right onto the ship. I don't remember much more, but It didn't seem very special to me at the time, and still doesn't now."

"Uh oh. I hadn't thought of this before. We may have less time than I'd thought."

"What is there to think of? Why are you so concerned? There's no dock there now, probably because some big storm tore it out. And with the war on since then, no one's bothered to replace it."

Travis paused before replying. Beneath them, the horse walked along, unconcerned while continuing up the slight incline. Oddly, it seemed as fresh as it had when they had begun their trek.

"Lorne, I had been assuming that the raiders would be unloading their men and horses back at the same beach they'd left from, because that one was the easiest along this stretch to make landfall. But now I suspect that they only used it because they'd been running from the army and couldn't get to this closer one at the end of this road in time."

"And... so, what does that mean?"

"It means that at the end of this road, ships can sail in much closer to land than other places along the shoreline. Which means that his men have probably not been following us on horseback along the beach the way we had to travel. Instead, their ship likely sailed south all the way down to where the dock used to be. They anchored, then lowered down the horses and men into the shallows and they just waded onto shore. That saved them a lot of time. They might have sent a couple of scouts ashore where we had been, just to make sure we had gone, but I'm certain The Otherside knew we were fleeing in this direction. Of course, I don't know all this for certain, but I'm guessing they are much closer to us than I'd hoped for."

"But we'll make it to Lieutenant Billings and his men when they set up their overnight camp this evening, don't you think?

Travis looked behind them, again seeing nothing of their pursuers, but noting that the daylight noticeably dimming as they continued their ride westward. Unfortunately, he also noticed their pace was slowing. The horse was finally weakening after the long day of carrying them both.

"I can't say. I don't know exactly when they decided to break camp, but it may have been as long ago as when the storm began. They'd have a very large lead on us in that case, even though they must have been horribly slowed down."

"So, there's no hope then?"

"I'd say that after all we've both endured, there's always hope." He kissed the back of her neck, then continued.

"I'd be willing to bet there's at least an even chance that when the commander realized how bad the storm really was, he marched his main body of soldiers inland only a few miles and established an emergency camp to escape the brunt of the storm. Then he sent out a few scouts on horseback to brave the rains and wind to ride on and deliver his message to command."

Lorne sighed, her shoulders slumping in despair. Travis continued.

"But it's also possible they may have stayed down there in their original camp and have only packed up and moved out this morning after the storm was all over, the same as us."

"So, they may be right around the next bend?"

"Anything's possible, Lorne. We do need to keep moving if we're to get to them, and more importantly, keep away from those that follow."

"Travis, how do you know those raiders are really behind us? You'd think they'd have better things to do than follow a couple of folks who have no money or gold."

"It's really just a... strong feeling I have. His men are the ones who destroyed your home, but you managed to escape, so you're a symbol of unfinished business. As for me, in the past I had an... encounter with their Captain that didn't go so well for him. He wants revenge. So, the both of us still being alive are two very good reasons for him to come chasing after us So, as far as he's concerned. the mere fact that both of us are still alive makes two very good reasons for his men to come chasing after us."

Lorne stiffened, her voice shaking with rage. "I see. You'll be fine Travis because I'll have my vengeance upon their horrid Captain first." She reached down to lay her hand upon the sheath containing the Bowie Knife she still carried."

Travis said nothing.

The forest had become denser as they moved inland along the road. They continued for another few hundred yards, neither speaking again of the horror that stalked them, until finally the growing sluggishness of the horse became too apparent for them to ignore.

Travis stopped to dismount in the deepening twilit gloom. He removed the pack with their provisions and passed Lorne a ration while taking one himself. He gave the horse some of the fruit they'd found earlier, then slung the bag over his shoulder, took the reins, and walked on.

"If we're to have any chance of catching up to the army, we have to keep moving. I'll lead the horse until we either find them, or it's almost too dark to see anymore, then if we have to, we'll bivouac off the road as best we can. We'll have to hide behind some brush and trees."

"But Travis, it's a wide road, and I do believe the moon is close to full tonight. Don't you think we should just keep going?"

"We certainly can't travel in the dark through this forest. Only the barest slivers of moonlight will get through this thick canopy above us, and that's assuming there are no clouds, which we can't count on because we saw them rolling in earlier. Besides, even if we push ourselves and get lucky, the horse can't keep going all night. She'll have to rest. In fact, I'll take a couple more items off her."

He transferred to himself not only the bag with his modified spear inside, but also the sleeping roll he'd carried on his back for so long.

Only twenty minutes later, it happened.

They were still trudging along the road. Travis again glanced over his shoulder, an action now become habit during this long day of both retreat and pursuit. Nothing odd was to be seen within the shadowed sides of the forest as the darkness behind them crept closer every time he looked. He knew they would have to stop soon to find a suitable clearing for their bivouac before movement became impossible when utter blackness closed in around them.

Lorne dozed, while the horse below her, having carried the two of them most of the day with very little to eat, was run out. Travis hated to stop but knew they must. He began to wake Lorne so they could find a clearing off the road and rest for the night.

Then he heard the noise. Still holding the reins, he covered his ears, but it made no difference. The sound bored into him from nowhere and everywhere. He dropped to his knees in agony, hearing a malevolent clawing cacophony of sharp talons rending fissures deep into human skulls, gurgled moans scraped from within slit throats, and the broken twisting of iron flayed bone.

He could not escape the shrieking peals of pain drilling into his head.

The horse went drum-head tight. All signs of the beast's exhaustion had completely fled as it snapped its head back, whipping it from side to side.

Travis felt his hands burn bloody as the horse ripped the reins from them. The beast shivered in place, shaking its head, perhaps struggling against the alien manifestation that had invaded it. Now controlled by The Otherside, the animal that held Lorne had transformed into a dark creature of doom, silhouetted against the last shards of twilight.

Taking advantage of the pause, he grabbed its mane, and reached with bleeding fingers to again secure his grip on the reins.

In the waning light he watched as a scar appeared across the horse's back. That same mark had been there, then not, and was now there again. Somehow it had been disguised by The Otherside's arcane power. The scar was the same as he'd remembered it. This horse was obviously the same one they'd been riding before, the same beast that had been searching for them with the others.

"So! This horse has been under the sway of The Otherside all along! It was just waiting for its chance! We must escape!"

Suddenly the animal ceased shivering. It shook and stomped about with decision.

"LORNE! GET OFF THE HORSE! LORNE! GET OFF!"

Her head lolled toward him, eyes and ears uncomprehending. He reached up intending to yank her from the crazed animal's back. As he touched her, she seemed to rouse from the strange enervation that had seized her when the noise had begun. She lifted herself from the sprawling position along the neck of the creature, attempting to leap free from her ever more savage mount.

"I'm dizzy Travis! What is that ghastly sound? Help me! Help!"

The horse pranced a circle of four-hooved violence. Travis was scraped and stepped on, then finally beaten to the ground, forced to release the reins. Only the thick boots he now wore saved his ankles and feet from complete destruction.

Worst of all, his smashed and bloody hands could no longer hold on to Lorne.

Immediately after he'd released her, the animal broke away at full gallop, off the road and into the murk of forest shadows, deftly avoiding obstacles. Lorne lay low along its back, gripped in place by potent forces unknown.

Travis was laid low, sprawled twisted amid rocks and clumps of dirt kicked free upon the road. The big beast had banged hard into his head during the frantic half-minute of chaos and kidnapping. Now, watching Lorne carried away into darkness, he forced himself past pain to almost stand, at least managing a bent crouch.

Ignoring the disgorging blood from his broken nose, he shifted the burdens carried on his back, made sure the firearms still sheltered within their holsters, and then began a slow but steady shuffle in pursuit, his mind more clumsy than his stolid and determined gait.

Above him, the full moon's silver sheen battled nightfall, a bright slash through the forest, a spite to fell gloom. Below, he could see, at least a bit, what he needed to keep from falling on his face.

One goal propelled him beyond human endurance... to rescue Lorne from the animal that had once helped save their lives but had now become a kidnapper, another sad hostage to the mind-warping powers of The Otherside.

Oblique patterns of moonlight snared Travis within a crazy quilt of shadows as he trudged the brush and dirt below, so not seeing the horse's dead body until he tripped over it shouldn't have been a surprise. And it wasn't, for he had no room for any more emotions now.

Sprawled across the cooling body of the beast, he lay atop a length of fabric partially wrapped around the carcass. He pulled it free.

He held the shredded remnants of the dress she had been wearing.

"Lorne! Lorne! Where are you, Lorne?"

There was no reply.

His fist shook, heavy with the torn fabric it clenched. The dead silence of the forest muffled hammers of rage pounding inside his skull.

He stood. Assessing his options, he attempted to calm himself. Finally, he dropped the cloth and peered into the moon-lit darkness.

A violent scene of struggle and death surrounded him. The twisted body of what could only be one of the raiders lay contorted among broken branches and... something else.

Travis went closer to the body. A large hilt protruded from its chest, directly above the heart.

It was the Bowie knife that Lorne had carried.

With an effort, his weakened grasp managed to remove it. He wiped the blade clean of gore upon the dead man's shirt. Nearby lay Lorne's broken belt, the scabbard still attached. He affixed it to his own belt, then replaced the big blade within the leather sheath.

An iron focus had replaced his blind blood rage.

"Well, she did manage to kill at least one of her abductors. I hope it was the one who ripped her dress off... !"

It was obvious that she had fought back but had not been able to stop the others. Why the horse was dead was a mystery. Either the raiders had killed it because its job was finished, or perhaps the poor critter had just given up, tired of being a puppet for evil.

Travis wasted no more time considering what had happened here. He knew that he must continue his pursuit. But which way now? He moved one way, then another, spinning in circles, lost in the forest. Finally, he stopped, staring straight forward, mind's eye filled with visions of revenge.

Delirious by blood loss and seething with fury, he began to see that what should not exist... for before him, a pinpoint of brightness formed in the dark, while along the forest floor, shadows began glowing, pointing a phosphorescent, blue-green path toward the slowly expanding light ahead.

"Impossible... that can't be here in this forest or anywhere else! I must be going mad. Or dying. Or both."

Dizzy and stumbling forward, his attention on the shimmering turf beneath him, he struck a low hanging branch full on with his forehead. A loud pop briefly echoed off the nearby tree trunks. His last thought before blackness overwhelmed him was the terrible memory of Lorne, helpless, slumped forward, her arms akimbo as the horse crashed away from him.

His exhausted form collapsed and lay still, heaped hopeless and cold.

The white light before Travis swelled wide, engulfing him. There was a brief flash, then waiting darkness returned to claim the dying man... but he was gone.

Only muted rage remained.

14. BREATHING WITHOUT A BREATH

Travis awakened, thirsty. His mouth hung open, painfully dry, yet unable to breath otherwise. Thick wads of some cotton-like substance plugged both nostrils, sealed in place with his own hardened blood. He lay on his back, chill on one side, warmth soaking the other. Red firelight glow reflected from the ceiling.

He rose slightly, hoping to see more, but that was a mistake. His head whirled one direction while the world's orbit spun the opposite. Immediately exhausted from that one small effort, he fell back and struggled to remember what he'd briefly seen.

He'd found himself within a cavern where a small fire burned inside a stone-lined pit dug into the floor. He could feel the breeze of a slight draft that pulled smoke from the cave. Stacks of cut wood lay nicely trimmed along one wall. Shelves and nooks along the walls held various implements, oddly shaped tools, and other items, organized by an unknown plan.

And... a woman had looked up from a book, dark hooded eyes boring deep into his own.

Trying to raise himself again, he found he could not. He had many questions, yet his weakness crushed his voice to a croaking whisper.

"Lorne... "

The eyes he'd just seen now loomed above his, and a hard, somehow familiar, woman's voice whip-cracked his ears.

"I brought you here through the Between. You have lost much blood. Your skin was cold. I could not rouse you after you had fallen. Do not speak. Do not move. You still may not live."

She reached over, out of his sight, rustled about briefly, then brought an earthenware cup over. She lifted his head slightly, pushing the vessel to his lips.

"Drink. Drink as much as you can, and then more. It will bring strength.

Again, came his torn cough of words, "Who are... ?"

"Quiet, fool! I know you heard me! I know you are not deaf, yet you act as if you are! Do not attempt to speak or move!"

She tilted the cup's liquid into his mouth, shaking her head in dismissal as the hot syrupy substance poured into him.

"It has been said that you should not die. Not that I care."

Too weak to turn away, he swallowed the brew as he'd been ordered. The pungent liquid passed his lips, almost burning them as it did so. As it flowed down his gullet it cooled more quickly than was natural, suffusing throughout him from core to extremities. A heavy cloak braided of winter's chill and bright fragments of polar light soon lay upon him. Then, heat grew within, melting the ice of his bruised and broken bones. Soon he felt as if the sun itself had burst inside him.

Again, the eyes came close, the lips spoke,

"This is powerful medicine. You will be more than you are now. Ha! If you survive. But... it is your only hope to overtake The Otherside in time! Oh, and that female you obsess about. Ha!"

He gazed deep into those eyes. Within them, specters danced behind the tattered edges of a curtained stage. He forced himself to turn away, then rasped words again.

"You. I am sure that I've never met you, yet... you are familiar. Do you know me? Have we somehow met?"

"You insist upon speaking! I see it is no use telling you not to, you will not obey. Well, perhaps the medicine will fail, and I won't have to listen to you again. Ha! Of course, I know you, not that you know me, not that I ever cared. Not so long ago, when the night brought the searching horses nearby, it was suggested that I protect you and your woman as you slept inside your tiny house. It was I that made the horses turn away, convincing them that there was nothing which their loathsome master sought."

He croaked out another question.

"But it was a horse, one of the same, that took her last night! We heard a horrid noise and it attacked me, then galloped off with Lorne. Why didn't you stop that?"

Her voice cradled the crack of spines snapping in two.

"I was busy! Do you think I have nothing else to do? Do you think your problem is the only crisis on this Earth? Ha! If you only knew! Besides, I wasn't warned this time, as I had been before! The Outer Forces cannot be watching every time, and all across the wheres! They're not omnipotent, even if they act like they are! Ha!"

She settled close to him, face leaning in, her anger splashing bloody outlines around every word,

"They are not horses! How do you think that darkness means nothing to their vision? Why do you think the one that stole your woman followed a commanding sound like a dog? They are not of this realm!"

She took a breath and leaned back.

"Forget your questions, listen to me, and be grateful, even if you cannot find it in you to be smart! Before that night, I had already saved your life! You were inside the house helping fight the evil men on horseback. You were alongside your woman, although you did not know she would become that then, when I shot the raider on the porch! He was aiming straight between your eyes! He would have easily killed you. Ha! The Otherside would then be staying for another thousand years, and I would have to linger here as well. The joke would be again on me, a good laugh. Ha!"

Travis struggled to speak around the numbness now seizing his lips, tongue, and throat.

"What? Another thousand years? What are you speaking of?"

"Again, will I tell you this. Do not you speak. Do not move. Do not think. Do not try to make sense of what is happening. I try now to save you, but this medicine brings either fast healing and great power, or poisoned rank deformities and faster death! But... it decides! The medicine sees who you are, what your true self is within. It knows how you are made of what you are made of! After you awaken in the still and hidden place, we shall see how long you live, and if you have grown strong. I would try to wish you good luck, but that is not important to me."

She moved away, now intoning enigmatic syllables of a language already a thousand years dead. Occasionally her arm swung into sight as it moved in time to her strange, primeval chanting.

Suddenly, the most piercing shaft of intense blue he'd ever seen streamed in from just past his vision, beyond where the woman sat. It was as if a door leading outside had momentarily been opened and something rushed inside, out of the cold. The blanket around him grew even heavier, the force of the invisible energy from beyond laid upon it. Finally, the bright blue light fled, leaving only a tinge of faint purple that twisted shadowed fissures, until it too was absorbed into the rapidly forming shell around Travis.

The stink of low tide filled the close space, while her chants changed in form and timbre, becoming a jostling, cajoling murmur, as if calming a skittish lapdog during a storm.

Searing chill overtook his prone form, bubbling up outside his body, first enveloping the boots he still wore. It rose ever upward, hugging his skin to form a sealed body cast of living, frozen flames around him. Soon he was encased from soles to skull, only his face clear.

From the effects of the potion within and the... *something*... from without, his battered body was newly assailed and twisted, transformed entirely, seized by writhing, inky frost that seeped into every fragment of his being. Soon he chilled beyond shivering and the translucent blue fire flowed upward to cover his head completely.

Travis was unsurprised to find that he was

breathing without a breath. It was just a fact, another impossible reality. He didn't care anymore. All he wanted now was to find Lorne and kill The Otherside.

His thoughts shrunk inward from the effects of the elixir, devolving into memories from childhood, *"I bet I look just like a spit-bug... all cased up like a mummy in froth and bubbles. Now to find out if I get squished like one or not."*

Darkness veiled his eyes and mind. He stopped thinking and did not see what happened next.

Appearing from beyond the ceiling, a strange rift mangled the realities of then, now, that way and over there. It grew within the room, pulsating, alive with purpose. Its eddies crawled, forming a vortex of violet-blue energy that reached out to engulf the cocoon. Within it, Travis moved from the cave's stony confines to enter the interstices of the Between, where blazing bright forges wrested bone and flesh to hammered pulp, then reformed them, twisted new.

Unknowing, unconscious, yet secure and newly altered within his pod, Travis hurtled across time and distance toward an island that he'd seen before, but only from above.

"Heat. Must get out from under the sun, away from this heat."

The sun beat upon Travis from directly above. He lay on the deck of a small vessel that gently bobbed in its mooring. The peculiar cocoon he'd traveled here in was gone.

Hemp ropes were strewn around beneath him. He felt as if he'd been carelessly tossed into the boat. His back creaked with a dull ache, awkwardly bent across a bundle of tightly lashed together bone-white wooden branches.

The clothes he wore seemed to have shrunk. His motions met with an overall tightness from his garments, which ripped at any sudden movement. When he raised his hand to his nose, the sleeve burst, revealing an oddly unfamiliar arm. He knew it was still *himself*, but now larger and more powerfully constructed.

"Constructed?" He looked his arms, legs, and chest. All were larger and more thickly muscled. *"I think RE-constructed."*

His strange new hands probed his broken nose. It was clear and cleaned of blood, and the pain had gone. It was healed. But was he?

"She told me that if I lived, I'd be more than what I was before. Is this what she meant? A bigger body, fatter fingers? But also... "

Travis reached down to check his oversized boots. It was as he'd suspected. They fit perfectly now.

"That's an unexpected blessing! What else has changed? I suppose I will find out soon."

He looked around at his surroundings. The boat bobbed gently with his movements. It was tied up at the end of a man-made canal which led off about a hundred feet away, then turned sharply where water faded into surface mist. He could not see around the bend, but guessed it must lead to some outlet, most likely the ocean.

A tall wooden wall extended away on both sides of the canal, continuing off out of sight. He could see that many thousands of driftwood bundles had been tied together with ropes woven from thick grass cords to make it. Everywhere he looked, he could see that the palisade wall continued unbroken around the jungle clearing that surrounded him.

Outside, gusts beat upon the perimeter relentlessly as winds shook random sections with dry clatters. Yet only the slightest breeze occasionally passed between stormy exterior and placid interior.

Indeed, the atmosphere inside was held immobile in this static slice of time. The hot stillness was oppressive. The only clothes he wore were his old trousers, and his torn, blood-stained shirt. Both were much too tight. As he started to get up, he found another item nearby on the hot decking. He grabbed it to examine.

It was an odd, wide-brimmed, oblong hat made of what he thought might be leather, but of a type he'd never seen before. The brim was crushed, and the hat seemed to have been carelessly tossed there, merely an afterthought.

He felt his face slowly burning. He pulled the hat over his head, molding it into passable shape, a shield against the furnace above. Shortly, he felt the temperature around his entire body drop noticeably.

"This hat does seem to keep me uncommonly cool. Is this another item from that woman? Or something from the Outer Forces folks? Either way, it's good to have."

Even as he lay cooling beneath the shade of the odd hat, he knew he must move soon. His initial confusion had passed, and laying here was uncomfortable, between the furnace above and the ropy needles below. It seemed to him that the spiky fiber coils of hemp rope upon which he lay nuzzled his flesh with sharp thorns of spite. Someone had tossed his unconscious form here for a reason, or just didn't care. He really didn't either.

He was happy to be alive, to be able to continue the hunt for Lorne, and to enact revenge against the Otherside, whose evil minions had abducted her.

"Ha! As that woman would say." He flexed his arms, moved his legs. *"I'm still alive. And changed somehow, improved, maybe? I guess that drink she gave me decided that I was worth saving, after all. But none of this means anything if I can't find Lorne! Where is she? And... where am I? Still by the beach, or at another one, perhaps? And how many days have passed? How far away from her am I?"*

Carefully, he peeled himself free from the awkward sprawl and sat up slowly, worried about the debilitating vertigo he'd suffered the last time he'd done so. His body was bruised by unremembered pummelings somehow suffered while unconscious, but his head, remarkably, was clear now. He stood, the hot decking reflecting sun back into his eyes. He looked around. No ill effects were evident other than a strange difference of perspective, as if he were seeing his surroundings from a slightly higher vantage.

"I've grown taller. Things look different... they are different, and so am I."

He pulled the hat from his head, and immediately felt the heat again. He rearranged its folds and brim to a better fit, then replaced it. Again, it immediately dispelled the rays of the unrelenting sun to something tolerable.

He surveyed the little ship he found himself on. About twenty-five feet long, with a single mast supporting two furled sails, it nevertheless had a short curved stern funnel, providing exhaust for what he assumed was a modern steam engine below. The vessel was moored to a pair of small pilings that had been pounded deep into the sandy earth.

No one else was in sight.

On the decking behind where he'd awakened, propped up against bone-white driftwood, was a large bindle wrapped in a gum blanket. Many large protuberances of unknown device jutted haphazardly forth, unseen, under the material. It was tightly bound around itself with several leather straps, one of which he recognized.

"Be damned if that ain't my gun belt. But where are the weapons?"

He undid his belt from around the bag. It was stained a slight green, the leather sprinkled with shards of crackling seaweed. Some had also caught in the buckle. It was obvious that it had been exposed to sea water for a time. When he removed the other straps, he found they held similar artifacts of their journey across the water.

The heat was relentless inside the stockade of clattering sticks in which he worked. Travis was thankful for both his odd hat and the occasional wisp of sea mist that snuck inside on a vagrant breeze. That pittance of moisture reminded him that, although his strength and health were recovered except for a few painful bruises, he would need fresh water very soon.

Finally, the last strap released; the gum blanket fell, open, its contents revealed.

His eyes hooded, he looked over the items now exposed. He could see why there had been so many lumps and bumps sticking out. Everything seemed to have been quickly tossed into an untidy heap, then jammed together with a tight wrap.

Most of what he found were familiar items, possessions either his or Lorne's, that had been recovered from the site of the abduction, including her boots. A smaller work shirt and sturdy skirt had been wrapped around them. But there were other items as well. The first of those were two full canteens, both army issue and covered in standard thick cloth. Immediately he drank his fill from one, then continued with his hurried inventory. He knew time was crucial to his search; the more he lost here, the less was to be had for finding Lorne.

"And to discover where I am, and where that nameless woman in the cave has gallivanted off to. She's the only one who can tell me now, unless Mr. One or Alyssia shows up again."

He hadn't long to wait. While he dug his old items out of the pile, he came across a few new items which had obviously been added, like his strange, cooling hat, and a large shirt and pants that had been rolled up together and tossed in. While putting on the new clothing, he again almost tossed away the iron horseshoe he'd found at the beach, but for some reason, he once more changed his mind before dumping it, instead transferring it to the new shirt's front pocket.

Quickly, he clothed himself, relieved to find that the clothing not only fit, but also offered better protection from the sun than did the torn and tattered rags he had been wearing.

He was so hurried that he almost overlooked the square of folded parchment that fell out from the jumbled lot.

He paused, unsure of exactly what he saw. Then another zephyr blew gently by, pushing the light material around amongst the other items, partially opening a creased edge to reveal what could only be writing. He snatched it up before it blew away. Travis studied the blocky hand-printed text.

- YUR WELLCOM - YUR NOT DEAD - SURPRISE! YUR INSIDES MADE BETER I THOT YU WER - WUT YU DRNK HERE WEN YU WAS SICK - ALWAYS IT NOS INSIDES - MAK SOME TIME BIGGR MOST TIME DEAD - HA HA HA - I NO CARE - NOW YUR HEELD - AN GROWN - UP BIG STRONG TOOO - BUT - LISTEN CLOSE! - IF YU GET BIG HURT BY BIGGR - YU MUS EAT - EAT LEAFS INSDE SMAL POWCH - THIS WHAT I TOL YU I WUD GIVE YU! - WHA OUTR FORCES TOL ME GIVE YU - BUT BIG DANGR NOW - YUR ON HIS LAND NOW - YU WENT FAST THRU THE BETWEEN! - YU THER BFORE HIS BIG SHIP GET THER - NOW YU GET YUR LADY OFF BIG SHIP!! - NOW YU STOP TH OTHERSIDE!!! - NOW I DO TOOO CARE - YU KILL TH OTHERSIDE!!!! - GUD LUK - YUR WELLCOM -

He re-read the note several times, struggling with its meanings.

"Alright. She may not have been the friendliest woman, but she obviously saved my life to give me a chance to rescue Lorne and kill The Otherside, or maybe not in that order. Either way, it's clear that I have lived to fight

296

another day. But what did she mean by saying 'I'm on his land now, before his big ship come there'? And where is this 'powch' with a leaf inside?"

He kept an eye out for anything strange or odd while continuing to organize his inventory and dress himself. Both pistols were there, jammed inside their holsters. Their extra bullets and gunpowder were secure as well. However, the carbine was missing. He shrugged his shoulders at its loss. The pack of food was whole, and he ate a bit because he knew he should, although he had little hunger. Finally, he checked the case containing his spear.

On the tip had been placed a sort of sheath made of thin wood. It was tied tightly in place by a grass-like twine. A large "X" was scrawled on one side, on the other were two letters, "O.S.".

The hair behind his neck rose, and some primeval instinct gibbered its fear at him, forbidding him to untie the knot that held the sheath on. When, out of a foolish cat-like curiosity, he brought it to his nose for a tiny sniff, he yanked it away as he caught the faint whiff of a necrotizing stench, infinitely more mephitic than even the putrid drippings of a bleeding carbuncle. Poison. It violently assailed his sense of smell, momentarily deadening it, causing his newly-recovered nose to swell and itch.

"Haven't smelled anything even close to that reek since the men's feet were rotting off during the winter of 'sixty-three. Have to remember to be careful with that blade."

Travis replaced the spear inside its pack then stood, still acutely conscious of how his body had changed. He felt larger, heavier, more solid, and strong, yet at the same time seemed to be lighter on his feet. He estimated that his height had actually increased by a couple of inches, and perhaps as much as double that across his chest. Both arms and legs had grown proportionately as well.

"Obviously, the whatever-it-was that I drank and whatever happened inside that pod not only saved my life, it also turned me into some sort of brute. When all this nonsense with The Otherside is over, I could probably make a living as a boxer. If Lorne approves, of course. But first I need to find her. Which means I have to find a way out of this corral and get going."

As he gathered up and re-equipped from the disorganized pile, he made a pleasant discovery. A new sheath made of lightweight metal now held the Bowie knife secure on his belt. Its length was scribed with a flowing script, unlike any he'd seen. He checked the blade. It was sharper than ever before.

Travis eventually found the "powch" and checked inside to find the promised dried leaves. Unlike the stink of the horrid spear blade, the leaves had a pleasant, if faintly medicinal, aroma. He finished draping himself with the weapons and supplies. Thinking to ascertain how long he'd been putting himself back together here inside the palisade wall, he glanced up toward the sun. Unmoving, it remained still and motionless, where it was when he first regained consciousness, almost straight above his head.

"Or is it really EXACTLY above me? How can that be? I've never seen the sun that high before, I didn't know it could happen. And where is my

shadow?"

Now he looked around him. Indeed, every object in sight had no shadow, nowhere for darkness to hide and fester.

"Where am I that such a thing is possible?"

Even with the strange cooling powers of his new hat, the spongy air swathed him like overheated shaving lather. Unmoving and wretched, it clamped the heat within its cloying grasp to thwart even the delusion that any refreshing breeze might have ever existed here since time primeval.

Then he noticed the complete lack of natural sound from anything other than the brush of wind, or a muted crash of sea. He was unable to hear anything living, anywhere, around him. Thinking he must be mistaken, yet afraid he might be right, he paused, listening intently.

"No gulls. No bugs or buzzes. No critters rustling along their paths inside the tall grass. Just what's outside the barrier. I wonder what else this wall is keeping out, and why the sun seems to be locked at high noon. Or maybe, it's keeping something in. That certainly includes me, so I'd better find a way out if I'm to have time to meet the big boat that Lorne's on."

Laden with his goods, supplies, and weapons, yet feeling lighter than before, Travis began to appreciate his new-found strength as he explored inside what he began to think of as a "pen".

"My prison. A pen for a pet goat. Or one awaiting slaughter."

After searching along the enclosure, he found no door, Travis looked up again. The sun had not moved. The wooden fence shivered, again struck by an outside gust of wind. He tried to rip apart a section, but to no avail, even with his increased strength, somehow, he could not tear apart the strands of grassy rope to create even a smallish rift he might be able to slip out between. It was as iron in his grasp.

Frustrated, Travis picked up a loose branch of driftwood, aimed toward the fence-top, and slung it over. It spun as it flew, pinwheeling in a fast arc toward the outside. As it passed over, its spin slowed while a soft hissing emanated from around it, like sand showering over a taut canvas tent. It faded into nothingness before leaving his sight.

"Alright. No door. But goats can jump. Let's see how far I can."

Unable to ascertain which direction he faced since the unmoving sun gave no reference, he assumed that the ocean was the source of the occasional rattling gusts. He faced away from that direction of the wind, keeping it at his back, wishing to attempt his leap inland, rather than toward the sea.

"Of course, it all depends upon me making it over that barrier in the first place, and not falling flat on my face."

Backing up several yards, he gauged the leap, then made a couple of test jumps from a dead standstill. He rose more than twice as far as he'd ever managed before, and still felt light enough on his feet, even loaded down with all his gear, that he could jump even higher. Without further thinking, he set off with full bore strides toward the wall.

One, two, six, ten paces, more quickly than any he'd run before, then...

"NOW!"

His feet left the ground. He rose higher and the top of the fence came closer as he hurtled inexorably forward. Pulling his legs closer to his torso, up he still went, clearing the barrier's top by several inches as he passed its peak.

Instantly, the viscid heat and bright eternal noon of the enclosure was replaced by a moist darkness cloaked in an essence of fear.

He had thought his jump was aiming inland, away from the ocean, but he landed on his feet, charging toward the water. His momentum carried him several steps forward after what could have been a harrowing landing, since it had taken his eyes a few seconds to adapt from blinding daylight to the moonlit tableaux he now found himself within.

Shocked at how easily his strides had carried him over the fence, and how quickly he'd been able to, somehow, sense the terrain to land safely while still unable to see, he fought down his own disbelief. He wondered what the limits of his new-found abilities might be.

"If I'm going to be fighting The Otherside, I'll surely find out."

Yet, like so many of the recent events that ranged far beyond what he or any other sane man would have considered normal, this latest supernatural incident had now become just another matter of acceptance for him. These were facts, and nothing good would come of ignoring them, as chilling or outlandish as they might seem at first.

The long dead voice of an old friend he had never known chanted softly in his mind, *"The enemy of mine enemy, thou art my friend."* It was, he surmised, a memory of dust dredged from the life of his own ancient ancestor.

"Another something that never happened, at least not to me. Or perhaps, not yet."

Unlike the area within the walled anomaly in which he had awakened, there was no dearth of sound along this edge of jungle. Skitterings and trembling shifts among the leafy fronds and branches surrounding him betrayed the unseen presence of countless nocturnal denizens.

"Either hunting prey or trying not to become it. Or both. The law of dog eat dog. Or maybe out here, it's snake eat snake." Travis looked around, seeing only shadowed glimpses of movement within the foliage.

"Or more likely, something worse is stalking around out here. Much worse if I know what kind of toys The Otherside enjoys playing with."

As if to punctuate that last thought, low pitched human-like moans emanated from the jungle's phantom gloom. He tensed, standing still while he listened. *"Sounds like I'm certainly not alone out here."*

The ever-more insistent vocal articulations surrounded him both near and far. Louder and faster they wailed, their morose beseeching now amplified into a soul-piercing cry from ten thousand undug graves.

"Only The Otherside could invite this many happy folks to a party. At least now I know I'm getting close to that diabolical S.O.B.'s playground."

Shuffling crashes banging amongst underbrush became louder, moving slowly closer under cover of the night. Travis saw a hundred pairs of chalk-white eyes staring back at him from the jungle as they approached. The clash and clatter went on, ever louder. He moved away from the awful noises, toward the water again, toward the moonlight, toward anywhere away from the dark and eerie cries of undead spirit hordes.

"They're everywhere, whatever they are! Even sharing lunch with The Otherside almost seems a better bet than this nightmare!"

Still on the move, he again glanced behind him into the blue-edged jungle. This time, several two-legged shufflers could be seen coming out of the overgrowth, slowly limping or lumbering toward him along the moonlit sands, their intent clear. He moved away even faster. Then his anger welled up, prompting a decision to speak to these once-human creatures, to at least try to communicate. He abruptly stopped to face them, yelling.

"Hey boys, I'm not the one you're after! He's my enemy too! I mean to kill The Otherside bastard. I'm on your side, fellas!"

And with that, the spectral wailing stopped, silence descended. The phantom forms turned away, melting back into the shadows of the jungle. They had heard, and they were gone. The sounds of four-legged critters going about the deadly business of their nighttime lives resumed.

"Well, how about that. Sometimes it pays to talk. It worked! For now."

15. LITTLE JAMES AND BILLY BILL

Travis lifted his eyes out toward the glassy sea, seeing where his true enemy now lurked in this time and place. He recognized The Otherside's vessel as it steamed closer. It was the selfsame ship that had played its part as bolt-hole for the evacuating raiders on the beach. Now that gray and black juggernaut loomed ever larger, cutting moving scars across the water as it approached the dock, bearing its master's implacable intent.

Off to one side, almost midway between zenith and horizon, and dominating the sky behind the grotesque shadow of the vessel, lay the gleaming moon. As he stared toward the brightness of that mystic orb, it was as if the silvered path reflected across the surface of the sea to the shore invited him to walk out, and upon, and all the way up to it.

He was not foolish enough to try to replicate that miracle.

"Only one man was able to walk on the waters, and I'm not He. Besides, I don't think I need to go to the moon. What I need is to find a way aboard that demonic vessel."

He could see lanterns, few and shuttered as they were, carried by jerking figures moving with gnat-like agitation to and fro across the vessel while they carried out their abysmal duties.

"Heartless fools consumed by greed! They're burning their souls for The Otherside, a blind

exchange for swag and plunder!"

Wrapped with rage, he stared hard at the approaching ship, then gripped the hilt of the heavy blade hanging from his belt, loosening the deadly knife in its sheath.

"But now I'm here to show anyone who gets in my wat that there's no future in that. Lorne is somewhere on board that ship. Nothing will stop me from rescuing her."

A distant *"CHUG CHUG CHUG"* came to him from the approaching vessel, which looked much larger from this angle than it had when he'd been spying on it from his perch up in the tree with Lorne. An errant wave surged in, sloshing over his boots, and bringing his focus back to the danger steaming toward him.

"Alright. If I can see them, they can do likewise. I'd be better served by getting out of this surf and backing into the shadows of the tree line behind me."

Travis hastily backpedaled, toward what he thought must be the driftwood wall, but then stopped. There was no wall to be seen.

"Why am I not surprised? After all, it was a wind-blown day inside there, yet out here it's a calm sea, probably sometime after midnight."

What he'd seen before from inside as a driftwood barrier wall, was perceived from out here as the worm eaten bottom hull of a shipwrecked hulk. It lay on its side, partially buried in the sand, overhung with thick leaves from the cornucopia of plants and vines now growing over and through it. The keel was consumed by its own rot, and the entire hull, or at least what he could see of it, lay unbroken an unknown distance back into inky jungle. Looking up, he saw the cracked decay along the top edge of the hull, exactly where he'd come over on his leap out from the sunbaked enclosure inside.

"I may need to get back inside that corral at some point, so I'll need to know where to find it within all this foliage. This jungle's thick with plants... and animals too."

Green life teemed in profusion around him. Travis searched for a suitable trunk on which to carve a mark of some sort. A large patch of dark wood stood out prominently just below the area from which he'd jumped. He pulled out the Bowie and quickly hacked strips of bark away in a foot-long segment an inch or so wide to reveal the fresh white wood underneath. To him, this slash of exposed inner pulp shone bright and was noticeable even in the jungle gloom.

"If you know what you're looking for... that mark is obvious. If not, it's lost among this maze of vines and leaves.

Only a few minutes had passed, yet when he turned his attention back to the sea, the approaching ship had grown noticeably larger. As it slowly glided forward, the tenor of the ship's steam engine changed, now only a low rumbled clanking of hiss and thud. Faint shouts could be heard from the crew as they yelled curses at one another while preparing to dock the ship.

The milky sheen of the moon guided his steps. Finding his way toward the ship in the glowering light, Travis became as one with the other dark creatures of the night. He hugged the murk and mess along the jungle's edge, boots silently racing along the thin strip of sand which the narrow beach grudgingly lent.

For several minutes he hurtled along the skinny path, dodging strewn about fallen logs or leaping over the occasional snapped-off tree limb. Focused on his objective, he ignored this leftover evidence from earlier storms. He ran without pausing.

The ship passed around the bend and left his view. He increased his pace, not wishing to lose any chance to see Lorne when, or if, she was brought down the gangplank.

In front of him he saw a strange, coiled mass, protruding far out from the jungle and spreading long into the sea, that seemed to be a high wall of greenish black leaves blocking his way along the beach. A doorway faintly revealed itself as part of the barrier. This wall blended in with the profusion of growth nearby and seemed like any of the other natural barriers he'd already passed tonight. He decided to just leap across it.

As he strode toward a leap that would have before been an impossible task of human strength, he again counted in his head the steps that led to his departure point, in this case a fallen tree trunk only some eight feet from the hurdle he challenged.

"One, two, six, ten... NOW!"

Once more the power of his enhanced body launched him over the obstacle with a more than human force. As he arced above it, a patrol of three men came into his view. They lounged about a campfire, joking, and passing a bottle. Obviously, they were making only the minimum effort to keep watch on this far extremity of The Otherside's citadel.

Beyond the lazy trio, on the far side of a second wall, he could see a series of three docks.

308

The two nearest him had only a few of small vessels tied up, with no men at work to be seen.

In contrast, on the dock closest to the center of the settlement, the activity was intense. Stevedores working by lantern light grappled with ropes and heavy lines flung from the ship, snugging her to anchor.

All this he noticed in the few heartbeats while airborne. He landed on the hard-packed ground and drew his knife.

The guards had given themselves no such opportunity of observation. Three men had been sharing a bottle and a joke amongst themselves when the fast moving silhouette of motion flicked the corner of their eyes. Boozy torpor interrupted, bawdy laugh forgotten, they twisted their heads in the direction of this new and unexpected threat.

What they saw was an echo from the distant past, a swordsman with his weapon pointed at their throats.

"Wal, Gee Oh Dee! Who's that? Where'd he come from, Billy Bill?"

"Don't matter! Git 'im, Little James! Shoot 'im, kill 'im now!"

The two men who spoke reached for the weapons on their hips, drunken reflexes slowed by the alcohol they'd consumed.

Deep memory stirred within Travis. He pounded toward the frantic group, the big-bladed Bowie in hand, ready to strike.

"Those names... seems like I should know... where have I... ?"

Then he remembered. These two would have butchered him, had he not lain under a corpse inside a shallow trench.

"You two! I know the both of you, Little James and Billy Bill! You greedy cowards were killin' my wounded brothers after we were overrun on the battlefield! And then you were going through their pockets! I watched you both!"

The accusation startled them both into a brief pause, while the third man, spasmodically flung the almost empty vessel toward the fast approaching man. Travis moved easily to one side, the glass projectile passing him by.

"Must make this quick and quiet, can't let them fire off their weapons."

After tossing the bottle, the third man scurried off, not bothering to even pick up his rifle from where it lay. Travis glanced back to see him open the barrier's door wide, escaping into the jungle blackness beyond. That door now hung open, caught on some overlarge vine or undergrowth sprouted besides the ill-maintained wall.

Their moment of short-lived indecision past, the two before him sputtered enraged grunts from their besotted lips.

But it was too late. His voice as iron, Travis had become a hammer of imminent revenge.

"How many of my army's wounded men did you sneak up on and murder after a battle, while they lay helpless and crying for mercy?"

The raider called Billy Bill managed to draw his revolver from its holster, bringing it up to aim at Travis. He growled his answer while pulling back its hammer.

"Plenty but plain to see it weren't enough, since you ain't dead yet!"

Travis moved in, wielding the big blade. He could see the raider's finger begin to tighten on the pistol's trigger. But he was faster. The razor edge of his knife was as a guillotine, slashing down to strike and sever hand from arm. Billy Bill's naked wrist fountained away its warm red life, spraying down on both gun and his former appendage, fingers still gripping the weapon where they lay entwined as one upon the sand below. Silence strangled screams as he grabbed his stump, choking on incredulity.

A few feet away was Little James, he staggered drunkenly, fearful and fumbling with his holster, unable to clear his pistol to shoot. Travis spoke to them both, his voice now a gravel path to the graveyard.

"You two cowards joined up with your so-called Captain 'cause after the war was over you couldn't keep on killin' and stealing like you had been, could you? No more war, no more easy pickin's. So now you boys and that ugly foreign bastard just carry the war around with you, rapin', killin', and stealin', whenever you want. Well, not after tonight you don't. Those days are done for, and so are you."

Billy Bill couldn't staunch the blood flowing from his stump despite his frantic efforts. Knowing his end loomed close, his desperate heart was suddenly filled with the same fear and terror he'd enjoyed watching in his many victim's eyes while they tried to escape his brutalities.

Travis wanted no part of inflicting painful punishments, only wishing to insure they could not alert those inside. If killing these raiders was a payback for a small part of what he owed them, all the better. But the priority was Lorne. He had to get inside. He must save her, at any cost.

The inebriated Little James never could quite

get a bead on the intruder. Even as he was finally able to aim his weapon in the general direction of Travis, he was dead before he knew it, for the man who held the big blade leapt close to slash deep slices into quivering flesh. The brigand dropped the pistol and died as he had lived; just another mean, confused drunk.

The other man was on his knees, attempting to peel his own dead hand from its death grip around the weapon with his other. Looking up, Billy Bill ground out an oath from between clenched teeth and foaming lips. He spoke with unfocused rage as his bleary eyes sought to penetrate the darkness in which Travis stood.

"You're a demon!"

"I'm not, but your Captain is!"

Travis swung his fist into the grave-robbing raider he'd promised to repay, striking his nose square on with all the force of his enhanced strength. The man's head shot back with a rip-cracking snap; the bone structure of his nose driven deep into his brain. In his agony of expiry, the grotesquely clothed pistol that he'd been fumbling with in anger only an instant before dropped onto the bloody sand from doubly-dead fingers. Neither remained a threat.

The severed wrist leaked his dead fluids out. Watering the thirsty sand.

Travis surveyed the scene. His way was clear in his search for Lorne.

"How did I manage all that? Potions and spells? Maybe... maybe not." He looked at the ship on the far side of the inner wall, now drawn up and lashed still against the planking, engine silent, with its cargo being hoisted down and carried off into hidden recesses of the town. *"But*

312

none of this matters if I can't find Lorne. Time to clean up here and move on."

Keeping his attention on the activity over at the ship, he went back to the green-black wall that he'd just leapt over. Strange scratchings and the occasional sound of semi-human snuffles from beyond the wall betrayed the death that lurked there.

He dragged the two corpses into the surf to obscure footprints and tracks, then back to the wall by the far door that still hung open, where he unceremoniously chucked each one through. Their corpses crashed to the ground, treats for the hungry jungle denizens who waited there.

Thinking back to the flesh-melting, soul-sucking final resting spots afforded the last batch of used-up men who had been soldiering for The Otherside, Travis felt that this type of disposal was at least as consecrated a fate as the alternatives that awaited anyone in this so-called Captain's employ.

The heavy thud the second body made as it crashed onto the dirt nearby the lifeless husk of its former comrade had hardly dissipated when the sounds of a different commotion came from the busy gangplanks near the ship. He saw nothing different than the same activities he'd already seen, but the tone and timing had changed, and somehow, he knew.

Suddenly, he sensed that now was the time when Lorne was being prepared for something on the big ship. He didn't know what it was, not that it mattered. He knew for a certainty that she was on board. He ran away from the beach to jungle's edge, racing toward the docks while skirting the brighter moonlit pools, always seeking shadows in which to hide.

Determined to not make the same mistake of overrunning his objective again and being thrust into another fight he knew he had no time for, he slowed as he approached the interior boundary wall surrounding the town. The shouts and yells that came from the men working were now more excited than what he'd heard earlier, more strident with intent and urgency. Travis kept his focus on them all with a fevered resolve.

"Something's fixin' to happen with them Captain's boys any time now. I've got to get over there. Got to save Lorne, somehow."

Reaching the base of the second wall, he saw that the top stretched upwards about ten feet from the ground. Without another thought he braced, crouched, then leapt high into the night air. Reaching above, his hands scrabbled blindly, seeking purchase, then his fingertips caught and held. He quickly pulled himself up to lay flat along the top, high enough up to allow a view of the dock and the town behind it.

He swept his gaze along the length of the wall from his position. It encompassed the entirety of the town's perimeter, from jungle hills down to the beach and into the water, where it continued for some distance. His next thought was to merely drop down inside next to the barrier, then continue into the town.

But as he peered over, he saw that would be impossible. Rank upon rank of sharpened stakes and broken lengths of old swords, along with various rusty spears, had all been planted deep in the ground along the length of the wall. This field of pickets extended from the edge of the wall to at least thirty feet away. Several white skeletons lay impaled, their flesh-eaten bones and mummified tatters of skin a testament to those unlucky creatures who had already hazarded the crossing but failed.

"Too far to jump over, even with the extra strength I've been graced with, and it doesn't look like I'll be able to march into the jungle to get around that way either. If I try to swim it from the other direction, they'll surely see me in the water and start firing before I'm close enough to take a shot at them myself. Besides, it would be a hundred to one, and all I've still got are my two pistols. And the Bowie, of course."

He continued studying the situation. He noticed a pattern in the many sharp stakes spread out beyond him. It was narrow back and forth path, invisible from the ground, that led from the wall to the town He memorized it.

Also revealed from this angle atop the wall was a feature that was disguised on the jungle side; a metal frame set within the stonework of the wall. A heavy iron door hinged within it.

It was closed, seemingly impassable and... invisible to anyone approaching the town from outside.

"That gate must be locked, but no sense in not giving it a push to make sure. That's if I can find where it's hiding over here."

He made note as to its approximate distance from him, then dropped lightly back down outside the wall. He paced over to where he estimated the portal would be, hugging close to the stonework to judge its general fabrication. He strained to see within heavy shadows as his fingers searched the wall, seeking any deterioration or flaw of construction. But all he touched was frustratingly solid.

When he thought that he'd arrived at the position, there was nothing to betray the existence of the hidden gate. He pushed the stones in every direction, prodded at any larger ones that protruded more than others, and scraped his fingers in between to test the mortar for any tell-tale cracks. Nothing moved.

"Yes, it's supposed to look like it's solid as rock, but I know what I saw. There is a door over there, so this side must have one as well.

Beyond the stone and concrete by which he stood, the noisy commotion at the wharf suddenly intensified. Travis knew that time was running out.

"That's got to be either Lorne or The Otherside coming down the gangplank, or hell, maybe the both of them. I've got to get across somehow, now! Everyone will be watching them, and not paying attention to what's happening over here."

He redoubled his efforts, hands frantically clawing across the stony face in all directions; down, up, side- and cross-ways. To no effect, other than some broken and bloody fingernails.

Hearing the ongoing fracas playing out unseen along the jetty and knowing that Lorne could be sacrificed or worse at any moment, lent fanatic madness to his efforts. Each stone and the mortar between them became objects of intense scrutiny. As his work progressed along its length, he knew that he'd passed the point at which the door on the opposite side lay. He looked back, searching for what he had missed.

"Somehow it must be here, somewhere. I've just got to find the key stone to solve the puzzle.

WAIT! That smooth section... there!"

He had been half-right. It wasn't the stones themselves that were the key, but the hardened cement paste between them. Or rather, what *looked like* that gray substance.

Just slightly higher than eye-level, nestled between two innocuous stones, was a section of mortar slightly wider and deeper than any other he'd yet seen or felt along this section. He reached up, placed his forefinger along the indentation, and pushed slightly. It moved inward, connecting with a lever cunningly hidden within the wall itself. He heard a faint "click" as metal moved inside, then a small "thud" that announced the release of the locking mechanism. A narrow section of wall swung back away a fraction of an inch, just enough for him to grab hold of. Restraining himself in the face of whatever dangers surely lurked beyond, he forced himself to a more deliberate pace, and slowly pulled it open.

But instead of revealing a view of the docks and their loud commotions he knew lay just ahead, a stuffy mildewed darkness lay heavy and moist within.

"Clever bastards used some kind of rubber substance to mimic the mortar! And everything else about this gate joined up exactly next to the stones beside it, a perfect fit. No wonder it took so long to find it! But where in the hound's hall of hell is that other door hidden?"

Spurred on again by the increasingly excited shouts and anguished cries he heard, he stepped into the hollow space within the wall. As soon as he'd done so, another hidden mechanism began to pull the spring-loaded door shut behind him while releasing the lock on the inner steel gate that opened onto the field of spears beyond. Instinctively, his reflexes now faster than he thought possible, he reached back behind him and lay hold of it tightly, intending to prop it open.

The task quickly proved a more daunting challenge than what he'd expected, even with his larger size and enhanced strength.

"Whoever made this gate REALLY did NOT want anyone paying a visit to those docks! If I'd tried a stunt like this before I was enhanced, my arm would have been crushed."

He struggled against the power of the coiled steel spring within the heavy door, beginning a search of his immediate area for anything within his reach that might prove an effective chock to bar the door from closing. His strength, even improved, was quickly waning in its battle with the steel spring.

Discerning nothing much hidden within the deep gloom, he had almost decided to let it close and pass through the inner door, into the town beyond. But a primeval fear of it closing before he could reach it, and then being trapped within this dead and dark tomb-like space had already gripped his heart, inflaming his refusal to give up. He continued his search, gritting his teeth against the rippling pain burning ever hotter down his arm.

He shifted his feet to get better purchase as he fought. A light "CLANK" briefly touched his ears. It was a sharp but soft noise barely perceptible above the riotous sounds emanating from the crowded docks. He looked down.

"And there it is, just inside the wall!"

Dust covered, and more than half buried it lay, a large section of broken sword blade, snapped off and lost here from a previous battle along the wall's perimeter. His boot heel had jarred it loose when he'd shifted his weight. Just enough dusty sand from the steel had been scraped away to allow a slight reflection. It cast a bleached glint of hope.

"Strong as I've become, I'm not a match against these coil springs. I know the only way to fight iron is with steel... so, steel it shall be."

Bracing himself against the door's insistent pressure, he reached down and picked the old blade. Though a heavy and solid artifact, the tip was severed. Perhaps it was outside, sunk into the earth, now part of the field of blades.

Travis shoved the pommel and what was left of the rusted grip into the workings of the door hinge, then let go. It swung to close but caught on the steel obstruction, leaving the door blocked open about six inches. He would be able to push it open easily should he return this way.

His burning muscles relaxed, but he could not.

Lorne was still missing.

The other opening was three steps away, offset at an oblique angle from the first door. Hand on knife, he walked cautiously through the foul passageway. Reflections from the big ship's glowering lanterns guided his steps.

"Looks like whoever made this set up didn't ever want both doors open at the same time. They built it with no straight line access too, forcing any invaders into a dog-leg to slow them down. But why? What could be so dangerous out there in that jungle, that a town

full of armed killers is this afraid?"

16. SUPPLE LIVING WHIPS

The intensity and volume from the large crowd that had formed at the bottom of the gangplank was much louder over here, on the city side of the stone wall. Still within the passageway, Travis gaped at the spectacle through the iron door's gap.

His mind went cold as he took in the barbarity of the primeval scene before him. He watched the proceedings with disgust, taken aback by the beastly power of archaic ritual splayed obscenely before him.

All around, hundreds of smoky torches burned the cold blue moonlight ruddy as bloodstained flesh. From every nook and corner came the slow thrumming echoes of deep, heavy drumming, shaking his chest from inside. Oil lanterns hung aloft on lines along the gangplanks leading from the vessel, each bright light a pinpoint dagger to the eye.

More than a hundred men were dressed in identical midnight black uniforms. In time with the drumbeats, they strode a slow cadenced march from ship to shore. Each held aloft a tall banner, its swirling fabrics haughtily emblazed with arcane symbols and blocky twisted letters of other-worldly origin. Guided by the shouts and curses of their commanders, the men formed up into columns. Their lines were like the spokes on a wagon wheel, with all attention focused on the center hub, the forward deck of the ship.

As soon as the last man took his place, a large door behind the forecastle groaned open, revealing a large cage on wheels, its wide crisscrossing bars gave it the appearance of a mobile jail. Travis estimated it was about eight feet square, and perhaps six or seven feet high. The axles squealed as it was slowly winched out from the darkness.

Travis knew his time grew closer. He focused on the increasingly dire situation at hand. He had not seen Lorne yet, nor any way to go within the ship that didn't court certain death.

"At least I was right about one thing, no one's paying any attention to this wall."

He needed to move, to mingle with the large number of civilians who milled about behind the troops. Yet it was necessary to keep this door ajar. He searched the vicinity for a suitable object to block its closure. Even though it now stood slightly open, he feared that could change upon the instant, maybe even as soon as he left the confines of the wall's interior.

"As soon as I stepped in, this door jumped open. Maybe there's some underground trigger built in, that releases the locks. I don't know, and I don't really care. I only want to be able to get in and out of this unholy town of perdition and escape back to that little boat with Lorne when I need to. We can't get trapped here."

Without having to wrestle with this door as he had the other, the task took little time. He soon found a brick-shaped stone just inside the wall's structure.

"That must have fallen loose from the inside. I'll move it where it will do me some good."

Swiftly kicking it over to the jamb's edge, he nudged it in tight across the threshold in a position that would keep this inner door from closing all the way if its spring-loaded lock reactivated.

"I don't want to have to tinker about with another locked door if I'm being chased. If we do come back this way there's a good chance it'll be in a hurry."

The crowd's attention was still fixed upon the macabre scene playing out aboard the ship's forecastle.

"Alright. I've got my chance, it's time to go. Now!"

He stepped away from the door, now left slightly ajar, grateful to have an option for an escape route away from the town. Dodging the spear points of sharpened death poking up from the ground on either side, he moved quickly along the narrow path away from the wall's environs. The skeletal remains of those unlucky denizens impaled upon the blades leered with grotesque humor while he ran by. Even as he tried to avoid looking at their skulls and empty eye sockets, he found he could not ignore what they had once been, and what they were now.

"The Otherside is responsible for all this. He's got a lot to pay for."

The craniums of these broken creatures did not display the rounded bony dome normal to humanity. He noticed what hadn't been obvious before when seen from above; each lifeless brain-box had been inhumanly pulled and twisted as an infernal taffy might be, then hardened into hideous position within the frozen caverns between the outer worlds. The curving shell of bone above the brows had the look of having been formed of melted wax drippings from a sputtering candle, the skull made useless for the task of retaining the seat of human consciousness.

Still, each dead figure retained the general aspects of a man, though all had been left to sullenly rot, the unburied flesh picked clean by scavengers and others of their breed. Many still held weapons, rusted axes, and cudgels now worthless, in the bony clutches of once livid rage.

"Looks like these ugly ol' boys from the forest tried an assault that didn't work out so well. Well, maybe they'll do better next time."

He slowed his pace to an inquisitive amble when he cleared the area surrounding the wall, stepping forward to join with the ragged outer fringes of the mesmerized crowd. He noticed that his clothing didn't look much out of place among the townsfolk, except possibly his odd hat.

"I shouldn't have too much trouble fitting in around here, since what I'm wearing probably came to me courtesy of the stores these bastards left behind in those busted up crates."

He found a place behind the throngs of teeming sycophants before him. Travis looked over their heads at the town's square. It faced the sea and docks, with high hills breaking upwards behind him. Those slopes were studded with tightly packed houses and workshops, sprawling a hundred or so feet up the hill. All were lit with lanterns, many of which were made with rounded paper enclosures, a type he'd not seen before.

He slouched, wishing to be less conspicuous. Moving farther around the crowd and cautiously working his way closer, he remained well clear of the ranks of uniformed raiders now lined up at attention.

Back on board ship, workers finished dragging the cage out for all to see. Travis watched the large enclosure, finally realizing that it was not just a cage of large, crisscrossed iron bars, but that many thick sheets of glass were fitted and sealed between them to create a huge watertight corral. Water would occasionally slosh over the upper lip of it, as if it were full of liquid.

"Why would The Otherside go to all the trouble to have that big thing built? What could he possibly have that needs a huge tank of ocean water?"

The answer was not long in coming. Soon, another series of splashes shook the water's surface as several huge glistening tentacles shot out from within, hungrily probing the area around their watery pen. Between the bars above the open top, they reached over the edge, then whipped around searching in all directions, again and again, as they hunted for prey. Nothing was in reach... so far.

"Right now, they can't reach anything. Or anyone. But I'll wager that's going to change real soon."

Travis's guts churned, recoiling from the inhuman motions of the supple living whips. Their probing explorations scraped along the decking below the cage. They were at least twenty feet in length, covered in quivering suckers that dripped a viscous liquid resembling coagulated saliva. Thicker than a large man's leg at the top, they tapered down along their snake-like forms, narrowing to a wrist-sized terminus. From that, there protruded a pair of sharp and bony hooks, clacking incessantly while they opened and closed.

They dragged along the decking, seeking flesh.

Without warning, The Otherside appeared on deck. He stood just a few steps out of the flailing monster's ravenous reach. In the dark behind him were three smaller figures, cloaked in robes of a strange and foreign cut, at times illuminated from within by powers unknown.

The crowd bellowed in adulation, *"CAPTAIN! CAPTAIN! CAPTAIN!"*

Before them, basking amid smiling deception, The Otherside presented his gruesome leer to the assembled throng. He raised his arms high to their chants, preening back and forth. The crowd cheered with over enthusiastic applause.

"Finally! The real monster makes his entrance! A fearful display he puts on, to be sure, and uglier now than I remember. He's worse for wear since my bullet tore half his cheek off! But so far, no sign of Lorne. She wasn't taken off the ship yet. If The Otherside has plans for his slimy pet whatever-it-is of his to touch her in any way, I'll do whatever I can to put a stop to that. And, come what may, I'll at least have my revenge upon him. Or die trying."

Several more tentacles rose from the vile waters of the cage to join their brethren outside. They also swung ominously to and fro, hunting. Their chittering claws continued to blindly probe their surroundings, opening and closing.

"Or maybe not so blindly! What dread horror lurks within that glassy cage? Is that an eye... a giant eyeball that I see within?"

The crowd around him choked out an exhalation of sick surprise, lurching back en masse a step. He was jostled back as well, cursing under his breath, but then he saw it too, between the crossbars, a nightmare come forward out of the water's deadly murk to press against the glass. It was indeed a huge and lidless eye surrounding a black slit of an iris, contracting and expanding as it gazed upon the crowd. It blinked slowly, looking at them all. *Food!*

"It's beastie's feeding time and The Otherside is letting everyone know their proper place within his scheme of things... stay in line, don't say or do or think the wrong thing, or else... you're just another meaty tidbit."

Hunger flung the sea monster's coiling tentacles about. Unconcerned, the large man with the toothy rictus stood nearby them, but not too near, and began to speak to those assembled with his inhumanly loud voice.

"Trusted servants and able citizens of this, our first city founded here on this island on the far side of the great ocean, I thank you for your unceasing courage and never swerving dedication to our great cause!"

More applause. He raised his arms, palms up, while the intensity of adulation increased. Slowly he swiveled his head back and forth, scanning the upturned faces as he then lowered his arms to his sides. Immediately, the cheering applause ended. A shivering quiet smothered the eerie tableau. Only the occasional slap of water was heard as the tide sloshed along the ship's hull below. The Captain continued.

"Truly, immense things we have done... no, no, I should say... that YOU have done in my employ while laboring for our shared vision, and again I state that I am grateful. For your reward,

I will direct the kitchen laborers to provide an increase in your daily ration of fish sauce for the entirety of next week!"

More cheers and happy shouts came in a studied show of dutiful appreciation. Every upturned visage seemed printed with the same broadside of wide-eyed, but paper-thin exuberance.

"And ALSO, you all are now eligible to partake of an additional bottle of your favorite drink, *THE MOST,* every day this week! In fact, not only eligible, but required to imbibe! This will help all workers to increase their production to meet our sacred goals! I am SURE that will not be a problem for anyone, will it?"

"NO!" The crowd shouted. Again, a wracking crash of hands acclaimed him, but Travis noticed the growing sheen appearing on the people's faces, sweat slowly beading on their foreheads, before running down.

"These townsfolk have been through this before. They know the Captain giveth, but they're worried about what he's going to taketh. If I were a gambling man, I'd put money on that being what's coming up next in this performance."

Continuing to maintain his slouching gait, Travis again worked his way back behind the edge of the crowd, keeping his hands low and near his six-shooters, just in case.

"Don't know how much good these few bullets would be against this army. Since every one of them soldiers standin' there's armed, ain't no way I'd ever be able to shoot my way out of this situation. But better a cold chance in Hell than a hot chance of none at all."

The hands of The Otherside lowered, signaling for quiet. Silence descended like a heavy sail before a storm. He gestured behind himself for something still hidden to be brought forth, then he spoke.

"But NOT everyone is worthy of rewards, some sad few are useful only as examples to anyone contemplating weakness or disobedience to their oaths! So now those who have not lived up to their commitments, those who have shown cowardice in the face of the enemy, and those who have let down our community and have BETRAYED not only me, but ALL OF YOU as well, shall face their punishment! Soldiers my forces, present the traitors!"

Travis watched as each rank of men arrayed in front stood to attention line by line, pulled their weapons to the ready, then turned to face the fearful people of the town, a barrier of bayonet and gunpowder between them and their evil overlord.

"I knew it. Now's the time for a blood thirsty lesson to his subjects, just to make sure they remember what happens to those who fail to toe his line."

From each soldier stared eyes of neutral cruelty. The townsfolk shivered beneath their gaze. Another detail of even more soldiers marched up from below decks to stand around the cage, just out of reach from the wet death within.

Soon, more soldiers dragged out five struggling men. The prisoners were dressed in crumbling rags, bound hand and foot with chains, and gagged with handfuls of a decayed and chalky plant-like substance that muffled their groans, screams, and wails.

A sergeant strode forth to bow deeply to his Captain, then turned to address the crowd.

"NO MERCY for filthy cowards who fail to fight, or the traitors to our One Great Cause! You know our enemies will give us no quarter, so we must do the same, and worse, to ANY who oppose the will of our glorious Captain!"

The Sergeant turned back to his soldiers, bellowing, "For the greater glory of our Land and our People, let the punishments begin! Expire the first prisoner!"

Four of the uniformed men hefted the starved and ragged man above their heads, beginning to fling him toward the sloshing froth of the iron-bound tank. But before they could finish their toss, a wild-eyed man on the far side of the crowd suddenly screamed as he ran toward the gangplank, knife in hand.

"STOP! Stop, that's my brother! You can't kill him, he did nothing wrong!"

Without missing a step, four of the Captain's enforcers threw the struggling man within reach of the monster's writhing tentacles. Immediately several slimy tentacles shot out of the tank, curving over the edge in a high, steep arc that reminded Travis of a mortar round's trajectory. The result was just as deadly, perhaps even more bloody than canister shot.

As two of the sinuous cords wrapped themselves around the prisoner's body, the crazed knife-wielding brother gained his first step onto the gangplank, still spitting curses at The Otherside. The soldiers nearest the attack had already aimed their rifles at him.

Before the crazed brother of the doomed

prisoner had taken another step, another two of the creature's tentacles whipped out from the roiling waters. One attached itself by the many suckers that lined its writhing arm to the screaming victim's head, while its other did the same to the lower half of the doomed man's body.

While Travis watched in utter horror, he saw the look of bemused boredom that lay upon The Otherside, which changed to satisfaction as the hideous strength of the ocean creature pulled the man in its grasp in opposite directions.

Sharp claws started their incision at his belly, splitting his skin around the center of his body, separating it like a knife edge pulled around a banana. The other tentacles gripped his head and feet to pull in opposite directions, yanking skin off top and bottom in two red-soaked cowls.

Only a quaking inner core of living agony remained, staring at his rampaging brother through a blood-flayed pair of fleshless, lidless eyeballs.

The brother was able to choke out one more step, one more shout, as he flung the knife toward the creature he knew only as the Captain.

"I'll kill you! Die! Filthy demon from hell! DIE!!

The Otherside watched the spinning blade approach. He nonchalantly plucked it from the air and tossed it overboard.

A fusillade from the soldiers crashed into the enraged brother as one moving hammer of lead. The impact of the many projectiles shredded his skin and cracked his bones, making a still-living stew of perfect fish food as it swept what was now only a perforated meat bag over the edge of the gangplank, into the water below. He died as a feeding frenzy erupted where he'd gone in.

Their motions precise and machine-like, as if there had been no commotion, the soldiers moved on to the next prisoner. Their steady cadence of death was grinning evil personified. They lifted the man's squirming form, then flung him within reach of the watery beast's rending limbs. The unholy feeding process was repeated to the frenetic cheering of the crowd.

Under the thirsty eyes of The Otherside, each of the bound prisoners soon met their end. As each one died, it seemed to Travis as if the physical size of the watchful demon-like entity increased.

Was that strange effect just his imagination? After watching the spectacle closely, he was convinced of his first assessment.

"That wicked son of a devil is feeding himself from their agony!"

Travis had thought he knew the abominable depths of villainy the outerworldly beast was capable of, but even the horrors of what he'd already seen during the past weeks had not prepared him for this exhibition of barbarity.

"It's as if The Otherside is performing some stone-age blood rite of human sacrifice. This creature has obviously had a lot of practice. Probably been doing things like this, and much worse, to human beings for more than the last thousand years. How much pain and torment has this monster created, and how many victims have been cruelly torn limb from limb, just so he can feed on their agonies?"

After the last body had been skinned, cleaved, and consumed alive by the many tentacled sea creature, its agitations calmed, its monstrous hunger briefly abated. Occasionally a clean picked bone or jawless skull that had been scoured of flesh would fall from the orifice of the monster to lay atop the other relics of past feedings that littered the bottom of the cage in a deep, calcified layer of human remains.

Travis fought down a wave of nausea.

"I've seen much worse than this when I was fighting on the battlefield, but that war was fought between humans. And it's over and done now. The only war around here is between The Otherside and... everyone else in the entire world!

This incessant pain will never be finished while that thing is demanding his supper. For some reason, these people think their Captain is here to help them, but their minds have all been tricked sideways! They don't know he's really The Otherside, come to eat them all alive!"

And if they didn't like it, the town was full of his stoic, loyal soldiers, every one of them ready to do their precious Captain's bidding.

"This whole town is a big people farm, keeping all these penned up two-legged critters working hard... until they fumble into some minor infraction, and then it's off to the kitchen with 'em. They're nothing but human hogs fattening up on the Captain's slops to be his supper, or a snack for that sea creature."

He looked at the spasming sinews of fear etched into the people's faces as the watched the watery scenes of depravity before them.

"Have to admit, if you want to scare people it's quite an impressive display to remind them what their options are. Or aren't."

The cringing throng gave a shiver of revulsion as the caged creature again flung another pair of ropy limbs out to languidly probe about for more nourishment from its human hosts. Finding nothing yet, they pulled back inside their watery enclosure.

"In this case, none. No options at all. Their best option has already passed them by. That would have been never joining up with this crew to begin with. Now, the only way out is at the cost of your soul."

A bellow erupted from the sergeant on the ship.

"Townsfolk! It is now time for the night workers to return to their duties! Gunpowder still needs making, and the cannon balls and bullets won't cast themselves! Those who are to return to work at daybreak, go to your dwellings and rest swiftly until the morning town bell awakens you! Be you not slovenly tomorrow in your labors for what The Captain has decreed! You will drink your bottle of *THE MOST* with the morning meal to banish fatigue and clear your minds! Concentrate upon your needful tasks! He is counting upon us all! We are with the Captain! We are with the Captain!"

"WE ARE WITH THE CAPTAIN! WE ARE WITH THE CAPTAIN!" repeated the crowd, a false veneer of fervor overlaying every word of the chant.

Travis watched as The Otherside spoke a few words to his Sergeant at Arms, who then scurried off out of sight. The monster who looked like a man then turned, slowly scanning the docks with his piercing and outerworldly eyes. He still displayed the unhealing stigmata of bone

334

and tooth beneath a torn rift of fleshy cheek. For some time, he watched the crowded docks of people going off to do his bidding. He nodded approval, then turned away, vanishing into the serpentine corridors of his ship.

As the people trickled away from the docks back to their homes and workshops, a numbing alarm washed over Travis.

"All that murderous havoc, and still no sign of Lorne! Maybe the information the Outer Forces folks gave the witch woman wasn't right? Could it be that Lorne's not on that ship at all?"

Then a thought came like a brick shattering a pane of glass.

"What if The Otherside decided she was too much trouble to keep alive? What if he figured she just wasn't worth enough for the effort? What if he's already fed her to that THING that just devoured those men?"

Imagining her bones mixed with the human remains that lined the cage's lower depths was almost enough to trigger a do-or-die suicide attack on The Otherside. Blinded by rage, he reached for his pistols and took a half-step toward the ship that held the otherworldly madman, but then halted his motion before it was even fairly begun. Sanity returned. Taking several deep breaths, he turned on his heel, hunched even further down, and walked with the crowd as they trod back into the winding warrens of the haunted town.

"Fool! Stop! Strong and fast as I've become, I wouldn't get more than halfway up that ramp before being shot by a hundred rifles! I must believe Lorne still lives! I must stay alive to

335

rescue her! I will find a better way to get on board that ship."

He left the immediate vicinity of the brightly lit docks. Here, the streetlamps were few along the large square, and darkness filled the twisting spaces between them with a quilt of blackness.

Travis sought a hidden place to watch the ship unseen and wait for his chance to board it.

"If what that fella, Mr. One, told me was true, my family has been trying to kill that monster for a thousand years. Right now, I've got more reason than any of them to do just that."

He glanced over his shoulder while he kept sidling away. Not attracting attention was high on his priority list.

"But The Otherside is just too damn well protected! His soldiers and personal guards swarm around him like a rolling brick wall. I'd be cut down in a few seconds if I tried anything stupid, like I almost did. I must wait a little longer. My time for revenge will come, but is it already too late for Lorne? WHERE IS SHE?"

The crowd had almost dispersed. Only a few groups of stragglers remained, people either too tired to shuffle off to their midnight labors once more, or too infused with the manic excitement inspired by their "Captain" to wish leaving the scene of what they considered his latest triumph over their enemies. The ranks of soldiers remained at ready, blocking the gangplank to any other enraged fools clamoring for the blood of The Otherside. The guards remained overconfident and bored, but Travis could sense their attention turning toward the dwindling number of citizens who still loitered about. He had found a small degree of safety by hiding

336

within their numbers, but now that was lost.

"Better git moving, somewhere, anywhere. Make 'em think I've got important work to do for the greater glory of their stupid Captain."

Travis tamped down his anger, hunching even farther forward in a false display of subservience. He shuffled off as quickly as he dared without attracting attention.

Looking up from the sandy dirt, glancing around for a bolt hole, he noticed one of the townspeople staring at him. The man ever so slightly inclined his head to make a gesture of imperceptible acknowledgment, then made a tiny jerk of his neck toward the buildings behind him. He shifted his eyes away, waiting more than just a moment longer than he might have, as if to underline his message, *'FOLLOW ME'*. Then he turned to stride into the narrow recesses of the nearest alleyway.

Travis immediately changed his direction to follow the stranger. As he walked, he noticed a small cluster of soldiers were breaking away from the main group behind him. From what he could see, their leader looked like an officer of minor rank, but one who carried himself ramrod straight.

"Uh oh. One of them young martinets who thinks he needs to do his job with more gusto than what's by the book... 'cause he's written his own. Another baby tyrant beating up his men and looking for a promotion. Of course, since he's joined up with this crowd, I already know he's trouble. He was probably drummed out of the real army. I'd best keep moving away from that bunch."

The furtive stranger Travis was following had

337

already disappeared into the alleyway. Travis imperceptibly picked up his pace, hoping to also round its corner and become lost to sight before the small group of soldiers behind called for him to stop.

He'd managed another ten paces to get within literal spitting distance of his goal, when a harsh command sprang forth from behind. It was the annoyingly high-pitched voice of the officer he'd marked earlier.

"YOU! By the alleyway! The townsman wearing the strange hat! Stop now!"

"Uh, oh. I knew it! Now what? Into the alley? Or stop? I really have no choice. I need to keep moving."

One more long stride and Travis was around the corner, out of their view. He figured he had about ten seconds before his pursuers managed to gain sight of him once more. He pounded down the alley.

"Where to go? Into the darkness ahead, for a slim chance to escape and find Lorne, or to fight in this narrow street? If I run, I'll soon be lost, or if I fight, I may have a long shot to kill them, but the rest of the soldiers will rally behind them and shoot me down before I can escape."

Stopping beneath the lone oil streetlamp, he hesitated, angry and wanting to fight. He clenched his fists, frustrated.

A hissing whisper came from above him. He looked up to the building's second story, where a window stood open, hidden in the darkness above the upper cowling of the lamp. The hooded eyes of the stranger he'd followed from the plaza flared wildly with a blue glowing phosphorescence that pierced Travis's gaze. He

338

held a coil of thick rope, ready to toss down.

At that instant, the detachment of shouting soldiers burst around the corner, crazed killing for the greater glory of... something... in their eyes. They ran toward Travis with rifles at ready. But the streetlight was behind him and shone in their eyes, while his transformed stature was now a looming shadow before them. He blocked their path, taking up almost half the passage.

The face in the window narrowed his eyes, then mumbled just loud enough to hear above the approaching clatter, "You have what you need in your possession. Don't fight them. Instead, brazen it out!" He disappeared inside, yanking the still unfurled rope back with him.

17. DON'T BLEED ON YOUR BETTERS!

Travis turned his full attention to the soldiers, planting his feet and placing his fists square on either hip. Playing the required part, he jutted his chin out aggressively. His sham persona spoke from behind gritted teeth, a facade that he hoped would seem to them as a higher ranking officer barely containing his raging incandescence at being detained and questioned by an obvious inferior.

"Gotta remember, I am, after all, a Sergeant who led my artillery battery into battle for almost four years of bone-busting war! I can do this."

With gusto, he heaped every moment of that hard won experience upon them as he quietly addressed the group with angry calm.

"You men! As you can plainly cogitate, I have been forced to delay my mission... thanks to your insufferable ignorance. I have stopped. Here we are. And... now?"

His firm, relaxed stance caught the small troop up in confusion born of their constant fear of some loathsome punishment for any infraction, no matter how minor. Not knowing the pedigree of this large stranger, the soldiers instantly opted for a cautious proceeding, hoping to placate the big man should he be someone of importance, while also ultimately being able to lay blame for any insult upon their disliked squad leader. They immediately snapped to

341

attention behind their commander, face forward, eyes studiously neutral.

These actions were unseen and completely lost upon their leader, whose oblivious ineptitude was legendary among the rank and file soldiers.

Travis spoke again.

"To whom do I owe the honor of my displeasure?"

Upset that this stranger from out of the unknown might show him up in front of his men, the martinet pushed his way forward to stand uncomfortably close to the glaring mien of Travis. Sour spittle coated every word of his contemptuous reply to the big man wearing the strange hat.

"You... ! Your displeasure... is irrelevant! It is MY displeasure we should be addressing!"

"And... why?"

"I am the commander of the shore detachment!"

"I see. And your name, shore detachment commander?"

The veins bulged on both sides of the shore commander's head as he forced himself to an infuriated approximation of calm.

"My orders are to be followed without question; I am the shore commander!"

"So you've already laboriously explained, shore detachment commander. Yet, all I do know is that undoubtedly there is a name attached to your rank, and that I've already asked for it once, without satisfaction."

Travis discarded the last vestiges of his slumping posture to stand tall, stretching vertically another half-hand's length, while leaning in to look closely at his adversary.

"I will not ask again. Now is your opportunity to comply, shore detachment commander."

Travis watched the soldiers behind the man he faced off with carefully. If they believed him, his stature over the commander would rise; if not, his odds would go down. He saw their feelings in their eyes and surmised he was close to winning at least this first battle of wills.

The soldiers listening knew well that whip-crack of authority underlying the unknown man's voice, instinctively standing even more solid and still, their eyes painfully unblinking while staring straight forward. They all knew this argument was well above their pay grade. Whatever happened, they could always plead the usually unimpeachable mantra that 'I was just following orders, sir.' to save their skins, literally. Nevertheless, every one of them wished to be somewhere far away. Silently wished, of course.

The martinet's nerves snapped. Spluttering a frothy series of unintelligible curses which made reply impossible, he raised his hand, pointing hard at Travis' chest. The shore commander intended to drive his next words home with physicality.

"My what? Did you say 'OPPORTUNITY'... ? I'll have you know that... *OW!*"

His poised finger came crashing down upon Travis's chest, smashing directly into the pocket containing the two-horned iron horseshoe. He struck it hard. The shore commander's fingertip almost broke, while his fingernail split in half, buckling upwards with sharp crackling pain and a spout of blood... lots of it.

"Shore commander. Don't bleed on your

betters."

With an infuriated twitch the squad leader pulled his injured hand away, then reached with his other, unhurt hand inside the pocket containing the horseshoe Travis had found on the beach. As soon as he pulled it out, a pallor of horrified recognition macerated his face.

He held the curved piece of iron with shaking hand. His eyes crossed while staring at the cursed metal.

Once the commander and his men saw the two-horned horseshoe, they knew exactly what he held; something only the hand-picked elite members of the Captain's own cavalry guard would have possession of. The soldiers managed to maintain a semblance of parade ground stillness even as they gaped before this unexpected symbol of power.

Instead of indignant fury, now the shore commander's quivering jaw spluttered with terror as the fearful lash of certain punishment covered his every word with layers of sycophantic syrup.

"Sir. I... was not informed... that the raiding party had returned from... "

"You ramble on yet have still not answered my question."

"Sir. My name is Lieutenant Samu... "

"Did I ask you for your former rank?"

"My former... ? Uh, no... Sir. No sir."

"Perhaps a lack of attention to simple commands explains why you did not inspire in yourself the effort to ascertain all the facts regarding the embarkations, whereabouts, and disembarking of those within the orbit of your authority, which is, exactly, where?"

"Sir. The shore, Sir."

"Once again, to where does your authority extend?"

"Sir. My authority extends to the shore. Sir."

"Precisely. Samu. Your responsibilities are matters of the shore. Not the sea. Not the fields, or these warrens of the town... nor those of us who report directly to our glorious Captain."

"Sir. No sir... Sir."

"Certainly, you don't feel responsible for meddling in the affairs of such as I, who serve only under the direct orders of our leader himself, which you just happened to interrupt tonight by your ignorant actions. Do you or don't you feel responsible for that, Samu?"

"Sir. No. Ah, I mean, yes, I was responsible, but no, I'm not supposed to be. Ah, I mean, my name, It's... not Samu, it's Samuel, Sir, Samuel Stittof. Sir."

If a chill wind had blown across the ocean from a pass between the high frozen peaks where this conflict had begun for Travis, it could not have been colder than what now filled the atmosphere between the two men.

"Alright, Samu. That's helpful to know. Very helpful. However, did I ask you to correct me?"

Travis paused while the shore commander realized his error. His arrogance had notably withered. *I guess that ole' devil-horned horseshoe has its uses. I'm glad I didn't toss it. It sure as heck shut these boys down in a hurry. But now what? I've got to either kill them all, which won't be easy or quiet, or somehow get 'em to keep their traps shut and walk out of here, peaceful like. I have to just brazen this masquerade out while I try to think of something."*

The commander's voice was barely a whisper, "Sir. No sir. Sir."

"I see. Your enthusiasm is very helpful. You know, Samu, I believe there might be some... slight... hope for you after all. First thing, return my property."

Travis thrust his hand out, palm up, demanding the return of the horseshoe.

The commander proffered the article requested. Travis immediately returned it to his shirt pocket.

Then, so fast that the motions were over before they had fairly started, Travis back-handed his adversary across his face. He fell in a heap before his men. *"Oops, maybe too much! No, he's moving. I'm glad I didn't hit this weaselly fool any harder, that would have killed him for certain!"*

Travis stepped forward, looking each man in the eye. His suppressed rage underlined every word he spoke.

"You two, there and over there! Lift your commander and hold him up!"

The selected men stepped up to follow the orders. The shore commander groaned, opening his eyes to get his bearings. He brushed off the men to either side of him to stand shakily on his own feet.

"He was only stunned, thank the good Lord. I didn't want to kill him, just teach him a lesson, and put the fear of his Captain into him in case he'd forgot. Not that that's anything anyone living here in this hellish town is likely to do."

"You men interfered with an investigation earlier. A secret inquiry into a traitorous cabal.

346

That's why you hadn't been informed. None of you need to know anything about a need to know operation! But now... I've seen your faces and memorized them all. I've looked into your eyes, and I believe every last one of you can keep a secret. Isn't that true?"

A thick enthusiasm enwrapped every man's oath of fidelity that they swore to him. Satisfied, Travis spoke again.

"Alright. In the interests of time, I won't pursue any actions against any of you."

Silent relief washed over the men.

"And... in the interests of your own selves, you won't mention any of what has transpired here tonight. That is an order. Understood?"

Again, they heartily replied in the affirmative.

"Now, when you go back out there someone might ask what took you so long in here. Well, you'll just tell 'em to take a look at ol' Samu's face! It's obvious to anyone that he just happened to trip and fall flat on his head! It took a few minutes for you boys to wake him up and nurse him back to life, isn't that right?"

Nodding heads and a scattered chorus of "yeps" and "sure 'nuffs" responded to his rhetorical query.

"Alright. Commander Samuel, I appreciate your enthusiasm. Just keep in mind where your duties begin, and more importantly, where they end. I don't want to ever see any of you before me again. It may remind us all of this little incident, and that would angrify me somethin' awful. None of us want that, least of all any of you. Now, return to whatever you should have been doing all this time, instead of having this conversation. Get a move on!"

They group turned on their heels and marched away, their commander slogging along, bringing up the rear before realizing his mistake. He quickly stalked past his men, angrily making sure to lead them into the square. They disappeared around the corner. They were gone.

Travis stood in the alley, breathing heavily, imperceptibly shaking as he realized he'd made it through a very tight spot. Now only Lorne filled his thoughts. He had completely forgotten about the man he'd followed in here, or the open window hidden in the shadows only a few feet above his head.

"If I hadn't been searching for Lorne, I never would have bothered with that nonsense. Would have done my best to just kill 'em all and let the cards fall where they damn well may."

Above him he heard a soft series of scratches, like a piece of wood or leather moving across iron. The stranger was still there, silently motioning for his attention. He dropped the rope down to him. Travis climbed up and into the window in a flash.

Stygian shadows sheathed him as his boots trod the stone floor within. Even the weak reflections of the oil burning streetlamp below the window swirled away, hammered out of perception by a dull flat dusk that filled the room.

He heard a sound. Or was it a thought? Travis didn't know, exactly, but he knew he'd it heard before, the same familiar cadence that spoke to him now.

"Travis Lehrman. Hear me. Your deception of the enemy using a token of their own Cavalry Guard is to be congratulated. The Guard are the

most highly ranked of all the forces serving The Otherside. As such, even the lowest-ranking Guard may command any soldier of the regular forces."

Travis looked around the room. He only saw the stranger who had beckoned him.

"I was right, it's the voice of Mr. One! The same and only who led me off across the seas to that battle up at the mountain pass! I'd know his voice anywhere."

"The ranks of this world's Roman Praetorian Guard were his inspiration. After being called here from beyond the outer gate of the Other Realms, this being known as The Otherside had personally witnessed the Praetorians in action over two millennia ago, hundreds of years after his arrival here. He trained his own Cavalry Guard to be even more ruthless."

One continued speaking. As if echoing his words, the lips of the stranger moved silently, his face haloed by a bluish tinge of illumination, his unseeing eyes rolled back into his head.

"The female you know as Lorne still continues her life but is diminished. The... restrictions that have been inflicted upon her must be removed before you will have the chance to defeat the one called by his followers 'The Captain'."

"You're talkin' about The Otherside, of course."

"Correct. For some reason only he would know, he represents himself to his minions as an officer called The Captain."

"So I've gathered. But back to what's important, I'm thinking I've got to find her before I can save her. So, what's my next move?

Where do I go? Where is she?"

"Her essence is trapped. Part of her is gripped tightly in another realm by the machinations of The Otherside and his Underlords, while the rest of her is bound on this plane of existence. Both worlds lay slightly offset from one another yet are separated by the universe itself."

"All that don't mean much to me, Mr. *One;* it's confusing. And you still haven't answered my question! None of this is helping me to find her."

The voice of *One* grew quieter, becoming almost personal.

"Travis Lehrman, listen well. The words your ancestor spoke when he cursed The Otherside were powerful a thousand years ago and are still strong today. Over these long centuries, they have increased in strength. You must memorize them! Use them when you fight the minions of The Otherside."

"What minions? I don't care about them. I'm looking for Lorne!"

"You must care about them, for it is those servants of The Otherside that have trapped both her and Alyssia! They use the same bonds of power that link this world with that of The Otherside! These Underlords now hold both in deadly thrall. Travis Lehrman, you must find their lair, destroy those who guard the alter where the evil ones would sacrifice them, and wrest the women free from their evil grasp."

"Alright, alright! Which words am I supposed to memorize?"

The answer came from *One*, slowly but clearly, and repeated twice.

"BLESTEMUL   MORTI...   BLESTEMUL

MORTI... ! "

"Okay Mr. *One*, I understand, sort of, anyway. But Lorne's hurt and trapped! I need to find her. What next?"

"Repeat the words, Travis Lehrman. Mark them well. Repeat them now!"

Travis didn't like being bullied, but if this was something to help save Lorne then he was willing to do what Mr. *One* required.

"Besides, it seems like his way of talkin' down to people is the only way of talkin' that Mr. One knows how to do. For better or for worse, that's just the way he is, seems like. At least he's not as much of a jerk as The Otherside."

"All right, Mr. *One*. Here ya go. BLESTEMUL MORTI... BLESTEMUL MORTI... ! Is that good enough for you?"

Silence.

There was no answer. It was as if the telegraph line to headquarters had been cut during battle. That had happened to his unit before.

Has Mr. One decided to leave? He can't do that! Lorne's life is hanging by a thread!

He tried again.

"BLESTEMUL MORTI... BLESTEMUL MORTI... I'm sayin' it, Mr. *One*! Now tell me where Lorne is hidden, and I'll go after her!"

He waited, motionless, watching the stranger for any sign of movement or response. Nothing. After several minutes he decided it had been long enough. The man nearby still shone with his unnatural blue illumination, although not as brightly as before. He leaned close to the stranger, speaking to him in an urgent whisper.

"Hey there, Mister *One*. I appreciate what all

351

you've told me so far, but it still don't seem to make much sense. Mister *One*, you still there?"

Dread silence lingered heavily around both men. No reply or further instructions were forthcoming. The stranger continued to stare unseeing at the ceiling, eyes rolled up behind fluttering lids, his tongue lolling helpless and trapped by unsaid phrases.

Travis turned his attention around the gloom thick room. He was tired. Today he had already fought and killed several men, seen the true enemy in the flesh, spoken with the mysterious *One*, and worst of all, still not found a path to Lorne! And... all that before breakfast!

"For that matter, all before lunch and dinner too. It must be well past midnight. I haven't been hungry yet, but I know I need to eat, if only to keep my strength up."

The faint blue halo around the stranger gave just enough light to see. Travis prowled about, careful with his steps. He found the room to be larger than he'd thought.

A deserted and dark street lay below. Along the side of other buildings were a few smallish windows such as this, but all others were tightly shuttered by thick panes of wood or had been covered up with a permanent seal of bricks and thick gobs of mortar. What might have been old blood stains covered large swathes of the stonework below deep scratches around the bottoms of the windows.

"Those scratches are scraped into solid rock. Whatever claws the critters sported that spilt all that blood along the walls, they were damn and more than damned strong!"

He moved away from the opening, exploring

the room. The stranger continued to radiate a smoldering gleam. Travis noted a folding pocket telescope like his, but somewhat larger. Next to it was a solidly-built box of wood. He opened it, and inside lay a triangular instrument of some sort which fascinated him. He examined it but was unable to ascertain its purpose. He replaced it carefully and moved on to another shelf.

The bluish emanations from the stranger abruptly increased. The room brightened, pushing the patchwork of shadowy gloom aside.

Travis heard sounds of shuffling scratches, as if a pebbled dirt path were being trod upon. Once more came the familiar voice of *One*, now a forceful cantor, a heavy whisper of such force that each word burst painfully within the room. The stranger's lips again moved silently along with what *One* said.

"You have memorized the words. Use them when needed. Now time grows ever more scant. Your presence here within the enemy stronghold is suspected, though they have not yet discovered the stillness of the sanctum-twist where you arrived on this island."

"You mean that hot blazing pen I woke up in, where the boat is? With the sun straight up above? It's a... what did you say...? a cinnamon-twist?

*"A sanctum-twist. It is a small bubble of refuge hidden from the eyes of evil. A small curve in time binds one tiny fragment of **WAS** locked in a perpetual **NOW**. At its creation, the sun was passing directly above, so there are no sidelong shadows in which the energies of The Otherside may lurk. Because of that, this sanctum-twist, and whatever is within it, are*

353

both undetectable and impenetrable to his senses, weapons, and defenses."

"No wonder the sun never moved. A place frozen in time. I suppose I shouldn't be surprised anymore by what you can do. You Outer Forces folks have more tricks up your sleeves than arms."

A small hint of concern tinged the aloof voice of *One*.

"*Where did you hear that term, 'Outer Forces'?*"

"The old woman who healed me up, better than new, and sent me on my way with a poisoned blade with The Otherside's name on it."

"*Bah. She is very useful but has always talked too much.*"

"Guess she didn't think it mattered. Somehow I got the impression she didn't expect me to survive either my injuries or her treatment."

"*Bah. She is correct, yet some... always do.*"

"You sound like you wish I hadn't."

"*I do not 'wish'. I calculate probabilities. Based on facts. That is all.*"

"You can't tell me that you don't still wish I would have killed The Otherside way back at that mountain pass you dragged me off to."

"*The removal of that creature has always presented a probability of greater benefit for everyone on this world, than the alternative of violence and terror that permeates all he touches. Therefore, I work to better the odds supporting his elimination. You are merely part of that calculation, Travis Lehrman.*"

"But why me... why me in particular?"

"*Bah. This is meaningless. I would not need to explain myself to a hammer or a nail.*"

"Be nice, Mr. *One*. I know I'm more useful than either of those. Just a few words are all I ask."

"In short, when your ancestor vowed his revenge, he spoke a particular curse that he had learned from one of the surviving gatekeepers who had originally opened the barrier that allowed The Otherside access to this world. That curse formed a link between him and descendants of his line. The last of which is, perhaps unfortunately, you."

"Alright. I'll try to do better. But this command tent, map-table stuff is way above my pay grade, so I'll take your word for it all. I'm done tryin' to figure out your strategy anyway. It won't make a hill o' beans' difference in the outcome, just like you said. I'm ready to save Lorne and kill that blood-thirsty bastard. He's been causing trouble for way too long. Two thousand years he's been here? Yes, that's way too long! Alright. You said time is short, so let's get a move on."

"Hear me, Travis Lehrman. Hear me. Both Lorne and Alyssia will be found within the 'The Fist'... somewhere. This man must accompany you, for he knows that which you do not about that evil place. He will lead you to their prison when you awaken. His hatred of The Otherside is even greater than your own, revenge his only nourishment."

Red-rimmed fear washed up from within Travis. He needed to move!

"Wait! What is this 'Fist', and why should I awaken when I'm already awake? I can't sleep now! What about Lorne and Alyssia?"

The bluish aura dimmed quickly. Light fled

from the chamber while the voice of *One* receded as if he were walking away down a long hallway.

"Danger must be minimized. Preparations are in motion. Afterwards, follow the mate, do whatever he says. Trust him with your life. Trust me, Soldier Travis Lehrman. This is the only way."

"NO! Wait!"

There was nothing else said. Then a stunning fatigue swept Travis down, spinning his head, buckling his knees. From outside, hideous croaking wails of fury from once-human throats started to yowl and yap. His last glimpse was of the iron-faced shutters slowly swinging shut to block the open window. Darkness returned.

After a brief and futile struggle to maintain wakefulness, the imperious arms of Sleep enfolded him. He succumbed within them as the screaming beyond the window began in earnest.

Hearing nothing more, he lay still upon the floor's gentle pillow of stone.

18. VISIONS, VOICES, SPIRITS!

Alyssia stumbled after banging her toe on a stubby three-legged stool in the center of her small chamber. Cursing, she kicked it away. She missed having her sword as she paced within this floating prison made of oddly angled bars.

They canted to and fro, a solid yet strangely moving pattern of inexorable confinement surrounding her. Every molecule of their dark crackling material howled the utter wrongness of their existence on this earthly plane. Merely looking at them pained the eye; they would not allow prolonged examination.

Floating outside her prison, Travis once again found himself out of body, this time far, far above the ground. He was nearby the alien cage, and could see Alyssia struggling, trapped within its harsh embrace.

Both the cage that held Alyssia prisoner and his own position were offset at an angle perpendicular to the great mass of Earth, which hung in space off to the side of them both. They were turned sideways in a ninety-degree axial tilt, as if the plane with which they were aligned owed its allegiance to some strange reality far from the here and now in which they existed.

As a demigod of yore might have done, Travis gazed past his shoulder at the sphere of Earth alongside him, for such he instinctively knew it to be. The planet loomed before an eternally black void spangled by the sharp facets of a million stars and more. Below, the lands and peoples of the world lived and died beneath both light and shadow.

The awesome sight was beyond measure, yet to Travis it was merely another diversion from his mission. His attention flashed back to the despised cage before him. He willed himself closer, shouting to its captive within, calling past the imprisoning bars made of tormented infinity twisted upon itself.

"Alyssia! Alyssia! What is this place? Is Lorne nearby as well?"

The confined woman jolted to a stop and looked directly at him. Her angry warrior spirit infused each word.

"Soldier Travis of Earth! I had sensed your presence, dimly, as soon as you had left the tiny sanctum-twist that shielded you. Your physical self lies now in the town founded by The Otherside. The prison where I'm trapped lies there, within a nearby docked ship... and, yes...the woman known as Lorne is also here!"

"But where is she? I see you but not any sign of her."

"We are both here... she is diminished and unseen, but safe for the time being. We have been locked together in bondage to the evil one. We must be freed together, or not at all."

Travis clenched his fists. He looked around, as if hoping to catch and fling The Otherside down the long fatal fall to smash upon the hard packed soil of Earth. But nowhere was the monster seen.

"What happened? How were you both captured? I know that when the horse Lorne was riding answered its master's call, she was paralyzed somehow, then dragged away into

358

the forest. But you are more than a human, are you not? How were you so fooled?"

"I had tried to save her in the forest, after they yanked her from the horse. I was late, but she had fought her captors, killing one. When I arrived, it looked as if there were only one remaining, but nearby were more raiders hidden within twisted folds of the Between. Unseen until the last instant, they attacked, overpowering both Lorne and me."

Self-admonishment lay heavy as she continued,

Travis Lehrman, I am not 'more than a human'. I am of a different breed, that is all. My kind... also makes mistakes."

"Alyssia, I am of a breed that must destroy this evil plague! You and Lorne are trapped! Mr. One said you were inside something called The Fist! This cannot stand. I must destroy The Otherside now!"

"No! Not yet! He will keep me as a final flail to smash your resolve should you be close to gaining victory. While I'm imprisoned, the mere threat of my destruction makes me a weapon in his hand, and you will never persevere. You must free both Lorne and me from his Underlords first! While we remain locked within this vile enclosure, we are unable to fight alongside you. You will require our aid to annihilate The Otherside and his lackeys, Soldier Travis of Earth."

Angry, he tried to reach past the eye-blistering bands surrounding her confines, but his hands were deflected away by a base and primal force, as if he'd tried to compel the ends of two like-ended magnets close together. It was impossible.

No matter how hard he pushed, his aching hands slipped away from the bars, their cold flames burning his skin.

At the same time, the glowing cage drained his strength from him, stripped away and gone, perhaps feeding it to some slavering otherworldly entity consumed by hunger. He was forced to retreat.

Frustrated, he cried out to her.

"Alyssia! What manner of cage is this? Nothing made by men, I'm guessing."

"Yes and no. Made by men no longer men. Little of human flesh or breath or dreams remain within their brittle and corrupted shells. Having now become something base, they live only to serve The Otherside and those beyond the gates of the Other. These are the selfsame Underlords of the past, the few that have survived the centuries, their lives extended, existing only by the dark powers doled out by their overlord. They were tutored, given the knowledge and instructions of how to construct this unholy box and so many of their other devices."

"How will I destroy it when I find you?"

"The Underlords hold its key within themselves and their machines. They keep this cage bound here against its nature. Defeat them, and this enclosure will dissipate back into the reality they wrested it from."

"Tell me where you and Lorne are within the Fist! I will come!"

She answered, but her words were now a jumbled garble. The cage dulled, fading away. She screamed out her location, but her last words were nonsense to his ears as the eye-rending glint within each bar diminished to an opaque dusk.

By her supreme effort, she managed to shout four words clearly.

"The Fist! The Fist!"

He heard, but they made no more sense to him than before.

She said no more as the cage around her transformed into a terrible twilight gray. Its light now skewed from stiletto strikes of focused pain into an oubliette absorbing life's bright energies, seeking to make all creation dark and hopeless.

Travis willed himself to attack it in some way. He again shot forward, fists flailing, hands reaching for purchase. He wanted to wrench apart the alien contraption, but felt only frozen slivers of eternal cold, and soon even that withered from his grasp.

"Too late... too late!"

He swung his hands about, now clenched in fruitless rage.

The cage had disappeared.

Immediately afterwards, Travis had trouble maintaining his perspective above the currents of the world. Below was bedlam. He fell from the limitless domain of the gods down into the chaos of Man. His consciousness swung a seesaw descent through clouds and rain and smoky storms above vast oceans.

He was lost. Bereft of Alyssia's counsel, he had no idea where his physical self now lay, only a terrible certainty that he must not fail to return to his physical body before it awoke. That fear gripped him as he called out for help.

"Mr. One! Are you here? Anywhere nearby?"

He had never been a sailor, there were no

landmarks in the surging sea.

"Can you show me where to go, Mr. One?"

There are no instructions when the teacher has left the room. Travis dropped toward tumultuous waves, the featureless ocean reaching away in all directions. No land in sight. No sense of direction.

No reply.

Suddenly an invisible gale caught him, dragging him away. The weather in the physical world around him got rougher. He felt himself flung and twisted, moving more quickly than he'd ever thought possible. Rushing seascapes below his flight changed to land then back again. He finally slowed after passing through an enormous surging storm. It was moving westward, every minute gathering more swirling strength.

Directly in the storm's path, yet still hours from the giant gale behind him, lay the island of The Otherside. Relief washed over him. He knew that now he would be able to find the room in which his sleeping form lay.

Bright green jungle overran the steep hillsides surrounding the town, cascading along the shores, helping to disguise the settlement from casual view.

"That place is indeed hard to see, it looks like uninhabited jungle. You can only get a glimpse of it from beyond one small opening off the point if you're at sea. Or, if you obtain a view like this from above, but what navy is ever going to fly?"

His trajectory took him over the great open funnel that lay between the masts of The Otherside's ship. On deck below him was the cage, the watery outline of its many limbed terror moving within. After its latest feeding frenzy, soggy piles of new dismemberments lay strewn about, the victims a hodgepodge of dripping red chunks, too many to count. Even the incessant hunger of the sea creature was, for a time, suspended. So much had it eaten that it could not gulp more flesh within its maw.

While his being passed over the ship, Travis noticed more slaughter, with many unmoving bodies strewn about. He was grateful for this incorporeal point of view, as he was among the carnage, but not of it.

"At least for now. My turn to fight and maybe die will come soon enough."

The condition of the corpses varied. Some lay still and mostly whole without major desecration. Other bodies had been torn limb from limb, leaving torsos lonely and skulls empty, save the eyes that dangled loose.

The instigators of this widespread destruction were revealed. In the final minutes before returning to the stone room, he saw a group fighting and feeding below. Travis recognized them from when he'd first arrived.

They were the deformed husks that remained after the failed experiments by the Underlords upon their human subjects. Creatures that had been banished beyond the walls, sent out to die.

But they had survived, and now ignored the pain of their ruined bodies, for this was their time for revenge.

A group of them surrounded several soldiers of The Otherside. The men fought and screamed and died in terrible failure. The dead soon became food for the insatiable shamblers, who rent and chewed and fed with drooling glee.

"That's Samu, the lieutenant I faced down in the alley! Right there in front of me, getting his throat ripped out by those brutes from outside the walls!"

Travis was pulled away from the bloody scene, along the narrow street of his last encounter with the dead man he'd just seen, then inside through the shuttered window where his body still lay dormant.

"My fault! It was me! Those gates! After I came in, I blocked them open! They must have gotten into the town last night! An entire army of them!"

Even though it was difficult to work up much sympathy for the denizens working for The Otherside, as he returned through the heavy shutter of the stone room's window, he felt a shade of dishonor.

"My actions managed to kill a man I knew, even if he was an enemy, yet I can't be bothered to remember his name, except for what I made up to insult him with."

His teeth clenched with anger as he rejoined his waiting physical form.

Travis woke. His face lay flattened against the floor within the stone room. The left side felt nothing, dull and numb as a wooden shingle. He recalled when his jaw had been knocked numb by a billy-club in a tavern brawl while on leave. Now, as he'd done then, he reached up to affirm his teeth were still in their proper places. They were. He was grateful for that.

From beyond the closed window, weak beads of light crept within, prodding darkness to gleam dimly. But even heavy steel-faced shutters could not muffle the agonized cacophony of shrieking torment while the voracious shamblers fed in their special ways.

Those noises never lasted long.

He lurched up from the floor, intending to stand but finding himself too unsteady to manage more than a cross-legged sitting posture, at least for now, so took the time to get his eyes adjusted to the dimness of the room. He wanted to eat but his hunger was interrupted by a new voice.

"You ain't gonna kill me are you, mister?"

Having forgotten to remember the stranger, Travis cursed himself for another foolish misstep. Before he even saw the man, who sat leaning back on a chair's two legs in the deepest of the dark recess of the stone room, he began answering as emphatically as possible, while twisting around to look him in the face.

"Hell's bells and buckets of blood! From what I've seen there's already enough killin' been going round this accursed town!"

Silence lengthened while the stranger slowly brought out a wooden phosphor match. He swept it along the table, lighting a nearby candle, then his pipe. He kept his eyes square on Travis the entire time, who for his part, was beginning to wonder if he'd made the wrong decision in coming here, no matter what Mr. *One* had said. He began to rise from the floor but stopped short when the stranger spoke.

"Naw, don't do that, you're just fine where y'all good and sat right now, fella. Now... I've got another question for you."

The stranger took a draw on his pipe. Travis noted that he had a blanket laid over his legs which also covered his lap, even though the room hadn't too much of a chill. Unless you were sitting on the cold stone floor, of course.

"Okay. Shoot."

The briefest of smiles crossed the stranger's face before continuing.

"I want you to tell me who Alyssia is."

"What? How do you know... ?"

The stranger held up his hand, again stopping Travis. He spoke.

"Now listen boy. That's the second time I've asked you a question you ain't answered proper to. From what I know there's chores a-plenty needin' done right now, but we ain't goin' nowhere till I get answers I like. Now, who is Alyssia?"

Travis answered in a matter-of-fact growl. "If it's any of your business, stranger, Alyssia is... a friend of my fiancé."

The man by the candle set his pipe aside with one hand, while the other, unseen under the blanket, made a slight movement. The sharp sound of two metallic "clicks" sprinted about the room. He pulled the blanket away. In his lap lay a sawed off double-barreled shotgun, pointing directly at Travis. The stranger had lowered the hammers back to the "safe" position. He quickly turned it aside and set it on the table with a bitter laugh.

"Not exactly what I was told but close enough, I suppose. From what I've heard, it sounds like we've got a lot to do."

Confused, but relieved that he'd passed some sort of test, Travis began to rise. The stranger jumped up first and reached his hand out to help him up off the floor.

366

"Thanks for not shooting me, mister. My name's Travis."

"I'm Andrew. I go by Andy to my friends. You look a mite done in. I imagine you're hungry. Here, have some chow."

He opened his small pantry and set bread, butter, and fruit on the table. They both dug into the meal.

"Well, I hope I'll be able to call you that one day, Andrew."

"Ha! You're halfway there if you're a friend of Alyssia."

"Perhaps a friend, at least another comrade in arms, I hope."

"Mebbe so, mebbe so. She thinks very highly of you. From what she and that other fella told me; you got the best chance to get us rid of that so-called 'Captain'. Nothin' but demon spawn, that one."

"What other fella are you speaking of? You talkin' about a fella that calls himself *One*?"

"Hell, I think that's what he called himself. He recruited me a few years ago. Wanted me to keep an eye on this place. Said to just lay low and learn what I could. When it was time to make a move, he'd let me know. Never talked much at all but made it clear that it was important. I was glad to get a chance to get back at that coward of a Captain. He put my last employers out of business, and I lost everything. He's crazy, and his people are crazier. Thinks they're gonna somehow rule the world from this island. I was happy to pretend I'm part of his crew if I could help throw a cannonball or two into their plans. Outside of the heat, it's not too bad here, if you like fish and that tonic everyone washes their chow down with. Gotta admit, that stuff keeps you goin'."

"Seems like it must, Andrew. But if that Captain is gonna be stopped, we've got to rescue Alyssia first, and I've no idea where she is, exactly, except that she's on a ship."

"Well, that's a start, and we know she's nearby."

"But there's not enough time to search everywhere, especially since these bloodthirsty beasts are all over. We'll have to avoid them too."

"Yes, but they've saved us a lot of trouble by killing off batches and bunches of the Captain's troopers. While you were napping, they somehow overran the town. I don't know how they managed to get over the wall. It's always kept them out before."

"Ah, Well... I think that might have been my doing. When I snuck into the city last night, I, ah, sort of propped the gates open. I didn't want to be trapped in here in case I needed to run. Especially if I had my hands full."

"Ha! That's a good joke on these unholy bastards! Using their own failed experiments against them! Those cannibals used to be human! A few times a year soldiers are taken to be "improved", made bigger, faster, and then to serve in the Captain's personal guard. The ones that make it without deformity or death end up bigger and stronger, sort of looking like you, come to think of it."

"Your guess about me is... close. I was about to die, but an older woman sent by the Outer Forces saved me. My body was also improved, but it was done by friends of Alyssia, not The Captain."

"It's a good thing you weren't mucked about by his crew. Only about ten or fifteen of a hundred come through in better shape than they went in. The rest end up twisted in body and mind, then kicked out over the barriers into the jungle to fend for themselves. They naturally hate this town, and everyone within, what their feeble brains remember of it, anyway. There's a lot of them out there, and they're always tryin' to get back in to take revenge."

"They're in here, now."

"Yes. There's a lot of food."

Andrew nodded toward the window. "That's why that outside shutter is faced with iron. Some of those critters can chew through the wood, but they have a harder time with the metal."

Travis wasn't particularly concerned about the shuffling husks of once human wreckage. He felt his improved strength and speed would keep them from the worst of it. Unless they got trapped by a whole drove of them, of course. But he had his guns and the big Bowie if it came to that. He finished his meal, then stood up and checked his weapons.

"Thank you for the food. I'm ready to go."

"Belay that big fella. We don't yet know exactly where to go, or how we're leaving after the rescue."

"Andrew. You're coming with me, then?"

"Of course. I told you the *One* fella said he'd tell me when the time was right. Well, he finally did. Yesterday. So did Alyssia. That's how I knew what you looked like and what questions to ask! Kid, of course we're going together. I haven't been rotting away here in this pestilential hell hole for all this time to watch you gallivanting off to save the world by yourself! Besides, you'll never get away from this island, let alone kill that idiot Captain, without me!"

"I didn't mean for you to think I didn't want your help. I was merely surprised."

"Ha! If you're that easily surprised, Travis me boy, maybe I don't want to come along with you after all!"

Travis didn't reply. He knew what the older man said was true. He'd already made more mistakes than he should have during his dealings with The Otherside. Any one of them might have killed him, or Lorne. He wasn't proud of any of those missteps.

"Alright, then. I'm not surprised anymore. Where do we go first?"

"That's what we've got to ascertain now! What did Alyssia tell you?"

"She was in a jail, more like a cage. I didn't see Lorne, but she said they were together, however that may be."

"That's where you saw her, alright. But what did she say, Travis?"

"Quite a bit, but... when I asked her where she was being held, the bars of her cell started changing, the whole thing went dark, and I couldn't hear her words clearly. All I could make out was her yelling, *'FIST, THE FIST!'* before she completely faded away."

"HA! We've puzzled out the first question, then!"

Travis lifted his hands, balling them into fists, waving them around to punctuate his words. "What do you mean? Mr. *One* said they were inside something called 'Fist', which is what I thought the cage she's in called, but maybe

Alyssia was talking about these! Obviously, she's angry, and she wants to strike back with her fists!"

"You've made an honest assumption, even if it's wrong. But it does make sense, in a way. Since you've just arrived, you wouldn't know. HA!"

"Ha, yourself. So, what is it I don't know, Andrew?"

"That I was First Mate on the good ship *FREEDOM*! That's the ship that the so-called 'Captain' stole from my old employers! What you don't know is... he's renamed it, and now it's called *THE FIST*!"

"The steamer that's docked out there? That ship?"

"Yes, the one and only. He got rid of all the old working crew, but I took a job here to fabricate spare parts for the boiler. That fake Captain rarely leaves it. Likes his privacy, I suppose."

Travis considered, he'd expected both captives to be hidden in some buried cell, deep within the cliffs behind the town. But for them to already be on the ship! Right in plain sight, with the macabre forces of the enemy aboard as well... there was going to be a fight, and probably more, he knew that. He spoke.

"Nobody said this would be easy."

"Certainly not. And it wouldn't be any fun that way, now would it, boy?"

The two men organized themselves. Andrew gathered his handfuls of brass shotgun shells and other supplies, while Travis told him about awakening upon the small vessel hidden inside the strange little harbor of eternal noon.

"It's a little more than a mile past the outer

wall along the shoreline. From this side of the barrier, it looks like the underside of a rotted old ship, overgrown with jungle. Nobody would look at it twice."

"But you say there's a vessel moored inside? Inside this harbor where the sun never moves?"

"That's where I found myself when I arrived. I know it sounds like the ravings of a mad man, but... "

Andrew nodded his head in agreement as he jammed the sawed-off shotgun into his jacket's long pocket. "Yes. I understand. Everything's a conversation from inside the insane asylum when having to deal with any of these Outer Forces people." He ticked off a list on his fingers to punctuate each word. "Visions, voices, spirits, flying, and nightmares galore! Sometimes makes me wish I'd said no when *One* and the others asked me for help."

"But you didn't, of course."

"No, because everything they showed me was true. I'd already seen and been forced to live with his evil before, so I knew. That stupid Captain, he's worse than just another bad one. He's got to be stopped; dead stopped."

Travis nodded. They both looked around the room, then back at each other. The time for speaking was over. They had their plan. It was time to go.

Andrew unbarred the door. They trod down the narrow staircase onto red spattered streets. Everywhere was littered with half-eaten brains and uncoiling entrails running with blood and other butcheries.

19. STEEL BLADE OF THE SNAKE!

Now the looming storm's heavy mists mixed with the gore swathed streets of the town, diluting the remnants of recent violence. It seemed a silent promise from the approaching deluge that it would soon wash the gnawed bones and blood away, from rooftop to gutter.

The two men walked carefully through the hazy wet streets side by side. No one, and no thing, were in sight. Andrew wore a waterproof cap against the coming storm. Travis pulled his own hat further down onto his head, the strange leather of the oversized brim flexible enough to cover neck and shoulders.

Empty human husks lay heaped in all directions. Even as they skirted the gnawed piles of flayed skin and cracked marrow-less bones, the two men could not avoid the pools of red sheen clotting the cobblestones.

They neared the ship. Its iron funnel spewed a thin flag of coal-dead smoke, which disappeared quickly into the advancing storm's windy gauntlet.

Two gangplanks at bow and center swung loose in broken disarray, as useless as the overloaded mass of lifeless human shard entwined within their cables and planking.

Travis pointed to the unmoving piles of half-eaten dead, and the occasional smashed weapon, "Looks like they tried to put up a fight."

Unimpressed, Andrew snorted in dismissal.

He increased his pace, heading off toward the stern, where no gangplank lay, only a heavy rope tied off from pier to ship. He yelled over his shoulder at the younger man.

"Fighting. That's the one thing these motherless bastards thought they were good at, and you see now how far it got 'em."

"Not many of them still left, in fact, none that I can see."

"What these raiders did best was stealin' horses, rapin' women, and killin' children. They'd always try to kill any men folk who were around from a distance, then move in to use their bare hands and blades for the other."

Andrew stopped at the dock's edge, almost directly below the vessel's stern, spinning around to face Travis.

"We're here lad, and I'll tell you what I think. The cowards who are left alive will be on board, hiding out with that stupid Captain. And I'll give you one guess where he is."

"With Lorne and Alyssia!"

"You win the prize. So now you get to go up first."

Beside them was a large cleat set into the edge of the dock. Above, a heavy rope hung from the big boat which wrapped tightly around it.

"Up first? You mean up this rope first?"

"That's what in front of us, isn't it? Time to go."

Travis looked up along the line, reached down and found his hands were just able to grip it. He took a deep breath and started to climb.

"Hey! Hold on there, big fella!"

He paused, looked back at the older man's exasperated expression.

374

"What's wrong?"

"Wait for me!"

With a fatalistic chuckle, Andrew climbed up on the big man's back, held on. "Alright, now. Make it quick, I wouldn't care to fall off into this feeding ground. Those fish swimming below us are at least as hungry as those poor bastards from beyond the wall."

Travis grunted, but found that with the improvements that his body had been granted, he only noticed the other man's weight if he concerned himself with it. As he climbed, his thoughts were of Lorne, an obsessive focus that almost caused him to forget that he must also rescue Alyssia as well. When they reached the top, Andrew spoke sharply.

"Getting close. Now it's my turn to go first. Get as far up as you can."

As soon as Travis touched the hull, Andrew leapfrogged up and over his shoulders. Squarefooted, he stood solid upon the rain-slick deck, his shotgun quickly out and at the ready.

Finding a dearth of adversaries, he turned, extending his arm to give Travis a hand up.

They prowled the deck, battered by swirling gusts of the rapidly windering storm, determined to destroy the foul chaff which held Lorne and Alyssia captive. Yet, no lackey of the Captain had so far been seen.

But soon Travis held up his hand for pause, faintly hearing through the noise of rain and winds a rhythmic chanting coming from the under deck.

"Below us, Andrew. There's a group of men down there, maybe singing, it sounds like."

"Ha! The Captain's toadies never sing, I don't

think he allows it. Now wait, don't give me that look, boy! I didn't say I didn't believe you! Listen, they never sing, so it's got to be something worse, much worse. But I know a way for us to find out for certain."

Andrew stepped around the piles of incomplete bodies. He made directly for an innocuous rectangular section of planking set into the hull. It was clear from the number of corpses nearby that brutal fighting had taken place here.

Pushing the cadavers aside, he reached down and unscrewed the brass finger screws that held the section of planking in place. It opened. He spoke matter-of-factually to the other man's unasked question.

"Access hatch for maintenance. Goes down inside the vessel. Along those catwalks inside, you can get everywhere. Don't worry Travis, we'll find these singers of yours soon. Ugh, this thing's a mess. Looks like these imbeciles haven't opened this hatch since they stole the ship."

They climbed down the steep ladder, entering the bowels of the ship.

Silently they passed along the darkened corridors and narrow crawlspaces, following the strange reverberations. Andrew led the way, his movements catlike and careful, then raised his hand. They both stopped. The sounds were clear now; the low voices of men chanting in unison.

"Just round this corner." Andrew whispered, "It overlooks the main hold. Sounds like they're having some sort of meeting down there."

Those who chanted sat in a broken circle on uneven piles of boxes and rusty ship's ballast. In turn, one by one, each spoke a few phrases, their words of ancient ritual carried through the strange mists swirling amid the group.

Several of the Underlords that had stood near The Otherside on deck yesterday were here. At some hidden cue, they began to chant in cadence to their living deity.

"We beg, we plead, we cry... for your protection from those creatures more ravenous than us! We beg, we plead, we cry... to grant us safety from those that have swarmed within to feed upon our people! We beg, we plead, we cry... and offer you these blood sacrifices!"

The Otherside sat above them, taking it all in as his due, his arms crossed, greedy lips curled back in a sneer of contempt at the proceedings before him. He made no move to help as his fearful minions beseeched him... he would wait until the sacrifices had been made.

One of the cadaverous Underlords shuffled over to a raised dais covered by a midnight black cloth. Gripping one corner with ancient bony fingers, he unveiled what lay sprawled across the hard material, unmoving within an immobilizing torpor.

It was Lorne. She had been dressed in a diaphanous gown covered in unknown symbols and lay surrounded on three sides by hooded beings. Their robes dragged the ground as they skittered about. It was a scene torn from the ancient world of human sacrifices to the bloody god Baal, now shifted across the ages and oceans into hellish existence before him.

Without another thought, Travis tensed and made ready to leap into the gathering. The Bowie was already in his hand.

Andrew's strong hand restrained him on his

arm and with a forceful whispered query. "STOP. What do you think you're doing!?"

"I see Lorne!"

"I see a lot of things, boy! That doesn't mean I jump into viper pits to dance with the devil when I do! Listen! We will get her out. Listen to me. I have a plan."

He shared his idea, and Travis slightly relaxed, then nodded. Andrew crawled back along the way they'd come, disappearing into the ship's hidden belly.

Travis waited, watching the sickening scene unfold below, ready to jump down instantly if Lorne's life was immediately threatened, no matter what the older man had said.

"Finally, I've found her! I was worried I'd never see her alive again after that demon horse dragged her off!"

Lorne's hand tightly clasped an iron chain locked round her neck. Attached to that was a small, intricately made amulet of some sort.

"That... filth... put a chain around my fiancé's neck! I can't wait any longer! I need to get down there! Where is Andrew? It's time to move!"

Just as he finished that thought, the smell of smoke seeped into the hold. ALL pleading and chanting stopped, then the big man that their fear had deified rose to his feet.

The age-old dread of fire on board a ship clawed beneath everyone, even the outer world instincts of The Otherside. He bellowed at his underlings,

"FIRE! GET OUT THERE AND STOP THE FIRE, YOU LAZY DOLTS! GET GOING BEFORE WE ALL BURN ALIVE! HURRY YOU FOOLS!"

The room almost emptied as most of the men

scurried out the main hatch to fight the fire that Andrew had set. After giving several sharp commands to the darkly mantled Underlords who remained positioned around the sleeping Lorne, their Captain stalked away.

"Presumably to keep an eye on things or bite the heads off any more of his soldiers that don't do their duty up to his standards, whatever they are today. Or both, I suppose. The Otherside's going to run out of men soon if he keeps that up."

Travis watched the three remaining Underlords chanting, then raise their chalky arms in supplication to a primeval ritual of evil, the ancient words writhing cold along his spine.

Their cowls quivered with unnatural motions, wrapping each face close. They surrounded Lorne, one on either side, another standing by her throat, who pulled from beneath his cloak a twisted knife forged in the likeness of a writhing snake. He lifted the blade high above Lorne's breasts, preparing to slice the life from her.

Travis knew time had run out. Rage red explosions swept his vision. He flung the big Bowie down, straight into the heart of the one holding the sacrificial knife. The impact knocked that Underlord away from Lorne, his reptilian blade spinning into the darkness beyond. Unclean blood oozed stinking from the still twitching corpse.

Travis leaped over the catwalk, seeing surprise on the two others below: *Where had this avenging human locomotive come from?* Yet, he was bewildered that neither of them showed any fear.

He soon found out why.

As one, they reached within their billowing cloaks for something unseen, muttering an arcane tongue. Their coal black eyes flared red with fierce powers stolen from beyond the outer worlds. Travis hurtled toward them, but the objects of his wrath now held strange metal objects from which poured a crimson heat, suddenly forming a blazing wall before him. Not only was it hot, it was unexpectedly solid.

Travis crashed hard into the barrier, feeling it give way a few inches before he bounced back. He felt burns on his face and hands, but the pain was only another goad for him to destroy these two creatures who stood between him and rescuing Lorne and Allysia.

Once more he smashed into the hot red shield with all his strength. Again, it moved slightly forward, but there it stopped. Through the crackling firestorm around his head, he watched the faces of the Underlords contort with pleasure as they watched him burn before them.

Travis suddenly realized he hadn't recoiled back out of the flames this time, and, even worse, he couldn't extricate himself from them now. Ruddy ropes of living fire clasped him tightly with deadly heat.

He was trapped.

Now the ancient Underlords of anguish spoke, their voices clotted with cobwebs past.

"See how its flesh burns! A cheerful sight! It will be another offering to those we serve!"

"Yes, and this one is powerful! Its sacrifice will gain much favor for The Otherside, our mighty Captain, as well as for us!"

So now he had become a sacrifice as well. Travis decided he would tear these Underlords limb from limb instead. But struggle as he might, He could not break free of the fiery cords. He knew he hadn't much time left before the burns inflicted on his body would become serious. He could see Lorne just beyond the two creatures before him. She still clutched the amulet upon the iron chain strung around her neck. Fighting intolerable frustration and rising pain, he lunged forward again, using all his improved strength.

Nothing.

Travis furiously howled in frustration and growing despair. Suddenly, a bright spark from within the amulet passed before his eyes, then a bluish glow filled the space around them all.

He heard an urgent, friendly voice, a familiar phrase... a reminder spoken as a fervent whisper in his mind.

"Soldier Travis of Earth... say it... BLESTEMUL MORTI... BLESTEMUL MORTI... !"

Hot air punished his face and throat as he drew the desperate breath, then bellowed out the phrase.

"BLESTEMUL MORTI! BLESTEMUL MORTI, you evil sons of bitches!"

Now the Underlords' grins of amusement disappeared. Their shaking hands flew up to cover their ears, but neither was swift enough. Travis repeated the ancient curse again and again, while its harsh syllables banged and clashed back and forth to break the power of the flaming weapon.

Then both the barrier and its heat were gone. Travis rushed forward to attack. The cloaked figure farthest away stepped back, and turned away, frantically searching for something.

"He's lookin' for that snake knife! I've gotta stop him!"

The closer Underlord still blocked his way. He again began to chant, while reaching under his flowing robes for another arcane weapon.

But Travis was faster. Even pained with burns inflicted by their powers, his speed outpaced that of the ancients. He reached the closest Underlord before the creature had the chance to activate whatever strange new weapon he'd grabbed. Travis already had his fist pulled back as he stepped within striking distance. He let fly his punch, striking the hated opponent square in what passed for its face.

No blow from club or mace on any battlefield of ages past had ever struck more fiercely than did Travis strike now.

Crushed and crumpled, the hooded entity keened a demented squawk of dismay. A stinking miasma of death filled the hull.

The thing's cloak fell open when it hit the deck, revealing odd meal devices. Travis had never seen anything akin to them. It wore several belts with various small boxes, cases, and strange mechanisms attached to them all. Each one of them had several colored lights affixed to it, pulsating with unknown energies. Even more baffling, one of the boxes emanated sounds, which Travis thought sounded like several demanding voices, all of them upset and inquisitive. But he could not understand the language to know for sure.

Startled by what he saw and heard; he knew that these boxes were something beyond what even Mr. *One* had revealed to him.

Travis was fleetingly distracted from the third

382

Underlord.

That ancient creature had recovered the wavy knife and shuffled back to the sacrificial dais. Once more was the steel blade of the snake raised high above Lorne, again prepared for the imminent plunge into her sleeping flesh.

The old one began a muffled chant from a distant time and place...

... it was only those rhythmic sounds that saved her.

For Travis heard the creature's rasping voice, turned toward it, and leaped across the intervening space, just as the snaky steel tip plunged downward, aimed at Lorne.

The same fist, that had so recently dispatched another Underlord, now reached out with unerring aim to grab the wrist which held the plunging knife. Travis stopped the deadly blade's descent mere inches from his betrothed. It was enough.

The Underlord struggled to force the knife into Lorne's breast, but Travis tightened his grip, eyes locked with the two black pits glaring at him from beneath the shroud. The pressure he applied increased, but the skeleton beneath the skin of the ancient once-human had transformed into another substance entirely. Instead of snapping, the wrist sagged like thick jelly, deforming under the pressure. The spongy wrist was more akin to the tendrils of the captive sea monster, rather than solid human bone.

"Nearby... that creature is somewhere nearby. I can hear it splashing in its cage and can smell its reek. Have to make sure to stay far away from that thing."

Travis kept squeezing the wrist holding the

deadly dagger. He shoved the hooded form away from the dais.

A painful yowling erupted from beneath its cowl, but Travis didn't let up. What should have been bone buckled and twisted like clay beneath the pressure of his fingers. On either side of his hand the Underlord's spongy flesh bulged out. Yet it still managed to hold firm possession of the deadly blade.

Travis continued shoving the knife-wielding thing closer and closer toward the hatchway the others had earlier scrambled out through.

Travis yelled past his burned face and lips, "Drop the knife, creature!"

It looked up at him, haughty contempt and trickery wrapping its every word, "Certainly I will, fool... into my other hand!"

Laughing, it did so, seizing the falling blade with its free hand. Straight toward the unprotected belly of Travis it went, who immediately released the empty wrist, grabbing desperately for the other.

Too late. The snake blade aimed toward Travis. Only a couple of feet separated the sacrificial knife from cutting deep into his vitals. Fast as he was, he knew he couldn't block or twist away in time.

Travis tensed, waiting for the viper's kiss of steel. *"Lorne! I've failed again."*

During their dance of death, the struggle had moved them both adjacent to the exterior passageway, and now the gloating Underlord stood upon its threshold. Laughing, the knife he held began its killing thrust. However, the ancient one's hood blinded him to the sea creature's cage just off to his side. It had rolled closer to the hatch as the ship was shaken by the increasingly stormy winds outside.

Oblivious to the monster beside him, the Underlord began to plunge the blade forward. But fast as it was, the beast was even quicker.

Two tentacles whipped around the corner of the hatch. Faster than the eye could follow, they shot forward, the lead one looping tight around the Underlord, pinning down both arms.

The deadly knife dropped from his hand, useless.

Travis leapt away, unscathed. He watched in horror as the second watery tentacle spun around the legs of its newfound meal, splashing murky sea-water around the room, a foetid bath of former feedings.

Wailing torment erupted from the Underlord as the powerful writhing limbs of the sea monster bulged and twisted, ripping the ancient one in half, finally ending its unholy existence.

Only two trails of bloody bubbling slime remained to mark the end of the Underlord, as both of his sections were dragged around the corner, out of sight. Soon, slurping and sucking sounds mixed with heavy splashes as reddish globs of water were flung from the tank.

The monster ate with mindless fervor. Travis turned away.

"Don't think I'll go out that way when it's time to leave."

Except for the sounds of frenzied feeding in the passageway, silence and stillness now reigned around Travis. Gathering himself, he made sure that Lorne was safe for the time being, then gingerly examined the burns he'd sustained, deciding there was no option other than to ignore their discomfort.

"I've seen worse on men who got powder flashed by a misfire. I'll live."

He went to the unnaturally cold corpse of the first Underlord he'd slain and yanked the Bowie from the sheath of chalky flesh into which he had plunged it.

While wiping off the blade, he decided to take one of the strange metal boxes from it. Reaching down, he tried to grab the closest of them off the belt, but it was secured too well to remove. Beginning to pry at it with the Bowie, he stopped upon hearing the agitated call of Andrew, who had returned atop the catwalk.

"Travis! Grab Lorne and let's git goin'! Make sure you've got that thing around her neck too! The fire's flaming but they'll have it out soon! We don't have much time!" He beckoned with dire urgency.

Realizing the older man was correct, he dismissed any more thoughts of the strange device and replaced the Bowie in its sheath. Going to Lorne, he lifted her up, noting that the amulet was secure. She did not wake, so he lay her over his shoulder and climbed back to where Andrew waited.

They fled.

The stink of fire, smoke, and dousing water surrounded them as they escaped from below, bursting out upon the deck from the same hatchway they'd followed inside.

Bullets cracked past as they fled back the way they'd come. There was no time to waste sliding down the rope, so Travis simply tucked Lorne under one arm, then grabbed Andrew with the other, and leaped the distance.

They crashed down onto the dock in a heavy but unmarred landing. Briefly, they were out of sight of their pursuers. Travis set his human passengers aside and turned back to the boat.

He pulled free both revolvers.

Their two pursuers soon appeared, looking for the three fugitives. They peered over the ship's rail, expecting them to be injured if not dead after the long fall.

But to the raiders' consternation, the strange trio below were uninjured, and the big man's pistols were aimed directly at them both. Frantic, they raised their rifles... too late.

Twin explosions rent the air, and both pursuers went down, hearts pierced through the center. Two shots, two hits.

"Improved strength, improved aim too. I can get used to this."

He holstered the pistols and again picked up Lorne, then turned toward the fuming Andrew.

"Next time you're gonna manhandle me like that, give me some warning! Nice shooting, by the way."

"Thanks. No time that time, sorry. We have to run; we're going back to the boat I told you about."

They began to run toward the barrier walls he had left breached the night before, racing past vilely maimed cadavers. Andrew spoke between heavy breaths.

"Right. From what you said, I'm guessing it's another boat I used to work on. A smaller version of the ship that fake Captain commandeered."

When they reached the overturned hull rotting in the jungle, Travis saw the bright white mark he'd hacked into the gloomy dark wood. Sounds of manic pursuit were a violent trickle behind them.

Andrew paced impatiently as he spoke,

"Well, is this it?"

"Yes, see that cut? It's just on the far side of this overturned hull."

"I'll take your word for it. Now what?"

"I'm warning you, Andrew."

"What? Warning me about what? Oh, that again! Well, get on with it, boy!"

The simple expedient of tucking them under each arm worked once more. He ran, leaped high toward the mark. They passed over the beached hull and entered the sanctuary.

Outside, search parties of angry raiders ran past in worried haste, thinking more of the punishments they would receive for failure, than the whereabouts of those they pursued.

Inside, all remained as it had been, a shadowless moment of grace, protected from the disembodied gaze of The Otherside.

Now freed from that diabolical influence, Lorne awakened.

Travis exulted, hugging her in joy.

He introduced her to Andrew, who was already working on the small ship that must lead them to freedom.

They left him to his work. Travis showed her the pile of clothing that he'd left here along with her boots. Gratefully, she dressed herself, then dropped the hated sacrificial gown overboard. Finally, she turned to him, falling into his arms.

Travis embraced her, "All three of us escaping! What a miracle!"

"Better than that, my love! All four of us!"

"All four? What do you mean?"

Lorne held up the amulet, Alyssia is also with us, here! But we must somehow set her free! Her essence is trapped within!"

An hour or so after the small band had left the sanctuary's confines, their little steamer chugged westward at full speed, boiler burning hot, sails full of the storm's wet winds. Their escape from the island of The Otherside seemed to be going well and Travis had almost begun to relax with Lorne. But it was not to be. Andrew leaped from the boiler room below, carrying an armload of ropes. He tossed them at the others, who sat inside the small ship's bridge.

"This here's a nasty squall we're already in, but there's a bigger storm coming, plowing along behind, pushing it forward!" He looked over his shoulder at the oppressive sky behind them and shook his head in dismay. "Never seen anything like this in twenty-five years at sea! It should be impossible! This next one is bigger than any I've seen before, maybe bigger than every storm I've ever been in, combined!"

Andrew looked at the others, expecting action, but they still sat unmoving, uncomprehending.

"Listen up you two! Those ropes aren't for staring at! You both need to lash yourselves onto something solid! Tightly! If you don't, you'll be banged about the bridge, maybe even tossed overboard! That would be... a big problem! So do it now!"

He ran from view, then returned. "Don't forget to save a few lengths for me!" He turned

389

again and ran off to make final preparations,

Since days primeval when the first crude rafts were set upon the waters of Earth, the seas have mocked the desires of Man. Now was no different.

Soon, howling winds stoked sledgehammer torrents that shoved them ever westward. For hours, towering waves pummeled the cabin as the fugitives clung on. Andrew had been right. Only the ropes that tied them to their seats kept them from being dashed into each other's skulls or flung crashing through the portholes into the raging sea outside, such was the violence of the vessel's frenzy.

The elemental Titans of the sea played with their toys. The boat spun around, traveling stern first and Andrew cried out that he saw the Captain's black vessel behind them. But then the juggling waves spun the bow forward again. No one else had seen anything.

Soon after, twilight became dark, and blackness shrouded the ship.

Within its gimbal housing, a small oil lamp flamed inside the cabin. The three people who shared that space occasionally took note of it, but all had long since ceased caring much about anything except surviving the ravening maw of watery death outside. Even the danger of The Otherside's pursuit had receded from their concern.

Fists of night and storm pummeled the vessel where and how they wished. Even the improved strength of Travis would have been lacking to guide the ship through the power of the surging waves, had he been granted control of the wheel by Andrew, which, of course, he had not.

By the dim light of their single lamp, Travis watched sheets of spray crash relentlessly upon the cabin. A storm torn fish came too near the intersection of its natural home and our alien habitat; he watched as it was yanked above the waves to be sent flipping across a porthole.

"That fish and I are both out of our element. I know I'm beyond my depth when dealing with the likes of Mr. One or Alyssia. Of course, if the Captain hadn't always been such a problem, my ancestor wouldn't have cursed him, and I'd probably be tillin' crops back home instead of being dragged by strangers through something called the 'Between' to fight The Otherside and his rotting creatures of worn-out sin. And now... ! I've ended up here on a boat that might sink any time! But... what else could I have done? I've seen enough to know that demon must be stopped."

He looked over at Andrew, who was doing what he could to keep the tough little ship afloat despite the pounding fury of the worst waves.

"And I'm not the only one caught up in this madness! Andrew was spying on The Otherside's island at the request of Mr. One, and Alyssia too. And then... there's the angry old woman in the cave who sent me to the island... she's not part of the Outer Forces, in fact she seems to like them even less than me! But what is she? A nurse or doctor, or perhaps she's something else. A witch of some sort? Impossible to say. She saved my life, but only so I'd have another chance to defeat The Otherside. Ha! I haven't had much luck with that yet, but... I must finish the fight. I must win this time... If I'm spared the dive to Davy Jones' Locker... "

391

Another turbulent wave lifted them high atop its crest, spun the ship around full circle several times, then dropped them back into the maelstrom.

"... but now it's the storm's own mercy that will tell the tale for all of us."

Travis gave thanks that the cabin door still held. Lorne sat nearest to it, one hand holding fast the metal artifact around her neck that held the thread of Alyssia to this world. He knew that if that precious talisman were lost, her existence would be forfeit.

"Losing Alyssia is the last thing we need right now. She said I'd need her help when I faced The Otherside again."

From within her cage, Alyssia reached out to Travis, hoping to reassure him, but found her power still diminished by the shackles of the outer worldly cell. She realized she must wait for the proper time and circumstances when her constraints could be broken. For now, all that was possible was for her to share in the deprivations of the others, who were together yet alone within their battered human shells, aching fatigue their only companion.

Behind them, their nemesis suffered no such enervation.

Travis sensed the inhuman eyes of their pursuer peering at them through the blinding storm with over two thousand years of unblinking determination.

A starless night and uncounted tons of churning waters stood between him and those he chased as the two vessels careened westward. But what was left of his facial ligaments slowly stretched into a shattered grin. He knew he was not far behind.

The Otherside caressed the shadows of his prey.

20. THERE IS NO DAY BUT THIS DAY

Violet streaks of first light tinged the high clouds standing guard along the horizon to the east. Sand fleas, stirred by the approaching dawn, began their daily hunt for critters even smaller. Little did they know they would go hungry for a while.

Today, all routines of big or small or tiny were to be shattered. Upon these sandy hunting grounds of birds and beasts and men lay the broken evidence of last night's stormy violence: two scattered shipwrecks hewn to pieces. They lay about a mile apart upon the beach.

Both hunter and pursued had been equalized in destruction. The fickle whims of sea and wind had laid them low and scattered across the sand. The hulls now breached by broken masts; the funnels once hot with steam, either lost or crushed.

Not so long before dawn, even while the furies of the storm began relenting, the smaller ship had been heaved upon the sandy dunes. Tossed outside the breached and broken wheelhouse, the exhausted companions lay scattered unconscious in the night. There they lay insensible for some time.

The brightening sky prodded Travis to no avail. The steady breathing of his deep sleep belied the exchange with Alyssia he was having.

"Soldier Travis. You must awaken. We have arrived. There is no day but this day for doing

what must be done. Travis. Hear me."

This time, he did not fly above the earth and sea, or plummet through the folds of the Between. Alyssia and her energies were still trapped within the outerworldly amulet. She had managed only enough power for a feeble contact. She pleaded but her cries proved futile.

She could tell that he wasn't seriously injured, and in fact, none of them were. What held them was an exhaustion so deep and wide the best cure would be a week of rest.

"Travis! Only death can wait a week. The Otherside will kill us all this day if you do not now awaken!"

Alyssia finally goaded him awake with the tiniest of stings, it was all the weakened energies she had at her disposal. He sat up, eyes slowly focusing. They sat facing one another on a blue and orange shadowed landscape, a false colored reflection of the physical world of dunes and scrub around them.

"That hurts! Alyssia? What are you doing?"

"Travis. Finally! You are with us once again!"

"I didn't know that I was missing. But... speaking of that, where are Lorne and Andrew? Where is the boat? And where are we now? This desert must be a land far away from the jungle that we left."

"Your friends live but scattered across the sands and unconscious as you were. Your boat is ruined, as is the enemy ship which pursued you. Last night's winds gave speedy flight and wrought similar destruction to both your vessels. The hurricane brought us far, far west across the watery gulf to this shore. It is known by your people as the lands of Mexico."

396

"Mexico! Just a few days ago I was next to the Atlantic Ocean!"

"Never underestimate the powers that surround you. Anyone might at any time be swept away within their grasp. They hold great destinies and fateful purpose. Be always ready for their task!"

"My task right now is to find Lorne, then get some more sleep."

"For you, today that cannot be. Unfortunately, Soldier Travis Lehrman, the law of planetary motion makes that luxury impossible today."

"Soon your planet's star will reach its zenith above this place, bringing light and breaking darkness."

"What? This whole beach will be like what's inside the hidden dock back at the island?"

"Yes, that sanctuary on the island is but a frozen page of time that holds the instant when shadows are no more. Such is anathema to the powers and senses of The Otherside, for it hides within the blind spot of the evil one. Now, here in this place, on this day, within a very short time, it will be our only chance to defeat him for another thousand years."

"Where is he now?"

"Inside his broken ship. Within the deepest hold. His wrecked vessel lays beached and on its side, never to sail again. He is recovering alone, without receiving the traditional salves of healing from his Underlords."

"Well, I had to get rid of them back at the island. They were going to kill you and Lorne!"

"I owe you thanks, Travis of Earth! But I sense that one of the Underlords is here, injured yet still clinging to life, its powers vastly reduced. However, destroying the others of their breed is a great and unexpected boon. We of the Outer Forces have tried for many cycles to eliminate those minions closest to him that helped augment his power."

"Those Underlord characters all looked pretty dead to me. But I'll take your word for it."

"I too have been weakened, Travis of Earth. I may be wrong."

"Okay, but I'll keep an eye out for this undead Underlord, while I'm going after The Otherside. In fact, if he's so weakened at this time, I should go and kill him now!"

"He may be weaker than he might have been, had he their healing ministrations, but so are you! And with one of them still living, I will not be freed from the prison of this amulet to help until the banishment of shadows, when the sun is, for a few glorious minutes, directly overhead! That will be our time, your time, to strike! To finally cleanse this world! To eliminate another thousand years of anguished sorrow that your unfortunate failure at the battle of the mountain pass allowed a millennium ago."

"Uh, yes. That's been a problem, I know. Sorry about that."

"You have not been the only one. Many tried to kill him. All failed."

"Then I must not fail again. But now, I need to wake the others."

"Travis. I know you still carry the medicine our old friend gave you. Make sure to take that before your battle. Do not forget."

He began to answer in the affirmative, but the odd twisted colors faded, carrying her away. Harsh morning reality surrounded him. He went from sitting on a rock to feeling like one. He yelled,

"LORNE!"

Pulling himself to his feet, he cried her name again and again. Nothing stirred as the first blinding sunlit sliver rose in the east. Even the birds that normally swarmed the tide pools for their breakfast knew that something was amiss and stayed away.

He searched methodically, clomping up and down the sandy hills and clumps of scrubby vegetation, he found Andrew first, embraced by prickling bushes. He was scratched but his fall had been broken by their thin resilient branches.

"Our ship?" he asked.

"Beached and broken hulled. I'm sorry, Andrew."

"Ah, she was a tidy little boat."

"We still need to find Lorne. Alyssia says that she's alive."

Andrew clambered up. "Yes, let's find your Lorne. So glad to hear she's still alive. We're all very lucky."

They found her sleeping, curled into ball, upon a cushioning bed of sand and spongy growth. She still clutched the amulet that held Alyssia's essence, unconsciously waiting for the moment when she could set her free.

After they awakened her, they returned to their beached boat and scavenged what they could from their scattered stores, managing to find enough rations for a meal. Andrew found the pack containing the deadly spear. Travis reloaded the pistols which he'd fired during their escape. He pulled the big Bowie from the scabbard to check it. The knife was sharp and bright under the tropical sun. Soon, all was ready for the fight.

While working, they had all kept an eye upon the broken *FIST,* looming sideways in the distance, menacing even while quiescent.

The sun climbed higher. Soon the time for battle would come. Then

Alyssia broke her silence. In their minds, to all at once she spoke.

"There is movement and purpose from the enemy. I cannot tell exactly... "

Suddenly came a piercing yowl of pain from Lorne. Sweating pain beaded her forehead as she spoke.

"It hurts! It hurts! The Otherside is attacking Alyssia! He uses me as his conduit!"

Andrew reached over, meaning to grab the amulet, to pull it from its chain around her neck.

"Well then, get it off you, girl! Don't give that lousy devil spawn any opening!"

She held tightly to it, pushing him back.

"No! She and I are bonded! My strength is hers; I cannot let her go! We fight together or not at all!"

Travis came to Lorne, putting his arm around her. He gave her a portion of the medicine from the pouch, then gripped her hand that held the amulet, willing what he could of himself to her aid. He felt her shivering as she fought The Otherside's attack, hearing far echoes of the invisible battle from what little contact he still had with Alyssia.

Andrew yelled in frustration, "What can I do?

I can't help her, but there's no one out here for me to fight!"

Travis answered in a leaden tone, his eyes shut as he struggled to hear Alyssia's faint thoughts.

"This would be a good time to ready the weapon."

"What weapon?"

"You must not touch its poison. It is deadly; made to kill The Otherside."

"Well enough. No poison on me. Where is it? What is it?"

"There are several sections of a spear inside the pack you found. Each will fit tightly into the next with a twist. Put them together. Again, mind the poisoned tip!"

Andrew set to work as Travis turned his full concentration to supporting Lorne in her battle.

Her shaking calmed as the old woman's remedy he'd given her took hold. He saw her eyes give him a glance of thanks before she closed them, going back to helping Alyssia fight against her tormentor.

Travis tried to help, but still found only punctured echoes of the outerworldly clash of arms. Opening his eyes, he saw the sun had climbed higher, while shadows had grown shorter.

"I'm not cut out for this kind of fighting. This part of the war is between these Outer Forces folks and The Otherside. I can't get in there unless they invite me. Now it's my turn to ask, what can I do?"

He had no time to seek an answer. Just then, came a booming roar from the direction of the enemy's ship. It was a sound he knew all too well.

"Cannon fire! Get down deep as you can!"

He hauled the sweating Lorne to the closest sandy valley and lay atop her back, a fragile shield of his own mortal flesh. Andrew also knew the sound, and, holding tight to the spear he'd just assembled, rolled into the lowest ditch among the dunes he could find.

The heavy iron ball trammeled the air into submission above their heads, a locomotive crashing by on worn-out tracks. It landed harmlessly in sand and disappeared into the scrub.

Andrew whooped his glee. "You see! I knew it! That dirty so-and-so can't do nothin' without his toady crew! Can't hit a barn's broadside!

Travis wasn't so sure. He cautiously looked up. Lorne was still sweating, fighting her own battle alongside Alyssia, a fight that he could not join.

"Andrew. He's just getting range on us. I believe he'll keep firing solid balls until he knows where to hit us, then switch to canister shot. At least that's what I would have chosen."

"What do we do?"

"Either dig in deeper or move our position."

He looked up at the sun. Even higher had it risen, along with the temperature. Rippling waves of heat shimmered in the air.

"Andrew, we don't have time to dig in, so we'll have to move."

"But if we run, he'll see us. There's no cover out here except in these dunes. Any other options?"

"One. We could return fire, but we haven't any cannon."

402

Andrew began to speak, but another crack of gunpowder from afar broke his reply. Both men resumed their tenuous positions. Soon, another solid ball thumped hard between them and their evil adversary, quickly burying itself unseen.

Travis stood, lifting the torpid Lorne into his arms. "Now, Andrew! We must move! He has our range!"

"Go back to our boat!"

Without further comment they scrambled the hundred or so feet over to the shipwreck, crouched low as they ran to minimize their profiles. He gently lay Lorne into the lowest nook of furrowed earth he could find.

Andrew crawled inside a hatch, still carrying the spear. He called out.

"There was a small cannon stored down here, never been set up on deck. It was to discourage boarding parties from getting too many smart ideas."

Travis remembered the cannon that Lorne and her sister had been working during the siege of their home.

"A pedrero? That won't have the range, Andrew."

"About the same, but it might be good for something. Besides, at least we've moved ourselves away from over there, like you said."

As if The Otherside was listening, his cannon barked again. The two men laid themselves low, Andrew inside what was left of the hull, while Travis again covered Lorne with his own body.

Seconds later, another shattering crash was heard, this time directly above the dunes where they had been. Speeding balls of hot iron exploded outward from the canister, peppering the empty ground below. A few of the deadly projectiles sped by them off to one side of the killing ground. No one was hit. Travis stopped holding his breath for a sigh of relief.

Suddenly, with otherworldly speed he appeared, consumed by rage and hunger. Cursing and clawing the bushes and brambles, The Otherside himself was now where they had been, tossing vegetation and sandy soil about willy-nilly as he sought his victims in the undergrowth.

Travis noted, as he gazed upon the wailing monster with terrible fascination, that the shadows cast by this foul being had shortened into nubs of darkened motion as he moved about on his destructive spree. The sun stood higher than he'd ever seen it, a livid white hot scourge to cauterize the putrid rot from under every rock and oubliette of darkness.

Lorne trembled, sighing deeply as if she'd been starved for air, then opened her eyes. She took a few breaths to focus, bringing her attention back from the other realms in which she and Alyssia had been fighting The Otherside.

"Travis!"

He quickly motioned her to silence, pointing toward the havoc being raised nearby. Whispering into her ear, he spoke quickly, explaining their situation. Nodding, she replied,

"The monster just disappeared from where we'd been fighting him. Alyssia turned away to follow, then our contact broke. Now here I am. I knew that you'd be with me, Travis."

"Always."

From amidst the destruction The Otherside came forth. Having not found his fleshy victims over there, he began to seek them everywhere. He paced around in ever-widening circles as he searched.

Travis and Lorne stayed low behind the wreckage of the little ship. Of Andrew, there was not a sign. The sun crawled toward its zenith at a much too languid pace it seemed to Travis, watching every shadow's slow retreat.

Without warning, The Otherside suddenly stood beside their hiding place, a snarl of victory on his lips. Travis felt himself lifted by hands that charred like burning coals, held high and twisted to and fro before the sneering eyes, then flicked away like trash to smash, rolling and tumbling, across the wooden hull nearby.

21. FROM NOW TILL PAST FOREVER

Landing in a hard heap, Travis had felt something snap within himself. Immediate pain radiated from the injury. He could not move without incurring nauseating agony. He watched, helpless, as the towering creature reached for the screaming Lorne, grabbing her arm to pull her up to his eye-level. His voice was molten slag, bellowed from a blast furnace.

"This one! so much TROUBLE from this very little one! Finally in MY POWER! You have been the FULCRUM on which the power of the HATED Alyssia rests for far TOO LONG! No more will you THWART MY REVENGE upon her! This was the LAST TIME, little pink GRUB!"

Travis reached for his pistols, but seething bands of liquid agony enwrapped his torso with paralyzing torment. Every move became a blinding red affliction. Frustrated banshees of loathing gripped him, when suddenly those angry voices calmed, spoke softly, and reminded him of the remaining medicine within his pocket. He reached for it, struggling it out of the pouch.

The Otherside continued his tirade, still holding Lorne, ranting to his audience of one, every former minion of his now deserted, dead, or missing. But Travis knew that speech could change to action, with his fiancé dashed into broken human dust before his eyes.

Ignoring the pain, he pulled the medicine out,

placed it in his mouth. It dissolved quickly. He swallowed it.

Simultaneously: the ranting creature grew tired of listening to himself and lifted Lorne high above his head, intending to smash her as he had Travis; Andrew reappeared from hiding in the wreckage of the hull, dragging out the *pedrero,* now loaded full of nails and shot and broken shards, aiming it point-blank upon the torso of The Otherside; and while Travis watched, his medicine took hold, and the sharpened prongs of pain within him dulled to vanish on a healing zephyr.

Not waiting another instant, Travis leapt forward to the attack.

Andrew fired the weapon, just as the surprised creature finally took note of him. The harrowing blast shocked him into dropping Lorne aside. It knocked him back several feet, tearing terrible flesh wounds along his body.

Travis saw Lorne fall, and broke off his assault to catch her. He used the power of his improvements to speed her to relative safety on the far side of the dune. Uncaring that her arms and hands had been burnt by the touch of The Otherside's volcanic demon-flesh, she still clung tightly to the amulet, waiting for the moment she knew was coming.

Although the shrapnel from the small cannon pained The Otherside, the projectiles did not penetrate too deeply, and could not for long damage his outerworldly body. He was still alive and raging when Travis returned to see the wounds slowly fade and heal.

Bellowing incoherent curses, the creature reached down to crush his new tormentor.

Andrew stood just outside the hatch from which he'd fired the first small cannon, taunting him.

"You always did talk too much, ya yammering jackass! Have another one!"

A second fire lit inside another iron tube. This time the load of broken iron crashed full into the outstretched arm, ripping off hot chunks of bubbling inhuman flesh.

Travis moved in close between them, pulled his Bowie, and stabbed the mutilated hand before it could snap the Andrew's neck.

Again, the damage began to almost immediately heal.

But their coordinated attacks did hold up the grasping fingers long enough to allow Andrew to make a scampering retreat back inside the hull. He hid, briefly out of the sun, out of The Otherside's sight.

His burning visage turned to Travis, regarding him with a temporary mask of sanity. The human stood, guns aimed and at the ready.

"So, AGAIN we meet! Your lineage is nothing if not PERSISTENT! Your ancient grandfather would have made a strong LIEUTANANT for my armies, had he not chosen to OPPOSE ME with his nagging MALEDICTION! Those accursed words he spoke DRAGGED YOU into his dispute across the barren CENTURIES! Do you not feel RESENTMENT at your FATE? Perhaps a YEARNING FOR MORE than what you HAVE? It is not too late to JOIN ME, Travis Lehrman of EARTH! This new land Is RIPE for the PICKING, we could BUILD AN EMPIRE to last another THOUSAND YEARS!"

"I remember the fate of your minions all right! Heads lopped off and souls singed to ash! No thanks! I've seen you at your work!"

"MY work? YOUR PEOPLE'S work! It was the work that was RESQUESTED, nay, it was BEGGED and PLEADED for by your fellow HUMANS when THEY called me away from my FEEDINGS on the OTHERWORLDS! I never ASKED to come here! They LIED to me! I never CARED who won or lost amongst your PETTY SQUABBLES! This world has ever PAINED me! It is pale with only thinnest GRUEL FOR SUSTANANCE. I only FEED so I may LIVE! That is ALL!"

Travis kept his pistols aimed at where the heart of a human would be, not trusting the ravenous monster, or his selfish tale of woe.

"That's all very sad to hear, but If you hated it so much, you could have left at any time! You kept alive the human Underlords who had brought you here all these years, they could have sent you back if you'd only asked!"

"They were ALIVE until YOU killed them!"

"You had more than a thousand years to leave before I came along! Don't blame me!"

"I blame you ALL, every one of you PUNY creatures! Fit only to SERVE and feed my NEEDS! Why should I have LEFT? Why leave my AMUSEMENTS behind, to be BORED for all ETERNITY?"

Done talking, the madness once again filled his eyes as he turned upon Travis.

"Your REJECTION of my FINAL OFFER is your DEATH SENTENCE, feeble one! Let this meeting mark the LAST of your LINE!"

Travis fired both barrels again and again. He emptied the cylinders as he twisted away from the burning grasp that sought him. The lead slugs struck, but unlike the wound his shot had inflicted in the mountain pass, this time the bullets seemed to have no effect. Dismayed, he watched as the perforated outerworldly flesh of the creature again healed before his eyes.

Rolling to his feet, Travis found purchase in the hard soil held tight by the scrub that coiled in arid patches along the dunes. He brought the Bowie knife to bear upon the stalking form that loomed above him, who now swung a fiery fist to smash him into boiling pulpy stew. High and hard it came, but Travis was too quick.

Dodging the blow, Travis struck, driving the blade's sharpened steel deep into the creature's side, low and on the left. Surprised at the speed of his prey, The Otherside grunted, then lashed out again, a back-handed slap that knocked Travis to the ground. He saw the Bowie knife still buried deep within the creature, even while the punctured otherworldly flesh began to heal around it.

The promise of slow death in his eyes, The Otherside smiled his mutilated grin and pulled the blade effortlessly from his side. It flung droplets of alien ichor about as he waved it at Travis.

"NOW shall you PAY! Watching your AGONIES as I SKIN YOU by my own HANDS will be an AMUSEMENT for me to REMEMBER for CENTURIES to come! You will DIE SLOWLY in tormented MADNESS when..."

The landscape *SHIFTED.*

Shadows were no more. The Otherside dropped the big knife and ceased ranting. He convulsed with an incomprehensible pain he'd never known, for his wounds from bullets and the knife had not fully healed.

Travis grabbed the Bowie and leapt away from the shaking monster. Above him, the sun shone hot with brilliant majesty. Shade and shadow had been banished for this fleeting time, and the outerworldly powers of The Otherside were suppressed.

Lorne appeared, crawling up from beyond the dune where Travis had carried her. In the burning gaze of the sun above, the iron chain around her neck became brittle, dissolving into ruddy orange dust. She still clutched the amulet. Now, she flung it hard and true at the shuddering form of their tormentor.

The surface of the artifact had dulled to a wispy, flaking shell beneath the cleansing light. It struck the smoldering creature's skin full on, bursting into actinic flames, a momentary rival to the sun.

A flaming beacon flashed, expanding before them, taking shape into a long and curving steel sword held by a warrior woman in full armor.

Lorne cried out, "Alyssia! You've finally escaped!"

Travis was awestruck by Alyssia's manifestation in this physical realm. Never before had he seen her here; only in the astral worlds of the Between.

Without a word, she flew in close to the still-writhing Otherside, her sword raised to deliver the killing blow.

Lorne saw the trap first and cried out.

"NO! Alyssia, get back, get away!"

Too late.

It had been a sham. The Otherside's agonies had been but a greatly exaggerated farce to buy him time, to lull his foes while he lined them up for unexpected slaughter.

The Otherside shook off the play acting. Too fast to follow, he swung a huge fist toward her, smashing into her wrist and jarring the sword free.

It fell to the sand. She tried to recover it, but his other hand blocked her way, toying with her as a bobcat might a mouse.

"Final VICTORY will be MINE, no matter how the sky may CHANGE! Admit that you are HELPLESS before ME! ADMIT that your FEEBLE POWER cannot withstand the SOUL-SHATTERING MIGHT of THE OTHERSIDE!"

Travis did what he could to help Alyssia recover her blade. Approaching from behind, he grappled with the demon tyrant. Sinews strained, hands burning from the fiery contact, every iota of his energy went into holding doom away from Alyssia, who still tried to recover her weapon. But strong as the improvements had made him, he felt himself losing the battle.

Suddenly, the monster roared in genuine mortal pain; with a yowling, piercing fear beneath it all, a warbling tone of petulance not before heard from the would-be ruler of the world. . He swung his hands down, grabbing at his leg as Andrew leapt away, carrying the spear with him.

Travis and Alyssia saw their chance. Both grabbed their blades and pierced The Otherside again... to little obvious effect. Even within his agony, he managed to slap them both aside, Alyssia knocked one way and Travis another.

Andrew moved in close again, thrusting the poisoned spear into the creature's leg a second time, yelling, "You always liked the sound of your own chatter too much, ye false Captain! Have another one!" He pulled the dripping spear from The Otherside's trembling right leg and drew it back over his shoulder as he might have done with a whaling harpoon in his youth. He began to let it fly.

Eyes blinded by the poison roiling within him, the stumbling creature still managed to hear from which direction his danger lay. He swung crushing blows toward them.

He connected. The soft brittle crunch of human tissue folding in on itself told Travis that Andrew's time had run out.

Bellowing in what he thought was victory, The Otherside again lashed out his fists with superhuman speed in all directions, hoping to find another kill.

Travis groaned, trying to rise to the attack again. It was hard to move. The side of his body where he'd been hit was a darkening bruise of deep, dull pain.

He dragged his pummeled body forward. He knew he must do something before the sun passed through its zenith and allowed the evil of The Otherside to respawn into a new and even more terrible menace to the world.

Travis rose slowly, keeping a watchful eye on his wounded nemesis as he weighed his odds.

Alyssia lay battered in the physical world, wounded now... or worse.

Andrew had given his life, landing a pair of punishing strikes.

And Lorne... she had been knocked behind the dunes just before Travis had been struck... or had she? His own battered memory could not quite decide what he had seen after the many head blows he had suffered.

Travis advanced on the raving alien fiend, determined to plunge his knife deep into whatever passed for its heart, hoping to kill it while the sun still held its shadowless sway above.

Thinking he'd be able to avoid its deadly fists, he jumped forward, his knife-point drawing blood. But then his arms were seized in a grip of bone-cracking power, and he was slowly lifted off his feet, brought face to face with the visage of ancient evil.

No words were spoken by The Otherside this time. He opened wide his far too-many-toothed mouth now for what it was truly best at.

Eating.

A miasma of internal digestive fluids wafted past the sharpened points of toothy razored fangs. Travis struggled, but even his improved strength was not enough to break the monster's grasp. Only inches from him now, the reptilian jaw hinged open even wider, enough room inside its reeking maw to swallow human heads in whole.

Oddly, a stray thought, irrelevant to the looming danger, danced into Travis' mind.

"Now I know what happened to his raiders inside that bloody little pond! Looks like I'm next."

But that fate was not to be his.

A lurch shook The Otherside, then another and a stumble, then a spasmed body jolt. The burning hands opened, weakness releasing them from within. Travis tumbled to the ground. He watched the struggling creature stagger back.

It wasn't the first blow that had caused The Otherside to drop him, rather it was the second, and then the third, and fourth.

Lorne had crept around the dunes in silence and stealth. She had taken the poisoned weapon from the hands of Andrew where he had fallen, then stabbed the thing that threatened her beloved.

After Travis was free, she made a final attack. Using all her strength, she flung the spear directly at neck of The Otherside.

But in his misery, he kept twisting round and round, futilely attempting to escape the ravaging poisons now coursing through him. She missed her target, yet by luck, still managed to deliver him a last dose of the deadly poison.

The spear point penetrated deep within The Otherside's left shoulder. His body spasmed, sending its outerworldly muscle fibers into howling palpitations of agony as they degenerated and died.

No scream or grunt came from his muted maw as he swayed and fell, dully thumping to his knees. The sun remained at zenith, its shadowless shroud preventing The Otherside from feeding upon the black powers of darkness.

His wounds refused to heal.

The deadly taint coursed deeply through what passed for cells and blood within the alien tissues of The Otherside. Caustic juices broke and burned the veins and vessels, tearing up and tossing away his outer shell of faux humanity. His form quickly withered before them.

First the damaged leg fell away, reduced to dust. Then, below the shoulder where the final blow had landed, the entire arm dropped off, burning with acrid fumes of hate.

Losing physical substance by the second, The Otherside was being reduced to his basic state of malevolence: a two-limbed malformed clod of flesh, not much more than a stomach with large teeth and a tiny brain tortured by unsated hunger.

As Lorne and Travis watched, it looked like The Otherside was dying at last, after so many centuries of stealing the gift of life from others. It contorted into a shriveled creature only three feet across. Rapidly shrinking, it seemed that its death was inevitable.

Exhausted, they waited together for the end.

But once more the landscape *SHIFTED*.

The metamorphosis stopped. The zenith of the sun had run its course. Now the shadows that nursed the power of The Otherside had returned to heal what remained of him... saving from certain death even the melted living stew of bone and sinew that remained.

That horrid mess of what-had-been was now an asymmetric, desiccated thing of scuttling nightmares. It clattered weakly among the bubbling remains of its former limbs and hissed, scaring off the sand-fleas.

The dark energies could not reverse the near-fatal damage that had been done, nor ever bring back the cloak of false humanity that had covered his swaggering evil. For the being once known either as the Captain to his deluded followers, or as The Otherside to his enemies, was trapped within this hideous new form, from now till past forever.

The couple embrace, relieved to find each other still alive, then went to find Alyssia, while giving the floundering creature a very wide berth.

As they passed it by, they felt the ghost of endless unsated hunger.

Alyssia lay where she'd fallen, the faintest spark of animation remaining within the armor-plated warrior. Once fiercely indomitable, she was now broken and dying, sacrificed upon the alter of good versus evil.

Lorne brushed her lips with water from their pack. Alyssia refused it, instead reaching out to them from mind to mind, as she'd done so many times before.

"I'd hoped we'd win the Final Battle against The Otherside with more festive circumstances after the outcome. But... in war there are the living and the others, and this was a very, very long war, with many, many others, both the counted and those unknown."

She coughed a wreaking sound of ruined lungs, fatal wounds she'd received while fighting the unseen war against their adversary, then lay still once more. They could begin to see the ground beneath her as her translucence increased. Her body grew less defined as they watched. She reached out again.

"Men like Andrew, he knew what he was about. He joined us almost before we asked him to. But the old woman who saved your life, Travis of Earth, she came to us only as a sense of duty to her people and for revenge, after her clan had been wiped out by the depredations of The Otherside and his followers. She, unlike you, has no lineage to trace, no future for her race. She is the last of her people. She knows that no matter what she does, her fight will

never bring a single one of them back. When you speak with her again, be kind."

A shudder passed within her. Before their eyes, Alyssia's body became thinner, more transparent.

"There were so many more casualties. So many beings suffered because of the selfish greed of a very few others. But their defeat has brought them punishments, the greatest vengeance reserved for the former Captain himself."

She opened her eyes and forced herself to sit up.

Alyssia stared across the dust blown sand at the ghastly creature twitching in the scrub before them. Its odious form reeked of evil, a vile effluvium which grew ever more loathsome as the thing lay baking in its juices under the noonday sun.

The fingers of the single arm which had survived were grown together into a sharp and scooping appendage like a spoon, while the end of that nearby wrist had become a sort of hoof. The withered leg was transformed as well, now more akin to a hairy spider's limb, small claws at the end of the foot where once toes had been.

Between those two extremities was the beady-eyed skull, still dominated by an over-toothed maw. The shrunken body had grown a short and bony tail beneath its gut, now a bulbous, red-scarred knot of greasy flaccid flesh, later to become a sac that would expand with entrails and gristle as the creature fed.

The former tormentor of the world, its would-be ruler, had now become merely an eater of blood-soaked entrails and the offal of four-legged beasts.

Alyssia slumped back, her fading form almost lost in the hard glare from sand and stone. *"An illusion. It is... as I suspected. The Otherside was only a construct of the masters of the otherworlds all along. Now, he has reverted to his true form."*

"It's awful to look at and worse to smell! What is that thing?" asked Lorne.

"A scavenger among the desert climes among the otherworlds. A killer when hunger makes them brave, rarely. Usually hiding underground in daylight, scuttling out for solitary nighttime hunts. They search for easy prey, the herd animals caught in pens, or pampered pets. Fearful yet ravenous creatures, they avoid anything that may prove a threat."

Travis watched as the ruin of the former Captain slowly scuttled off toward a dip in the sand. It dragged its new tail awkwardly behind.

Travis asked, "Can we kill it? Should we?"

Not easily. Eventually it will die, but these beings are very long-lived. It does not look like there's much food for it in this place. Still, it will be around for a long time, always hungry, never sated."

She opened her tissue-thin eyes, looking hard at the man as she shook her head.

"No. You should not kill it. Death would commute the punishment."

Lorne shivered despite the heat. She listened to the scrabbling noises the creature made as it dragged itself away, then asked,

"Alyssia, what is this thing called by your people of the outerworlds?"

Alyssia's being faded, drawn away from Earth

to where she had begun. As from a boat floating on a river a long distance away, came her echoing answer.

"It is called in our language: Chup a' cabra, meaning 'Teeth of the night'."

Then... she was gone. When they looked back over to where the strange and awful thing had been, it had disappeared as well.

EPILOGUE

*T*ravis and Lorne buried Andrew where he had fallen and flung the disassembled parts of the poisoned spear far out past the surf. Travis reloaded his weapons, then cleaned and honed the Bowie knife. The other goods they'd carried for so long were stowed back inside the pack.

Trekking north, they passed by the open cargo bay of the beached and broken FIST. They made a minor detour and explored inside.

A few rodent-like creatures scurried out the hull, carrying their stink and some oddly glowing baubles with them. The couple saw them leaving and were glad to see them go.

The man and woman continued their exploration.

Lorne saw it first. A small wooden chest, clad in ancient iron bands and heavy locks lay upside down amidst the watery debris. Somehow, it looked vaguely familiar to Travis. Perhaps he'd seen it in a dream. He used his improved strength, and a nearby metal rod, to break the seals.

They looked within.

Gold. More than they had ever seen or dreamt of.

It would help them start their new life in Texas.

THE END

Made in the USA
Monee, IL
26 June 2021

72382531R00256